OPERATION
TROJAN
HORSE

FIVE INDIAN AGENTS IN THE LASHKAR-E-TAIBA

OPERATION TROJAN HORSE

D.P. SINHA
ABHISHEK SHARAN

A NOVEL
INSPIRED
BY TRUE
EVENTS

HarperCollins *Publishers* India

First published in India in 2021 by
HarperCollins *Publishers*
A-75, Sector 57, Noida, Uttar Pradesh 201301, India
www.harpercollins.co.in

2 4 6 8 10 9 7 5 3 1

P-ISBN: 978-93-5422-517-8
E-ISBN: 978-93-5422-525-3

Typeset in 11/15 Adobe Devanagari at
Manipal Technologies Limited, Manipal

Printed and bound at
Thomson Press (India) Ltd

MIX
Paper
FSC FSC® C010615

To the brave Indian intelligence operatives engaged in battling terror. They remain faceless and nameless despite their priceless sacrifices for the country.

– D.P. Sinha

To India's 'Trojan Horses', who are its silent warriors, and all the families who have lost their loved ones to terror.

– Abhishek Sharan

AUTHORS' NOTE

The Soviet Union 'Red Army' withdrew from Afghanistan, the country it had occupied for ten years, by February 1989, stumping the world. The historical retreat did not ensure peace and stability in Afghanistan, however. Instead, the country became embroiled in ceaseless hostilities between the communist government forces of President Mohammad Najibullah Ahmadzai and mujahideen groups in their efforts to control Kabul. It virtually signalled the beginning of a long and enduring national security nightmare for India.

Concluded on 14 April 1988, the Geneva Accords had been signed by the representatives of the Soviet Union, the United States, Pakistan and the Republic of Afghanistan. The agreements were ostensibly meant to provide a framework for the withdrawal of the Red Army and a multilateral understanding among the signatories regarding the future of international engagement in the war-torn country. The Pakistani army and its intelligence agency, the Inter-Services Intelligence Directorate (ISI), meanwhile were left stranded by the sudden departure of the Soviet forces from Afghanistan. The ISI had stockpiles of weapons, explosives and battle-hardened mujahideens of different countries. The training infrastructure for the newly inducted mujahideens was also intact. The ISI decided to divert this against India – for creating mayhem in Jammu and Kashmir and, later, in the soft belly of the country – from 1989 onwards.

In its campaign to bleed India with terror, the ISI began using the Lashkar-e-Taiba (LeT) as its principal battering arm. The LeT was set up in 1987 by Hafiz Saeed and had the blessings of the Pakistani establishment in its terror campaigns against India from the very beginning. The LeT has conducted a spate of terror attacks in India, including the 26/11 Mumbai attacks that killed 166 people. Tackling the LeT's game plan to seek to pulverize India with mindless suicide attacks and blasts from 1989 onwards has presented a stiff challenge to the Indian security and intelligence agencies. The task of thwarting terror is not an easy one. It's a 24x7 mission. After its attempt to kill British Prime Minister Margaret Thatcher failed in 1984, the terror group Irish Republican Army had said, 'You have to be lucky all the time. We only have to be lucky once.'

Pakistan's hostility is ingrained in its approach towards India and is part of its strategic template. Back in the 1960s and 1970s, Pakistani leader Zulfikar Ali Bhutto had vowed to 'bleed India with a thousand cuts'. He had earlier also announced a 'thousand-year war' against India while addressing the United Nations Security Council in 1965. His dangerous, negative policy was continued by his wily and ruthless successor, General Zia ul Haq. From then on, sub-conventional warfare and the use of terrorism as a strategic tool to achieve its objectives against India became a norm in Pakistan.

During my long innings in the Indian Police Service (IPS), I had the opportunity of serving the country's premier intelligence agency and getting involved in security and counter-terrorist operations. Terror has no nationality, colour, creed or religion; the human race is its victim. Terror kills and maims the innocent and the unarmed who never expect to be its victims.

I had one mission during my long service career: to do my best to save civilian lives from violent and life-threatening terror attacks. That mission drove me, inspired me.

Operation Trojan Horse is the story of a handful of counter-terrorist operatives engaged in India's fight against Pakistan-backed terror. I dedicate the book to the brave, faceless and nameless Indian intelligence operatives who are engaged in battling terror. They cannot be identified due to national security and attendant constraints despite their priceless sacrifices for the country.

During my active service career, I hardly had the time to analyse and reflect upon the counter-terrorist operations I was part of. Even during my post-retirement assignment, when I held the statutory position of Central Information Commissioner, it was difficult to spare time and pen down my thoughts. I am really thankful to my co-author, Abhishek Sharan, for putting together my experiences in the form of a nail-biting work of fiction. For obvious reasons, actual incidents cannot be put in the public domain. With his imagination and creativity, Abhishek has been able to create and convey a sense of what could have actually happened on the ground.

Discussions with my wife, Rashmi, son, Dhawal, and daughter-in-law, Sonal, helped me focus on this endeavour and I am thankful for their encouragement. My daughter, Saloni, particularly, was a patient reader of multiple drafts and gave insightful feedback. I am also thankful to my brothers – Ujjwal, Alok and Dr Amit – for their support and enthusiasm. My late parents, Swayam Prakash Sinha and Usha Rani, have been a great influence on my life. Their guidance, teachings and strong value system played a huge part in shaping me. I would not have reached this stage of my life and career without their constant support and faith. My late mother had a photographic memory, a fraction of which I have inherited from her. She taught me to use this attribute at the opportune time and place for maximum impact.

In the end, I want to quote Abraham Lincoln, who said, 'Without the assistance of that divine being, I cannot succeed. With that assistance I cannot fail.'

D.P. Sinha
New Delhi, July 2021

∽

Who is a terrorist? Is a terrorist alone in his conscious insanity or is he the product of a process? Does a terrorist want a lot of people dead or a lot of people watching? These questions on terrorism, which is a major threat to humanity, have no easy answers.

During his stint as the UN Secretary-General (1997–2006), Kofi Annan had tried in vain to build consensus among countries about what constitutes terrorism to facilitate greater cooperation across issues, including deportation/extradition and the freezing of assets of suspects. In the 1980s, when two American academicians sought responses related to the attributes of terrorism from scholars, the exercise threw up as many as twenty-two key components.

Yet, there exists some unanimity around a broad set of ingredients that define terrorism: the use of unauthorized, deliberate, wanton violence against non-combatants and civilians for political ends. Terrorism's raison d'etre is to instil fear in the public, and this deadly challenge must be addressed holistically, according to experts. Terrorists want a lot of people watching and a lot of people listening and not a lot of people dead, according to terrorism expert Brian Jenkins.

Academicians also appear to agree upon a set of factors that contribute towards making a terrorist. These include the existence of perceived or alleged grievances that makes one receptive to new ideas or values, a body of ideology to make sense of the discontent and to propel it towards a certain direction, and the idea of being part of a group, according to academician Peter Neumann. According to psychologist-academician Professor

Fathali Moghaddam, the final stage in making a terrorist involves the side-stepping of the in-built inhibitory mechanisms against acts such as the killing of another human being.

As a political phenomenon, terrorism emerged in the late eighteenth century. The term 'Reign of Terror' came to be associated with Robespierre, one of the key actors of the 1789 French Revolution, when he began targeting 'counter-revolutionaries' in the 1790s. Later, the term 'terrorism' came to be associated with Europe's anti-monarchist forces, nihilists, anti-colonial nationalist forces, left-wing radicals, then right-wing vigilantes. The year 1979, when Russia occupied Afghanistan, marked the emergence of a strand of terrorism that was allegedly state-sponsored and made faith-based claims.

The world has suffered two of the most dastardly terror attacks in this century. One is known as the 9/11 attack of 2001 that killed around 3,000 people. It took place in the United States and was orchestrated by the Al-Qaeda.

The other tragedy is the 26/11 Mumbai attacks executed by Pakistani terror outfit Lashkar-e-Taiba, which killed 166 people in 2008. The LeT is accused of carrying out a spate of attacks across India – to wear India down as part of its strategy of attrition. LeT lures gullible youth for 'just war' in the name of dubious propaganda and 'propaganda of the deed'. It was set up in 1987 by Hafiz Saeed with the stated aim of attaining a theocratic, universal state through 'preaching' and 'armed struggle'. Its armed cadre got their first taste of combat in Kunar, Afghanistan, as part of the armed struggle against the Soviet Union. Over the years, it has acquired the reputation of being the alleged irregular special forces unit of Pakistani intelligence.

During my two-decade career as a crime reporter, I have seen – and felt – the ruinous impact of terror attacks. I cannot erase from my memory the sight of mangled body parts lying among charred metal pieces at blast sites. When I learn about a terror attack in any part of the world, the voice of a young mother, whom I met eighteen years ago, still reverberates in my ears. I can hear the desperation and the helplessness in her words. She had lost her husband, a cab driver, in the twin blasts that rocked Mumbai in 2003. But she could not afford the luxury to grieve as she had to make sure her young school-going children survived the trauma of losing their loving father. Her husband had had dreams of making them doctors or lawyers, and paying their school fees demanded her immediate attention.

Operation Trojan Horse is the story of India's fight against Pakistan-sponsored terror in the country. The Indian response is proactive and precise. The book is a work of fiction inspired by instances of supreme courage and sacrifice exhibited by a few young men who became part of secret projects like 'Operation Trojan Horse', choosing national service over lucrative careers to blunt terror. These men must remain nameless in the face of their invaluable sacrifice. The 'Trojan Horse' was a hollow wooden horse crafted by the Greeks to conceal themselves in and deceptively enter the city of Troy during the Trojan War.

Mr D.P. Sinha has been an exemplary, upright police officer and has an acclaimed record in counter-terror/intelligence operations. I am grateful to him for having faith in me and collaborating with me to bring out this reality-based fiction based on the world of shadows. Working with two brilliant editors, Siddhesh Inamdar and Shreya Dhawan, has been an absolute pleasure. They have enriched the book with their editing. I thank Siddhesh for believing in the book's premise from Day 1 and working towards being on the same page thereafter.

This book would not have been possible without the support of my family. I thank my wife, Neha, who is my fellow traveller in life, and our children, for bearing with my long hours at the laptop with a smile. I want to express my gratitude towards my late father, lawyer Tripurari Sharan Tatarvai, and my late grandfather, freedom fighter Krishna Chandra Prasad, who introduced me to the world of words, and my Ma, for their blessings and teachings. I am thankful to my niece, Aditi, for diligently proofreading the first draft and appreciating and criticizing it in equal measure. I thank my siblings, Jaya and Amit, and niece, Akansha, for their suggestions. I am grateful to all my contacts and friends in the police/security services from whom I have learned, and continue to learn, about crime and its ecosystem.

Abhishek Sharan
Mumbai, July 2021

1

'IF ANYONE MOVES, FIRE *MAARO*'

A sleek black mobile phone vibrated, a green light flickering in its top left corner. This was the third time the phone had buzzed in less than a minute. It glided a little to the left, then returned to its original position on top of a dark-brown coffee table made of sheesham wood. The table occupied the centre of the living room – a large space with white walls and black doors – in police officer Shekhar Singh's official residence in New Delhi's Lutyens' zone. It was 9.54 p.m. on 26 November 2008.

Shekhar had returned home after a long thirteen-hour workday just a while earlier. He got out of his car, a white Honda City, at the gate, which faced a lush green park. His walk to the front door was slow, one step at a time.

Shekhar rang the bell and was happy to see Anjali, his wife, when she opened the door. She was a professor in the English department at a well-known city college. Shekhar, forty-five, was of a dark complexion and six feet tall with a wiry frame.

'You seem tired. Was it another stormy day in the office?' Anjali asked. 'I have heated up water in the bathroom. You can have a hot shower, which will wash away the exhaustion. I'll get dinner ready for both of us.'

'Thanks, Anjali. Yes, it was a really hectic day at work. I had to do a lot of damage control as a project was in nosedive,' Shekhar said.

'You, of course, only talk in code, if at all. Only one of us gets that code and that's not me,' Anjali laughed.

Shekhar laughed too, patted Anjali on the cheek and headed to the washroom.

Two minutes later, though, he rushed out, a towel wrapped around his waist. Anjali had knocked on the door to inform him that his colleague, Vinay Rathod, an assistant secretary, had been calling continuously to speak to him.

Shekhar and Rathod were both senior officers working in India's premier domestic spy agency, the Counter-terrorism and Intelligence Cell – CTIC, informally referred to as CTC. The CTC was tasked with internal security, intelligence gathering and counter-terror functions. Shekhar, a joint secretary, was number two in the CTC's Operations Group hierarchy.

In his twenty years at the CTC, he had supervised the busting of several terrorist cells, most of which were controlled by Pakistan-based terror organizations such as the Lashkar-e-Taiba (LeT), the Jaish-e-Mohammed (JeM), its predecessor Harkat-ul-Mujahideen (HuM), and Pakistan's external spy agency, the Inter-Services Intelligence (ISI). In the eyes of his peers and seniors,

Shekhar had a knack for conducting challenging, audacious 'operations'. He took good care of his sources, whether human (informants and agents) or technical (gadgets and machinery). He was a no-nonsense boss, a tough task master, but stood up for his team.

Shekhar checked his phone and found that Rathod had called twice earlier as well. Three calls in less than sixty seconds. Why? What calamity had occurred and where? He braced himself for bad news as he dialled Rathod back. He was keen to find out what had transpired so that it could be dealt with effectively.

'Yes, Rathod, what is it? Is there anything urgent?' he said calmly, but unable to conceal the weariness in his voice. 'I was freshening up. I just got home actually.'

Rathod was apologetic but brisk. 'I'm really sorry, sir. But there are reports of firing happening in different parts of Mumbai, mostly south Mumbai. We don't know yet who is firing, at whom and why. This has been going on for the last twenty minutes or so. Mumbai Police is scrambling for a response. The police control room is in a state of chaos, busy dealing with the crisis unfolding.'

'Firing in Mumbai?' Shekhar said. 'This sounds like a typical mafia operation, but ... there is hardly any underworld there. Who is firing then and at whom? What is the police control room saying about the identities of the gunmen? How many casualties are there?'

'Sir, shots, suspected to be from AK-47 automatics, were reported to have been fired in high-profile landmark places that attract well-heeled locals and foreigners and at public establishments that attract a huge number of people. So far, shots have been fired at the Leopold Café at Colaba Causeway, the Taj hotel, the Chhatrapati Shivaji Terminus, and the Cama and Albless Hospital near St Xavier's College in Dhobi Talao.'

'That's strange,' Shekhar said. 'These aren't standard mafia attacks. The mafia is driven by money, and no money is to be made by killing random civilians. From the way they are carrying out their attacks and the type of weapons they are using, these gunmen seem to be trained operatives, with skills to act in an urban milieu with substantial police presence, like in the case of Mumbai. They could be terrorists – but who sent them and what outfit do they belong to? Contact Mumbai's joint commissioner for law and order and the commissioner of police. Find out the latest from them.'

'Yes, sir.'

Shekhar hung up, finished his tea and picked up an apple from the dining table. He informed Anjali about an 'emergency at work' for which he needed to rush to office.

'*Arrey*, how can you? Dinner is ready, Shekhar! You can't do this every time we plan to spend some time together!' Anjali was furious. But, a second later, she called out to Shekhar, who was at the door, and said, 'Take care and try to sleep for some time, whatever the emergency may be.'

As he stood on the porch waiting for his driver to bring around his Honda City, Shekhar caught a glint of streetlight reflecting off the dew-soaked shrubbery in the lawn outside. There was a nip in the air. The fragrance of the slender white Alstonia flowers, which bloom in Delhi's winter, wafted across to him.

Rathod was on the night shift and in charge of CTC's control room and technical communications wing, which was located in a Raj-era heritage building in a ten-acre complex on the Delhi–Haryana border.

The control room, often referred to as the operations room, was where tracking of targets, domestic and international, including terrorists, the mafia, wanted Maoists and narcotics traffickers, was done. Commands were issued to the Special Action Team to deal with emergencies, especially tasks requiring speed, use of force and stealth. The compound was outfitted with concealed telecommunication and interception equipment and remote-sensing receivers.

The Honda City cut through the late-night traffic, zipping through the streets. An hour later, Shekhar was standing in the operations room, assessing the frenetic activity going on around him.

Rathod briefed him on the latest from Mumbai. The Mumbai police had initially thought that the firing was the result of an all-out street war between rival underworld gangsters having access to sophisticated weapons, including automatics. Later, however, reports of bursts of AK-47 fire at Chhatrapati Shivaji Terminus (CST), targeting commuters, and the use of powerful hand grenades at the terminus and at the Cama Hospital a short distance away indicated the involvement of terrorists.

'According to eyewitness accounts available with the Mumbai police, both AK-47s and hand grenades were used,' Rathod said.

'Have the Mumbai police put up resistance anywhere? Is there a plan in place to deal with the carnage happening there?' Shekhar asked.

'A small team of railway policemen returned the fire, with their vintage Second World War .302 Lee Enfield rifles, driving two gunmen out of CST. But many people were killed; there are bodies strewn around in the open, pools of blood everywhere. Thanks to the policemen's fightback, the gunmen were forced to exit the terminus. The police are putting up a fight at the Taj hotel, the Oberoi Trident hotel and Nariman House, the Jewish outreach centre,' Rathod said.

'Are we hearing any chatter connected to these attacks? We have hundreds of numbers belonging to suspects linked with criminal and terror networks that are under surveillance. Is any such phone number active currently that may be relevant for us?' Shekhar asked.

While Rathod went to check on the phone numbers under surveillance, Shekhar's eyes wandered to the news coverage of the unfolding events on a large television screen in the operations room.

'There are reports of two black-and-yellow cabs going up in flames in Wadi Bunder and Vile Parle after blasts tore them up … the two taxi drivers died in the blasts,' a female news anchor informed her viewers.

Suddenly, Shekhar heard the footsteps of somebody running into the room. It was Rathod, who was visibly excited, a smile on his lips.

'Sir, one of the numbers under surveillance has just gone active. Conversations are happening on it. It seems a group of men are talking to one of the sets of gunmen active in Mumbai currently. It seems they are the controllers of the gunmen. Both the gunmen and their controllers are speaking in Punjabi laced with chaste Urdu,' Rathod said.

They both ran towards the terminal where the 'live' channel – the tapped phone number – was being monitored.

Shekhar, Rathod and the latter's deputy, Rakesh Tomar, hunched over terminal number twenty-seven, where at least twenty such phone numbers could be monitored. Rathod passed Shekhar a pair of headphones. Using a set of headphones, Tomar was listening in on the conversation occurring on the number that had been put under watch. He was making notes on a sheet of paper. Several voices could be heard on the same number, against which a tiny bulb glowed red. The number was 91-99107194XX, which was currently active in Mumbai. The Videsh Sanchar Nigam Limited (VSNL) control room had informed CTC that the call was being made to it from the US, using a virtual number, 00120-125318CC.

Rathod told Shekhar that there was one number that was active, sporadically, and several callers were in touch with it.

Tomar was attempting to locate the coordinates of both the target (referred to as Party A in technical intelligence jargon) using the intercepted phone number and the callers (Party B), who seemed like his handlers.

Shekhar asked Rathod to monitor the number closely and share any useful information the conversation might throw up that could aid in neutralizing those involved in the violence unfolding in Mumbai. He also told Rathod to keep CTC's Mumbai control room in the loop and ask it to alert the Mumbai Police if required. Just then, Tomar interrupted them.

'Sir, something serious is brewing. The target, the one whose number we put under surveillance, seems to be a small fry or a subordinate. He is talking, with respect and deference, to several men who are directing him,' said Tomar. 'They are speaking in a mix of Pakistani Punjabi and Urdu, but also using military jargon in English, like "stronghold", "hostage" and "burst fire". The one who is taking the orders has told his handlers that a man under his captivity says he is a teacher. The handler says he could be someone more important than just being a teacher. The minions thrash the captive and rebuke him for lying; saying the measly salary of a teacher cannot enable him to stay in a swank hotel like the Taj. His handlers told him, "*Maaro usko, jhooth bayaan kar raha hai* (Hit him, he is a liar).""

Tomar was interrupted by a flurry of loud sounds that emanated from the intercepted number. Amid the cacophony, the booming sounds of AK-47 burst fire and hand grenades stood out. Then, everything went quiet for almost five minutes.

Suddenly, the voices of the handlers and the target came alive.

Shekhar, Rathod and Tomar stood motionless, listening to each word in rapt attention.

Then there was a long conversation between the man whose number had been intercepted, Target (T), and those calling to direct his and his teammate's actions, Handler (H):

T: *Civilians chhat pe chaltey phirtey nazar aa rahe hain.*

H: *Jo nazar aa raha hai na, usse fire maaro. Jo bhi aadmi chalta phirta nazar aaye, harqat karta insaan nazar aaye na, usse fire maaro. Fire maaro use … thik hai na?*

T: Yes. How many died in our operation? What is the casualty figure?

H: What did you ask, brother?

T: What is the casualty figure being reported by the media? What's the media's casualty figure?

H: So far, hundreds have died.

T: Okay.

H: You must protect yourself; one of you must be in a state of alert always. Shoot at whoever you may see on the terraces in front of where you are, kill them ... What's the name of the Mexican woman who is among your hostages? What if she talks to the Mexican media and tells them about her plight and about the need to save her life?

T: Yes, we just made her talk to people in Delhi.

H: You must ensure that she does not blurt out any sensitive detail – like how many of you are there – as that will expose you to danger.

T: You are right, sir. She was opening up and was about to reveal more than what we would have liked. So, we snatched the phone away.

Shekhar, Rathod and Tomar were stunned by the conversation they had just heard. They looked at each other in disbelief. Neither uttered a word nor moved, as if they had frozen. An uneasy silence fell over the bay containing terminal number twenty-seven.

Shekhar called up his superior to update him about the situation in Mumbai and the fact that the attackers were in touch with their controllers, possibly located outside of the city.

Five minutes later, the number became active again. Silence descended upon terminal number twenty-seven once more.

H: *Yeh jo aapne abhi grenade phenki hain na, usse media mein shor mach gaya hai.*

'The man whose phone we have intercepted appears to be at the Taj hotel,' Shekhar told Rathod. The 'target' had received a call from a virtual number, which was used by a bevy of 'handlers' who spoke to the terrorists in Mumbai, Rathod explained.

A few minutes later, Shekhar and his team heard the conversation between the handlers and the target.

H2: Ashfaque had dictated a statement to you. Do you have that with you?

T: Yes.

H2: Speak to Qama till then, I am handing over the phone to him. He wants to dictate a couplet to you.

H3: This is Qama here. Do you have a pen and paper ready?

T: Qama Bhai, how are you? May the Almighty keep you safe and bless you.

H3: May the Almighty bless you. Now write this:

Ye sach hai ki andheron ka tasalluf hai magar

Shama bujhne na denge zulm ke iwanon mein

Aandhiyan zulmon tashadud ki bahot tez

Hum hi woh deep hai jinhe jalna hai tufaanon mein

H4 (Ashfaque): Tell the media what you would like to tell them, reveal your thoughts to them. Do not reveal your location and numerical strength to them. The media will run for hours whatever you may tell them. Tell the Indian youth to sacrifice their lives for jihad.'

H5: There is a wazir at your hotel, probably on the first floor.

T: Yes.

H5: Abduct him, and then all of India will kneel before you, will agree to your demands.

H1: Are you setting the fire or not?

T: Not yet. I am getting a mattress ready for burning.

H1: What did you do with the body?

T: Left it behind in the boat.

H1: Did you not open the boat's lock located at its bottom? You had been told to open the lock while exiting the boat … The seawater rushing inside the boat would have drowned it within minutes. You left a vessel brimming with evidence instead of sinking it all!

T: No, we did not open the locks. We left in a hurry. We made a big mistake.

H1: One more? What big mistake?

T: When we were getting into the boat, the waves were quite high. Another boat came. Everyone raised the alarm that the navy had come. In the confusion, Ismail's satellite phone got left behind.

The line went quiet again and Shekhar turned quickly to Rathod.

'Share the Mumbai gunman's number, the virtual number and the multiple handlers' numbers with the Maharashtra ATS. Request Uttam Saxena, the Mumbai station chief of the Research and Intelligence Wing, who has worked with the Maharashtra Police, to listen to the conversations between the gunman and his handlers. Also, share with the Mumbai CP and the Mumbai police control room whatever information of operational value that can be deducted from the intercepted communications. And ask the navy and coast guard to be on the lookout for the satellite phone on a boat or motor launch which brought these gunmen.'

'Yes, sir. Sir, we now know how this number came under our surveillance. It was you who authorized the interception of this number and two others around three months ago. You said the tapped numbers could be of help one day. The LeT must have procured the SIM cards for these numbers to give to its suicide attackers in India.'

Shekhar stared blankly at Rathod. Initially, he had no recollection of having authorized the surveillance. Seconds later, it all came back to him.

A senior Jammu and Kashmir police officer, Shrikant Bhaskar, had approached Shekhar around three months ago, giving the latter the opportunity to plant the SIM cards in the LeT. A Kashmir police intelligence department's operative, codenamed 'Mongoose', who had infiltrated the LeT and was able to embed himself in the local unit as a committed terrorist who specialized in supplying logistics for terror operations, had informed Bhaskar about the directive of his Lashkar 'commander' to buy thirty-five prepaid Indian SIM cards. Shekhar was delighted to get such an opportunity.

Shekhar had thereafter arranged for three prepaid SIM cards, purchased in Delhi, to get embedded in the LeT. Shekhar had had a hunch that the cards were meant for some big operation of the LeT in India.

Bhaskar was involved in several counter-insurgency and counter-intelligence operations, largely against the Pakistan-based groups in the state, in active cooperation with CTC.

'If one of those three SIM cards has become active, it means that the Mumbai attack is being orchestrated by LeT's men on the ground, since the cards were procured by the LeT's setup in Kashmir for sending to Pakistan,' Shekhar said.

The actual groundwork for this major breakthrough, which allowed a peek inside the secretive world of the shadowy outfit, and which enabled the CTC, Mumbai Police and other counter-terror agencies such as the Anti-Terrorism and Counter-Intelligence Squad (ATCS) and the Research and Intelligence Wing (R&IW) to listen in to the conversations of the attackers active in Mumbai, had begun around a decade earlier.

Ten years ago, the capture of a young LeT terrorist who had entered India illegally after crossing the India–Pakistan border had led to a series of revelations and developments that made CTC undertake a classified mission to slip into the heart of LeT's terror infrastructure in Pakistan and India.

The mission's objective was twofold: to prevent, neutralize and weaken LeT's terror attacks in India, and to destroy the Pakistani outfit, the terror mother ship, from within.

2

DAWN ABDUCTION

A ten-foot-wide road split off westward from the eight-lane Hyderabad–Mumbai highway to reach Rukhsar Ganj's three-hundred-year-old Al Aqsa Noorani mosque. A beautiful structure with tall, Prussian-blue minarets and a near-perfect white dome, the mosque was known to fulfil the wishes of a true *namazi,* a faithful who offers prayers. It was also the lower-middle-class locality's only claim to fame in a heritage-rich city, where the past coexists with the present. Five times a day, around a hundred faithfuls bustled through its halls and courtyards to offer prayers.

The brick road was narrow, with gaps, but was built like an arrow. Open drains flanked its sides. Two kids, bare bottomed and in white vests, sat on their knees. Two goats, one much smaller than the other and with a pink line across its white-brown fur, were challenging each other, their heads bent and horns clattering noisily. The air was laden with the smell of soil-coated bricks, wet since the previous night's rains, of the jasmine flowers outside a row of white single-storey houses, and of putrid drain water. The road was the main way of passage in Rukhsar Ganj.

A kilometre ahead, it came to a dead end. To its left stood the Noorani mosque, its campus spread over a rectangular plot of land, with decades-old banyan and tamarind trees standing by waist-high boundary walls.

Diagonally opposite the mosque, across the road, was the single-storey house of Saeed Ali, known as 'Ali sahab' locally, the imam of Noorani mosque. Ali's house was painted white and had a lemon and a tamarind tree outside it.

As the mosque's prayer leader for the last forty years, Ali was known for his soulful recitation of the holy words praising the Almighty, and for his love for the pious.

Ali counted himself as one of the beneficiaries of the mosque's divine blessings. To have a lovely daughter like Rahat, a twenty-seven-year-old with a master's degree in computer applications and a topper throughout, who had got her striking looks and candour from her late mother, was nothing short of a divine blessing for him. But the true confirmation of the fact that he was blessed, Ali would tell his close friends and relatives, lay in the fact that he had a son-in-law like Salim Khwaja Amjad.

A thirty-year-old automobile engineer-turned garage owner, Salim was perfect for Rahat, Ali reckoned. He took good care of her and their two young daughters and ran the garage well. Despite having spent the first eighteen years of his life in a Patna-based orphanage run by a trust, which funded his education till the completion of his engineering course, Salim seemed well brought up. He was the son Ali never had.

'Just look at Salim,' Saeed would tell his relatives sometimes. 'What a fine young man he turned out to be. He did not have a mother's lap or a father's hand on his head, which each child needs to grow up as a fine human being.'

A practical man, Salim kept a cool head and found a way out of the most trying times. He abjured emotion when dealing with an issue, except when it was about Rahat and his *deen*, his religion.

Rahat was his world, he would tell her. They had fallen in love after meeting a few times at a common acquaintance's house. They got married after taking Ali's approval. Their twin daughters, Chahat and Jannat, aged five, took after their mother in their appearance and easy-going nature and were sharp like their abba, Salim.

He could, on occasion, be as passionate as pragmatic. The atrocities perpetrated against the Muslim community in India was a topic that made Salim quiver with rage. He would grieve over reports of violence and killings during the 1992 Bombay riots. Some of the listeners would say his claims were exaggerated while Salim would manage to fill a few others with rage. Ali would see tears in Salim's eyes at such times. Salim would then talk about 'the duty of each able-bodied man to avenge the wrongs done to the community'.

Early on the morning of 13 July 1999, around 5.30 a.m., Ali's family was up and about. The flock of roosters, which stayed in the mosque compound, had just given their second call of the dawn. Ali sahab, who would be turning seventy-five the next month, was pacing up and down the corridor between his bedroom and the drawing room. Till late into the previous night he had been attempting to finish writing an article titled 'Duties of a Faithful' for a conservative Urdu weekly, *Paigham*. When Ali got up in the morning, his spectacles were nowhere to be found. He had to be at the mosque for the morning prayer in thirty minutes, though he was hardly prepared to start his day.

'Abba, I checked everywhere, where do you think you kept your glasses?' Rahat asked him. 'Salim is also looking for them but can't find them.'

She was of a slender build, fair in complexion and, at five feet six inches, looked taller than she was. Salim soon joined them in the corridor.

'Abba, don't you worry. Relax for two minutes. Rahat, give him tea and let him rest. I will lead the prayers at the mosque, he has trained me enough,' Salim said.

'But won't you get late for work?' Ali asked.

'I can manage. I will join you for breakfast before leaving for the garage,' Salim said.

Salim put on his leather slippers and left the house for the mosque. Rahat followed him out of the house.

Before crossing the road to reach the mosque, Salim passed by a newspaper vendor, whom Rahat had not seen before in the neighbourhood. She saw the hawker fold up his stall then rush towards a telephone booth a few metres away.

Seconds later, a black car with tinted glasses came hurtling towards her house but halted metres away from it, almost knocking over Salim. Two muscular men clad in safari suits and wearing sunglasses leapt out of it.

'*Teri maa ki* … don't you know how to drive?' Salim screamed.

But the two men were all over Salim in an instant, punching and kicking him.

A man clad in a white shirt and sporting black Aviator sunglasses sat inside.

'*Chalo*,' he said sharply to the other men, who then bundled him inside and left.

'Salim! Salim! Where are you taking Salim? Abba, they are taking Salim away! Abba, come out please ... Let go of him, where are you taking him?' Rahat shouted, running after the car. 'Who are you?'

Two hours later, Rahat was still at the Rukhsar Ganj police station with Ali, lodging a complaint about her husband's abduction.

Sixteen kilometres from the police station, at the Hyderabad airport, a lone chopper painted orange and white sat motionless on a tiny airstrip. The car suddenly appeared next to the chopper. A sedated Salim was shifted to the chopper. The car then reversed and disappeared in a flash.

3

WAITING GAME

His head felt like it was about to explode. The pain was agonizing. Salim put his hand on his forehead and pressed it. He suppressed the cry that was about to escape his lips, even as he realized that the crusty coating he felt was probably blood.

Salim sat in silence for a few minutes, trying his best to ignore the sea of pain throbbing through his body. Had he passed out? He tried to figure out where he was and why. He looked around the room he found himself in. It had white walls and clean granite floors, with wooden doors painted dark brown. Was it a government office? The memories, meanwhile, came flooding back.

He was heading to Noorani mosque when a black car had rammed into him from behind, he recalled. He was seething and had rushed to confront the burly men who had alighted. The duo, as if expecting Salim's response, were ready for him. One of them had kicked Salim on his left knee and that had made him wobble. He had fallen on the road. His two adversaries were waiting for that moment. The duo had then thumped Salim, raining blows on his chest and back, almost in a practised rhythm, wordlessly.

Were they professionals, trained combatants? They knew what they were doing, Salim thought. This thought made him uneasy suddenly. The fight was staged? He sank deeper in thought.

He recalled losing consciousness. Next, he remembered being in the vehicle, which was zipping past parked aircraft in what looked like the Hyderabad airport. He remembered a booming voice asking the men in the vehicle to put him in a chopper.

He was now lying on a mattress; his wrists and feet were bound. An orange plastic glass with water was kept on a stool nearby. A plate with two slices of white bread and an omelette was kept there too.

He looked around and saw a small crack in the door frame. Through the crack he could see brilliant golden light outside.

So, was it noon? Salim's mind was racing. He tried to stand but fell down. His knees hurt. For a minute he sat still, waited for the pain in his knees to subside and then dragged himself to the door.

His face pressed against the wall, he peered through the crack. Four men in jeans and T-shirts with cropped hair stood outside in what looked like a long, wide corridor of a three- or four-storey building. The athletically built men carried automatics, the Russian-built AK-47s and the German MP-5s. One of them was pacing the corridor with measured steps, the other three were chatting in a huddle. One of them carried a newspaper.

The building he was being held in seemed to be on one of the four sides of a square-shaped complex. He could also see two watchtowers, one on each side of the building, manned by men in civvies. They were bent over what seemed like long-range sniper rifles.

'Farhan Qureshi, get up, bastard!'

The moment Salim had been dreading had arrived. He shuddered and shut his eyes.

The door of his room was flung open. A lone bulb emitting a pale yellow light was switched on, and the two burly men who had thrashed him outside the mosque entered.

'Pakistani snake! *Aatankwadi, qaatil kahin ka*! Just see how we will screw you and your terrorist *baap, chacha*. And everybody in the cave from where you came!' one of the two men who had barged into the room screamed at Salim.

He caught hold of Salim's neck and landed punches on his stomach, one after another. The other man joined in. He pinned Salim's face to the floor and began slapping him hard. The thrashing continued for about half a minute. Then there was a knock on the door.

The pain from the blows did not matter to Salim. It was what they had dubbed him to be that bothered him – a terrorist. His assailants had also accused him of being a non-Indian – a 'Pakistani', to be precise. They had also called him Farhan Qureshi.

One of his two assailants went to the door and spoke in a low voice. When he returned, he and his companion began questioning Salim.

They had many questions:

'When did you reach Hyderabad from Pakistan?'

'Were you not preparing to kill dozens in serial blasts across Hyderabad during the city's annual Ganesh Chaturthi procession?'

For the next few hours, his interrogators treated him roughly but were surprised when Salim survived the ordeal without asking why he was being targeted.

'He is being thrashed on an hourly basis, sir, but he is yet to divulge anything. He has not winced.' One of the assailants was on phone.

Salim also heard another voice, which he recognized as the booming voice he had heard earlier, giving the command to put him in the chopper.

'Did he ask why he was picked up? Is he shocked or furious?'

'No boss. He has not asked who we are or where he is. He is a slab of stone!'

'That's nice,' said the man with the booming voice. He took out his phone and punched a number. 'We have the right man. Had he not been who he is, he would have been screaming out about why he got plucked out. But he has not. He knows he is busted and is scared now.'

4

'BREAKING' SALIM

'*Theek hai, band karo yeh,*' the man with the booming voice spoke sharply as he entered the room.

His rebuke startled Salim's minders. 'Yes, boss,' one of them said feebly. The duo stopped hitting Salim and stood in attention.

'Get a few chairs; make him sit on a stool,' the 'boss' ordered.

Salim was made to sit on a wooden stool that one of the men brought in from outside. He was given a glass of water. But it was snatched away even as he was taking gulps from it. He wiped away the blood on his forehead and at the corner of his lips while glaring at the man who had done that.

'What animal-like behaviour!' Salim scolded the man. 'Sir, what is this? Are you all goons?' Salim asked the 'boss', finally laying eyes on him.

The boss, who was at least six feet tall with a wiry frame and a thin moustache, was Shekhar Singh. It was he who had led the operation to grab Salim from the sleepy Rukhsar Ganj. Salim was now being held at the New Delhi zonal headquarters of Delhi Police's Special Squad, which worked closely with the CTC.

'Good afternoon, Salim,' Shekhar said, smiling. 'But who are you? Salim, a garage owner from Hyderabad and the son-in-law of a law-abiding imam? Or Pakistan's Farhan? When did you slip into Hyderabad?' Shekhar's voice began in an even tone. But it was rising rapidly.

'*Janaab*, there is some confusion, I am sure … I am Salim Khwaja Amjad. I am an automobile engineer and run a garage in Hyderabad. *Padha-likha, ek professional hoon, sir*,' he said.

'A "professional" you are, and well trained at that, if I may add,' Shekhar said. 'Let me ask you a few things: When were you dispatched to India from Pakistan? Did the Lashkar-e-Taiba send you? LeT's India operations boss Al-Cheema sent you, right? Who are you reporting to in ISI? You Lashkar men sent on long-term covert missions report to two masters, to LeT and ISI, right? What are you working on?'

'What rubbish is this? Sir, you are mistaking me for someone else. Your men thrashed me, kidnapped me from in front of my home. Is this how educated youth are being treated by whoever is running you? You can ask my family, my relatives in Hyderabad and Patna, who I am,' Salim's words came in a torrent. He seemed to be in a rage over Shekhar's accusations.

'Don't worry, we will ask your relatives too. Where are your parents? Tell me, where you are going to conduct your blasts?' Shekhar asked. His query appeared to have jolted Salim, who just stared at him.

'I know you already have the explosives required for the job. When is your return to Pakistan scheduled for, or will you stay back to carry out the mission yourself? Are you a fidayeen? A suicide attacker?' Shekhar asked.

'*Zulm hai yeh*, to defame an innocent person. This is an attempt to frame me,' Salim retorted, glaring at Shekhar. Shekhar smiled at him.

'But, considering the rat that you appear to be, even your Babaji would not trust you with a suicide mission,' Shekhar said, chuckling. Shekhar noticed Salim's jaw had tightened.

'Sir, I am not a Pakistani, I am from Patna; my parents are dead, and I was brought up in an orphanage there.'

For a few moments, the interrogator and the accused merely looked at each other. Shekhar turned his face towards one of the two men who had assaulted Salim. The muscular man came bounding down towards Salim, picked up his five-foot, nine-inch frame and threw him back on to the floor. He slapped Salim twice as well.

Fury turned Salim's face red. He had taken the thrashing with spunk but the slap had hit a raw nerve. Salim, to his acquaintances, was a character who never shied away from a physical fight and was known to be quite skilled in combat techniques. He was furious at being slapped around here. His 'teachers' had warned him against letting his anger get the better of him but he wanted to do just that at this moment. If he could free himself, he would tear the man to pieces for daring to slap him.

5

THE CONFESSION

Shekhar continued with the interrogation. Salim felt like strangling him for his provocative, direct queries. 'My men say that you are a coward, a spineless rat,' Shekhar began in a low tone. 'There's evidence that you came here to kill – kids, old men and women. And to do this, you resorted to deception. You deceived your wife, what's her name, yes, Rahat ... A simple girl, who trusted you, loved you but got deceived. She, your daughters and Ali sahab do not know that you are fake. In fact, you are a killer!'

Salim flinched at Shekhar's nerve, but said nothing.

'But you ran out of luck. We are here to host you, Al-Cheema's rat! Do you value your life, Farhan? Then sing!'

When Salim said nothing, Shekhar continued. '*Apne gunaah qubool kar, warna uparwaley ko kya jawaab dega tu, Farhan?* Who is your target? Which places have you visited so far? Who are your collaborators here?'

Salim ignored the questions. For a minute, he sat erect and unmoving. Then he bent his head a little, looking down at the black granite floor. Finally, he raised his eyes and met Shekhar's gaze without blinking. Shekhar sat on a chair; he sat cross-legged, with bare feet, on the floor three feet away. His eyes were bloodshot.

'*Hath khol dein janab, aukaat dikha dunga aap sab ki*,' he said in a low tone.

Shekhar was stunned. He looked at one of the two men who were assisting him in the interrogation. The man stepped up to Salim and slapped him once, then returned to the spot where he was standing.

Shekhar said, 'His Pakistani blood is boiling. He wants to talk to us? Speak up, save your life, Farhan.' He glared at Salim. 'Tell me, what's your work here? Why did you come? '

'I have told you already. I did my engineering course at a college in Phulwari Sharif, Patna.'

'Where did you stay? How far was the college from your home? Who did you know at your college? Who were your neighbours?'

'I stayed at Pathar ki Masjid Lane, Sultangunj, in Patna City. The college was some … er … twenty or thirty kilometres away, sir. I know my classmates, of course, and the teachers. Ahmed sahab … Ahmed sahab was my immediate neighbour. *Inteqal ho gaya kuch saal pehle*. His family is now in Riyadh. I don't have their numbers.'

Shekhar scoffed. 'Your parents and neighbour are dead. The dead neighbour's family is abroad. What a story, Farhan. What is your mother's maiden name? When did you complete the engineering course?'

'I completed my engineering course in 1992, from Abdul Bari Islamia Engineering College. Rasheeda was my mother's name.'

'Classmates' names? What was your roll number?'

'Roll number fifty-six. Tariq Khan, Ahmed Nabi, Muzammil Ansari and Anwar Sheikh were my classmates. I no longer have their numbers.'

Shekhar spoke to one of the co-interrogators in the room. 'Anvay, call up the principal of his college and get the current contact numbers of a few students of the 1992 batch. Check the original roll number fifty-six's mother's name.'

Shekhar turned to Salim. 'You are in big trouble, my friend. You will now see how we call your bluff.'

For a few moments, Salim kept staring at Shekhar, then shifted his gaze to a point on the granite floor. Minutes later, during which no one spoke in the lock-up, it was Salim who broke the silence. 'Sir, I need a cigarette,' he said in impeccable English.

Shekhar took out a pack of cigarettes from his shirt pocket and passed it to Salim. He gave him his tiny red lighter as well. Salim picked out a cigarette and returned the pack.

Suddenly, Anvay rushed in. 'Sir, roll number fifty-six's name was Salim, of course, but he is dead. The college keeps no record of a student's mother's maiden name but the principal knew the mother of Salim, the one who is now dead. The principal and roll number fifty-six's mother had studied together in college. Roll number fifty-six's mother's name was Saleema. Not Rasheeda.'

A smile spread on Anvay's face as he glared at Salim. 'This rascal's cover is blown. His handlers had prepared him well but that was not enough.'

Shekhar was smiling too but said nothing. He lit up a cigarette. 'Salim, are you the ghost of roll number fifty six?' he asked. Salim said nothing. He asked for another cigarette instead. For the next five minutes, the captor and captive blew out plumes of white smoke. Salim smoked as if he had all the time in the world and was at home.

On finishing his cigarette, he was quiet for a few minutes. He snapped his fingers at Anvay, then turned to Shekhar. '*Janaab*, what do you want? I will tell you.'

Shekhar was waiting for this moment. 'Which district in Pakistan do you belong to?'

'I am from the holy land, Pakistan.'

'Which district in Pakistan?'

'Bahawalpur.'

'When did you come here? To India?'

'January 1995. I am Farhan Qureshi. Salim is my assumed identity. You Indians did your homework properly this time!' Salim had a mocking smile on his face.

'Wipe the smirk off your face. What's the mission? Who are you planning to kill, or rather how many? Your collaborators? Where are the explosives and arms?'

'Those are not here yet. The attack will be staged in a month. Beyond that, I don't know what I may be asked to do.'

'How long were you to stay here?'

Salim laughed. 'Where would I go?'

'What is your mission? This is the last time I am asking you. Answer! Or you will be sent to meet your ancestors, wherever they may be!'

'*Sarey Hyderabad mein dhamaaka karna tha!* On Ganesh Chaturthi, bodies will be strewn around streets. The sound of the blasts will pierce the ears of the rioters of Mumbai and Ahmedabad and those who pulled down the holy Babri Masjid at Ayodhya.'

'Okay, then what?'

Salim looked confused by Shekhar's question and gaped at him. Shekhar stared at him without blinking. Salim gathered himself quickly. 'I was to coordinate with the ongoing projects of the Lashkar sleeper modules and ISI agents in India. I take the final calls for them, I have been authorized. I am the commander of sleeper agents in India. Target? There are many but with one aim. *Hindustan ko tabaah karna hai.* Till Kashmir, Hyderabad, Junagadh and the Lal Qila of Dilli join Pakistan, the mission is to continue.'

'You will just return to Bahawalpur in a shroud!' Shekhar taunted.

'Who is going back? Not me! I came here to live and die. Babaji told me to get buried in Hindustan.'

'Al-Cheema – your Babaji! He is your commander, your *ustaad*, isn't he? When did you join LeT?'

'Yes, Babaji's teams taught me how to assemble and defuse a bomb. And how to use Kalashnikovs, MP5 automatics, light machine guns, machine guns and PIKA guns. I did a twenty-one-day course, *Daura-e-Aam*, in which I underwent basic training related to weapons, explosives and physical fitness.

'There was a ninety-day commando course, *Daura-e-Khaas*, which included exhaustive skills training related to the use of weapons, explosives and unarmed combat. We were taught about our *deen* and its core teachings. I later did an advanced course on intelligence gathering and sabotage, *Daura-e-Ribaat*, whose duration was of three months.

'I did two additional courses in theology, *Daura-e-Sufa* and *Daura-e-Tadrib-Al-Musaleem*, meant to strengthen our knowledge about our *deen*.'

'Why Hyderabad? Why did you choose to come to Hyderabad?' Shekhar asked.

'I came to Hindustan in 1995 to run a PCO booth in Old Delhi, but it failed to take off. Then I went to Haryana, Mumbai and finally Hyderabad. Now, Hyderabad is where my garage and family are.'

'You will die. Your efforts have been wasted, Farhan,' Shekhar said.

'A moment spent in jihad gives you far more rewards than even a million prayers offered at the Kaaba, that too on the night of Lailat-ur-Qadr, the pious night of Ramadan, *janaab*. Babaji told me this.'

'You are a lowly killer, and so is Al-Cheema. Both of you will die like dogs. Your religion, the noble religion of Islam, does not have place for terrorists like you, remember that.'

Shekhar fell silent, and for a long time both men stayed quiet, exhausted. Shekhar lit up a cigarette again.

Shekhar signalled to Anvay to switch off the tape recorder and camera that were installed in the room.

Shekhar turned to Salim. 'It's late, Farhan. You will get your dinner, then you should sleep. We begin at 3 a.m. again.'

Half an hour later, Salim got his dinner. When he was done, he requested Anvay for another cigarette. He was given a bed sheet, a blanket and a glass of water at the end of his first day at the Special Squad's regional headquarters.

On the fifth floor, Shekhar was listening to the tapes of Farhan's confession for the third time. He had spent ten years dealing with Pakistan-sponsored terror and sabotage activities, but he knew that the current assignment could dwarf the challenges he had encountered so far.

Later, he sent an encrypted text message to his superiors: 'The Pakistani kid, who was nabbed at the border in 1996, had revealed Farhan's (alias Salim) presence in India. He spoke the truth. Hyderabad's Salim, who is in our custody, has confessed to being Farhan, who arrived from Pakistan to never return. He led a few LeT–ISI sleeper modules and had been plotting serial blasts on Ganesh Chaturthi in Hyderabad. Interrogation is on. I will update further. Shekhar.'

6

AN ENCOUNTER

It was pitch dark and silent. Not a soul could be seen on the wide Khemkaran–Kasur road in Punjab's Khemkaran town, which lies barely a few kilometres away from the India–Pakistan border. At 3.12 a.m. on 14 January 1996, the stillness was broken by bursts of gunfire that continued for a couple of minutes.

The bullets were being traded by members of a police night patrol team and unidentified persons who were using a truck as their shield. The patrol team had received information from military intelligence about the arrival of three Pakistani intruders on a specific terror mission and had been halting all vehicles on the roads for inspection. The occupants of this truck, however, had taken a long time to produce their travel documents and licences and had finally opened fire with their weapons, AK-47s, hidden only inches from where they sat.

Two patrolmen, who took the first volley of bullets, died instantly. The rest lost no time in overpowering the driver and the passenger who sat next to him. The duo was dragged out of the truck and thrashed. When the beating stopped and it was assumed that the targets were immobilized, one of them tried to scamper away, but a single bullet aimed at his knee broke his run.

Just as the patrolmen were about to drive away, with their two captives seated in the back of their armoured wagon, a deafening explosion made the vehicle jump in the air and turn turtle. A hand grenade had landed a few feet away from the wagon. Moments later, the patrolmen somehow made their way out of the vehicle and took positions around it to deal with the new aggressor.

One of the patrolmen, the team leader, Inspector Sumer Singh, took out a megaphone to communicate with the aggressor.

'Scoundrel … Whoever you are, wherever you are hiding, this is the first and final warning. Come out of the truck with your hands raised. Or die.'

The warning drew a volley of gunshots from the truck, which was loaded with bales of hay.

Singh fired five shots from his service pistol even as his team members also fired their AK-47s at the bundles of dry hay, which went up in flames.

'Come out, coward, your death awaits you,' Singh shouted.

A man clad in a white kurta-pyjama, with a black shawl draped around his shoulders, jumped out of the back of the truck, holding a Kalashnikov above his head. Two patrolmen jumped on him and pinned him down, raining blows on him. The automatic rifle, with a capacity to fire up to eighty rounds per minute, a favourite of Pakistan-sponsored terrorists as well as Indian security personnel, was quickly taken off him.

'Shine the torch on this rascal's face … let's see who he is,' Singh instructed one of his men.

The beam revealed an angry-looking, fair-skinned boy with burning eyes and barely any facial hair, who could not have been a day older than fifteen. Singh was stumped. He had never seen such a young killer sent across by the ISI.

'*Oye, uha seraph ik ladka hai.* He is just a boy. A killer boy! *Twada nama ki haiga*? Singh said.

'Jigar Singh.'

'Jigar Singh? What's your age?'

'Fifteen years, two months.'

'You three are terrorists? The Pakistani army and the ISI sent you here in the dead of night! We are asleep here?' Singh asked.

'No, I am an Indian. Those men you caught are my uncles, they are local farmers.'

'Farmers? AK-47s grow in your fields, is it? Come to the police station. Your uncles as well as your father will talk there.'

The police wagon left for the station. By then, an ambulance had arrived, and the paramedics were taking out stretchers to carry the two men to the district hospital.

'No wonder, sir, the Pakistan rangers have been firing since yesterday. They were providing cover for these terrorists to sneak in,' Singh said when narrating what had happened to his superior on the wireless.

Punjab's districts along the international border were not new to random shelling. India's security forces and intelligence agencies, however, knew that the shelling by the Pakistan rangers always had a purpose and was never random. In the 1980s and '90s, such shelling would coincide with attempts to launch trained Khalistani terrorists into India for terror missions.

There were several pro-Khalistan outfits whose top leadership was hosted and funded by the Pakistani Deep State, that is, the army and the ISI. The most active amongst the Khalistani outfits, operating out of Lahore and Karachi, were the Khalistan Liberation Commandos and the International Sikh Youth Group.

7

'LEADER IS IN INDIA ALREADY'

Four hours after the police encounter in Khemkaran, Jigar was yanked out of a cell at the Shahid Bhagat Singh police station. The station house officer, Hoshiyaar Singh, wanted to see him.

Hoshiyaar had spent the last fifteen years of his career on assignments in border districts and preferred the rough but direct method of dealing with people detained or arrested for alleged involvement in terrorism and espionage. He did not believe in the 'carrot and stick' technique, the employment of both soft and hard approaches to extract information from a subject.

For Jigar, a team was in place to grill him. Apart from Hoshiyaar and his aides, Constable Sucha Singh, Head Constable Sangram Singh and CTC's Shekhar were also there.

Shekhar had been woken up at 4 a.m. by a phone call from his boss. He had asked him to rush to Delhi's Palam airport, where a chartered chopper was waiting to take him to Khemkaran. From the Khemkaran airstrip, a police car took him to the Shahid Bhagat Singh police station.

His boss had also briefed him: 'A fifteen-year-old boy has been nabbed with two Pakistan-trained Sikh terrorists, who crossed over from Pakistan, then killed two cops in a midnight encounter.'

Shekhar was asked to find out why the trio had infiltrated into India and, specifically, why a fifteen-year-old boy had been sent.

The boy's questioning began at 8.15 a.m. Hoshiyaar began with the basics.

'What's your name, Junior? Your two uncles gave us your name, but I want you to confirm it. Speak up!' Hoshiyaar Singh screamed at the boy.

'You came here to plant bombs at movie theatres in Delhi on 26 January? At Minerva, Ram and Liberty theatres in Delhi's Connaught Place? Gift of death on our Republic Day, is it?'

When the boy refused to speak, Hoshiyaar continued. 'We know who you are, Junior! Do you want to talk? Your hands are already broken in several places; shall we break some more? You are young but mixed up with vile, murderous people…

'Confess to your crimes here, do your jail term and we can try to reduce its quantum for you, provided you cooperate. Then return home to your father and mother, brothers and sisters. Live your life there well, do something worth doing. Or else, you face hell here. You know, jails are not good places.'

As if on cue, Sucha leapt towards Jigar and slapped him hard. Jigar winced.

'I told you all who I am,' Jigar blurted out, a scowl on his face.

Sucha left the room when Hoshiyaar looked at him. Sucha returned seconds later, wheeling in an electronic contraption. He twisted Jigar's left hand. Jigar yelped loudly.

Hoshiyaar waved at Sucha, who stepped back. 'Talk, Junior. You are too young to survive these electric shocks. You may also turn impotent due to these shocks. Want to become impotent or a vegetable? Sucha hates your silence. Speak up!'

For a full minute, no one spoke in the room. Shekhar was watching Jigar closely.

'Stop beating me. I am not a Khalistani. I was only with the two men you caught with me. I have no knowledge of bomb blasts planned in Delhi theatres,' Jigar said.

Shekhar signalled Hoshiyaar to pause.

'Why did you accompany the Sikh men? Why is a minor running around with terrorists attempting to cross an international border? You have to be a terrorist. Aren't you?' Shekhar asked Jigar.

'Tell your Sucha to fuck off from here with his machine. I will tell you...' Jigar spoke calmly while looking at the contraption. Sucha left the room after Hoshiyaar nodded at him.

'Firoze Ashraf. My name is Firoze Ashraf. I am from Sialkot.'

'Why did you come here? Why did you join them? Did somebody force you? Or did you join them seeking paradise or money?'

'Money for what? Who can force me?'

'So, why did you come here?'

'Babaji ... Janaab Al-Cheema ... sent me here. I don't know who those two men are except that they work for the ISI and have some links with Babaji. They were asked to bring me to India for the Delhi job. I am the bomb-maker. These men only know how to plant bombs and fire a Kalashnikov. I can make bombs with delayed timers using Integrated Circuit chips.'

Hoshiyaar asked him, 'Where are the bomb-making materials, the detonators? Who taught you bomb-making? Where are the chips? How did you enter India? Who helped you from this side of the border?'

'Some of the bomb-making material is in the cavity beneath the driver's seat in the truck. The chips were to be bought at the Paris Electronics shop on M.G. Road in Khemkaran. Our Delhi contact was to arrange for a shelter and anything else we required.'

Jigar paused before continuing. 'The Khemkaran contact met us with a truck, which was stolen. He left after giving us the keys to the truck and the address of a dhaba that he runs on the Chandigarh–Khemkaran highway. We were to spend the next forty-eight hours at the dhaba, in the small rooms he has built for patrons, posing as transporters. From Chandigarh, we were to take a bus to Delhi after dumping the truck in a remote, forested tract near Chandigarh.'

'How did you enter India?' Hoshiyaar asked him again.

'We used gas-powered cutters to cut through the metal wires at the border, near milestone number 137, in the Khemkaran sector. There is a big ditch along the milestone, and we hid there for several hours after crossing the border at 9 last night. The cutters are buried north of the ditch, ten inches below the surface.'

'What were you supposed to do after the Minerva job? How will you return to Pakistan? What's your exit plan?' Shekhar took up the questioning.

'After the blasts, I was to take up a job as a hotel worker, then enrol in a school once my papers were made. Babaji told us that we will destroy India. They will have to answer for the Babri Masjid's demolition, and the victims of Bombay's 1992 riots.'

'How many men has Babaji sent to do what he said must be done?' Shekhar asked.

'I was asked to wait for further instructions. Our leader is already in India; he will contact me. Babaji said we will have to set up our network, our sleeper cells. They are to be activated for action, then wait for further instructions.'

'Why has your leader been sent to India? Where is he, what's his name? When will he return to Pakistan?'

'I do not know his name. He is settled in India. There is no exit plan for him,' Jigar said with a chuckle.

'No exit plan?' Shekhar was surprised. 'Why?'

'Babaji said he has been sending trained Lashkar mujahideen to Hindustan to settle down. Permanently. To wage jihad from inside, to create a local base of collaborators and mujahids to conduct or aid in doing direct actions, blasts...'

Shekhar couldn't believe what he was hearing. 'How many such men have been sent here by your Babaji?'

'I do not know much. But he often spoke about the leader, who was sent to Delhi in 1995. To run a PCO booth, but it did not work out and so he went somewhere else.'

'How many operations has the leader carried out so far?'

'None.' Jigar turned to Hoshiyaar and taunted him, 'Go, SHO sahib, find him if you and your Sucha Singh are sons of your parents!'

Shekhar signalled to Hoshiyaar to stay calm. He knew that the boy's cooperation was crucial for finding out more details about the LeT's unprecedented plan to send men to India to never return. Such a possibility took the challenge of dealing with Pakistan-sponsored terror to another level.

Shekhar stepped out of the interrogation room to call his superior.

8

BABAJI'S MAN WITH
NO EXIT PLAN

The plot to bomb several movie theatres in Delhi was nipped in the bud. The two Khalistani operatives and Firoze Ashraf, alias Jigar Singh, were grilled thoroughly and later kept captive in a Patiala jail. But the disclosure that Ashraf had made about the anonymous senior Lashkar commander who had come to India without an exit plan triggered a response that would have far-reaching implications.

The CTC did not know the commander's name or the names of his associates. They did not even have a sketch or a mugshot of him. All they knew was that their target's plan to run a PCO booth in Old Delhi had fizzled out over a year ago.

Over the next six months, informants, of both the CTC and Delhi Police, fanned out across the city's lanes, streets, slums and markets, especially in the historic Old Delhi. They were looking for any scrap of information on a man who spoke Urdu with a Punjabi accent and had tried to set up a PCO booth in Old Delhi three years ago. Several names cropped up and were duly investigated. But the exercise drew a blank.

At the Chanakyapuri office of the Mahanagar Telephone Nigam Limited (MTNL), the public sector telecom service provider, a sharp eye was being kept on Indian telephone numbers that received calls from known or suspected LeT phone numbers for any reference to the PCO operator. A few dozen suspicious numbers were put on a 24x7 tap, but without any lucky break.

Shekhar's bosses were contacting him on a weekly basis to find out if he had any leads on the 'PCO Man'. Exasperated, Shekhar went to Patiala twice to meet Ashraf, but he could not add anything more to the information he had already given.

Shekhar would often meet his colleague Agyeya to discuss the case. At one such meeting, he was feeling particularly frustrated. After ordering their standard tea and cappuccino, he decided to talk to Agyeya about what was troubling him.

'What do you do when you have nothing to show after months of honest efforts?'

Agyeya mulled over the question for a few seconds, stirring his coffee. Finally, he said, 'You need to double your efforts. It may still not be enough. Then, wait for a break; it will come.'

9

'MAN OF RESPECT' IN HYDERABAD

It was mid-monsoon and dark, but the Border Security Force (BSF) sniper had sighted his target with his infrared binoculars. The man was spotted crouching at the barbed wire fence at Abohar, near the Line of Control (LoC), the military control line between the Indian and Pakistani administered parts of Jammu and Kashmir. It was around 2 a.m. on 1 July 1998. After a heavy shower around an hour earlier, the ground was soggy and fragrant with the aroma of wet soil, crops and wildflowers.

The shots rang through the air, startling the birds sleeping in the fields on both sides of the LoC. A peacock called somewhere close by. The sniper switched on his walkie-talkie and informed his superior that he had shot an intruder at the border. Till now, this was a routine encounter between a Pakistani intruder and Indian security personnel.

Minutes later, two BSF commandos crawled to the spot where the man lay by the barbed wire, on the Pakistani side of the border. They cut the wires quickly, pulled the body through and dragged it to the regimental office. The dead man was clad in the typical Pakistani jihadi combat fatigues, with a rucksack containing almonds, cashews, maps of all the army cantonments across north India, a few thousand Indian rupees in counterfeit notes, magazines and two improvised explosive devices (IEDs) without detonators. He was also carrying an AK-47 and a revolver.

Pakistani wireless chatter intercepted a few hours later confirmed that the deceased was Abdul Malik, thirty-one, an LeT operative from Sargodha who had got separated from his team while making his way into India.

The encounter was covered prominently in the local and national newspapers as well as the electronic media. 'Pak terrorist killed at LoC by BSF sniper,' the headlines screamed. The BSF was happy. The regional army command made inquiries into the details of the killed intruder, while the defence ministry hosted journalists at a press conference to alert them about the foiled Lashkar plan to kill the then chief minister of Punjab.

Shekhar sent a junior CTC officer, Vinay Rathod, to run a routine check on the encounter and the recoveries made from the dead man. Rathod was briefed about the encounter in detail by the local BSF officers. He offered CTC's congratulations to the officers and expressed his desire to go through the belongings of the deceased Pakistani.

'Don't worry, we have already defused the two IEDs,' a BSF officer laughed. He was slightly irritated by Rathod's polite request.

Was Rathod questioning the BSF's ability to conduct the frisking of a dead man? That too, a week after the encounter?

Nevertheless, Rathod was taken to the BSF 'maal khana', or warehouse. He asked the BSF sentry accompanying him to wait outside the room as the operation was confidential. He began scouring through the recoveries – clothes, rucksack, the Fake Indian Counterfeit Note (FICN) bundles, the magazines and weapons.

Rathod was curious about the revolver as its chamber was smaller than that of the Webley & Scott revolver that he carried as a service weapon. He opened the chamber, but instead of a cartridge, he found a small roll of white paper about the size of a bullet. He quickly unrolled the paper.

The only thing scrawled on the paper was '01675-664444, Malerkotla'. Rathod took a photograph of the notation on the paper, took leave of the BSF commander after thanking him again, and caught the next flight to Delhi. Inquiries revealed that the number on the scrap of paper was the landline number of a PCO in Malerkotla, Sangrur, Punjab.

The Chanakyapuri exchange of MTNL was utilized to gather information on all the calls made from and received by the PCO in Malerkotla during the last few months. Several of the numbers investigated turned out to belong to known LeT operatives, including Lashkar boss (its chief of India operations) Al-Cheema's Jamaat-ud-Dawa Lahore office, which served as the LeT's command-and-control headquarters.

Over the next few weeks, an analysis of the call logs threw up three numbers in particular. One was Al-Cheema's landline number, the second belonged to the Malerkotla PCO and the third was a Hyderabad mobile number. There was a set pattern to the calls. Al-Cheema would first call the Hyderabad number, after which the man at the other end would call up the Malerkotla PCO. The person in Malerkotla would then dial Al-Cheema's number. The pattern suggested that the man in Hyderabad held a position of authority in the Lashkar ranks in India.

The Malerkotla PCO was put under 24x7 surveillance and was closely watched by Anvay and four 'watchers' under his command. A man was nabbed on the fourth day while conversing with someone who answered the call made by him to Al-Cheema's Lahore landline.

The man sang easily after receiving the 'treatment' from Rathod's team of interrogators at the CTC headquarters in Delhi.

He disclosed his identity as Pakistani LeT operative Furqan Khwaja, aged thirty-three. He had been sent to India two years ago by Al-Cheema and instructed to settle down in Malerkotla's Bashir Town Colony and wait for further orders. He had told his neighbours that he was a school dropout and a radio repairer.

The man who answered the Hyderabad mobile phone number, Salim Khwaja Amjad, was a senior Lashkar operative who had come to India in 1995. He was Furqan's commander and was directly in touch with Al-Cheema. At times, the commander would include Furqan in his conversations with Al-Cheema.

The commander lived in Hyderabad and ran an automobile business as a cover. Furqan said that Salim had been sent to Delhi by Al-Cheema to set up a PCO unit in Old Delhi, but it had turned out to be a failure. He had then moved out of Delhi and had eventually ended up in Hyderabad. Salim was a respected man in his locality, with a flourishing business. Recognized as a community notable with a following amongst the local youth, he taught kids science and Arabic for free at the madrasa attached to the mosque in Hyderabad's Rukhsar Ganj colony. His father-in-law was a retired army man and served as an imam on an honorary basis.

According to Furqan, Salim was passionate about world affairs and especially about what happened to the ummah, the community.

'Salim has two daughters and a good wife,' Furqan rattled off the details, wanting to end the ordeal of the ceaseless interrogation that he was being subjected to.

Furqan had revealed what the CTC had been looking for since the Khemkaran encounter, when Ashraf had first mentioned the missing 'PCO Man', the man sent by Al-Cheema as a resident terrorist to India. Based on Furqan's information, Shekhar and the CTC had been able to find Salim after all. The lucky break had finally come, as Agyeya had said it would. Shekhar smiled.

10

TRACKING SALIM

No time was lost in shadowing the PCO Man, Salim Khwaja Amjad. He could be the critical lead that the CTC needed to find out what the LeT was planning in Hyderabad and identify its sleeper cells across India.

Watchers were deployed around Salim's home at Rukhsar Ganj. From the time he stepped out of his house in the morning till the time he returned at night, Salim was under the discreet gaze of the CTC watchers.

On day one of the surveillance, Salim was sighted outside his house at 6.03 a.m., wearing a black tracksuit and white T-shirt, carrying one of his daughters on his shoulders and a water sprinkler in his left hand. He watered the bed of roses and the chameli, then plucked one of the roses for his daughter, who took it excitedly. He picked up the newspapers that were lying near the door before going inside the house.

At 6.30 a.m. Salim was seen again, this time in a white Pathani suit and skullcap. He walked briskly out of the house with his father-in-law in tow. The duo entered the mosque compound. The muezzin gave a call to the faithful for the morning prayers. Salim and his father-in-law came out of the mosque at 7.30 a.m. and returned home.

Salim left the house again at 10.45 a.m., this time in black trousers and a light-blue full-sleeved shirt. One of the watchers, Prakash, who was keeping vigil outside Salim's house in the garb of a municipal street cleaner, made a call to his buddy, Ismail, who was waiting on the nearby Shaukat Ali Road in an autorickshaw.

Soon, Salim appeared on Shaukat Ali Road in his blue Tata 407 pick-up van with a white roof. After driving along the road for about three kilometres, the van stopped. Salim got out and rushed to a PCO by the side of the road. He made a few calls but did not appear to speak to anyone. When he finally got through to someone, he spoke for less than a minute. He then got back into his van and drove off.

At 11.45 a.m., Salim parked his van at his garage, Sikandar Autoworks, and disappeared into a small office, which was visible from the road.

Prakash passed by the office in an autorickshaw fifteen minutes later. He could see Salim inside. He was sitting motionless in his chair, his feet propped up on the table as he looked out through the smoked glass panels of his cubicle.

At 3 p.m., Salim left his office and drove away in his van. He went to Old Hyderabad and stopped outside a restaurant, Chandni Biryani and Kebabs, at Malakpet. It was 3.45 p.m.

At 4.30, he left the restaurant. Half an hour later, he was roaming the streets and lanes of Avanti Nagar, a Hindu-dominated commercial-cum-residential area. He parked his van near a school, Ideal English Academy, and walked to a nearby Ganesh temple. He took off his sneakers and went inside. He came out twenty minutes later, a tika on his forehead.

From the Ganesh temple, Salim drove past several shopping malls, movie theatres, crowded streets and three other temples. He seemed to be on an evening out, just enjoying the sights and sounds of Hyderabad.

At 5.45 p.m., he parked his van in the lane that led to the Musi River. He walked to the riverfront and seemed to be soaking in the view of the majestic water body that flowed past him. He stood there for more than ten minutes, breathing in the cool air, his feet buried in the golden sand, and then left.

He was back home at 7 p.m. and was not seen for the next three hours. At 10, he came out in a black tracksuit and orange T-shirt and jogged to a PCO about 400 metres from his house. He was out of the booth in less than a minute.

Prakash and Ismail watched and followed Salim for the next four days. His daily routine was more or less the same, with the only variation being what he did after lunch at the Malakpet restaurant. On the second day, after lunch he went to a farmhouse located on the outskirts of the city, which bore a sign saying 'Al-Hilal Poultry'. He was there for two hours before he made his way back home.

On the third day, he went to meet somebody at Basheerbagh, a lower-middle-class neighbourhood in the north of the city. He stayed in the ground-floor flat of a three-storey building, which seemed to house government employees, for forty-five minutes before leaving for home.

Prakash, who was hanging around at a tea shop located nearby, casually asked a fellow customer who stayed in the ground-floor flat.

'Sukhram Tiwari. He is a senior babu in the municipal corporation's sewage department, responsible for handing out contracts to clean up the gutters and drains,' the customer said.

On the fourth day, after lunch at the restaurant, Salim went for a drive on the Mumbai–Hyderabad highway and drove as far as Viqarabad, a good twenty kilometres away from the city. On the way back, he stopped at a PCO for a minute before returning home.

On Sunday afternoon, Salim did not drive to his office. Instead, he went to Maulana Chirag Ansari's palatial yellow bungalow, known to locals as the 'Peeli Haveli', in Old Hyderabad. There, Salim was seen mingling with a band of young men who were practising with five-foot-long sticks and nunchakus under the watchful eyes of two tall wiry men who seemed to be their instructors. Salim joined in the practice and was even asked to show his moves to the rest of the class by the instructors.

Rathod was at CTC's regional office located in an unmarked bungalow in Old Hyderabad, poring over surveillance reports. One of his teams was keeping a watch on Salim, who was exhibiting his skills in stick-combat at Peeli Haveli.

Salim had received calls from and made calls to the Malerkotla PCO number under the CTC scanner at least a dozen times in the last three months. He had also received calls from a Lahore landline number, which was one of the four known numbers belonging to the headquarters of Al-Cheema. He had also made frequent calls to PCO numbers located in Mumbai, Ahmedabad, Hooghly and Kanpur.

'Salim seems to be making final preparations for D-day, which could be an attack on temples or on a religious procession culminating at the Musi River. He is ripe for plucking,' Rathod told Shekhar on the phone that same Sunday evening.

'Do it tomorrow, I am reaching Hyderabad tonight,' Shekhar said.

Exactly a month later, the Ganesh Chaturthi procession, a famous event in Hyderabad's social calendar, would make its way past the Ganesh temple that Salim visited often, to the Musi River. Shekhar knew he was running against time to prevent the carnage Salim had been planning for.

11

HOLDING BACK

The large TV screen in Shekhar's residence flickered. A female news anchor was giving an update on a recent encounter in Jammu.

'There were only two men, dressed in deep-blue pathani suits, but they managed to engage thirty-six-odd soldiers and commandos of the Indian Army's quick-response unit, which was deployed to smoke them out,' she reported.

'After a fierce gun battle lasting ninety minutes, a search of the site and the terrorists' combat packs revealed that they were carrying nine spare AK-47 magazines, eight hand grenades and two Pakistani army-issued curved daggers, meant for its elite Special Services Group commandos.'

At the crack of dawn, the two men had fired a volley of shots at the sentries standing guard at the army's residential compound on Sydenham Road in Jammu. The duo had rammed a truck into the entrance gate, broken it open and then jumped out of the vehicle with their guns blazing. They had then walked, in no apparent hurry, to the two-storey building located at the end of the road, which housed the mess, the games and recreation centre as well as a modest library. They had taken up positions on the first and second floors, shooting at anyone who came close. Two snipers from the army shot them in their heads eventually.

At the end of the firefight, the army counted its casualties. Seven had died, including the sentries and a twenty-four-year-old lieutenant who had joined the army's elite para-commandos only a month ago.

The chatter later intercepted by the CTC communications team and the army's signals wing caught LeT commander Al-Cheema rejoicing over the success of their operation led by just one commander, Abu Anas.

India's minister of defence, A. Bhadrakumar, warned Pakistan that it would have to pay for orchestrating a cowardly terrorist attack on the families of army men.

Shekhar switched off the television in his drawing room, wore his sneakers and went out for his daily four-kilometre jog. It was 7.00 a.m. He came back an hour later, bathed, ate a light breakfast and left his house. An hour later, he arrived at the unmarked detention facility where Salim aka Farhan was being held.

He was told that Salim had dozed off in his cell after having breakfast.

'Wake up the Pakistani rat and drag him to the interrogation room,' Shekhar instructed one of the guards.

Salim, his hands tied behind his back with a plastic restrainer, was hauled to the interrogation room. He had a scowl on his face and bloodshot eyes. He was asleep when the guard arrived in his cell and kicked him.

His tone mocking, Salim addressed Shekhar, 'Good morning, *janaab*. You're here early today. *Khairiyat hai*?'

Shekhar stared at him but said nothing.

'Did somebody die?' Salim said, a smile dancing on his lips now. 'Now also think of those who were crushed under your army's boots in Kashmir!'

'You knew about this attack today? They were your men – Babaji's men, I meant,' Shekhar asked.

'Perhaps. Are you referring to Kashmir? *Upar waley ka reham ho toh sab ho sakta hai*,' Salim replied.

'Your men died like dogs. You will meet the same fate. But later. First you will tell me when the blasts are going to take place. Where are your accomplices?' Shekhar asked.

'You nabbed me, so who will do the blast now?' Salim was in no mood to talk.

'Why do you go to temples? You want to bomb the Ganesh temple? The clerk you used to meet has exposed you. He said you went to bribe him for a contract to clean the manholes and gutters in the city. Why? Aren't you running a garage? So why shift to municipal contract work?'

Salim was silent for a while before finally answering. 'The blasts were to be set off by two boys who would enter India via Bengal. But they will no longer be coming as there won't be any signal from me. I do not know anything about the temples or any clerk.'

Losing patience, Shekhar instructed his men, 'Take him to his cell and make him understand. He stays alive today if he talks!'

The guards dragged Salim to his cell, where two CTC men, experts in persuading suspects to 'talk' their hearts out, took over.

12

WHAT IS SALIM HIDING?

Three days after he had been picked up and put under sustained interrogation, Salim was yet to give a full disclosure. His strategy was simple: reveal something only if his interrogators had an inkling about it and were asking. Shekhar was looking for some new information related to Salim's bomb plot, hoping it might provoke him into revealing what was unknown to the CTC.

Shekhar called for the files on Salim that had been compiled by the surveillance teams. He also requested Rathod, Anvay, who had supervised the watch, and another colleague, Srinivas Reddy, an inspector with CTC's transport wing, to join him.

'Be seated, all. Reddy, you were earlier with the Hyderabad police?'

'Yes, sir.'

'So, for a policeman in Hyderabad, what is the prime priority in terms of measures against a terror attack?'

'If there is a general terror alert, no chance is taken as there could be a bomb blast in a crowded place or a targeted attack on a high-profile authority. Frisking, roadblocks to conduct random checks of vehicles and their passengers, and intensified patrolling at sensitive locations are some of the measures taken. You never know which of these preventive checks may net a suspect.'

'What else?'

'There is the routine preventive policing work that is so crucial to preempting criminals. The police stay on high alert this time of the year as a month later, in August, the Ganesh visarjan takes place. The city's majority population looks forward to this religious event. Thousands participate in the procession, including the elderly, kids and women. In the past, fundamentalists and extremist elements have attempted to disrupt the procession, especially since the Babri Masjid demolition.'

'Can you tell me the route of the Ganesh procession?'

'Sir, yes, it begins from—'

But Shekhar interrupted, 'Does it pass by a few temples? Is Avanti Nagar's Ganesh temple on the route of the procession? And does it end at the Musi riverbank?'

'Yes, sir. The Ganesh temple is a key halt for the procession. The temple is old, at least a few centuries. It's a tradition. The procession moves ahead after paying respect to the deity.'

'Oh, I see. Thanks, Reddy. You may leave. I will call you later for an assignment we have for you in Kashmir.'

Shekhar turned to Rathod. 'Now, we know what he was up to probably. Salim was planning to set off blasts along the route of the procession. He is out of the game. So, who will organize the bombing in his place now and who will plant the devices? Who has the explosives now and who will assemble the bombs? Who brought the explosives into Hyderabad? We have a key member of the team but the rest are on the loose and dangerous.'

'It does seem like he was preparing for the procession, indeed,' Rathod agreed.

'Anvay, pick up that fellow, Moosa, from the restaurant that Salim used to visit. See if he has any idea about what Salim was up to. Thrash him, tell him to cooperate. He could be looking at twenty years in jail for being part of a terror plot, tell him that.'

'Yes, right away.'

Shekhar continued, 'Also, get details from interstate toll booths around Andhra Pradesh on Salim's vehicles, both his pick-up van and his bike. I want records for the last six months. Let's have them fast. Sound out the relevant authorities in Gujarat, Karnataka, Maharashtra, Orissa, Tamil Nadu and Kerala right away.'

Rathod quickly made calls to his police contacts in all the states that Shekhar had asked him to check with and sought the records on the van and the motorcycle. His contact in Tamil Nadu said that there was no record of either of Salim's vehicles entering the state. He had better luck in Ahmedabad – Salim's van had crossed the interstate toll booth.

Rathod also received confirmation from the authorities in Karnataka, Maharashtra and Gujarat that the pick-up van had paid toll tax at their booths a month ago, on 1 and 2 June.

At 6 p.m., Rathod met Shekhar. 'On 1 June, Salim went in his pick-up van to Gujarat, the toll authorities have confirmed it,' Rathod said.

'Salim must have gone there to meet or receive the explosives from his contact. The explosives must have been smuggled in via the sea. They could have been loaded on to a speedboat off Keti Bunder, near Karachi, and dropped off on the Gujarat coast. A fishing trawler could have received the consignment to hand over to Salim so he could bring it back to Hyderabad by road,' Shekhar was thinking aloud while puffing on his cigarette.

'Yes, could be, sir,' Rathod said.

'Have Salim's vehicles picked up immediately and call in a forensic team from the Central Forensic Science Laboratory. We have to look for hidden compartments and the presence of explosives, narcotics and DNA samples like hair strands to establish who all have used it recently,' Shekhar told Anvay.

'By the time I confront you again, Salim, I will have you figured out. No more hide-and-seek games, you will be begging for mercy,' Shekhar said grimly.

13

POULTRY FARM YIELDS 143 CHICKENS, 380 EGGS, 2 PAKISTANI 'GUESTS'

'*Aao Salim miyan*, have a seat,' Shekhar said as two guards brought Salim to the interrogation room for the second time that day. It was around 8 p.m. As Salim took a step towards a wooden chair, one of the guards kicked it away. The other guard and Shekhar laughed.

'You came here to kill. You expect a chair to sit? Sit on the floor!' Shekhar said.

Once Salim sat on the floor, Shekhar spoke again. 'And you are also a liar. I asked you for all the details related to your bombing plan in Hyderabad but you are a sly and dishonest character. You did not reveal anything about where the explosives are and who your accomplices are in the conspiracy! You lied and said there is nothing to reveal. But, well, your sidekick, Moosa gave away all your secrets. *Tu gaya*,' Shekhar said.

'I have no plans that Moosa would know about,' Salim said flatly, unblinking.

'Aren't you planning to bomb the Ganesh Chaturthi procession? Isn't that why you wanted the sewage works' contract? So you could plant explosives in the manholes along the route of the procession that could then be triggered during the procession?' Shekhar raised his voice. 'Moosa knows all your secrets. And the man who supplied you the explosives in Gujarat sang too. I know about your trip to Gujarat on 1 June. No point in hiding, Salim, my foot is on your neck!'

The claims about Moosa and the tracking of the Gujarat supplier were lies, shots in the dark to shake Salim up. They hit their mark.

'I am a foot soldier. I did what I was told. Babaji said to kill as many people as possible, to let them burn,' Salim said.

'Who was to assist you in carrying out the blasts? Who sent you the explosives? Forensic tests have found traces of explosives in your pick-up van, so there is no point in denying anything,' Shekhar said.

'I acted alone. I don't have the explosives yet. I would have rigged the manholes next week on getting the contract,' said Salim.

Shekhar asked the guards to take Salim away. He told them to serve him tea and give him a single cigarette. Shekhar had an urge to smoke and was about to walk out of the room when Salim stopped him.

'Sir?' Salim said.

'Yes?'

'You are a God-fearing man; your family must be waiting for you at home. But you waste your time here, with me! Your children, your wife need you there. What do you want? The explosives? Send a team to Techpoint, an electrical appliances shop at Toli Chowki. Check out its shutters.'

Shekhar was stunned. He looked at Salim for a few moments, then asked the guards to take him out of the room.

Shekhar sent a team to the shop in Hyderabad the next morning. From inside the shutter's cavity, they recovered three kilos of a soap-like black substance that seemed to be RDX, thirteen detonators, six cheap phones, seven pre-paid SIM cards and an AK-47. Salim wasn't bluffing, for a change. Shekhar wondered about the reason behind Salim's generosity. In the meantime, Anvay and his team had picked up Moosa and brought him to the CTC office. A little 'treatment' there straightened him out. Moosa wanted to talk.

'I know Salim as a Kashmiri mujahideen who is here in exile. I help him with money if he needs it for the family, nothing more,' Moosa told Shekhar.

'You are going to jail for harbouring a terrorist. How do you propose to save yourself?' Shekhar asked.

'Sir, I am not involved, I am a law-abiding citizen. Keep this to yourself, but Salim has stationed a few young men at his poultry farm on the city's outskirts,' Moosa whispered.

'I hope for your sake your information is correct,' Shekhar said. 'Go now, you will be called again for your statement. Be ready; don't leave the city without seeking my permission. Here, write down the poultry farm's address.'

A raid at the poultry farm, which Salim ran unknown to his family, yielded 143 chickens, 380 eggs and two young men, Akmal Abbas and Jehangir Khan. Abbas and Khan were interrogated for three hours by the CTC. The realization that their 'commander', Salim, was already in CTC's custody and talking about their involvement in the terror conspiracy convinced them to cooperate with their interrogators. They accepted that they were Pakistanis and members of the LeT. They confessed to being part of Salim's blast conspiracy.

Abbas told Shekhar, 'We came to India last month, on 1 June, from Karachi to deliver RDX and bomb-making materials to Salim. His job was to help us settle down here so that we can do some *"bada"* action whenever Babaji sends us the instructions.'

'How was he planning to settle you here?' Shekhar asked.

'He had been told to find a safe, spacious but shabby-looking establishment to host infiltrators like us. He took the poultry farm on lease to avoid attracting any attention. As part of the planned building-up of our cover profiles, Salim was planning to procure a second-hand fishing trawler for me and a PCO booth for Jehangir.'

'What about the plan to bomb the Ganesh Chaturthi procession?'

'We know about it, he kept us in the loop. But he is too proud to take our help. Also, this project was assigned to him by Babaji, and he wants to carry it out on his own, spectacularly,' Jehangir explained.

'As Salim said once, his project will fill the streets with bodies,' Abbas added.

Shekhar could not tell if Abbas felt anything about Salim's wish. Or was it that he felt left out of the 'project' and was envious of Salim?

14

A TOOTH FOR A TOOTH

The text message that Shekhar received that night was a one-liner: Meet at 7 a.m., Office of Operations Chief.

CTC's operations wing's headquarters were located in an unmarked British-era mansion in Delhi with manicured gardens and a patch of woods, also home to a family of peacocks. Shekhar would have to skip his morning jog to make it on time for the meeting.

Shekhar wondered why the meeting had been called. He guessed it must be about the preparations to ensure that the Independence Day celebrations took place peacefully. As per custom, the prime minister would be addressing the country on the occasion from the ramparts of the Mughal-era Red Fort, with its impregnable walls, perfect arches and maze of dark, damp tunnels and chambers.

When Shekhar was ushered into the chief's office at 6.55 a.m., he was surprised to find three other officers present, who he knew were senior CTC officers. The chief usually met his officers one-on-one. Shekhar felt a rush of adrenaline, expecting a challenging assignment.

'Gentlemen, you are aware of the neutralization of an LeT sleeper cell that was being run by Salim Khwaja Amjad in Hyderabad. As you must have figured out by now, Salim is no ordinary Pakistani terrorist. He came to India to never leave,' the chief began the meeting, direct and to the point. He was a busy man and had no time for elaborate speeches.

'There are several others like Salim, all Pakistani Lashkar terrorists, who are deepening their roots in our towns and cities as we speak. They will have to be identified and neutralized. Our team is taking care of that,' he said.

The chief signalled to his orderly, who had just come in, to get tea and coffee.

'But, more importantly, at this moment, we need to take a deep breath and assess what we are up against so that we can adequately prepare for the latest challenge staring at us,' he said. 'What is Al-Cheema trying to do by embedding men like Salim Khwaja Amjad in our midst?'

The chief let the question sink in for a few moments before continuing. 'He is creating a local cadre of killers, bomb-makers and saboteurs who are trained, ready and at his beck and call to incite and encourage our disaffected youth to take up arms and turn into traitors. Till recently, his trained murderers would come for specific attacks and would die while executing them, get arrested or return back home. Not any more. Al-Cheema is being unconventional and is upping his game by a few notches.

'So we have to respond to this new, deadlier threat to India's well-being from the LeT. We have to respond with a strategy that should be imaginative, audacious and capable of foiling the terror plans of the ISI and its puppet, the LeT. It must defang both of them, devastate their evil citadels. I want to hear your plans on this. Gentlemen?'

'Let us begin by picking up all his suspected over-ground workers in India, booking them for supporting terror and drawing out whatever information they might have on Lashkar's operations here,' said Ankush Singh, who headed a group at the Pakistan desk.

The chief nodded. 'Do that, but without messing it up. The grounds of arrest should be strong and must stand up to the court's scrutiny. Taufiq, what do you propose to do?'

Taufiq Sheikh had spent five years with the CTC and was known for his nearly perfect record in operations.

'Sir, we must net LeT's Gulf-based operatives, who are involved in radicalizing men from the Indian diaspora there and also in guiding recruits from India to their destinations in Pakistan for training and indoctrination. We are planting our resources in their ranks as well, as you know,' Taufiq said.

'Who do you have in mind?' the chief asked.

'Hyderabad's Shahed Qasim and his elder brother Rehan, who is an engineer and employed with a luxury watchmaking MNC, are both in Riyadh. Mumbai's Salman Agarbattiwala, who is also an engineer and works with a petroleum major in Dubai, is another. These three are key Lashkar recruiters and must have supplied a dozen new recruits to the LeT in the last two years,' Taufiq said.

'Get them here through legal channels or otherwise. Talk to the authorities of the country concerned. Have them deported and flown in,' the chief instructed.

'Sir, if Al-Cheema's terrorists are here, we have to be there in Pakistan as well. Inside his lair, inside his group, invading his body and soul, to destroy both,' Shekhar erupted. He seemed confident about the proactive, aggressive stance he was proposing.

'We will create a cadre of men, of converts, if required, to get inside ISI's terror factories to learn what is happening there. Our boys will earn their confidence by staging a few minor operations for them, but will trip them up when it comes to big operations. These moles will help us in busting other LeT cells, seizing weapons and explosives, and foiling their next attack,' Shekhar continued, the excitement in his voice palpable.

The chief smiled. 'That is exactly what I have in mind as well. Let's put a Trojan Horse at the heart of Lashkar and Pakistan's terror-sponsoring infrastructure. Our men will have to infiltrate into the LeT to learn all about its terror operations in India to neutralize them.

'The 1993 Bombay blasts orchestrated by Dawood Ibrahim and ISI exposed our limitations in knowing what goes on in the coastal and international waters off India and Pakistan. Petty landing agents like Rehmat Kanse were able to smuggle in thousands of kilos of RDX, hundreds of AK-47s and AK-56s, hand grenades and magazines while we remained clueless, twiddling our thumbs.' The chief's tone was rising in anger as he drummed two fingers of his right hand on the table.

'There are a few social organizations that are in touch with our contacts and officers. I will tap them for recruits whom we can get inside the LeT,' Shekhar said.

'Tap your contacts among leaders of the fishermen's cooperatives. Maybe they can suggest candidates who can become part of the LeT's marine wing,' the chief suggested.

'Gentlemen, it's decided then here. Operation Trojan Horse begins with immediate effect. Information is to be shared on a need-to-know basis, and I must be kept in the loop. At the end of each day, I won't mind if I am sent an update on the mission's progress via encrypted channels. It could even be a single line,' he said.

'We will meet again in a fortnight,' the chief added before dismissing the gathering and turning to a small black landline phone that was ringing.

15

OPERATION TROJAN HORSE

The air was crisp and nippy. At 4.45 a.m., it was still dark outside. Somaiya Prakash, his face hidden under a grey monkey cap and clad in a white T-shirt, a black sleeveless sweater, khaki shorts and black sneakers, emerged from the staircase of the B wing of the Sahyadri Enclave residential society in south Delhi. There was nobody else in sight.

He paused for a minute to take several deep breaths. He then stretched his legs wide and bent, first over his left leg, then the right. After a couple of minutes, he straightened up and began walking towards the road, gradually quickening his pace until he was jogging.

Somaiya had been unwell for the past three days, but he hated missing his morning jog despite his wife's repeated advice against it.

'*Arrey baba*, it's okay. Have you ever heard of anyone being knocked out due to jogging? I will be back in thirty minutes; please keep my tea ready,' he had told her before leaving his flat.

Suman, his wife, was not amused. 'Oh, yes. If you don't jog, heavens may fall,' she had retorted.

As Somaiya jogged down the road towards the neighbourhood park, he stopped briefly to scold a neighbour for dumping a bin full of leftover food on the footpath. He soon arrived at the park, whose watchman was sleeping outside on a bench.

'*Jaag, bhai, Tiwari,*' Somaiya told the watchman. A group of children and their parents greeted him and, after some banter, began running with him.

Somaiya was back home at 7 a.m. and was ready to leave for work two hours later. By 9.45 a.m., he was at Connaught Place, where his colleague, Harsh Ahuja, was supposed to meet him at the Outer Circle. Ahuja was nowhere in sight. He finally appeared at the scheduled meeting place at 11 a.m. By then, Somaiya had bought two newspapers from a local hawker and devoured their pages, barring the classified columns.

'Hello, Mr Somaiya. What a fine morning it is! Let's go, Mr Chaudhary is waiting for us,' said Ahuja.

'Ahujaji, it's close to noon now,' Somaiya said and smiled.

They both walked briskly to Cappuccinos, the 24x7 coffee shop on the Outer Circle, where Ahuja preferred to meet his business clients. They both ordered their coffees, Ahuja his latte and Somaiya his filter coffee.

Chaudhary joined them half an hour later. And it was business as usual.

'So, Chaudhary sahib, don't worry. Our men will secure your bungalow as if it were their own home. They are razor-sharp as far as alertness is concerned. Almost like commandos, sir, and better than the most ferocious Alsatians,' Ahuja made his enthusiastic pitch.

Somaiya squirmed. His part would come soon.

'We are known for this, Chaudhary sahib. Ahuja A-1 Security means the very best private security in Delhi. No one can match us,' Ahuja said.

'Mr Somaiya Prakash, a retired police officer, will testify for me. He was a Grade-A officer with CTC, India's premier counter-terror unit, until around six months ago, when he retired. He is now our director of security. He chose to join us, to share his security skills with us and our esteemed clients,' Ahuja beamed.

Chaudhary and Somaiya shook hands. Polite conversation followed.

Somaiya hated himself from the bottom of his heart for every word he had to utter at the meeting. He hated himself for being there, especially with the likes of Ahuja and Chaudhary, who had already become friends and were tucking into their plates.

Somaiya hated himself for becoming old, too old for CTC, where he had spent thirty-six years of his life in investigative and intelligence-gathering roles. Six of those years with the CTC had been spent in Pakistan and Iran on covert assignments.

'Welcome to the civilian world as a retiree,' he mumbled to himself. Suddenly he stood up and told Ahuja he was going home as he was unwell and would be in the office the next morning at 10 sharp. Ahuja was busy enjoying his lunch and merely waved at him.

As Somaiya walked quickly out of the coffee shop, his cell phone rang.

It was Suman. 'Why are you not taking any calls? Your old CTC boss, Shekhar, has been trying to get in touch with you!'

'What does Shekhar sir want from me?' he wondered.

'I was in a meeting with Ahuja, a business meeting. I will call you back,' he told Suman and hung up. He quickly dialled Shekhar's number.

'Good afternoon, Somaiya ji, how are you?' Shekhar asked him warmly.

'I'm fine, sir, thank you.'

'Hope you are not enjoying your retired life too much? I want you back on an assignment, on short-term contract basis,' Shekhar said.

'Yes, sir, it's … it's a very quiet life.'

'Sounds like you may be getting bored at home already. Good!' Shekhar chuckled. 'Listen, CTC needs you again. You would be joining us as a consultant for six years, with a 10 per cent increase in compensation. You don't need to come into the office daily; you can be your own boss,' Shekhar laid out his offer.

Somaiya was stunned. After a few moments of silence, Somaiya thanked Shekhar. 'Thank you, sir, really. When do I begin?'

Operation Trojan Horse was now under way.

16

THE YOUNG DRONE-MAKER

The fifteen-year-old was spoken of well by his teachers at Tuticorin's St Xavier's high school but was seldom seen browsing textbooks at home by his family. No one knew how he found the time to study as his post-school hours, till he called it a night, were crammed with a series of activities barely connected to academics. A port city in southern Tamil Nadu, Tuticorin (known as Thoothukudi since 2018) is on the tip of the Gulf of Mannar in the Indian Ocean. It began as a small fishing village, then developed into a booming Portuguese colony in the sixteenth century and further expanded during British and Dutch occupations.

When the boy's class ten exams were around the corner, his family was panic-stricken. But Vishal Iyer, 'Vishu' to his family and friends, wondered what the fuss was about. Yes, there was an examination ahead, but he had been preparing for it. No last-minute scamper for him. As for the doubts related to his focus on studies, he did not care to respond. On the few occasions that he was caught with books, they were either on physics or algebra, or both. Sometimes, Vishu would be found bent over slim booklets on obscure or 'pointless' (his father's words) scriptures – a Bhrigu Samhita or a Garuda Purana – on the rain-soaked terrace of his family's large cottage, with its red Mangalorean tiles, a sprawling banana orchard in the back and flower beds in the front.

Vishu was fond of sports magazines, especially those covering Brazilian soccer or Chinese martial arts, but reading them was not exactly an academic pursuit, and his family made sure he knew that. His father was especially hard on him. Vishu, the school's champion in chess, karate and debating, was an 'embarrassment', who had no purpose in life other than being a loser, his father, Srinivas, had snarled in one of his darker moods.

Srinivas owned a well-known local restaurant that specialized in Chinese cuisine apart from the staple south Indian dishes. He was also the treasurer of the management trust of the Perumal temple in the neighbourhood. He did not visit the temple too often. Religion, for him, was not for public display and was one's private concern. He chose to perform his puja at home.

Vishu's mother, Madhavi, had no particular opinion on his academic excellence or the lack of it, but was sure that her capable son would take care of his studies, as he did with most affairs in his life. She doted on him and took him to the Perumal temple with her every morning when she went to offer her respects to the deity.

Vishu's twin brothers, Shiva and Varun, were eight years older than him. They felt protective towards him. At times, they would also pull him up for being too much of a 'free spirit'. The twins had dropped out of their BA and BCom courses respectively to assist their father at the restaurant, even though Srinivas had never asked them to do so.

Atharv, twenty-eight, Vishu's eldest brother, a lawyer by profession, was a loser too in his father's eyes. Atharv took no interest in the restaurant, the chores at home or the affairs of the Vishnu temple. Three years ago, Srinivas had asked him to put in a few hours at the restaurant in the mornings, when it wasn't as crowded as in the evenings or at night, so that Srinivas could pay a little more attention to his fledgling career as the leader of a pro-Hindutva party.

Atharv had dismissed his father's request. He had accepted an offer to study at London University, famous for producing eminent economists of a Marxist bent, for a postgraduate course in law. Srinivas had not been pleased at the news of his eldest fleeing to the 'land of half-communists', as he described the UK, with its strong tradition of liberal and left-of-centre politics.

Atharv doted on Vishu and was impressed with his 'ideas'. Atharv was the only one in the family who knew what went on in Vishu's life.

The drone that Vishu had made three months ago would be representing Tamil Nadu at the National School Science Congress in Delhi. But he was unlikely to attend as he was committed to delivering a lecture on the topic 'Does science challenge the Hindu faith?' in Pune the same day. He would be presenting his views at a gathering that would include learned men from Hindu temples and organizations from across the country.

Vishu was proud of his drone nonetheless. He had researched the science and engineering that went into its making for eighteen months. The battery-operated drone could soar to a height of 1,000 feet, had a speed of 100 kilometres per hour and could stay airborne for at least eight hours. He had already applied for a patent certification from the state authorities for the drone and planned to meet potential investors for its commercial production.

Vishu had big plans for the drone, whose prototype he had named 'Antariksha 1', but there was so much more to do before it took off. Batteries, for instance. He had flown the prototype with special lithium batteries that his friend Joseph had procured from Russia. Joseph's uncle, Rex, was doing a course in medicine at Moscow University and had purchased the batteries on his nephew's request. The batteries had run out and Vishu had ordered another set via his friend.

At 8 a.m. on 6 November 1999, Vishu was literally running, with Atharv in tow, to Joseph's house, which was about two kilometres away from his cottage. The drone had to be fitted with the fresh batteries that Joseph had helped procure before it was given to the vice principal of his school by noon that day. The vice principal would take the drone later that night to Delhi for the science congress.

17

AN AMBUSH

'Anna, run fast, we have to reach Joseph's house before he and his family leave for their picnic,' Vishu said sharply.

Their neighbourhood, Annamalai Nagar, was tightly packed with cottages, row houses, villas and multi-storeyed buildings. The main road to Joseph's house was flooded due to the incessant rain since the previous day, so the brothers took a short cut.

The short cut took them through a narrow alley, which snaked through a maze of concrete and stone-mud structures. The alley was typically dark even during the day as it was shadowed by overhanging balconies and awnings. It was so narrow that in order for two people to cross one another, one of them would have to press back against the wall while the other passed.

When they were halfway down the alley, the brothers heard the sounds of light footfalls and whispers. Vishu slowed down and then halted.

'Wait, Anna … there seems to be a big group ahead at the turn. We will have to make way for them,' he said.

'Okay, no sweat, bro,' Atharv said.

Within seconds, the group of passersby became visible. Six men, all taller than Vishu, were standing not ten metres ahead, one behind the other as if in a queue. One of them, standing at the end of the queue, had a black shawl draped around his shoulders. The man who stood at the head of the group indicated that he and the five others would take to the wall, while Vishu and Atharv passed by them.

The brothers had almost slipped past the group, without a word being spoken by anybody, when the man in the shawl suddenly pushed Atharv, who fell to the ground. Taken aback by what had just happened, Atharv turned towards the man who had pushed him, when Vishu let out a blood-curdling scream.

'Aaaaahh, Anna, he is hurting … stabbing me.'

Atharv sprang to his feet and rushed to save Vishu. He landed a few punches on the man assaulting Vishu, when somebody hit his head with what felt like an iron rod.

As Atharv collapsed, the world became dark in front of his eyes. Through his blurred, dimming vision, he could see two of the men holding Vishu by his arms as the man with a dagger kept assaulting the fifteen-year-old drone-maker.

Suddenly, Atharv received a kick in his stomach. The man with the dagger was now standing over him, kicking him.

'Son of a bitch! This is a message from those mourning the death of our brother, Sadiq. You must suffer as we suffer. You must cry for your brother, as we do for Sadiq,' the man with the dagger was screaming, kicking Atharv in the stomach maniacally till he lost consciousness.

Twenty minutes after the two brothers had been assaulted and lay unconscious in a heap, with Vishu in a pool of blood, they were found by Joseph, who had decided to deliver the drone's batteries to his friend himself after the latter did not turn up at the scheduled time. Joseph screamed for help and a man who lived nearby called for the police and an ambulance.

Hours later, Atharv regained consciousness in the same hospital that had released Sadiq the previous night.

Vishu, however, did not make it.

The previous month, a major fist fight had broken out when the Perumal temple's office bearers, including Srinivas, had objected to the faithful, who had gathered at the nearby Mughal Masjid to offer Friday noon prayers, loitering near the temple and leaning on its walls. The temple's priest, Muthuswamy, had shouted at the young men for leaning on what he said were old, holy walls and casting disrespectful gazes towards the deity.

The men had made fun of the old priest and his potbelly. The priest's attendants had then badly roughed up two of the youth. One of them, Sadiq Mir, a software professional and the son of the mosque's sixty-eight-year-old muezzin, had fallen to the ground and hurt his head badly after being shoved by one of the attendants. He sustained serious injuries and slipped into a coma.

The mosque's imam had lodged a complaint with the police against the priest, the temple's managing committee and the priest's attendants for assaulting Sadiq and his friend Imran, who had received only minor injuries in the assault.

Sadiq's family members, including his wife and two young daughters, spent the next few weeks praying for his recovery and keeping a vigil outside the intensive care unit where he was being treated.

Then, on Friday night, the doctor attending to Sadiq had told his father that Sadiq could be taken home as there was no chance of him recovering. He could die at home, if the family so wished. The doctor's advice had despaired his family. Sadiq's daughters had cried for hours.

Vishu's father and mother were stunned by what had happened to their innocent son. His mother, unable to bear the shock, suffered a heart attack and passed away the same day.

Atharv had to prepare for two cremations.

Relatives, friends and acquaintances were expected to arrive for the funeral by 4 p.m. The last rites were to be done before the sun set.

Srinivas's friend Somaiya was also expected to arrive that afternoon. The two had done their master's in history from Delhi University and had shared a hostel room at the time. They were good friends and had kept in touch.

Somaiya had been posted in Tuticorin for six years while working with the CTC. He was the one who had advised Atharv to become a lawyer, though Srinivas had scoffed at his son's career choice. Somaiya had been close to Vishu too and had taught him the mechanics of tiny heat-propelled toy boats.

Somaiya was hurting. Atharv was crushed with sorrow but had no time to grieve. He had to assemble the pyres before the sun set.

18

MURDER AND RETRIBUTION

The news about Vishu's murder spread like wildfire through Annamalai Nagar, stunning the sleepy neighbourhood and plunging it into an uneasy silence.

Hundreds began walking towards Srinivas's residence with prayers for Vishu's and his mother's departed souls and curses for the killers on their lips. Srinivas's family was among those who had lived the longest in the area and most of the residents knew them personally. Almost all of them had had a meal at his restaurant at least once in their lives.

The ladies of the locality knew Madhavi and had often interacted with her at the temple or at social gatherings. Vishu was a member of the local cricket club and had aspired to play for India as a fast bowler. Some of the teenagers had either studied with him at some point or had shared his enthusiasm for science and martial arts.

The mourners, who stood around in small groups, could not stop talking about the tragedy. They shared their outrage at the two deaths and how the young boy and his mother had not deserved it. Vishu had been butchered by goons who had lain in wait for him in the cramped alley. The question troubling many was how the assailants had known their prey would be in the alley at that time. Was it a coincidence or a conspiracy?

'He was too young to have harmed anyone. He had no time for negativity. He was Tuticorin's prodigy but did not live to see the day his drone would get the rave reviews that it was destined for,' rued an architect, Michael, who knew the family.

'People will talk, talk and talk, for hours, days and weeks, and then they will forget about it. Till they are reminded periodically by news reports about the case, the arrests made by the police, if at all, the bail granted or not granted to the accused and, eventually, his conviction or acquittal,' a neighbour of Srinivas was heard telling another neighbour.

Another neighbour, Suleiman Shaikh, an office-bearer of the Majlisi Defence League, also spoke of the loss of Sadiq's life in an unwarranted act of arrogance and violence on the part of the temple guards. He spoke about Sadiq's orphaned daughters, their uncertain futures and the fact that Sadiq's wife was inconsolable and had gone mute. He tried to remind the group he was standing with about Srinivas's decades-long association with a right-wing organization, Hindu Ekta Manch.

Srinivas was seen at the spot when the assault on Sadiq had happened, but neither he nor his colleagues in the temple's management trust had bothered to visit Sadiq's house to pay condolences. 'My heart weeps for Vishu but so it does for Sadiq too,' Suleiman continued with his rant, without noticing that no one in the group had uttered a word, of support or otherwise, in response to his opinions.

The bodies, draped in white, were carried out of the Iyer residence on the shoulders of their dear ones: Srinivas, his three remaining sons, two brothers, two nephews and Somaiya, who had arrived just in time. The bodies were accompanied by the wails of relatives, the holy chants of the priest and the deathly silence of Srinivas, who seemed to be in a daze.

The mourners left for the cremation ground, which abutted the waters of the Vaippar, one of the main rivers that sustain Tuticorin's communities.

'Why? Why was my kid brother butchered? Who would have the heart to knife him repeatedly? Sadiq's relatives?' Atharv screamed at Somaiya after the funeral. He took Somaiya by his arms and shook him. Somaiya looked Atharv in the eyes for a moment, put a hand on his shoulder and looked away. They were both crying.

'I want to avenge Vishu's death, I want to pluck the hearts out of the killers' chests with my bare hands. You were with the central intelligence, right? Something named CTC, right? Help me, for you are in a position to. And, I have a debt to pay for Vishu,' Atharv whispered to Somaiya. Somaiya heard out Atharv without uttering a word.

Atharv repeated his request when he visited Somaiya at the latter's modest hotel room two days later.

When Somaiya spoke, he did so matter-of-factly. 'Ismail. Ismail is the one who led the attack. Ismail was waiting for you and Vishu in that alley that day. He is the one who stabbed Vishu. He is related to Sadiq but is not a local. He was sent here by someone. He is a professional killer who works for the mafia in Chennai, and his associates have criminal records as bulky as his.'

'What?' Atharv could not make sense of any of this. 'A professional criminal attacked us that day? What's the connection? How do you know all these details?'

'I spoke to the Tuticorin commissioner of police two days ago, before I left Delhi to fly here. The police are looking into who ordered the killing and hired Ismail. There is a good chance that Ismail came here on his own to avenge Sadiq's death. But the attack seems more like an orchestrated crime, meant as a trigger for communal violence as assembly elections are around the corner.

'Phones of some suspects were monitored. As per the intercepted chatter, Suleiman Shaikh – of the Majlisi Defence League – and his goons could have been involved in issuing the contract. The police suspect that Suleiman has ties with the Pakistani ISI. It is to be verified if the orders to kill Vishu came from his Lahore-based handlers. ISI is forever trying to create communal disturbances here, associating itself with organized criminal gangs and using them as hirelings for various purposes,' Somaiya said.

Just then, he got a call. After hanging up, he said, 'It was the commissioner of police. Ismail and his three friends were suspected to be hiding in a lodge on Old City Mall Road. A police team went there to nab them, but the goons opened fire at the police. In the firefight that broke out, Ismail fled while three of his friends were riddled with bullets and are lying like dead dogs in the city's morgue as we speak.'

Atharv erupted with joy. 'Were these three part of the team that attacked us? Where is Ismail now? I want him dead more than these three scoundrels.'

'Ismail is missing. It is too early to say, but he may soon be spirited out of India via Bangladesh, Sri Lanka or the Maldives by Suleiman and his ISI handlers. Suleiman has been missing since yesterday after the local police station summoned him for questioning in relation to Vishu's murder. It is likely that both Suleiman and Ismail will lie low until they are able to flee the country.'

'So, what can you do about this, Uncle?' Atharv asked.

'Well, I plan to hunt them down somehow, Atharv. This I will do for Vishu, and also Srinivas, who is my old friend. But I also feel responsible for avenging the hundreds, young and old, who die without reason thanks to the bombs and bullets of Pakistan-sponsored terror in India. I am responsible for hunting down their killers too and will work till my last breath to do just that,' Somaiya said, his words clear and sharp. They fell like rapiers on Atharv and made him feel small.

'What can I do for you?' he asked.

'Nothing,' Somaiya smiled a tired smile. 'Sorry, I got emotional; it's probably the stress and the sorrow that has loosened my tongue.'

'No, please. I want to avenge Vishu's death. I have to account for all those who are linked to his murder, whether it is Suleiman or his Pakistani handlers. You must tell me what I can do for you.'

Somaiya remained quiet for a long while before finally saying, 'Will you go to Pakistan, Atharv? To fight for India? And to fight for me? In Pakistan?'

Atharv was stunned. 'What, are you crazy, Uncle?' he blurted out. 'Who on earth will go to Pakistan to fuck with the ISI? For what?'

'Well, young men who love India and are ready to die for their motherland are going there. I am sending them there. We need to destroy the Pakistani Deep State, the ISI and its illegitimate terror offspring like the LeT and JeM. We need to cripple their terror infrastructure,' Somaiya said.

Atharv was still shocked by Somaiya's proposal but managed to say, 'Let me think about it and call you in a few days.'

Somaiya did not take Atharv's promise seriously and returned to Delhi the same day.

A week later, Atharv called, however. It was 28 December 1999. 'Somaiya Uncle, I thought deeply about all that you said,' he said. 'The details of how and why Vishu was killed came as a rude shock, let me tell you. His killer may be dead but I will be frank with you. I want to reach his bosses, the ones who run, nurture such murderers. That day, my retribution will be complete. Vishu will get true justice.

'What you asked me to do, however, did shock me! I am a lawyer, not an army man, or a cop or a spy. But I see the point. Due to the deep personal loss that my family has suffered, life has brought me to that bend in the road where I can decide the direction of my onward journey. I am a patriot, and I can make sacrifices for the country. I also want to help in bringing to book the bastards who kill innocent children like Vishu.'

He took a deep breath and continued, 'I and two of my friends, Anant Nair and Nirav Pillai, who share my love for the country, will join you in your mission. For a few years only. I am in my mid-twenties, as you know, and can always return to my law practice, which is currently unremarkable anyway, a few years later. My friends are both around twenty-eight. They have postgrad degrees in commerce and have been unemployed for the last few years.

'So tell your CTC to take good care of us when we put our lives in danger by being part of this plan. We can be the tip of India's spear.'

Somaiya was taken aback. He hadn't expected Atharv to take his offer seriously. 'Atharv, I cannot thank you enough. The country will not forget your sacrifice. You and your friends are welcome aboard. Once the countdown begins, you will be paid a monthly honorarium of Rs 60,000 and a golden handshake of Rs 50 lakh after five years.'

'Sounds fair, Uncle.'

'But first, you will have to get trained and acquire special skills. You will then enter Pakistan. If you do not survive the rigours of the training or decide to leave it midway, we will let you return home with honour. No questions asked. You will then forget all about us and vice versa.'

'We are ready to do whatever is needed, Uncle. Just tell us where we need to go for the training,' Atharv said.

19

NEW RECRUITS

Clad in white track pants and black-blue check T-shirts, a hundred young men and teenagers were performing a combination of army-style physical exercises, karate moves and stick–sword drills in the large grounds of Jai Ambey High School and Junior College in Mumbai. The school, located in Kurla East, had been set up sixty years ago by the founder of the Bharatiya Vikas Parishad (BVP), which described itself as 'a Hindu socio-cultural group'. A 'patriotic' outfit, its members believed in action for the 'right' causes, according to BVP. The school, among the hundred such set up across the country, was established as part of the socio-cultural initiatives undertaken by BVP founder Shankarrao Abhyankar (1905–1970) to uplift Hindu society. Abhyankar, who had participated in the country's freedom movement as a Gandhian, later turned apolitical and devoted his life to community service, including in the fields of education, culture and socio-economic upliftment.

The morning meeting-cum-exercise session of the BVP volunteers went on for about half an hour under the watchful eyes of Vyayam Pramukh (Exercise Head) Vishnu Kelkar, a lawyer-cum-social activist. The session ended with the congregation paying its respects to the national tricolour and the BVP flag, which had motifs from the flags of iconic medieval Indian warrior-kings Maharana Pratap and Prithviraj Chauhan.

The seventy-year-old Vishnu, fondly known as Vishnu dada to the BVP volunteers, was about to kick-start his rickety blue Vespa scooter when his old friend, Raghuvir Sawant, arrived.

Sawant had retired as an assistant secretary with CTC five years ago and still performed select assignments for his old agency. He was called in for tasks that required the set of skills and contacts he had acquired over the thirty-five years that he had worked for CTC. Operation Trojan Horse was one such CTC mission that would require Sawant's services.

Shekhar had called him two days ago and had requested him to be a part of the operation. He had asked Sawant to find suitable recruits for Operation Trojan Horse, men who would be willing to go to Pakistan. Sawant had promised to do his best for CTC, as always.

'Vishnuji, namaskar! How are you? How are the BVP and its followers, your wards?' Sawant asked.

'I am fine and so are the BVP and my children. All thanks to your blessings, Raghuvir ji. Tell me, what brings you here after all these months? All is well, I hope?' Kelkar asked.

'I am back at work, Vishnuji. My organization needs my services. It brought me out of retirement, again,' said Sawant. 'I need volunteers for a secret mission that will need supreme sacrifices, including personal, from the participants. Excellent care will be taken of the volunteers, in terms of salaries, of course. The volunteers must be told that they will have to re-invent themselves as per the needs of the mission and there is no choice to say no once they commit.

'They will have to stay and work overseas whenever required. We will take care of the logistics like their travel expenses and their passports. Do you have anyone who would have it in him to take up these challenges for a minimum of five years?

'Take me on, Sawant bhai. *Rashtra ke charnon mein khud ko arpit kiya hai,*' Kelkar said.

'You and I are now old, Vishnuji. It is time for the young,' said Sawant, laughing. 'Do you have anyone?'

'We can offer two lions for this mission. Rohit Joshi and Sahil Purandare. Both are graduates and have just qualified in the Mumbai Police examination. Instead of doing routine jobs and having an ordinary existence, they would happily be a part of such a prestigious task for a higher cause,' said Kelkar. 'Won't you? Rohit, Sahil?' he added, turning to address two young men who were standing by a Hero Honda bike parked next to his scooter.

Kelkar had noticed the duo's arrival a few minutes ago and also calculated that they must have heard parts of his conversations with Sawant. He knew the two to be fearless young men who were aware about the world around them. They were also among the BVP volunteers who never skipped the morning drills.

Sawant valued Kelkar and his followers. For ten years, as a senior intelligence officer with the CTC, he had kept a watch on Kelkar, the BVP and a clutch of other right-wing outfits, on the lookout for any development that might threaten law and order. He had also worked to develop assets or moles inside the BVP.

Along the way, a few BVP office-bearers, especially Vishnuji, had taken a liking to Sawant and appreciated the fact that the CTC was at the vanguard of the nation's fight against its external enemies and had made sacrifices in this war. He understood that it was Sawant's job to keep an eye on the BVP's activities and did not resent him for that. Over the years, Sawant and Vishnu had helped each other whenever they could.

'Vishnu dada, for the country, we will do anything,' Rohit said. 'We can write the Mumbai Police examination again in four years. I am only twenty-two and Sahil is twenty-two as well.'

'I am in, tell us the plan,' Sahil added enthusiastically.

Sawant beamed.

With the recruitment of five 'intelligence agents' for Operation Trojan Horse, Shekhar began engaging, almost on a daily basis, with their CTC 'handlers', Somaiya and Sawant, to give shape to the fledgling operation. He asked them to instruct the five – Atharv, Anant, Nirav, Rohit and Sahil – on the need to create a plausible alibi for their work with CTC, which would involve years of secret, perilous work in India and abroad and long absences. He told the handlers that the agents must inform their families that they had bagged lucrative jobs with multinational corporates in Dubai or any other city in the Middle East. The agents were asked to also tell their families that while they would be staying overseas for prolonged periods, they would keep in touch with them and send a portion of their salaries regularly.

20

BUNGALOW NUMBER 105

Roughly a kilometre and a half to the north of India Gate lies bungalow number 105. It sits at the corner where the bustling, tree-lined Copernicus Marg and Chamberlain Road meet.

To the average passerby, the bungalow, despite the sprawling grounds in which it is built, would not merit a second glance. Indeed, it may seem like an oddity in the midst of its well-appointed neighbouring bungalows, which are visual treats. Their façades, boundary walls and French windows wear fresh coats of paint in shades of white and orange. A peek inside their compounds reveals manicured lawns, flower beds, walls festooned with bougainvillea, fleets of luxury cars and uniformed private guards in their specially constructed cabins at the gates.

Bungalow number 105, on the other hand, with its plain white façade and boundary walls, looks stuck in a time warp, forlorn. It has only a few windows, almost as if they were added as an afterthought.

It sits at the centre of a large campus. Apart from the bungalow, there is no other noteworthy structure inside. There is a garage, with a car or two parked, but they are unremarkable in terms of the colour, make and model. The grass on the lawns is unevenly cut and could do with a regular supply of water. There are no flower beds.

The black paint on the entrance gates is peeling off. The white paint that covers the entire bungalow has turned grey-brown where it is exposed to the rains and the scorching summer sun.

Two watchmen wearing shabby blue uniforms sit in front of the garage, their eyes trained on the gates. Apart from the watchmen, there is no sign of life or human activity either in the bungalow or the compound. No one can be seen on the lawns, in the portico on the ground floor or on the balcony and verandah on the first floor. The windows remain closed at all times. The cars in the garage do not budge from their spots. No visitor's vehicle is found parked at the gates. There are no sounds of kids cracking with laughter coming through the bungalow's walls; young men and women, in business suits or casuals, do not leave or enter; grannies and grandpas are not to be seen out on their daily stroll.

It was at this bungalow that Atharv, Anant and Nirav arrived at 5 a.m. on 1 May 2000.

Somaiya had instructed Atharv to get out of the taxi 500 metres before the bungalow and to then walk around to the back of the compound to a small, inconspicuous gate located in the service lane, where they were to wait for a 'receiver'.

After waiting for the receiver for about twenty minutes, Atharv and his companions ran out of patience. They scaled the walls and jumped over. Moments later, they saw two security guards running towards them, batons in their hands. The guards attacked them with the batons, letting out a volley of the choicest expletives in Hindi.

Atharv took two blows on his arms but managed to snatch one of the batons and land a few punches on its wielder. The second guard kept raining blows on the other two, Anant and Nirav, and eluded their grasp.

Just then the receiver, a tall man clad in navy blue hooded track pants, arrived and began screaming at the guards for mistaking the guests for intruders.

'*Guests hain!*' the receiver shouted. Identifying himself as Sunil Singh, he took the trio inside the bungalow after apologizing to them for the guards' gaffe. The guards retreated to their cots outside the garage. A portable CCTV monitor lay on one of the cots.

Unknown to Atharv and his two companions, Sahil and Rohit were already at the bungalow. They had arrived there at 3 a.m. as per Sawant's instructions. It was pitch dark then. There had been no receiver at the gate for them either, and the duo had also scaled the walls to jump over. They had been greeted by three dogs who had come charging out of nowhere to attack the boys as soon as they entered the compound. The black German Shepherds were barely visible in the dimly lit backyard. The duo had run for their lives, zigzagging across the grounds, trying to elude the lunges of the lean canines. They had charged back to the wall they had scaled, climbed it and stood on top, out of the dogs' reach.

Just then, the receiver had finally arrived and, with one glance, had figured out what had happened. He had barked out commands to the dogs, which withdrew meekly and were soon out of sight.

The receiver had then offered a barely audible apology to Rohit and Sahil as he had them inside the bungalow.

As the young men were soon to discover, bungalow number 105, an eighty-five-year-old Raj-era relic, had certain advantages that only its users were aware of.

The eight rooms and four halls inside the bungalow were spacious and well-ventilated. Two sides of the bungalow were not visible to the outside world, including to the residents of the neighbouring bungalows, thanks to the tall trees and shrubbery that acted as an impenetrable natural screen.

The bungalow's location afforded it easy access to most parts of the city, especially Old Delhi, with its maze-like alleys and cheek-by-jowl tenements, where several operations had played out in the past.

The bungalow also had a state-of-the-art indoor shooting range and a laboratory, where all kinds of scientific training, from making IEDs to dismantling them, could be imparted. Shekhar preferred the bungalow as a base for his covert operations due to the availability of the shooting range and the laboratory. These two facilities were not available at any of the other fifteen-odd 'guest houses' of the CTC located in Delhi.

21

A STEP INTO THE PAST

At 10 a.m., around five hours after the two sets of 'guests' had arrived at bungalow number 105 and were lodged in two spacious, air-conditioned suites in its basement, a hall on its first floor was waking up to activity. Men in civvies were going in and out. Its white-painted walls seemed to accentuate the glow of the concealed tube lights. A six-foot-wide corridor split the hall in two neat halves, from north to south. Wooden benches and tables were arranged on both sides.

The hall was known as 'Hillary Point' among those who stayed at the bungalow. Very few in the CTC could recollect why it was so named, though some suggested it was named after the Hillary Point that veteran climbers know of as the bend which is connected with a steep stretch to the summit of Mount Everest. The hall was used for key strategy sessions by the CTC's operatives before launching covert operations.

At 10.15 a.m., Atharv and his two friends entered the hall and took the seats on the right side of the corridor. Minutes later,

Sahil and Rohit arrived, taking seats on the left. The two groups exchanged glances, sizing each other up, but said nothing. It was the sound of footfalls, faint initially but increasing in intensity, that broke the uncomfortable silence enveloping the space. Somaiya entered the hall accompanied by two men, one of whom moved with the precision and assuredness of a commando.

It was this gentleman who was the first to speak. 'Good morning, tigers! My name is Sameer and my colleagues here are Somaiya and Sanjay, whom you may already know. I hope your stay here has been comfortable?'

'Good morning, sir. The bungalow is impressive. The stay has been better than the welcome,' Nirav, Atharv's former classmate, said tersely. His jaw was still sore, having taken a punch from one of the guards during the scuffle just a few hours ago.

'Good, but don't get used to it. For, you are standing at a point in life from where you will leap into a world of infinite opportunities and danger. You are getting the chance to fight for your country against its most hostile neighbour, Pakistan, by taking the fight to the enemy. History is a witness to the fact that those who are incapable of protecting themselves have only ruin awaiting them. Look at what happened to our country centuries ago to understand what I am saying.'

'Please elaborate, sir.'

Sameer looked at the boys to make sure they were listening. 'For centuries, external military adventurers have been drawn to India. They killed hundreds and thousands of soldiers as well as the unarmed, non-combatant citizens. They enslaved many and sent them back to their masters abroad. They looted the country's wealth.

'Beginning with Muhammad bin Qasim, who came to India for three things – wealth, land and expanding political–cultural influence – all of them left a trail of blood and sorrow behind when they were done. More than the armies in India, it was the civilians who bore the brunt of these invasions.'

'What were the Indian rulers of the time doing? Why could they not repel Qasim's attacks?'

'Qasim, a nineteen-year-old Arab from Taif, which is now a part of Saudi Arabia, came here to conquer Sindh. There was utter mayhem in flourishing cities like Debal, near what is now Karachi in Pakistan's Sindh, ' Sameer said. 'Like now, the civilians then too had nothing to do with the battles and wars of the states, big or small, ruled by kings or chieftains. Not with the victories, nor with the defeats. Yet, Debal, which prided itself on its position as an outpost of international marine trade and offered a good life to its residents, was burnt to the ground.'

'That is what happens when there is no unity among those who are facing the same threats, sir. The local rulers may have thought that the threat was to others, not to them.'

'Correct, Nirav. Then there was Mahmud of Ghazni, of the Turkic Ghaznavid dynasty, who attacked India seventeen times, beginning from 1001 AD. He went as far as Mathura in Uttar Pradesh and Somnath in Gujarat.'

'You are conducting a tutorial on India's history in brief. I was a laggard in history in school but here is another chance for me to brush up my knowledge. So, thank you, sir!'

'It's never too late, Nirav. Anyway, so I was saying, in the eighteenth century, the Persian king Nader Shah Afshar trounced the weak Mughal ruler Muhammad Shah Rangila's forces in the Battle of Karnal and took the keys of the city of Delhi, then the pride of Asia. Nader's 1,50,000-strong army comprising musketeers and horsemen carrying swivel guns put down the resistance of a million-strong army of the Mughals. Delhi then was a city of riches, history, *adab* or humility, and *tehzeeb* or manners.

'Nader lost no time in making himself comfortable in the royal apartments of Mughal emperor Shahjahan in the magnificent Red Fort. The next morning, there was an altercation between the rough, aggressive Persian cavalrymen and a grain merchant of Paharganj in Old Delhi. There were casualties on both sides. When the news of the killing of his soldiers reached Nader, he was filled with rage – the rage of a victor against the temerity of a defeated country's population to confront his soldiers. He gathered his troops and marched at their head, riding a tall horse and wearing full battle gear. He reached Chandni Chowk, unsheathed his sword and raised it to the sky, signalling the attack.

'Nader's army then began what is known as one of the worst chapters in Delhi's history, the *Qatl-e-aam*, killing one lakh helpless civilians. He stopped killing only after he was paid a ransom of Rs 100 crore and took away a big war booty, including the Mughal bejewelled Peacock Throne, Koh-i-Noor and Darya-i-Noor diamonds and Timur Ruby.'

'What about the British invaders? Do enlighten us on how they ruined us?' Rohit asked.

Around four hundred years ago, on 31 December 1600, the English East India Company was incorporated in London through a royal charter. The mandate? To conduct trade with India and

Southeast Asia. It had the right to set up its own army, just like the French East India Company. It began as a monopolistic trade body but transformed quickly into a brutal, exploitative tool of British imperialism. The company's defeat of the Portuguese in India in 1612 secured for it trading concessions from the Mughals.

'The company traded in cotton, silk piece goods, indigo, tea, spices and salt petre, among other things, and gradually began acquiring political and military ascendancy in parts of India, beginning with Bengal in 1757. Then Bengal ruler Siraj ud-Daulah and the French East India Company were defeated in the Battle of Plassey by the British company's forces. A 3,000-strong British company army, led by Lieutenant Colonel Robert Clive, would trump the numerically superior Bengal–French troops that were 50,000 strong, with better battle manoeuvres and tactics.'

'What do you mean by better tactics when talking about a mid-eighteenth century battle?' Atharv asked.

'The British used the artillery more efficiently and also ensured the absence of one-third of the Bengal army from combat by buying the loyalty of Bengali traitor Mir Jafar. The British could also ensure that their artillery shells remained dry when pressed into action as it had rained on the battle day, 23 June. The British had just remembered to carry tarpaulins, unlike the Bengal army. The British lost less than 50 lives; the Bengal army lost around 1,500.

'The company acquired revenue rights in Bengal. Its repressive and exploitative policies targeting Indians triggered the First War of Indian Independence or the Indian Mutiny of 1857–59 that involved British Indian soldiers, Maratha and Mughal soldiers. The

British army crushed the rebellion with extreme ferocity. Hundreds of soldiers were bayoneted or fired from cannons, while the Mughal royal family was wiped out, in reprisals by the British.

'The British government, which took over the control of India after the 1857 mutiny, was no less ruthless in dealing with dissent. As you know, a few dozen British soldiers under Brigadier General Reginald Dyer on 13 April 1919 opened fire on a peaceful crowd of 10,000 men, women and children at Amritsar's Jallianwala Bagh ground, sealing off its exits. Around 400 lay dead, while around 1,200 sustained injuries. Most of those who had assembled there that day had come to protest against the oppressive British Rowlatt Act while some were there to celebrate Baisakhi.'

'What was the reaction of the British government to the massacre?' asked Sahil.

'The British government set up a commission of inquiry, the Hunter Commission, which asked Dyer to resign. But the House of Lords praised Dyer's barbarism and gave him a sword inscribed with "Saviour of the Punjab". It was a typical case of British hypocrisy. Right after India and Pakistan attained freedom from British rule in August 1947, our neighbour stabbed us in the back. In 1947-48, it dispatched hordes of wild, armed-to-the-teeth tribesmen from their North-West Frontier Province to massacre civilians and forcibly and illegally acquire Jammu and Kashmir. J&K was then an independent kingdom that was delaying the call on acceding to either India or Pakistan. And since then, while on the one hand that country's government engages in dialogue with us, on the other, it covertly deploys its sponsored terrorists and saboteurs to bleed us.'

Seeing that the boys were beginning to look tired, Somaiya decided it was time to end the session.

'That's it for today. We will meet tomorrow, same time. There is an Olympic-sized pool at the back of the bungalow for those inclined to take a swim. There are volleyball and basketball courts in the campus here too. Enjoy the rest of your day.'

22

TRAINING

The following morning, Sameer continued the session. 'Gentlemen, yesterday I told you about the many foreigners who came to India to enrich themselves at her expense...'

The boys were taking an interest in Sameer's lectures.

Atharv was absorbing each word spoken by Sameer. He had a sombre expression on his face; his eyebrows were furrowed as he jotted down points in the small diary he always carried with him. He was, however, waiting for the classes to end and the mission to begin.

Nirav and Anant said they were relishing the history classes that were rich in 'quirky, shocking anecdotes'.

Rohit and Sahil had not made any comments on whether they were enjoying the classes. Rohit asked a few pointed questions related to the Jallianwala Bagh massacre. When the queries were being answered, he wore an agitated expression, while Sahil's face reddened.

Halfway through the morning session, Somaiya took over from Sameer.

'Boys, you are here for a specific reason. The country calls for you. The blood of each innocent killed or injured by terrorists, spies and subversives sent by Pakistan calls out for you. Will you avenge them?'

The five-man audience erupted in unison, 'Yes ... we will!'

Somaiya smiled. 'You will be trained here, get amazing skills for the mission. We will prepare you for every step of the journey. It could be a lonely one. But don't worry; we will be there, guiding you.

'You will be at ground zero, in the enemy's lair. Your skills, courage and the ability to think on your feet will come handy there. These attributes will let you live. Through your actions you can ensure the well-being of the country. You know what our mission is – the destruction of the Pakistani state's instruments of terror, the Lashkar-e-Taiba and its mentors in the ISI.

'When ready, you will set out like missiles to take out the enemy's lair. Won't that be fun, boys?'

The boys nodded.

'All of you have certain commonalities. You are educated, intelligent, driven, courageous and young. You could have been elsewhere, but you chose to be here.

'You have that X factor that separates you from the average Joe. And so you are here, at Hillary Point, preparing to scale the summit of your life. Only a few get such an opportunity.

'Tomorrow you will be given new identities. What you learn in this group must stay in the group. If at all your paths intersect, it will be for executing a task jointly, and you will get information on a need-to-know basis. Apart from your immediate handler in the CTC, you will share nothing about your involvement or work with the CTC with anyone. Is that clear?'

'Yes, sir,' the boys chorused.

Somaiya looked pleased with the recruits' enthusiasm. He turned to Sahil and Rohit. 'Boys, like you, I too have a link with Mumbai. The name of that great city brings back the memories of Ahaana, who was like my daughter. Her father, Vinay Kamthe, was my classmate at St Xavier's School. We used to call him Rana.

'At six feet, with a muscular frame, he was our school cricket team's fast bowler. Not only was he fast, he could swing the ball too, which was a gift. Anyway, if you were a friend and in need of help, you would find Rana there, especially if somebody needed to be bashed up.

'Rana settled down in life, got married and had a daughter, Ahaana. She was a delight. At six years of age, she was never short of stories to tell – they could be about some game she played, or the birds, cats and dogs she had seen from the balcony, or about her friends Ziah or Jiaan. When I went to visit, she would look at me with curiosity and smile, with a twinkle in her eyes. It would make my day.

'But then everything changed on the afternoon of 12 March 1993. On that day, Rana had taken his daughter to his office for the first time. He worked for Canara Bank, and his office was in the Alankar commercial complex in Nariman Point. His office building was next to the Air India building.

'Rana took Ahaana to his office that day because he wanted to take her to Byculla zoo in the afternoon. He had promised to show her Whitey, the Siberian tiger, the zoo's newest crowd-puller.

'At around 2, as Rana was getting ready to leave with Ahaana, a loud explosion shook the entire building. Outside the window, Rana caught a glimpse of a cloud of dust billowing from the neighbouring Air India building. Within seconds, the floor and walls around Rana and Ahaana had cracked open. The floor caved in, taking everyone including Rana and Ahaana down with it. The two of them were among the hundreds of victims of the Bombay serial blasts of 12 March 1993, the biggest terror strike that had been perpetrated on Indians thus far.

'The terrorists had used IED-rigged cars and scooters, as these bombs are particularly effective in blowing up buildings. The Air India complex and the Bombay Stock Exchange were hit. There were hand grenade attacks on the fishermen's colony in Mahim.

'Rana did not survive the blast. Only his right hand, its fingers still clutching two Byculla zoo tickets, was retrieved from the tonnes of rubble that he lay buried under. Ahaana lay injured and semi-conscious a few feet away from her father. She would later tell Kasturi Bhabhi that all she could remember was her Papa pushing her away after a loud boom shook the Alankar building.

'Ahaana recovered, but she lost her speech. Kasturi Bhabhi got a clerk's job at the bank, on compassionate grounds. Rana had been a senior zonal manager and had looked after his family well; now they are struggling and alone. Their planet lost its sun.

'Ahaana seems to want to say so much to me when I see her. But I can't meet her unblinking gaze. I can't bring her Papa back. In moments like these, you realize how small and powerless we are in the face of matters of life and death.

'She may no longer be able to speak, but I know what she wants to tell me. Ahaana wants me to go after those who took her Papa away. Ahaana and the loved ones of all those who died or were injured in the March 1993 blasts, orchestrated by Dawood and his friends in the ISI, want revenge.'

Somaiya paused and looked at each of the boys in turn. 'Somebody needs to avenge Rana's death for Ahaana...'

Sahil glowered at Somaiya and attempted to say something but his words were inaudible. No one else uttered a word.

23

GIVING INDIA A 'THOUSAND CUTS'

The next class picked up from where the last one had ended – the 1993 Bombay serial blasts. It all began with Atharv asking Somaiya for some 'inside story' related to the blasts' conspiracy and their alleged orchestrators, Dawood Ibrahim, Tiger Memon and their ISI handlers. Somaiya said the blasts were the biggest acts of terror in India till 1993 and were the result of the ISI deciding to use mafia operatives to damage India.

'In early December 1992, trouble was brewing over the issue of the Babri Masjid in Ayodhya, Uttar Pradesh. The mosque had been built, according to some historians, after demolishing a Ram temple that had stood on the same spot and where, legend says, Lord Ram was born. A section of right-wing leaders had been calling for the destruction of the mosque and the building of a temple dedicated to Lord Ram. After months of mobilization of popular support and resources, matters came to a head and got out of hand, and the Babri Masjid was destroyed by kar sevaks. The law of the land was violated,' Somaiya began the day's lecture.

'For Pakistan, the demolition of the mosque was a golden opportunity to inflame, radicalize, recruit and train young Indian men for terror attacks in the name of revenge. For some time, the Pakistani terror machinery had been baying for new frontiers in the proxy war it was waging against India, especially as their efforts to create a movement for a separate Sikh state, Khalistan, were not meeting with the desired success.

'Apart from Punjab, the Pakistani Deep State had its eyes on Jammu and Kashmir, which had chosen to accede to India after Independence. Refusing to accept this accession, Pakistan decided to gain control over the state by force and orchestrated an invasion of Jammu and Kashmir shortly after Independence, deploying tribesmen from the North-West Frontier Province for the attack. However, Pakistan's aggression was unsuccessful as the Indian Army gave them a fitting reply and drove them back to Pakistan. Unable to defeat India in multiple conventional wars, Pakistan adopted another strategy over the decades. They decided to inflict on India a "thousand cuts" through a sub-conventional proxy war, with the help of terrorists.

'The Pakistani army and the ISI created the Lashkar-e-Taiba, a band of terrorists under the leadership of Hafiz Saeed, an Afghan jihad veteran, in 1987. Saeed had done his post-graduation in Arabic and Islamic Studies from Punjab University in 1974 and become a lecturer at Lahore's University of Engineering and Technology. He later graduated from Riyadh's King Saud University. The army gave the LeT's parent, the Jamaat-ud-Dawa (JuD), a religious organization of clerics, land free of cost at

Muridke near Lahore. The base at Muridke would later serve as the training ground and command headquarters for waging a war of terror in India, especially in Jammu and Kashmir. They shed blood in India in the name of the imperative to make Kashmir a part of Pakistan and thereby reverse history. After Kashmir, the rest of India became their target, with attempts to recruit disaffected youth and organize them into covert cells.

'But now let me get back to the tragedy that was the destruction of the centuries-old Babri Masjid, an episode that is a black chapter in India's modern history. Pakistan smelt blood and went for the kill. They used Bombay's absconding gangster Dawood Ibrahim's muscle power, money, and gold and silver smuggling cartels working out of Bombay and Dubai – led by men like Tiger Memon – to orchestrate a frightful series of bombings in Bombay in March 1993 in the name of "avenging" the destruction of the Babri Masjid and the loss of lives in the Bombay riots that were triggered days later.

'The actual aim was to cripple India's financial hub, Bombay, and the targets for bombing had been selected keeping that in mind. They attacked Dadar in central Bombay, the diamond trade hub of Zaveri Bazaar, the Bombay Stock Exchange and the Air India building. Property worth Rs 57 crore was destroyed and 257 lives were lost. The synchronized bombings, thirteen of which went off one after the other, sought to kill Bombay's and India's spirit.

'While Bombay took the blackest day in its history in its stride and moved on, the terror attack put the spotlight on the gaping holes in India's security and intelligence networks.'

'We were ... caught napping? Day dreaming?' Rohit asked. He had a nervous smile on his face.

'You put it rather bluntly, Rohit. But that's the truth,' Somaiya said, his face turning pale as he looked at Rohit unblinkingly. For a few moments, there was hushed silence in the hall.

'No offence meant, sir…'

'None taken. It's a fact, isn't it?'

'From January 1993 onwards, thousands of kilograms of deadly, military-grade RDX, AK-56 automatics, Pakistani army-issue Austrian hand grenades and other small arms were being offloaded by ISI speedboats in the high seas off the coast of Maharashtra at Sindhudurg and Ratnagiri. For this, Dawood and Tiger used the sea routes and landing spots favoured by their silver and gold smuggling operations. The landing agents were paid well and also radicalized with talks about acting to avenge the wrongs suffered by the Muslim community during the 1992 riots.

'At least nineteen men from Bombay, picked by the Indian conspirators, were sent for training to ISI-run terror training camps in Pakistan, via Dubai. They returned the same way. And all this while, we who were in the security, intelligence and enforcement agencies, who are tasked with protecting the country and knowing what's happening on the ground, had no clue.'

'Where were Tiger and Dawood operating from to prepare for the blasts?' Rohit asked.

'Tiger and his Pakistan-trained men were at work in the parking lot of where he stayed, Al Husseini residential building in Mahim. Tiger, once he had tasted success in smuggling activities, had bought two duplex flats in the building. Since January, these flats had become the headquarters for planning the bombings. Through the evening and night of 11 and 12 March, around a dozen bomb-makers and bomb planters were in the parking lot.

'They were rigging jeeps, scooters and cars with RDX and giving finishing touches to the IEDs' detonators and triggers. They joked, spoke loudly, swore, ate and smoked even as they kept preparing the bombs, a young girl, an eyewitness, would later tell the police. At the crack of dawn the bombs were ready to take an unsuspecting city and its people by surprise.

'One by one, the planters left the Al Husseini building's parking lot on the fateful morning of 12 March to bring death and mayhem to the city.'

'Beyond darkness, there is light,' Atharva said. Atharva, when he was in the mood, wrote short stories and notes on whatever moved him in his diary. 'Tomorrow is a new day… the day of redemption for you and me.'

'We have a poet amid us. A warrior poet, are you?' Somaiya smiled at Atharva.

'No, sir. Where is the time for poetry?'

'Around the same time as the 1993 bombings in Bombay, the ISI was attempting to harvest the disaffection among the Muslim youth over the 1992 riots and the mosque demolition in Ayodhya. It was drawing in educated men like Dr Kamil Ansari of Bombay,' Somaiya continued.

'Kamil and other conspirators, looking for retribution, orchestrated over fifty IED blasts on long-distance trains across India to register their protest.'

'How many died?'

Sameer, who had been listening to his colleague, pitched in.

'Thankfully, only two lives were lost in the bombings. But again, we just did not know what was happening.'

'Kamil had suffered in the 1992 riots in Bombay?'

'In fact, his terror activities had begun before December 1992. He was found testing his bombs in the sands of a river in Malegaon years before the mosque was destroyed. The ISI has been trapping our disaffected youth with their propaganda quite easily. Often, we just do not know.

'And that is where,' Sameer finished, 'you and this mission, Operation Trojan Horse, come in.'

24

THE GAME BEGINS

Somaiya is furious at Pakistan this morning too, thought Atharv.

After greeting the boys, he wasted little time in beginning his lecture. 'There is no end to Pakistan's treachery; we need to always be vigilant. In 1999, as per information shared by army intelligence, Pakistani troops drawn from its specialized mountain warfare unit, the Northern Light Infantry, captured heights on our side of the Line of Control in Kargil in Jammu and Kashmir. Reports suggested that they had built reinforced concrete bunkers on those hills and accumulated weapons, ammunition and food and water for the troops. It required a limited war and the sacrifice of hundreds of young Indian soldiers and officers to eliminate the Pakistanis entrenched on those icy heights.'

'So we failed to spot again?' Atharv asked.

'No, the army and intelligence had some information but no timely or adequate action could be taken till intrusions began appearing like an invasion. The Pakistanis occupied peaks during winter, when both the armies withdraw from snowcapped peaks only to return later.'

Sameer took over from his colleague. 'Their defeat in the Kargil war did not deter Pakistan's efforts to create mayhem in India. To this end, they started pushing into Kashmir all the trained foreign militants, including Pakistanis, who were twiddling their thumbs after the end of the Afghan jihad theatre.

'We have to stop Pakistan's attempt to begin another war against us in the name of azadi for Kashmir. Kashmir is the pride of India, our idea of inclusive nationhood. Kashmir is where Sufism and Shaivism have interacted and prospered together.

'Remember, only fools would believe that Pakistan, the ISI and their terrorists are at war with us because they want to "liberate" the Muslim-dominated Kashmir, Hyderabad or Junagadh.

'LeT's founder Hafiz Saeed has warned several times that it will be at war with India until it captures the entire country. *India ki barbadi tak, jang rahegi, jang rahegi, unki maut tak, jang rahegi, jang rahegi.* That's their motto. Hafiz Saeed has spoken of the inevitability of a Final Battle for the Land of Hind. He called it "Ghazwa-e-Hind". They claim an army from Afghanistan, carrying black flags, will rise to conquer India.'

'What's going on right now as far as ISI's war against us is concerned?' Atharv asked.

'Foreign mercenaries, thanks to the ISI, are still coming here to destroy us, just that their profiles have undergone a change. You may have heard about the arrest of Salim Amjad in Hyderabad and of the two trained LeT suicide attackers. Salim was supposedly a Hyderabadi, but the CTC investigated and found that he is actually a Pakistani. The two LeT men are Pakistani terrorists too.

'Salim is a long-term resident terrorist sent to India to never return. He was to stay among us, as one of us, to help destroy us. We need to pluck out such embedded Pakistani terrorists as each of them is a ticking time bomb.'

An eerie silence descended on the room. Somaiya and Sameer were seemingly exhausted and were assessing the reaction of the recruits. Just then, an orderly entered the hall and passed around glasses of cold water and biscuits. The glasses were emptied at once. But no one touched the biscuits as if the mention of Salim's treachery had tamed their hunger.

'We cannot let another tragedy like the 1993 serial blasts happen in India. Trojan Horse will seek to be India's eyes and ears in Pakistan. The mission believes in the adage that attack is the best defence. The time has come to deal with Pakistan on its own land and under its own skies,' Somaiya said as he exited the hall.

25

SHOOT TO KILL

The soundproof shooting range of bungalow number 105 was built two floors beneath its sprawling compound. Now that the initiation of the five trainees was over, it was time for the three instructors, Sameer, Somaiya and Sanjay, to turn them into capable covert operatives.

Sameer was waiting for the boys as they walked into the range at 6 a.m.

'Welcome to the range, trainees. You will learn all about weapons here, from handguns like the Italian Glock, which is light and accurate, to AK-47 and AR-15 automatics, which are the weapons of choice for commandos seeking accuracy and a higher kill percentage. How many of you have fired a weapon before? An air gun?'

'I once went to a firing range in my city. I have fired a handgun, but I don't remember what it was,' said Atharv.

'Okay, then let's start with you, Atharv,' said Sameer. 'Pick up that Glock from spot "A", marked by the placard. That is the spot where a shooter needs to stand and take aim at a target that is between 10 and 60 metres away. Go ahead, shoot.'

Atharv, a tad uncertain about what was expected of him, ambled to spot A and picked up the Glock pistol kept on a rubber mat on the floor. He stood sideways, took aim with his right eye and pulled the trigger with his right hand. *Thwack*, a heavy metallic sound resonated in the large and empty space of the shooting facility. Atharv had missed the mark, placed 10 metres away, and the pistol's recoil had injured his palm.

'Forget about how Inspector Vijay shoots in the movies, with one arm, body turned sideways. That is all filmy,' Sameer said. 'We will teach you how to shoot the professional way. You will learn how to shoot to kill. Your instructor, Uday, will teach you how to fire and how not to fire over the next three months.'

As if out of nowhere, Uday, a six-footer, appeared in the range. He was attired in a white T-shirt and khaki trousers.

Nodding to the boys, he addressed them. 'Boys, you will pick a weapon for yourself, and from now on, you will consider it to be an extension of your being, your body. Your mind, body and the weapon should be in perfect harmony. If you take good care of your weapon, it will save your life during emergencies.'

Uday looked at Atharv. 'Atharv, go to spot A again and stand there.'

Atharv walked back to the spot.

'Don't stand sideways, stand straight, facing your target.'

Atharv adjusted his stance.

'Stand at ease and spread out your legs. Just enough for you to be balanced. Bend your knees a bit. Don't hold the pistol with your right hand alone. Use both your hands to hold the butt. Now, take aim, either with both eyes or with one eye.'

Atharv did as he was told.

'Make sure that your firing hand is gripping the pistol firmly, while the four fingers of the supporting hand – in Atharv's case, the supporting hand is his left hand – are beneath the trigger section. Such an action allows you to take good aim, increases your accuracy and protects you from the adverse effects of recoil.'

When Uday was satisfied with Atharv's stance, he instructed him, 'Come on, aim at your target and fire six times.'

Atharv missed his mark twice. But by the third shot, he was more comfortable in his stance. He was aware of where he was standing, where his firing arm and support arm were. Although he missed the mark again, shots four, five and six hit the bull's eye. He let out a loud 'Yes!' as he raised his right hand in the air with a clenched fist.

'Atharv, remain in your position and fire sixty more rounds. Pause for a while after each round of six shots. Hit the target every time.'

Uday turned to the rest of the boys. 'Remember, every bullet is meant to hit the target – head, shoulder or a limb, as per your situational need. *Ek goli, ek dushman.*'

For the next fifteen minutes, Atharv fired at the target. Thirty-nine of the sixty bullets that he fired found their mark.

'Not bad for an amateur,' Uday said as Atharv fired the last shot. 'But for a trained CTC operative, it should be fifty-six or fifty-seven out of sixty!'

Atharv, who had been feeling quite pleased with his performance, walked dejectedly back to join the boys on hearing Uday's comment.

'I will wrap up today's session with some safety tips. One, always treat a firearm as if it is loaded, even when you know it is not.

'Two, always keep the firearm pointed in a direction where any accidental firing would cause minimum harm. So, keep it pointed downward.

'Three, keep your trigger finger off the trigger and even the trigger guard, unless you have decided to shoot.

'Four, always be sure of what lies beyond your target to reduce the chances of a mishap.

'For beginners like you, it is important to keep some additional tips in mind to prevent accidental injuries. One, a two-handed grip is advisable. If you are left-handed, your left hand should be the gun hand. You hold the gun with it and shoot. Hold the butt of the gun firmly as this will allow you to control the recoil better. The other hand is the support hand, with which you also grip the gun with four fingers beneath the trigger guard or section. And two, stand with your feet apart. Understood?' Uday looked around at the boys.

As they nodded, he said, 'Okay, that's all for today. We will assemble here every day at 4 p.m. for firing practice.'

'Yes, sir,' they responded in unison.

26

KRAV MAGA, KALI AND TRACKING SKILLS

Chamberlain Road, lined with eucalyptus trees, runs straight as an arrow and, with a width of 120 feet, is broader than a typical two-lane street. After six kilometres, it splits into two roads – Kennedy Hill Street, which branches to the left, and Manchester Street, which turns to the right.

Manchester Street takes you to the town's well-known Chinese Quarter, the preferred fast-food destination of tourists in Lansdowne, the British-built hill station in Uttarakhand, nestled in the lower Himalayas. Beyond the Chinese Quarter lies the Lansdowne Royal Club, which draws sharply dressed patrons with old money from the town.

Lansdowne was developed as a military garrison under the British government in India, and the Indian Army's Garhwal Rifles Regiment still trains there. The air is fresh, the climate is cool, and its location makes it an ideal place for quick summer getaways as well as training for athletes.

In May, when most of India faces oppressive heat, Lansdowne stays cool, wet and pleasant. Residents can be seen enjoying the weather, taking walks along its wide, leafy roads and lakeside promenades, eating at the roadside eateries offering cappuccinos and lattes, steaming plates of Maggi noodles, fried river fish and savory snacks like pakodas. Tourists do all that in addition to trekking, climbing and whiter-water rafting.

Lansdowne has an unhurried pace of life. It lives in the moment but takes pride in its rich heritage. The town is dotted with white stone bungalows from the British era, with low boundary walls, French windows, carefully manicured flower beds and sloping roofs. The town also has several centuries-old Gothic churches with tall spires, mostly empty prayer halls and moss-laden walls enclosing sprawling grounds.

Kennedy Hill Street, on the other hand, winds up the steep slopes of the hill and lies deserted during most of the day, barring the occasional vehicles, cyclists and walkers. The road does not take you to any popular food destination or swanky watering holes. It leads to around two dozen Victorian-style bungalows built on the hill, near which are a smattering of old bakeries, restaurants and tea and coffee houses.

There is also a single-theatre movie hall, the Albert, which shows popular Bollywood movies during the evenings and old English movies during the day. Farouk Mistry, the seventy-six-year-old manager of the Albert, had been hired when he was twenty-five as a rookie accountant by the theatre's Anglo-Indian owner, Michael Soosairaj. Mistry had excelled at his work and, in no time, the management had entrusted him with the task of running the theatre's affairs.

A hundred metres away from the Albert is Wellesley Mansion. A 147-year-old Victorian-style bungalow, Wellesley Mansion sprawls across a 1,000-yard plot and has twelve rooms, twelve bathrooms and three kitchens.

The mansion is the CTC's preferred guest house-cum-secret training establishment for operations, especially those that call for equipping trainees with experience on the street and building their endurance and strength. The colonial relic's east side faces Kennedy Hill Street, with an orchard of apple and pear trees between the mansion and the compound's large black entrance gate.

A narrow pathway leads from the gates to the mansion. On the mansion's west side lie rows of flower beds and a boundary wall. Beyond the wall, thick woods cover the hill's face right to the bottom. Standing by the wall, one can get a bird's-eye view of the town lying below. At certain times of the day, especially in the morning, groups of monkeys sit on the walls, their backs to the town, peering at the happenings inside Wellesley Mansion.

At 5 a.m., the mansion was cloaked in darkness. Fifteen minutes later, lights flickered on in some of the rooms, the bathrooms and one of the kitchens. By 6 a.m., the darkness began to melt away as the sky lightened.

Sawant, the retired CTC operative now back in action on a special contract, took centre stage in the main drawing room while addressing the Pakistan-bound recruits.

'Gentlemen, I hope you all had a good night's sleep? I am assuming you have done your morning chores and had your tea and biscuits?'

'Yes, sir!' replied Anant.

Rohit added, 'Yes, sir, we are ready to hit the streets. Compared to Delhi, it is far more pleasant here. This is the perfect place for endurance training, I would think.'

Sawant smiled. 'Wonderful, boys. So, let's roll.'

The team of six, all in their track pants and sweatshirts, charged out of Wellesley Mansion.

After they had covered about a hundred metres and had just crossed the Albert, Sawant shouted, 'Slow down, jokers! It's a six-kilometre run, not a sprint! So, run at a pace you can comfortably maintain till the end. Your last lap will need more than the last ounce of energy you have left. It will require the kind of strength that comes only from your unshakable will to finish the run – as the winner.'

At the end of the jog, Anant emerged as the winner, followed by Atharv. The other three finished the race too but came in over two minutes after Anant and Atharv.

'Not bad for your first day, boys,' Sawant greeted them on their return to the mansion. 'After breakfast, we will climb up Kennedy Hill through its western face, which is steeper. After having a hot delicious lunch at Wellesley, you can enjoy your time, explore the town, and do what interests you. The sun goes down early here. Tell strangers you all are athletes and are undergoing specialized training. There will be an hour of gym work from 7 p.m. to 8 p.m., followed by dinner. Let's do it and enjoy.'

Three weeks later, during which the recruits underwent rigorous endurance and strength training, two visitors, one from Kerala and the other from Maharashtra, joined the team at Wellesley Mansion and instructed the boys in the art of unarmed combat.

Stanley Xavier, from Kerala, taught the recruits Krav Maga, a synthesis of techniques from a variety of martial arts, which the Israeli armed forces also practice as part of their training regimen.

Rahul Sardesai, from Maharashtra, instructed the boys in the Filipino martial art form of Kali. The deadly forms helped develop the skills needed to come out unscathed from violent street-fight-like situations, using bare hands as well as sharp objects like daggers, swords, curved axes and long, slender wooden sticks.

Atharv, fondly called 'Sniper' by his fellow recruits on account of the comparatively better skills he displayed in shooting at bungalow number 105's range, excelled in these fighting arts again. It turned out he had a black belt in karate too. Rohit too took to the Filipino techniques like a fish to water.

Twelve weeks after the five recruits were brought to Wellesley Mansion, Shekhar finally appeared before them.

'How is the training coming along, boys?' he asked them.

'We are surviving, I suppose. How are you, Mr Shekhar? Lansdowne will do you a world of good; you should stay here for a few days,' Atharv replied.

Shekhar was surprised by Atharv's informal response. He knew from the reports he had been receiving that the boy was 'sharp' and excelled in the tasks and exercises given to the recruits, but that he also had a strong streak of independence.

He will be an ace operative one day, if moulded properly to hone his skills and temper his ego, Shekhar thought to himself.

Aloud, he said, 'Hello, Atharv. I am glad to hear you are doing well. I am here to give you a task. In our line of work, tracking targets and evading trackers is our primary skill. Success or failure in both skills can determine the corresponding outcome of an operation and can secure or endanger our own lives and those of our colleagues. So, let's do a test, to assess how well you boys can tail a target or can wriggle out of a target's gaze.

'You will follow Sawant from Wellesley Mansion to the Chinese Quarter on foot. First, Sawant will leave, and five minutes later you will follow. An unmanned aerial vehicle will be monitoring you. Every time Sawant sees you, he will touch the back of his head. If you are spotted even once, Atharv, you will both return. Your punishment will be to trek up and down Kennedy Hill three times after a five-kilometre jog. You may take the help of the other recruits if you want.'

'I am good, sir. No help required for now,' he replied.

By the time Atharv left the mansion, Sawant had already crossed the Albert theatre. Atharv climbed the hill to use the vegetation as cover as he jogged ahead to get Sawant within his sights.

An hour later, Sawant reached the Chinese Quarter and entered a cafeteria. He chose a table on the first floor, from where he could keep an eye on the entrance. Atharv reached the cafeteria twenty minutes later and hesitated before entering. He finally crept into the cafeteria, attempting to make no noise or any noticeable movements. Sawant spotted him with delight. He went down the stairs at the back of the cafeteria and exited, even as Atharv continued to survey the crowd inside. He never saw Sawant.

Outside the cafeteria, Sawant looked up at the sky and patted the back of his head.

Atharv was seated in a corner of the cafeteria when Sawant appeared from behind him, as if from nowhere, with a tray of English biscuits, chips and coffee.

Atharv sat up with a jolt. 'What the—!'

Sawant laughed and escorted Atharv outside, where a Mahindra jeep was waiting for them.

Back at Wellesley Mansion, Shekhar addressed the recruits again.

'I have taken accounts of what happened in the exercise from both Atharv and Sawant. This is called debriefing. When I instruct you to do a task, it is called briefing. Atharv tried his best to track Sawant while staying in the shadows but got plucked out by his target. He flunked the test.

'How did Sawant succeed? To trap his tracker, Sawant entered the cafeteria, but he took care to plant himself at a spot from where he could keep an eye on everyone who entered. In intelligence parlance, this is called laying a cut-out. Atharv entered and Sawant spotted him. The reason behind success or failure in such a task may vary on a case-to-case basis, however. Think on your feet.'

Shekhar turned to Atharv. 'Atharv, you were caught. You endangered your team and the mission itself. The main aim when tracking somebody is to ensure you never lose sight of them. To ensure this, you deploy multiple trackers, who can be stationed at pre-determined points to cover the target's journey. Multiple trackers also means that the target will not see anybody twice.

'You refused the option to take help from the others but that was a blunder. In our line of work, only the execution of the task matters. The individual is not important, as you will realize during this training period.

'You could have tracked Sawant till Kennedy Hill Street, Anant could have taken the Manchester stretch and Rohit could have continued from the Chinese Quarter.'

'Sir, understood,' Atharv responded.

'Another important thing is communication. The strength and security of our communication system will decide whether a mission succeeds or fails, whether the operatives survive or are trapped by hostile forces. As we go along, we will teach you the art of secure communication. We will instruct you on how to use code, utilizing numerals, letters and everyday words. You will always use public telephone booths, never a listed residential or office landline.

'At times, we will use email, which is newly gaining popularity, for communication. You will go to a computer, access an email service provider's services, open a personal account and then send an email to the others from this email address. For instance, atharv2000@hotmail.com can be Atharv's email address. Atharv will have to select a password, say, blackbeltAtharv23, to access his account and send an email.'

Atharv broke into a chuckle at the mention of the proposed password. 'Yeah, by now, everyone respects the black belt considering the beating they got from me.'

Shekhar smiled. 'Right. So, we will create a common email address for all of us. Say, atharv2000@hotmail.com. We will have a common password too, blackbeltAtharv23. To communicate with each other, we will log in using the email ID and the password and then will write a message. But we will not send the message. We will save it as a draft. We will therefore have to access the drafts folder to read the message. Then, we can respond and act accordingly.'

'The email mode is a little tricky, but exciting!' Atharv said.

'It will be easy, trust me. You just need to practise. In our line, practice not only makes you perfect, it saves lives.'

27

THE MIND OF NAWAZ

From one forest to another
From one cave to another
From one mountain to another
From one peak to another
She runs, she runs
A young pursuer following her
No other woman has lips as beautiful, as luscious, as hers
No other woman gives an embrace that is as warm and fragrant
as hers
She is Laila
Laila of this young man who is after her
She is dearer than life to him
The man is in love
Do you know who Laila is?
Do we, who are assembled here in this open ground, under the
comforting shade of a tarpaulin that shields us against the severe
sun, know who that crazy lover and Laila are?

The raspy male voice, its pitch rising and falling as if in a practised rhythm, was killed abruptly. The Murphy tape recorder placed on a small table was switched off by Shekhar.

The five trainees and their four trainers, including Shekhar, were seated on cane chairs in two rows which faced each other. The session was being conducted in Merlin Hall, one of the largest halls in the CTC mansion. Apart from them, there was a stranger sitting with the trainers.

He had a light complexion, a wiry frame and appeared to be in his mid-fifties. Clad in a grey Pathani suit, he sported a beard that was dyed orange. While the tape recorder played, the man had watched the trainees like a hawk for any signs of reaction. He had not uttered a word since the session began.

Shekhar smiled at the trainees. 'I told you we would hear the speech of an interesting person, but I did not mention his name. We will find that out when we hear the rest of his speech. For now, let me introduce you to your new teacher, Mr Imran Hussein, who is also a long-time friend and colleague. He will conduct special classes for you. Hussein sahib has come here from Hyderabad to teach you the basic tenets of Islam. We are a secular, democratic country and all religions, including Hinduism, Islam, Sikhism and Christianity, are respected and treated equally under our Constitution.

'But once you finish your training, you will be given a special assignment that will take you to new places. You will meet new people whom you may not like but will have to work with nonetheless. You will have to befriend them, become their confidants. You will have to take on new identities, for which we will prepare you. Your job is to pay attention, absorb what is being taught to you and be prepared to execute tasks without any error.'

Shekhar turned to the man. 'Hussein sahib, please take over. But first, let us listen to the gentleman who wants to tell us about Laila and her Majnu.'

Shekhar switched on the tape recorder.

The raspy voice rang out again:

Let me tell you who Laila is, who her pursuer is. Laila is death itself, her lover is a Kashmiri mujahid. The mujahid begs Laila to take him in her embrace. He is a broken man. His heart is shattered because of the oppression and other acts of injustice committed by the Indian Army.

He says, 'Please accept me, Laila.'

Laila says, 'No, kill two more Indian security men.' Later, she says, 'Kill four more.'

Laila is still not ready to embrace the mujahid. But he needs her.

Her lips are crimson red. No other girl has lips as inviting as Laila's, as sweet as Laila's.

You must have heard about King Solomon? He was a prophet of the Jews, a just and wise ruler of the Jewish people. Suleiman had a beloved bird. One day this bird had a fight with his wife. The bird scolded her, 'Shut up or I will throw Suleiman's throne at you!'

Suleiman's throne required 28,000 men to join hands and lift it, but this bird thought he could fling it at his wife.

Baadshah Suleiman was passing by and heard his bird's claim.

He called out to the bird, 'Did you say that you would pick up my throne?'

'No, no, my lord, how dare I do that?'

'Then what did you say?' Suleiman demanded.

'My lord, I was arguing with my wife. Sometimes, I need to show my authority over her by exaggerating the extent of my otherwise negligible power, to keep her in control. Or else she will always defy me,' the bird said.

These Indian security forces and their prime minister are just like this bird. Weak imbeciles, but exaggerating their strength.

These authorities, these representatives of India and the United States, they warn us, tell us to stop or they will kill us.

That death will visit us, the mujahideen.

But Laila will come to meet the mujahideen, this is what we hear. So tell me, is that threat supposed to scare us? It is like telling a lover that he will be shut in a room with his beloved for twelve hours as punishment.

So then is it a punishment?

Give us death, we say, with smiles on our faces.

We love death, we covet it.

Maut badi meethi hoti hai.

Maut badi pyaari hoti hai.

What is the use of this life if it cannot be sacrificed?

There is no point in living this life. I choose death. Do you? Do you want to meet Laila? Do you want to savour her lips?

(A chorus of male voices erupted) Yes! We will meet Laila; we want to savour her lips!

(The raspy voice continued) *You will meet her? You won't run away? Will you disappoint Nawaz?*

(The male voices rang out again) *'Never, janab Nawaz, never!*

Jiye Pakistan! Jiye Pakistan!

The tape stopped and silence descended on Merlin hall.

Atharv was staring wide-eyed at the tape-recorder. 'Who is that toxic man? He is spewing so much venom against India. What a vile character!'

Sitting calmly with his arms crossed, Rohit asked, 'So, who is this scoundrel crying for death for India? I will pump his chest with bullets.'

'He is Nawaz Azhar, a top Pakistani terrorist-cum-recruiter,' Shekhar said. 'He is from Bahawalpur in Pakistan. He can make stones weep with his words. He spews hatred and venom at India in his speeches while mesmerizing his audience with distortions, lies and pure propaganda. He is LeT's topmost recruiter and radicalizer and is widely respected by other pro-jihad organizations in Pakistan. A silver-tongued merchant of death.

'He is an expert in brainwashing impressionable young minds, leading them to their doom with talk of religion, revenge and martyrdom. His team prepares the most committed suicide attackers, the fidayeen. This is part of a speech that Nawaz gave last month to eighty fresh recruits of his tanzeem, the Jaish-e-Mohammed. The recruits had completed their training in the three-month-long *Daura-e-Khaas* commando module.'

'Nawaz fought briefly in Afghanistan against the USSR army,' Shekhar continued, 'and subsequently, with the help of his mentors in the Pakistani Deep State, he has focused on attacking and hurting India with his cadres of fidayeen that he keeps churning out. He, along with LeT's commander-in-chief Abu-Lakhvi and its head of India operations Al-Cheema, is one of the top terrorists who are wanted in India for their roles in orchestrating terror attacks.

'Bahawalpur, which is in the Punjab province of Pakistan, is a major recruitment centre for both LeT and the ISI. The literacy rate there is about 35 per cent, which is a shame. Ninety per cent of the land in that district is held by ten-odd families. Most of those who have jobs are employed as daily wagers in fields or state-held factories. Private enterprise is next to nothing. Barely 45 per cent of the people have access to primary healthcare and schools,' Shekhar explained.

'Last month, on specific intel provided by the CTC, six LeT suicide attackers were located in downtown Srinagar. Their hideout, in an abandoned two-storey building, was put under siege, and the Lashkar terrorists were asked to surrender, but none of them did. A team from the Rashtriya Rifles division of the Indian Army picked out four of them with precision firing, putting them down like a shooter puts down clay pigeons. Two others died while they were trying to escape. The siege ended after thirty-six long hours.

'For their commanders sitting in Pakistan, and especially Al-Cheema, the fact that two of their boys had taken bullets in the back while escaping was a disgrace. His boys are trained to face Indian soldiers eye-to-eye. The option of escaping or surrendering is not even discussed in Al-Cheema's training facilities. The speech you heard was given after the Lashkar debacle in Srinagar. Nawaz is banishing the fear of death from his recruits' hearts. He distorts facts and spreads lies about religions to suit his requirements,' Shekhar said and then turned to Hussein. 'Hussein sahib, you may take over from me.'

Hussein stood up to address the trainees. 'Let's hear this messiah of terror again. Nawaz does not think twice before deciding to kill a hundred here to achieve the goals pursued by him and his ISI handlers.

'I am making you listen to his speeches so you can understand the kind of power these terror propagandists and recruiters have over their trainees, who are often poor, very young, with impressionable minds, jobless and school dropouts from Pakistan and misguided Indian youth. How these terrorists fill the hearts of young men with hatred and fury.'

Hussein pressed the play button on the tape recorder. Once again, Nawaz's voice filled the room:

In Pakistan, we have a different atmosphere. The old men are chasing dollars, a few are chasing sixteen-year-old girls as third or fourth wives; most are looking at acquiring land.

The middle-aged are busy looking after their wives and children, fulfilling the responsibilities of their nine-to-five office jobs or businesses.

The young cannot take their eyes off their TV sets and Bollywood heroines. When they are free, they cast their lusty eyes on our young daughters and sisters in the lanes and roads outside their houses.

No one is worrying about our community, the poor, the oppressed in Kashmir and Uttar Pradesh. Where our community is suffering. Where goons razed the Babri Masjid.

Except for some young men, whose blood boiled at the injustice meted out to the community.

Among such men was Rashid Tariq. Our Rashid, from Sialkot in Pakistan.

Rashid, who was blessed by the Almighty, and is in Paradise now.

Rashid was just like you. Young, with dreams in his eyes. He took forty-nine bullets from the Indian Army last summer. He was only twenty-two.

Rashid's mother is here in Sialkot. She is not waiting for her son. She says she will meet her son in Paradise. Because Rashid Tariq, her son, is a martyr. He died for jihad. Seventy-two beauties, blessed with eternal youth, fall over each other to be with him.

I heard the Indian prime minister say the other day that he will buy weapons from America and Russia. Let them buy weapons. But before that, they should buy wood. Because our lions, young men with broad shoulders, have left for Kashmir Valley. They will kill Indian soldiers. The families of these soldiers will need plenty of wood for their pyres. So I say again, let them buy wood before they buy weapons.

Hussein switched off the tape recorder. No one spoke as the recruits processed Nawaz's blood-curdling message.

Finally, Hussein broke the silence. 'So, you have a fair idea now of how these terror masterminds distort religion and facts to recruit impressionable young men. You can see how deftly they use questionable imagery and narratives to create accounts of the oppression of Indian Muslims, especially Kashmiris. Islam is a religion of love and peace, just like other great religions of the world, like Hinduism and Christianity. Criminals and deviants like Nawaz are not connected to any religion since no religion will have any place for a man like him.

'I made you listen to him to understand the kind of threat that such people and outfits like LeT and HuM pose to us. The LeT and its allies in India, like the Hindustani Majlis and its charismatic absconding leader, Malik Sarfaraz Rehman, reject the Indian state. They want to establish a theocratic state by overthrowing the constitution-based system of our democracy.

'LeT distorts religious, political and social issues for its own vested interests and those of its master, the ISI. They want to destroy India, plain and simple. During the medieval period, even the Arab, Turkish, Afghan and Mughal conquerors that came here had gradually developed an inclusive governance model, which considered non-Muslim subjects as protected, upon the payment of a religious tax. But in LeT's extremist world view, there is no space for those who don't subscribe to its ideology.

'So, let me tell you a few things about Islam. Let us know who is a Muslim and what it takes to be a Muslim. What is their ideology, what are their beliefs and social practices? Pay attention to what you will be taught here as this information might save your life one day. Knowledge about the salient features of the religion will help you as you will be operating as Muslims in your upcoming assignment. I hope you all know that?' Hussein asked.

'Yes,' Atharv said. The other trainees nodded in agreement.

28

KEY CONCEPTS

'Islam is the name of a religion whose followers are referred to as Muslims. Like Christianity and Judaism, Islam also emerged in the Middle East and is a world religion. Let us first talk about the basic practices and institutions of Islam. It is important for you to learn these as you should not be found lacking in your knowledge because knowledge, as they say, is power. And it can save lives too,' Hussein said.

'The word "Islam" literally means surrender and it forms the core of the religious idea – that the faithful, or the believer, accepts surrender to the will of God. Another cognate of the word "Islam" is the Arabic word for peace, "salam". It is a religion of love and peace. The mosque is the centre of a devout Muslim's religious life. In a few countries, most mosques are managed by the local communities while some are run by state authorities.

'The religion is based on five principles or pillars of religio-social organization. There are five steps, comprising both words and deeds, to take to the faith. These have to be followed with complete sincerity and belief.

'The first step is the profession of faith. The profession of faith must be recited at least once in one's lifetime, correctly, audibly, with an understanding and acceptance of its essence. The second pillar, salat, is the observance of prayers five times a day. There are five obligatory daily prayers, each preceded by ablutions, to be offered at particular times, and therefore each has a specific name. Special congregational prayers are offered on Friday. The Friday prayer service consists of a sermon. Friday sermons usually are on socio-political and moral questions.

'The third step is the paying of zakat. A portion of a Muslim's earnings must be donated annually towards fulfilling the needs of the less fortunate and the destitute, among other welfare measures.

'The fourth pillar, sawm, is fasting during the holy month of Ramadan, the ninth month of the Muslim calendar. It begins at daybreak and ends at sunset and, during the day, eating, drinking and smoking are forbidden. The month of Ramadan is a time for introspection, communal prayers in the mosque, reading the scripture and practising self-restraint.

'The fifth step is undertaking hajj, the pilgrimage to the holy city of Mecca, which must be undertaken at least once in a Muslim's lifetime, provided one can afford it and has enough provisions to leave for his family in his absence. This pilgrimage brings divine blessings.

'"As-salaam-alaikum" is a common Arabic greeting, meaning "peace be unto you", among Muslims whenever and wherever they meet and interact. The standard response is "wa-alaikum-salaam", which means "and unto you be peace". It is said that you will not enter paradise until you believe, and you will not believe until you love one another. It is said that the love will come if you greet each other with "salaam". So, at the end of his prayers, a faithful turns his head to the right and then to the left, greeting fellow believers with "as-salaam-alaikum wa rahmatullah", or "may the peace and mercy of the Almighty be with you".' Hussein paused, sat down and sipped water from a glass.

'What an awesome lesson, Hussein sir. Despite being concise and to the point, you taught us a whole lot. Thanks,' Atharv said.

'Welcome, Atharv, my pleasure. All the religions that we have in India are noble and great,' Hussein said. 'We will meet tomorrow.'

29

THE SACRIFICE

It was 6.30 a.m. and Sawant had returned from his daily three-kilometre run half an hour ago. As always, he had woken up at 4 a.m. for the jog. At that time, Wellesley Mansion and the surrounding area were an enclave of tranquility. The absence of sounds was almost unnerving. Every now and then, however, the calm would be pierced by the call of birds from the nearby forest.

After freshening up, Sawant had a cup of steaming 'cutting tea'. As he drank it, he thought about all that could go wrong with the training, and finally the mission, in the days ahead.

He was snapped out of his musings by the buzzing of the intercom. It was Shekhar, asking him to come to his room.

'Come in, Sawant sahib,' Shekhar welcomed him in the study of his suite. Shekhar was clad in dark blue track pants and a white T-shirt. He too had just returned from his jog.

'Dr Mohit Garg will be here at noon to conduct the circumcisions of the five recruits,' Shekhar said. 'As you know, this is the most delicate part. It is a brief surgical procedure, but it will have a permanent impact on their bodies, and no one likes this fact.' Shekhar sounded worried. 'But, for the mission, which will take the recruits deep into the lawless regions of Pakistan, getting circumcised is a must to blend in and not get caught. And shot.' He took a deep breath before continuing, 'So, Sawant sahib, what is your assessment? How many of these five will quit?'

'All five boys have strong personalities, but they are also very focused on the mission. They may not want to get circumcised, but their commitment to the cause for which they are here may drill some better sense into them, and I am counting on that,' Sawant said.

'But how many do you think will quit?' Shekhar asked again.

'Atharv will not quit. The other four will be sixty-forty in favour of quitting.'

'Okay, let's see what happens, Sawant sahib. If any of them quit, it will be a huge setback. We have invested so much time and energy into training them. Let's meet them in the lecture hall in two hours,' Shekhar said.

At 9 a.m., the five recruits, clad in their track pants and T-shirts, were seated in the lecture hall waiting for the day's session to begin.

Shekhar entered and cut straight to the chase. 'Good morning, boys. As you know, many in Pakistan undergo circumcision as per their customs. The practice has religious, hygiene and health-related aspects. For the mission, you may be required to go to Pakistan at some point and you will need to interact with men of the LeT and other organizations there. The idea is to blend in … and so you are required to undergo this procedure. I will let Hussein sahib guide you on this.'

'What are you saying, sir?' Sahil erupted, raising his voice.

'You were told at the outset that the mission asks for personal sacrifices from those who become a part of it,' Shekhar said in a flat tone.

Hussein stood up. 'Circumcision is an ancient social practice that involves the removal of the foreskin from the penis. The observance of circumcision is part of the refined practices, which include the shaving of pubic hair, plucking out the hair in one's armpits, cutting one's nails and shaving off one's moustache.'

Atharv asked, 'But why? What are the benefits of circumcision?'

'It is said that the practice is good for maintaining hygiene. Health-wise, it is still being debated whether it has any benefits, but some men of science claim it can protect one from infections and sexually transmitted diseases to an extent,' Hussein explained. 'A doctor will be here at noon to do the needful for you. Let me assure you, circumcision does not impact your manliness, manhood, health or ability to procreate.'

There was silence in the room for a few moments. Then, Rohit erupted angrily. 'How can we undergo circumcision? I am a devout Hindu. How can you even discuss it with us?'

Sahil agreed, 'Yes, we can't do this. We just can't do this. Sorry, Shekhar sir.'

Before Shekhar could say anything, however, Atharv jumped in. 'Rohit, Sahil, we are here to fight for India in Pakistan. Whatever it takes, we should do. The rest is up to you.'

'I am in this mission with all my heart and soul!' Rohit said with feeling. 'But this is a different issue; it is about our religion, which doesn't allow such a thing. On the contrary, it is the duty of all men to protect their manliness. If I lose my manliness, I am letting my body and spirit be defiled.'

'I agree with Rohit,' said Sahil. 'You may not have heard of this ancient Sanskrit shloka, "*Veer bhogya vasundhara*", the brave shall inherit the earth. A brave man is able to protect his dear ones, his country, and the entire earth, thanks to his manhood. *Purushartha gaya toh kya rahunga main*?!'

Atharv burst into laughter. 'Thanks, brother, for enlightening me on the duties of a brave man. It might surprise you, but I know a bit of Sanskrit as well, though I am from the south. From whatever little I know of Hinduism, a brave man thinks of others first before thinking about himself. Sacrifice for one's country is far more important than any concern for the self.

'*Api swarnamayi Lanka na mei Lakshmana rochtey,*
Janani janmabhoomischa swargadapi gariyasi.
Which means, O Lakshmana, though Lanka is a land of gold, it does not appeal to me … For mother and my motherland are greater than even heaven.
'And here is another shloka:
Namastey sada vatsaley matrubhumi tvaya Hindubhumi
sukham vardhitoham,
Mahamangale punyabhumi tvadarthe patatvesh kayo
namaste namaste.
It means, I salute you, motherland, the land of Hindus where I live happily, I salute my noble mother for whom I sacrifice my body.'

Atharv stopped. He had become emotional and his eyes were moist. He wiped the tears away and looked at Sahil intently, waiting for the latter's reaction.

Sahil remained quiet for a few seconds before finally saying, 'I too will do that, brother. Thank you, you have removed my doubts.'

He then walked up to Atharv and hugged him. Rohit too stood up and hugged Atharv and Sahil.

Rohit then said, 'Sawant sir, Shekhar sir, we are ready for the doctor. Let's get done with this procedure quickly.'

A few hours later, all five recruits had been circumcised, much to Shekhar's relief.

'Phew, we just ducked a bullet, Sawant sahib,' he said, smiling, as he lit up a cigarette.

30

'ONCE IS A COINCIDENCE, TWICE IS ENEMY ACTION'

The intercom was ringing. Atharv was drinking a cup of black coffee and reading the newspaper, his feet propped up on the small table kept in front of his chair. 'Who is it?' he asked no one in particular as he stood up and walked towards the blue intercom.

Nirav was still asleep in one of the two bedrooms of the small suite that the two were sharing in bungalow number 105. The team had returned with their trainers from Lansdowne the previous evening.

'Hello, Atharv here,' he said, when he picked up the receiver. 'He is up, getting ready. Why, what has happened?'

He listened intently before saying, 'Okay, sure. I will bring him along.'

As soon as Atharv hung up, he rushed into Nirav's room. 'Get up, Nirav! Man, it's 9 a.m., are you planning to sleep all day?' Atharv shook Nirav by the shoulder. 'Be ready in two minutes.

Shekhar sir has called us. It must be for some tutorial. As if we have not had enough already.'

When the two finally got to Shekhar's room, he took them to a spacious hall, where the others were already gathered.

'Boys, you are inching towards the starting line. Right now, like runners, you need to stretch one last time before the pistol is fired to mark the beginning of the race. That is why you are going through last-minute preparations. Do you have any questions or doubts you want to share?' Shekhar asked the recruits.

'No, it has been quite clear. We know the aim of our mission and you have prepared us for it,' Nirav replied.

The other four recruits nodded.

'Good,' Shekhar said. Then he called out, 'Milind, come in!'

A stranger stepped into the hall. He was six feet tall with an athletic build. A black cotton scarf covered his face. His eyes were hidden behind black Ray-Ban sunglasses. Clearly, Milind was too important to reveal his identity, even to CTC trainees.

'Milind is a seasoned intelligence operative,' Shekhar introduced the CTC officer. 'He has the experience to teach others, like you.'

'Is Milind his real name?' Atharv popped a query at the visitor.

'Milind is not his real name, only a functional name for today's session. He is here to teach you some basic counter-surveillance and intelligence techniques. When you are launched, or, in other words, made operational, your every move, every action will be crucial for the success of the mission. So, it will be necessary to know and ensure that you are safe and "clean" and are not being followed by LeT and ISI spies. How do we do this? I'll let Milind tell you,' Shekhar said and sat down.

'So, how do intelligence professionals ensure that they are not caught? And, at the same time, they also achieve their targets while working under the gaze of unfriendly or enemy entities?' Atharv's question was directed towards Milind this time.

'Hello, boys! Thanks for asking, Atharv. Let me begin with the basics of the world you are going to enter. In the world of intelligence operatives, there is no such thing as too much security nor is there space for complacence. You need to be alert and vigilant, always. But you should not make your vigilance obvious,' Milind began.

'In a secret mission like yours, you can't afford to be foolish and get caught. That will put the mission and your life in peril,' he warned the boys.

'So, tell us, what will you do if you have to perform an important task? Like if you have to meet somebody in Karachi to collect something important or pass on crucial information?' It was Rohit's turn to ask Milind.

'Okay, so if you are talking about Karachi, let's say you have to meet somebody discreetly somewhere around the Manghopir Lake off Naya Nazimabad football stadium. The rule, in the world of intelligence, is that if you are caught once, there won't be a second chance. So, you have to ensure you are not under the enemy's surveillance. For that, apart from taking a set of measures to ensure you are not being tailed by the enemy's counter-intelligence watchers, you must know how to determine whether you are being shadowed by the enemy or not.'

'How does one know whether he is being followed?'

'First of all, begin early. Prepare well in advance. Know the topography of the area where the meeting is going to take place.

To find out if you are being shadowed, you should prepare what is known as a surveillance detection route or SDR.'

'An SDR, what's that?'

'The SDR helps you determine if you are being followed, if you are being watched. We should always be in a position to keep the enemy under watch and not vice versa. To know if we are being followed, we have to take note of any person, or car or bike or any vehicle that appears more than once around us on a given day,' Milind explained. 'For, once is a coincidence, but twice is enemy action, as we say.'

'Sir, how do you create an SDR?' asked Atharv.

'I'm coming to that. To create an SDR, pick three or four places in different parts of the city. Find plausible reasons to go there, for example, to visit an office, a bank, the post office, a hospital or a restaurant. The last location should be selected with a view to exposing anyone shadowing you. A long narrow alley, or a bridge, work well for this. Anyone shadowing you will have to follow you into the alley or on to the bridge and will be easy to spot.

'While visiting the places you have selected, keep an eye out for any person or vehicle that you spot more than once. If you see a person or a vehicle twice, you have been found out. You need to disappear, escape from their trap, at once.'

'What next, sir?'

'So, the locations of an SDR should be such that they allow you to hoodwink the tail and escape. Run and lie low till a fresh plan, a more careful plan, is drawn up by you or your superior.'

'Tell us more, sir! These are interesting tips you are sharing with us,' Atharv said.

'Another crucial thing in a hostile setting is being able to communicate covertly with your contacts. Let us say that you have arranged to meet your contact on a particular date. When the set date is approaching, a vigilant operative will first check if it is safe to meet the contact. For this, he will use the SDR, of course. But he may need to communicate directly with the contact as well.

'Here, knowing how to use discreet communication techniques will come in handy. You and the contact can decide on a safety protocol, a secret communication mode, to send messages regarding matters of importance. Such a communication protocol can be used to send your contact a message regarding whether it is safe for the meeting to go ahead or not.'

'What are the signals that one can use, sir?'

'The signal could be anything simple. It would be ordinary in its mode but extraordinary in the message that it conveys. So, you could use chalk to scribble a sign at a pre-decided place, for example, a cross on a metal pole at a bus stop or restaurant or a departmental store. You could also drop a banana or orange peel outside a pre-decided location. The sign could be an affirmation or a negation.

'To ensure your safety, you must never utter a word about your mission to anyone. Not to your wife, not to your parents, not to your friends or girlfriends. You will be in possession of sensitive, privileged information and national secrets. Such knowledge could be dangerous to those for whom it is not meant. If you reveal information to those who are not supposed to know it, then you are putting them at risk. So, here at CTC we follow a policy of sharing information strictly on a need-to-know basis.

A natural corollary to this policy is that what you don't know can't hurt you.'

'Thanks, Milind sir. Please lay out the basic precautions that an intelligence operator must take?'

'Basically, as a rule, prepare for the worst. Always have a Plan B and a Plan C. In this line of work, if something can go wrong, it bloody will. So, stay prepared.

'Also, the mission is always bigger than all other things, such as a lack of ability, incompetence, failure or weak hearts. The mission does not need these distractions,' Milind said. 'Our job is to achieve the mission's objectives. If you think that an objective is impossible, know that we do not acknowledge that as an excuse.'

Milind looked around the room. 'Any more questions, doubts?'

'What do we do if we get caught?' Atharv asked.

'Don't lose heart. Be like a tiger. Even in the face of adversity, a tiger stays untamed, dangerous and a survivor,' said Milind. 'Never lose sight of the fact that even then the security of the mission is the only important thing, apart from your life, of course. So, do not admit anything, deny everything and divert the enemy.'

Shekhar looked at his watch and stood up. 'Okay, boys, we are done for now. Thanks Milind! That was a fascinating peek into the shadowy, dark world of intelligence,' he said, a smile on his face. 'Now let's go try the mutton biryani that awaits us in the dining hall. We meet again at 5 p.m., same place.'

When the boys returned to the hall at 5 p.m., they found Hussein waiting for them.

'Hello, boys, come in, sit down. This evening's lecture is about Arabic, the language of the Almighty and the religious language. So, just like Sanskrit is the religious language of Hinduism, classical Arabic is the religious language of Islam. Colloquial Arabic includes several spoken dialects, including those from Arabia and Iraq.

'The language has lots of letters that require the use of guttural sounds. Its alphabet has twenty-eight letters,' Hussein began explaining the rules of Arabic.

After their session with Hussein was over, Shekhar met the recruits one-on-one in his cabin. Atharv was the first to see him.

'Atharv, I hope you liked the Arabic lesson? You will have the opportunity to learn the basics of the language through a short course,' Shekhar said.

'Well, Hussein sir is trying his best, but it is not easy for us. We are struggling. The phonetics, the characters are all different,' Atharv said.

'No language is easy, and Arabic developed in west Asia. Give it time.'

'Yes, sir, I will work hard on mastering at least the basics.'

'Good. But that is not why I wanted to meet all of you. Atharv, the time of reckoning has come. The five of you have been trained in the skills that you will require to battle for your country behind enemy lines. It will soon be time for you to be launched.'

Atharv's eyes widened. Finally, the mission would begin.

'Here, take this folder,' Shekhar said, holding out a file. 'It has the details of your cover identity, the assumed identity with which you will enter Pakistan to face the wily ISI and the dangerous LeT. Never underestimate their capabilities to destroy us, they are vile and deadly!'

'From now on, you will be Mohammed Imran Syed, a lawyer. The file has the complete history and particulars of your assumed family. Your "father", Tahir, was a cloth trader with business ties in the Gulf. He was burnt alive by a mob comprising the followers of a right-wing organization. The tragedy occurred days after the demolition of the Babri Masjid in Ayodhya. The incident left you bitter and angry, and you have been looking for answers to questions such as who killed your father and why. Now, years on, you want to avenge the slaughter of your sixty-eight-year-old father by zealots.

'You believe that with the right-wing Rashtriya Pragati Paksha ruling at the Centre, Muslim youth like you must terrorize the government and the state's coercive machinery to create a situation wherein the Muslim community will rise to get what is due to it.'

Atharv nodded.

'Read the file, memorize it. Then burn it. I have a copy. Call me on the number given in the file.'

'Yes, sir. Wish us luck,' Atharv said.

He was nervous, but excited. The time for preparations was over; it was time to act. Atharv loved action. Mere words did not interest him.

'*Feliz viaje* – that means happy journey in Spanish,' Shekhar said.

'Thank you, sir.'

It was 5 January 2002.

'The training of the five recruits is complete. We have to activate these new operatives,' Shekhar texted his boss after Atharv had left.

'How long will it take for them to sneak into LeT's Pakistani apparatus?' his boss asked.

'The five are divided into two groups. One has three boys from south India, the other has two boys from western India. The challenge for them now lies in being in a position – say, within two years, by September 2003 – to be interviewed by LeT's senior commander and top recruiter Al-Wali, in Karachi or Islamabad.'

'Best of luck!'

'Thanks. I will keep you posted.'

31

FIRST CONTACT WITH
THE ENEMY

'All praise is due to the Almighty, we laud Him. We seek help from Him and ask for His protection. We trust Him alone and we request His protection against evils and the mischief of our souls and from the adverse results of our actions. Whomsoever He guides on the right path, none can misguide him, and whosoever He declares misled, none can guide him on to the right path,' intoned Hashim Qasmi.

It was Friday, some time in the afternoon of 23 August 2003, and Qasmi had just begun the first part of his sermon, having led an impressive congregation of the faithful in offering the Salatul-Jumu'ah, or the Friday prayers.

'The Friday prayers, preferably offered in a congregation, are obligatory, barring a few exceptions such as those who are sick, blind, disabled or are on a journey. The prayer fosters a sense of oneness and equality in the community,' Qasmi said.

The nineteenth-century Bengal Sultanate-built mosque saw at least a few dozen faithful who offered prayers five times a day. On Friday, however, the number swelled to over three hundred for the afternoon prayers. Apart from the regulars, who were mostly from the city, those found in attendance came from afar – from the neighbouring districts of Katihar and Araria. Some whispered there were faithful who came all the way from Nepal and Bangladesh. The charitable donations made to the mosque enabled the running of several social welfare projects, including a primary healthcare centre, a vocational training institute for girls and women and a madrasa.

The sixty-five-year-old Hashim Qasmi, his hair dyed orange, was the imam at the 155-year-old Jama Masjid Qudsia. The mosque, its walls and minarets decorated with intricate floral carvings, was located off Al-Husseini Road, the main street in Kishanganj, in northeast Bihar.

The mosque had spacious prayer halls. Their walls were painted green, while the ceilings were off-white and dotted with ceiling fans for the comfort of the believers. The floors were made of marble and buried under thick floral-patterned carpets.

Qasmi continued, 'Today, let us talk about the power, the beauty of a good deed, and about what the performance of a good deed does for us.

'All true believers must devote their lives to performing pious deeds that serve the cause of humanity and defeat the designs of evil. The Almighty rewards the pious with Paradise. He created Paradise for the virtuous believers. It is said that the bliss, the pleasures that Paradise provides to the righteous in his or her afterlife are so great that they cannot even be imagined. It is like being a child in the womb, who cannot imagine how big and magnificent the world outside is as he or she has not yet seen it.

'The divine spirit, Gibreel, once tried to measure the length and breadth of Paradise. He flew over an area that can be covered by 30,000 years of flying but still came up short. He repeated the same exercise innumerable times, but it was still not enough. Then a houri approached Gibreel and asked him, "Why are you wasting your time? You have so far not crossed even my courtyard!"

'Paradise does not know emptiness and sorrow. Old age and sickness do not exist there. There is absolute peace and contentment there,' Qasmi said.

'Excuse me, imam sahib, you are my elder and I respect you a lot, but I have two queries. Would you be kind enough to answer them?' said a youth who was standing towards the back of the congregation.

The youth was around five feet and eleven inches tall, dark in complexion, with an aquiline nose and unblinking eyes behind black metal-rimmed spectacles. He was clad casually in a navy-blue T-shirt and black trousers. A white skullcap only partially covered his head.

'*Bolo beta*. What do you want to ask today? You seem troubled. I have noticed this during your visits here over the past few weeks. You always ask questions and I try to answer them, but you lack patience. You interrupted me, though I was yet to be done with my sermon,' Qasmi said, a tinge of irritation in his voice.

The young man was seemingly unfazed. 'You said Paradise does not know old age or sickness and does not have space for the doers of wrong deeds, that there is absolute peace and contentment there.'

'Yes, I said that, so?' the imam asked impatiently.

'My abba, a sixty-eight-year-old retired schoolteacher, was killed by a mob in my village when a riot broke out.' The young man's eyes bored into Qasmi as he waited for an answer.

'May your father's soul find peace and succour, may he get accepted in paradise. May the wrongdoers repent for their sin. May the Almighty give solace to your wounded heart, may you get the strength and forbearance to get over your pain,' Qasmi said, haltingly.

'However, son, I notice a sea of anger welling up inside you, thanks to the misfortune that befell your family as you have just described. Be wary of anger since it clouds your judgment. Those who wronged your father will need to account for their barbarism on the Day of Judgment and will be sent to hell.'

'What do I do, where do I go and for what? How will I know if those killers get what they deserved? How will I know if my abba got justice, something that he did not get from the authorities?' the young man demanded, his voice heavy with anger.

'Have patience,' Qasmi said.

'Easy for you to say that, imam sahib. You have probably handed out the same empty nonsense to the victims of the Bhagalpur riots of 1989 in Bihar and the 1992-93 riots in Bombay. You must be an agent of the oppressors, not a spiritual leader of the hapless!'

'Watch your tongue! Throw him out, take him out of here,' Qasmi bellowed. His eyes were burning, his body shaking with anger.

A group of men grabbed the questioner by his collar and dragged him out of the prayer hall and then outside the grounds of the mosque. There, they decided to punish the young man for his temerity, raining blows on his head, face and chest.

'You come here to insult the saintly imam? How is he responsible for your father?' said one of the attackers.

'You rascal, do something about your intelligence before you dare to bombard the imam with your questions,' said another attacker.

Eventually satisfied that they had taught the impudent young man a lesson, they left to return to the prayer hall. Only one of them stayed back to rain more punches and kicks on the man, who was writhing on the ground by now.

'Bastard! *Hai kaun tu*? Tell me, or this bullet will make you meet your maker,' the attacker said, pointing a pistol at the man on the ground.

'All of you are agents of the oppressors. I spit on you instead,' the young man said.

Enraged, the attacker fired at the bespectacled man before fleeing from the scene.

An hour later, the wounded man found himself in a local hospital. Two bike-borne men had seen him slumped by the side of the road as they passed by the Qudsia mosque. They had managed to carry him to the nearby government-run Sushrut Emergency Hospital. The bullet had only grazed the flesh of his left leg, causing superficial injuries. He was allowed to leave two hours later.

Outside the hospital, as he was hailing an autorickshaw, a speeding Maruti Gypsy screeched to a halt in front of him. Two men jumped out and dragged him inside. He could feel the touch of cold metal on the back of his neck.

'Don't look back, sit tight.' It was the attacker who had stayed behind to beat him up some more.

The bespectacled man complied with the order but said nothing.

'Why did you insult the imam?' A punch landed on his nose, bloodying his face.

'It was a genuine question, mister. My father was killed during a riot three years ago in Thrissur, Kerala. The goons of the local right-wing outfit, Samaj Sanstha, went on a rampage, burning down homes and stabbing several innocents who were caught alone on the streets,' the man said.

'They also killed my father. All of this because a rumour spread that the men who had killed a young woman were of my community. Maybe they were from my community as the allegations went, maybe they were not, I do not know. But those who died, like my father, were innocent, and this is certain,' he said.

'So what will you do now?' the abductor asked.

'I do not know, but if I get a chance, I will take revenge as I am still hurting from the pain,' the man said. 'The police case was closed because there were no witnesses apparently, and the perpetrators could not be identified.'

'Why did you come to Kishanganj from your Thrissur?'

'My family exports cotton garments to Bangladesh and the Middle East. I came here to supervise our office here, along with two of my brothers.'

'How many brothers do you have?'

'There are six of us.'

'Where are your two brothers?'

'They are at the office. They are as desperate and angry as I am.'

'I see,' said the abductor.

'Who are you? Why are you beating me? Why have you detained me?' It was the bespectacled man's turn to be the interrogator, once the flurry of questions directed at him had stopped.

'What do you think?'

'I know you are a policeman or someone from the intelligence service. A special branch tasked to monitor mosques?'

'I am also a businessman like you, with international customers, not a policeman. Had I been one, you would have been in deeper shit,' the attacker replied. 'I also feel as strongly about my community as you do and run an NGO that is involved in health and educational projects.

'My men have kept a watch on you this past week, after you came to their notice for troubling imam sahib at the mosque during the Friday prayers. They told me that you could be a genuine victim in need of some community help. My name is Roshan Ahmed Baig,' he said, revealing his name finally.

'Your father was killed, as you described at the mosque. You want to avenge that. Once you do that, will you be a contented soul?'

'I want to make my father's killers pay. I want to teach a lesson to all those who oppress the weak and the innocent. I, and my two brothers who are here, won't stop after fixing the Thrissur goons,' the man said.

'Fine, let's see if you and your two brothers have it in you to walk the talk! If you can avenge your father's death and the wrongs against our community. I will put you in touch with a few men who are fighting for the dignity of the community and helping victims of majoritarian tyranny seek justice.'

'I am also a trained lawyer, sir. What do I have to do?'

'Ah, you are a lawyer? A lawyer who did not get justice from the courts of the kaffir?' The abductor burst into laughter. 'Meet me in two days, at 7 p.m., inside the Qudsia mosque compound near the back gate.'

'Okay,' the bespectacled man said, offering his hand to the man who had just offered to help him avenge his father's killing.

'Do not worry. You will be among friends and well-wishers; just be there on time.'

The man nodded.

'I can't believe that I have not asked for your name yet. Though we have checked out where your office is and where you sleep. So, what is your name, brother?'

'I am Imran, Mohammed Imran Syed.' Extending his hand, the bespectacled man, who was actually Atharv, smiled.

Atharv, Anant and Nirav had been waiting for this 'break' since January 2002, when they finished their training with the CTC. Finally, Atharv had the chance to make contact with the LeT's talent spotters.

32

BREAKTHROUGH IN KISHANGANJ

'*Masla kya hai, Imran miyan*? Roshan told me about you, about the insults you hurled at the old and respected Imam Qasmi. Is it that India's condition has worsened suddenly or is it that you were expecting much from tyrant rulers?'

The man talking to Imran was tall, fair complexioned and looked to be around forty years old. His long hair was tied at the back in a ponytail and he was sporting a black bandana around his forehead. He was clad in a deep blue Pathani suit. He had a deep, clear voice and spoke in an unhurried manner. Imran could see what appeared to be the barrel of an AK-47 peeking out from under a pillow next to the man. He was introduced to Imran as Zaheer, or 'Doctor', by Roshan.

Roshan had met Atharv as promised, at the Qudsia mosque, two days ago. Of his own accord, Atharv had brought his two 'brothers' along for the meeting. Roshan was fine with Atharv's decision to bring his younger brothers, Tahir – who was actually Nirav – and Sadiq – which was Anant's alias. Both were introduced as engineers and greeted him with warm handshakes. If Imran was inducted by Zaheer, his brothers may join with him; the more the merrier, Roshan thought to himself and smiled.

Roshan had asked Atharv and his brothers to meet him the next day at noon at the taxi stand on Chakulia Road, from where they would take a taxi to go see an important man. The next day, as planned, Roshan and the three brothers took a cab to the Jogbani India–Nepal Integrated Check Post (ICP), which was 114 kilometres away, in the neighbouring district of Araria.

From Jogbani, the four men took another cab to cross into Nepal and travel to the city of Birat Nagar, which lay around seven kilometres from the ICP. Half an hour later, the cab reached its destination in Birat Nagar, Badi Husseini Masjid. The mosque was around a century old, with a large prayer hall.

It was in the mosque that the brothers met Zaheer. The five men were now seated in a room with white walls and no windows on the second floor of the Badi Masjid.

'The mob killed my father during a communal incident back in Kerala. Goons regularly bully our people staying in Thrissur by taking out street processions through our settlements every second or third day. The processions last for hours and no one can object to them,' Atharv, aka Imran, said.

'What do you want to do? What can you do?' the Doctor asked him.

'What can I do? I don't know. But I am ready to do anything,' Atharv said. 'I want to hit people who have been tormenting our community for the past decade. I want to hold each of them by his collar and tell him to show respect to our people. I want revenge,' Atharv roared.

'Your thoughts and intentions are noble. But there is a big difference between talking and doing. To do, you will have to confront the truth, which can be uncomfortable at times, and you may have to do unpleasant things and see unpleasant things and sacrifice the self. You will have to bury your current existence and build a new one that can choose martyrdom. We want revenge as well. But who will make the sacrifices required for it? Can you and your brothers do that, Imran?' the Doctor asked Atharv, his eyes boring into the latter's.

The Doctor's face was reddening, he was screaming now. 'Will you take revenge? Or have you come here to waste my time? A decade ago, that L.K. Advani led two lakh kar sewaks who brought down the Babri Masjid in Ayodhya. The spot is located some 700 kilometres from Kishanganj, a Muslim-dominated district,' the Doctor said.

'We kept protecting ourselves, while they destroyed the mosque to build the Ram temple. Our cowardice was so great that even our existence appears to be a favour bestowed by our enemies,' the Doctor's voice was heavy with emotion for a moment.

'And what happened after the mosque was destroyed? The azaan that had resonated from the Babri Masjid since the sixteenth century was silenced, but we kept quiet. Not one Muslim country boycotted India,' the Doctor shouted.

'Babri Masjid offered its martyrdom to awaken the drowsy, selfish youth of this community. Till when will you sleep? Take up the sword for jihad and the community,' he continued.

'The Jews forcibly captured the Aqsa-e-Masjid while political speeches and deals were being made. In Bosnia, the Christians of Serbia decimated the local faithful. Closer to home, hundreds of Kashmiris have lost their lives in their struggle for independence against the Indian armed forces. Men from our community have been killed and subjected to unspeakable torture in police stations,' the Doctor claimed, looking agitated.

'They have spilled so much blood, the Jhelum has turned red. All of this calls for you and I to avenge the murder of your father and the atrocities committed during the Bhagalpur and Bombay riots.' The Doctor fell silent and looked at Atharv, as if assessing him.

'*Izzat se jiya toh ji lengey ya jam-e-shahadat pee lengey*. If I am denied a life of respect, I will have the drink of martyrdom,' Atharv said. 'Perhaps, like the Babri Masjid, my father was not killed. He offered his martyrdom to wake me up to avenge the atrocities committed against the community,' Atharv said.

'I and my brothers, Tahir and Sadiq, today take an oath in the name of our father, and in the name of the soil that accepted the blood oozing from his body, that henceforth our lives will be the property of the community. We will do whatever we need to do to restore the respect of the ummat,' he declared. 'So tell us who you are. And what do we brothers do next?'

'We are committed to the community, for it we are ready to sacrifice ourselves,' the Doctor replied. 'As to who we are, we belong to the pure and believe in the majesty of the religion. We believe that there is no truth other than the apparent in matters of faith.'

The Doctor turned to the door and called out, 'Mukhtar!'

Mukhtar, a tall man with a bulky frame and hawk-like gaze, appeared at the door carrying an AK-47.

'Get the maps and the forms,' the Doctor instructed him.

Mukhtar returned with what was asked of him in no time. Taking the papers from him, the Doctor turned to the three boys.

'What was the stream of your engineering courses, Tahir and Sadiq? And Imran, what was your specialization?' he probed.

Nirav and Anant told him that they had specialized in metallurgical and chemical engineering, respectively. Atharv said that he had specialized in criminal law.

'Criminal laws. Framed by the British, then the Indians post Independence?' the Doctor scoffed. 'The only laws we believe in are those that are approved by our community.'

The Doctor then spread out the maps of Kishanganj and Thrissur on a table and told Atharv and his brothers to point out the locations of their offices and homes. The three of them also had to fill up forms in which they listed the names of their close relatives as well as their residential and business addresses. They had to write down their educational particulars as well.

As the Doctor read through the forms and inspected the maps, Atharv silently thanked the CTC officers, especially Shekhar, for having anticipated what would happen and providing them with strong and detailed cover profiles.

Half an hour later, the Doctor gathered up the forms and the maps and left the room. Mukhtar stood motionless in the room, his eyes on the three brothers.

Atharv could hear the Doctor's muffled voice. He sounded like he was on the phone having a conversation with somebody important.

He was back in twenty minutes. 'Come with me, you three,' he ordered the boys, who trooped out of the room, following him.

They were led out of the mosque to the lane behind it, where a Land Rover was parked. Mukhtar slid into the driver's seat while the Doctor sat next to him. The brothers sat in the back seat. Roshan sat behind the brothers, holding Mukhtar's gun as if he were used to it.

'We are going to Kathmandu, so relax, have some dried fruit and water,' the Doctor told the boys.

Nine hours later, the six reached Thamel in Kathmandu. It was 11 p.m., but the locality was waking up to life. Classy discotheques and bars, restaurants and street hawkers dotted Thamel, the shopping-cum-nightlife district of the capital of Nepal. Its streets and warren-like alleys throbbed with foreign tourists, shoppers, knick-knack sellers and street musicians looking for appreciation and American dollars. Deals were being made with hawkers, funky music blared out of bars, a few junkies could be seen keeping a sharp look out for their next hit of dope.

The Land Rover stopped outside a hotel, the Kathmandu Guest House. Of all the hotels in Thamel, with their fancy architectural and decorative features, this one was the most inconspicuous. There was a lone guard at the entrance. The hotel seemed deserted. The guard knew who the Doctor had come to meet and gestured to the men to follow him.

He took the six visitors to the third floor, to a room at the end of the corridor, and knocked twice on the door.

'Come in,' said a voice from within.

The guard opened the door and ushered the six men inside. He then gave a stiff salute to two men seated inside the room.

They were dressed in identical dark grey suits and pointed, black leather shoes.

'Zaheer! So, these are the three Indians you had mentioned,' said one of the men, who was dark and mustachioed.

'Yes, janaab, I have brought them here to meet you. Please do the needful to your satisfaction,' the Doctor said.

'Show me their forms,' the man said. He looked at Atharv and his brothers and asked, 'What are your names? And what do you want to do?'

Atharv spoke first. 'I am Imran, a lawyer. These are my brothers, Sadiq and Tahir. We are businessmen, based in Bihar's Kishanganj, with family roots in Thrissur, Kerala.'

He continued, 'My father became a victim of a communal outbreak, and we have joined for jihad, under the guidance of Doctor bhai, to avenge our father's murder and the atrocities against our people.'

The two men in suits listened to Imran intently. They then read carefully through the forms that the three boys had filled up.

Finally, the mustachioed man spoke. 'Fine, we believe you. You will get a chance to pay your debt as a faithful and redeem your community. But be warned – if you turn out to be agents or spies, your real families will get only pieces of you, while your souls will turn into ghosts looking for your bodies.'

The three boys merely nodded.

'We will provide you with Pakistani passports, under false names, in an hour. Get ready to join Zaheer's training camps in Karachi and elsewhere. In a few weeks, you three will turn into able soldiers of the ummat, ready for LeT's jihad in India,' he told them.

An hour later, Atharv, Anant and Nirav received their Pakistani passports, under assumed names. Atharv was now Zakir Ahmed, Anant was Akram Ahmed, while Nirav was Abdul Qadir Ahmed.

'Your flight is for the day after tomorrow. You will fly Pakistan International Airlines, which will take you to Karachi via Dubai,' the mustachioed man told the boys as he handed over the passports. 'I am Salem and I am from the embassy. My colleague here is also from the embassy,' he finally introduced himself.

'Congratulations on getting your Pakistani passports. Your stature has increased, and you are no longer meek now,' the Doctor said.

'Thank you,' said Atharv. 'Doctor bhai, why do they call you "Doctor" and what do you do here in Kathmandu?'

'Doctor is Doctor as he has a degree in unani medicine,' Salem responded on behalf of the Doctor.

'A few years ago, the Doctor killed two Indian Army doctors in Srinagar.' Salem's colleague, who had not identified himself so far, spoke for the first time. A smile danced on his lips. The Doctor just looked at him and smirked.

The Doctor later told Atharv that Salem and his friend were from the 'agency', as the ISI was sometimes called by its operatives. Atharv smiled. The game had begun.

33

ROAD TO THAMEL

'They say Kashmiris are unfortunate, miserable and lonely. Some in the ummat say that Kashmir's men and women, young and old, are suffering. Their blood is being shed; they are targeted by the Indian Army.

'But I say they are very fortunate. They are not miserable, unfortunate and lonely because they have the qaum with them.

'It was not Assam, Manipur or Bengal, not Punjab, Hyderabad, Uttar Pradesh or Maharashtra, but Kashmir that was chosen as the stage of Ghazwa-e-Hind. Is that a misfortune or fortune?

'You die every day, of diabetes, in a road accident, by falling in a pothole, or because of addiction to alcohol and drugs. But the people of Kashmir have the chance to attain martyrdom. When you attain martyrdom for your religion, the doors to Paradise open for you.

'The alcoholics will queue up in the line for alcoholics; the vile will queue up in the line for the vile, but the Kashmiris will enter Paradise in a royal manner, in the line meant for martyrs, wearing the crown of martyrdom,' said the man dressed in black trousers and a white and blue checked shirt.

With his lean, five-foot-ten-inch frame, Malik Rehman, who had brown eyes and a sharp voice, seemed taller than he was to his listeners at Indore's Tipu Sultan mosque.

Malik – alias Bade Bhai, alias Instructor, alias Trainer – was the fugitive chief of the banned Hindustani Majlis (HM), whose stated aim was to overthrow the democratic government in India and in its place set up a theocracy under the leadership of Afghanistan's terrorist group, the Taliban. He often held such discussions as he found them useful for spotting new talent for his group, which was committed to jihad in India.

'There will be a Ghazwa-e-Hind. There is a long list of devouts who have fought to realize the promise of this Holy War against India, from Muhammad ibn Qasim and Muhammad Ghori to Ahmed Khan Abdali and Aurangzeb. And let us not forget Syed Ahmad and his band of Wahabi fighters who fought against the Sikhs and attained martyrdom in Balakot in 1831.

'When will we pay our debt to the likes of these venerated men? I ask you: Why are you alive? What is the purpose of your life? Fattening your bank balance? Watching cricket, Sachin Tendulkar and Azharuddin? Listening to music, Hindi and English?

'The youth of today have no conscience or sense of belonging. They are busy playing video games, watching movies and gyrating to Bollywood's obscene songs. I see them standing at street corners, whistling like wolves at young girls, casting amorous eyes on them.

'Your people are suffering in Kashmir, but you spend your time watching the bat and ball instead.

'In times gone by, if there were two brothers in the house, they would take on the whole world to protect their sisters and the family. So, I ask again, why are you alive? *Is zindagi se toh maut hi behtar*. Have your hands fallen off? Do your shoulders droop? Are you a man still?

'Then wake up, avenge the atrocities committed against the community! Pick up the Kalashnikov, join jihad, and pay your debts to your brothers and sisters in Kashmir, to the ummat.

'You will live a better life, the shaheed don't die, and the doors of paradise welcome the pious.'

No one spoke after Malik Rehman delivered his speech. Silence enveloped the room; only the chirping of a sparrow sitting on a wooden beam overhead could be heard. Malik sipped water from a steel glass and wiped the beads of sweat off his forehead with a white handkerchief.

'You talk of jihad, of martyrdom. Do you have any plan on how to conduct jihad? Have you done any such thing?' a sharp voice rang out.

All eyes turned to the questioner, a young man of sturdy build who seemed to be about twenty-seven years old. He was clad in a white shirt and black jeans. Like the others in the room, he was sitting on the green mattress that covered the floor.

'Be warned, young man! Think before you open your cursed mouth! Or is it that you have strayed into this mosque thinking that it is your usual street corner where you spend your life, making a fool of yourself?' Rehman spat out, bristling with anger.

'*Malik sir naraaz ho gaye lagta hai*,' the young man said, a smirk on his face.

He felt Malik's icy glare on him but continued nonetheless. 'You must be thinking who am I and why am I talking the way I am talking, right? I will tell you my story. I am from Mumbai. I belong to a conservative Muslim family. Five years ago, when I was in my final year of college, I used to attend lectures at Dr Syed Mujtaba's clinic in Goregaon West.

'We would discuss all the biggest challenges before the community, from the intifada in the Jewish-controlled West Bank and Gaza in Israel, to the massacres in Bosnia, to the destruction of Babri Masjid and the riots in Meerut, Bombay and Bhagalpur. Talk of killing and dying, killing and dying – *jihad aur shahadat*. That is all we heard for two years on every Friday at Dr Syed Mujtaba's clinic.

'Eventually, I got bored and tired and left. That majlis was of people from Hindustani Majlis as well,' the young man said.

'What is your name? Where are you from? And what are the names of your father and grandfather? Who are you staying here with and where?' Malik asked.

'Usman Sheikh, twenty-eight. I am a computer engineer. My father is the late Mohammed Khwaja Sheikh; my grandfather, the late Khwaja Syed Sheikh. I was born in Mumbai, but my family is from Faizabad in Uttar Pradesh,' the young man, CTC operative Rohit, said.

'It is good, Usman, that you shared your doubts. Doubts are the traits of a ticking mind,' Malik said. 'Now let me clarify these doubts.'

'For one, in spite of what you think of the people who work for Hindustani Majlis, they are not doing badly. They are talking about jihad and shahadat. At least they are not sleeping like most and are doing something. Second, it is futile to waste your time complaining about others in the community when you already know what needs to be done.

'I have no time for whiners. Just go ahead and do it. There are many youth who have risen above their personal desires and goals to submit themselves to the needs of the community and the will of the time.

'If you wish to do something for the community, then do something about it. *Jigar le ke saamne aao.* Look around, you will find a way. You may meet other devout believers like you,' Malik said.

Rohit looked at Malik and raised his right hand above his right shoulder in what was a snap reaction to what the latter had just said. 'Can't agree more,' Rohit said.

Malik pointed at a man standing at the edge of the room. 'Kabir,' he called out. 'Kabir assists us in our community work. He will assist you in finding your path, be with him.'

34

THE EAGLES ARE FLYING

'Meerut, Bhagalpur, Babri Masjid, the Bombay riots. The oppressors are on a high; they have gotten away after hurting our people. They have bloodied this land,' Malik said to Usman – Rohit.

Rohit was sitting with Malik. He had brought along his 'younger brother' Zafar – Sahil – a practitioner of unani medicine.

After Malik's sermon, Kabir had told Rohit to meet Malik two days later at the mosque, at 8 p.m.

Malik, Rohit and Sahil were sitting on the floor. Kabir stood a few feet behind Malik. A table lamp stood in a corner, and the smell of burning incense suffused the room.

'Revenge and rejuvenation. Get trained. Stand and fight. No longer can the community keep taking blows. Take the fight to your enemies, make them pay. Attack. Prepare for a long journey, both of you. You will learn what you need to elsewhere, as it is too dangerous here,' Malik told the two young men.

'HM is growing, but it is still small. It needs capabilities in bomb-making and urban warfare to take on the rulers. We also need arms and ammunition.

'After your training, you and Zafar can become able operatives of HM and teach your skills to your inexperienced brothers here if you choose to join us in our work. Otherwise, you will primarily work as the operatives of a Pakistani organization committed to the cause of the community. Kabir will make the arrangements,' Malik said.

After the meeting, Kabir left the mosque and took an autorickshaw to the Sankatmochan Hanuman temple at Awantipur. He entered a PCO booth across the street from the temple and dialled a number. He let the phone ring twice at the other end and then cut the call. He dialled again and repeated the process. As he lit up a cigarette, the phone rang.

'Good evening. All is well. Classes are going well. Two came for admission,' Kabir said.

'Okay,' the Doctor, who was sitting in the basement office of Gorakhnath Transport Company on Shri Krishna Street, the bustling commercial district of Birat Nagar, said softly into the phone.

'Please arrange for the teachers. I will speak to them tomorrow,' Kabir said and hung up the phone.

The Doctor then dialled a number.

'*Haan, janab*. Two examinees are to go to school. I will bring them to you, please prepare the admit cards,' he said.

'Fine, bring them tomorrow, at 8 p.m.,' said Salem, the undercover ISI agent stationed at the Pakistani embassy in Kathmandu.

Twelve hours after Kabir had made the call to the Doctor, he was back at the same PCO outside the temple, waiting for a call that would disconnect after four rings. He didn't have to wait long.

He answered the phone and listened briefly. 'Okay, thanks,' he said curtly and hung up. He then left the booth and went to another one 300 metres away to make a call.

'Get ready, Usman, you and your brother Zafar leave tonight for Jogbani by train, via Patna,' Kabir said.

'Okay,' said Rohit.

Rohit and Sahil smiled at each other. Like the three other members of Operation Trojan Horse, Rohit and Sahil had been working hard to be recruited by the LeT since January 2002, when they had finished their training with the CTC.

Thousands of kilometres away, Shekhar's encrypted phone was abuzz with calls as he received updates about the latest developments in the mission.

Finally, he made a call to his boss. 'The eagles are flying,' Shekhar said softly into the receiver.

It was 28 August 2003.

35

KARACHI APPOINTMENT
WITH LeT BOSSES

'Our friend in Nepal said you feel strongly about the wrongs done against us by the idol worshippers, the Christians and the Jews. But have you taken any action so far against the enemies?' the forty-something man, who had introduced himself as 'Al-Wali' a few minutes ago, asked Atharv. It was around 3 p.m. on 2 September 2003.

Atharv stood before Al-Wali, who sat on a wooden chair, next to which was a small table with a lamp. The two men were in Al-Wali's 'office' in Defence Officers Enclave in Karachi. This was one of the several LeT hideouts in Pakistan. Only a handful of senior operatives knew of its location. Al-Wali was one of them.

Al-Wali had been with Abu-Muzammil's team for carrying out operations against India for at least a decade. Abu-Muzammil trusted Al-Wali and often sent him to LeT stations located near India in Nepal, Bangladesh, Sri Lanka and even the United Arab

Emirates to coordinate and instruct Indian operatives directly for operations under way. Both Abu-Muzammil and Al-Wali were key members of Lashkar's anti-India 'Operations' team. Al-Wali was Abu-Muzammil's deputy. They had earlier worked together for LeT's terror formation in Jammu and Kashmir in the mid-1990s, where they had 'distinguished' themselves for their outfit by orchestrating numerous terror attacks that killed security personnel as well as civilians. Abu-Muzammil had led the Kashmir Lashkar formation and Al-Wali was his deputy there too.

Abu-Muzammil, over six feet tall and a 'combat veteran', who flaunted his two bullet wounds on the right shoulder, had a certain swagger and a penchant for talking big. Al-Wali, five-feet-eight-inches tall and with a sturdy frame, was a networker, kept notes of important details related to operations and personnel, and possessed an almost photographic memory. Abu-Muzammil reported to LeT operations chief Abu-Lakhvi, alias Chacha.

'I offer namaz five times a day; I have been to Saudi Arabia on holy pilgrimage,' Atharv offered, haltingly. 'I may not have yet learned the texts by heart, but I know the core teachings, customs and traditions.'

'You are a good Muslim!' Al-Wali said. 'But are you also skilled in carrying a gun or even a knife, fabricating an IED and shooting at an enemy? If not, I have no use for bookish, intellectual types here. It seems the Doctor erred in sending you here ... I will have to talk to him about this.' Al-Wali was stern.

'*Ji, janaab*, I may not have done these things before but I have two other traits instead. I think I have it in me to attain proficiency in all of these functions if you train me well and, secondly, I have the burning desire to turn out as a loyal soldier of the community who will make all of you proud one day,' Atharv offered. He knew he will have to impress Al-Wali with claims of having a strong commitment to LeT's agenda against India to get inducted as he did not have any combat background to show. He was getting the sense that Al-Wali was a driven jihadist and was probing his commitment.

'Do you know what is jihad?' Al-Wali continued to question Atharv.

'Our elders teach us how to submit ourselves for the good of humanity, how to become God-fearing, honourable persons and good Muslims. Jihad is the struggle to make oneself better and the fight to get justice and what is right. This is what I have understood,' Atharv said.

'Let me tell you something. Even a moment spent in jihad will get you more divine blessings than a million hours spent in namaz at the holy place. You will understand this one day,' Al-Wali said.

'Jaan doge kya yalgaar pe? The path on which we travel makes us put shrouds over our heads,' Al-Wali said.

'I want to offer my life, which is the goal. The spectacle of death is what that put me on this journey, sir. My life is not important. What is important is restoring the community's respect and enhancing its prestige,' Atharv declared.

'You are a passionate young man. We need men like you,' Al-Wali said approvingly while looking at Atharv unblinkingly.

'Here, these are the forms that the five of you, the friends of the Doctor, have to fill up. You need to provide information on your immediate family, your friends and your educational qualifications.'

Al-Wali further added that the forms, once filled, would be handed over to Naseer Javed, who was in charge of training recruits and was a Kashmir veteran. Naseer had been deployed in Sopore in Jammu and Kashmir for six years and had had several encounters with Indian security forces.

'Sure, we will fill them up,' Atharv said.

Apart from Al-Wali and Atharv, in the room were Nirav, Anant, Rohit and Sahil. Rohit and Sahil stood a little apart from Atharv, Anant and Nirav.

Al-Wali had been told that the five potential Lashkar recruits had been sent by the Doctor, LeT's commander for operations in Nepal and Bangladesh. The Doctor was known to have an eye for spotting and recruiting men from among the most driven, angry youth of India. Recruits sent by the Doctor had so far distinguished themselves in the 'battlefields' across Kashmir, Ahmedabad, Gujarat and Uttar Pradesh. When praised for his work, the Doctor would simply say he was totally reliant on men who worked for him across India. Baig and Malik were two of his star 'spotters'.

Al-Wali knew that the Doctor had provided some of the most capable sleeper agents – covert operatives – that were currently active in India. The ISI had asked the LeT to restrict the use of Pakistani nationals and resources for their India operations as these could be traced back to Pakistan.

'You can use Indian youth who are angry due to the injustices meted out to the community,' Brigadier Hashim Shah, the chief of ISI's elite 'S' Directorate, which handled operations in India, had told the Lashkar top brass.

Post the deadly 9/11 attacks on the US by the Al Qaeda, as a top US decision-maker had warned Pakistani president Pervez

Musharraf, Pakistan was either with the US in its so-called 'war on terror' or against it, and its actions, rather than its rhetoric, would now determine whose side it was on. America was moving towards a zero-tolerance policy for cross-border terrorism. It was therefore doubtful whether it would continue to shut its eyes to Pakistan's India-centric terror infrastructure that had spawned groups such as LeT and HuM. That was why ISI was keen to ensure that Pakistan was not linked to any terrorist operations in India.

An hour ago, Atharv and the four other CTC operatives had been escorted from Karachi's Jinnah International Airport to Al-Wali's safehouse in Defence Officers Enclave. The five recruits had arrived in Karachi from Kathmandu via Dubai, as planned. They had begun their journey from Kathmandu's Tribhuvan International Airport roughly twelve hours ago, their forged Pakistani passports tucked into their pockets.

The Doctor had also arranged for fake Nepalese visas for each of them, just in case immigration authorities asked for their details in Nepal, India or Pakistan. The Doctor had told the five to submit their Indian passports to Kabir. It was an order that had to be complied with.

Kabir had asked Atharv to wear a yellow hat on reaching Karachi airport. He had also told Atharv that his contact man in Karachi would approach Atharv with the query, 'Did you come by PIA or Cathay Pacific?' Once the recruits' identities were confirmed, the contact would take them to the safehouse in Defence Officers Enclave, a middle-class suburb on Karachi's outskirts.

As the five men had cleared immigration, a tall, wiry man with sunken eyes had come rushing up to Atharv, who was wearing a yellow hat as instructed.

'PIA or Cathay Pacific?' he had asked.

'PIA,' Atharv had responded.

The tall man had nodded and escorted them out of the terminal building, even as Atharv had noticed a few uniformed guards giving crisp, silent salutes to the contact.

The man had ushered the five recruits into a black Land Rover SUV with dark tinted windows, which was waiting outside the building.

As the SUV drove away, the contact had finally introduced himself. 'I am Hamza, Abu Hamza. I am with the Lashkar-e-Taiba and I welcome you here on behalf of the Doctor. I hope your stay here in Pakistan will be wonderful and productive, with the grace of the Almighty.'

He had then asked the five to hand over their Pakistani passports to him.

'Firdaus', Al-Wali's safehouse, was a sprawling bungalow with an old-world charm. The walls were ivory white, topped with a sloping, red-tiled roof. The bungalow was at the centre of a large compound landscaped with flower beds and shrubberies.

After a sumptuous lunch, the five were taken to Al-Wali's room. They now took the forms from him and completed them, after which they helped him and his assistants locate the addresses they had listed on their forms – for instance, their homes and their schools and colleges – on a map of India. Al-Wali also asked them to point out potential sites for targeted attacks or bombings. The whole process was recorded on a camera.

'Tomorrow at 2 p.m. you will catch the Karachi Express train to Lahore. It will be a twenty-hour journey,' Al-Wali informed the recruits. 'Here, take these letters of recommendation.' The letters stated that they were eligible to undergo terrorist training in Pakistan-occupied Kashmir. 'You may now go back to your rooms. Rest. Tomorrow will be a long day,' Al-Wali said, finally ending the interview.

The following day, as per the plan, Hamza escorted the five recruits first to Lahore, then to Islamabad. From there, the six took a bus to Muzaffarabad, the capital of Pakistan-occupied Kashmir. An SUV was waiting for them at the bus station. They were driven to Bayt al-Mujahideen or the House of Holy Warriors, the headquarters of the LeT for operations in Jammu and Kashmir and the seat of its military commander, Abu-Lakhvi alias Chacha.

36

DAWN AT
BAYT AL-MUJAHIDEEN

The black Pajero carrying the six men – Hamza and the five freshly inducted Lashkar recruits: Atharv, Anant, Nirav, Rohit and Sahil – had turned off the highway on to a narrow dirt track that led to Bayt al-Mujahideen. It was around 9 p.m., and the SUV's headlights illuminated the thick vegetation on both sides of the ten-foot-wide track. The forest was unusually noisy, with crickets chirping in the bushes abutting the dirt path. However, inside the SUV, there was an unnerving silence.

Sahil, who was fatigued, finally broke the silence to ask, 'Is there anyone in this part of the jungle? Are there leopards here? Any watchtowers?'

There was no response from Hamza. It was as if he had not heard Sahil.

Sahil asked again, 'Any leopards? Bears? Jinns? Is anyone around here? Or is it just us, janaab?'

Hamza, who was driving the SUV, turned his head slightly towards Sahil. 'You cannot see them,' he said in a flat tone, adding, 'but that does not mean no one is watching you.'

Suddenly, the SUV came to a screeching halt in front of two massive black metal gates that seemed to have materialized out of the dark. Four tall, well-built and armed men sprang out from the shadows and surrounded the SUV. Hamza killed the engine as he and the other occupants heard the unlocking of the AK-47 automatics held by the four guards.

'Roll down your windows, janaab,' barked a fifth man, who had suddenly appeared next to the driver's side of the SUV. Hamza rolled down the window and identified himself.

The fifth man said, 'Oh, as-salaam-alaikum, Hamza bhaijaan. Please proceed.' He issued his commands: 'Farooq, open the gates. Ask Ismail to escort the SUV to the office.'

The gates opened, revealing a wide road that stretched ahead as far as Sahil could see. As they drove in, an SUV parked on the side of the road pulled out and drove ahead, leading them into the compound. There were street lights at every 100 metres on both sides of the road. Dark silhouettes of what appeared to be large tents and single-storey structures could be seen along the road, rising above thick shrubberies and trees.

The SUV that was escorting the six men finally halted in front of a single-storey building. Ismail jumped out of the SUV and was soon joined by the six arrivals. They entered the building and were led to a large room by Ismail.

'Come, Hamza bhai, I was waiting for you; Mubarak bhai, our head of training, is here too,' a middle-aged man in a white salwar kameez said loudly, flashing a smile at the six visitors as they entered the room.

'Sorry, we are late, Yusuf bhai, it's almost 10 p.m.,' Hamza said.

'No problem. Ask the brothers to show me the documents; after that, Mubarak will guide them,' Yusuf said.

The recruits handed over the documents that the LeT had given them on their arrival in Pakistan. Yusuf put on his steel-rimmed glasses and inspected them carefully.

Yusuf Ibrahim was the administrative head at Bayt al-Mujahideen. He kept a record of everything that moved or did not move in the complex: the recruits brought there for training, those who left the camp and the details of their onward destinations, the trainers, weapons and ammunition that entered the camp, and all the logistical resources, from the number of tents and beds to the rations for everyone in the complex.

The administrative building was named after an LeT suicide bomber, Wali Mohammed, who had fallen to the bullets of the Quick Response Team (QRT) commandos from the 36th battalion of the Indian Army's Rashtriya Rifles. The encounter had occurred inside a forest in the Rajouri sector of Jammu and Kashmir. The QRT commandos were pressed into action by the Indian Army to track and kill terrorists based on specific intelligence received either from army intelligence or the state police. The QRT was referred to simply as 'Hunters' in army and police circles.

'All is fine, brothers. Mubarak sahib?' Yusuf said, shoving the recruits' documents into one of the drawers of the large table that he was seated behind.

'Introduce yourselves, brothers from Hindustan!' said Mubarak.

The visitors identified themselves as per the cover identities assigned to them by the CTC.

'Enjoy your stay here,' Mubarak said. 'You will leave for the LeT's main training facility, Abdulla bin Masood Maaskar, to undergo the Daura-e-Aam, your basic training. We will see if you are up to it physically and mentally,' Mubarak said before leaving the recruits to settle in and have a late dinner.

At 3 p.m. the next day, the five recruits set out with a guide, Hussein. Hamza had left the training camp that morning, after breakfast. Hussein had provided the recruits with hiking shoes, light sweaters and small rucksacks, each of which had a blanket, a packet of dried fruit, a torch and a hunter's dagger with a long, curved blade.

Hussein led them up a long, winding road at the back of Bayt al-Mujahideen's 150-acre campus that disappeared into the adjoining forest. After walking for around four kilometres, the six travellers arrived at the base of a mountain that must have been at least 800 metres high. It rose above the forest like a tower.

At the top of this mountain lay Abdulla bin Masood Maaskar, the Lashkar's premier terrorist-training facility. From the base of the mountain, it was a six-hour trek to the camp. At the Maaskar, new recruits were put through the three-week Daura-e-Aam and then the Daura-e-Khaas, a specialized 120-day commando training course that imparted training in weapons, explosives, bomb-making and unarmed combat.

'It will be a tough climb, so do not rush ahead like fools. Climb with sure feet and be careful where your feet land,' Hussein said matter-of-factly.

The five new recruits were soon out of breath but Hussein kept going. 'It is getting late. You can't let Abdulla Mountain's shadows fall on you as, after the sun sets, this becomes a playground of the wild bears, foxes and leopards,' Hussein yelled. 'Come on! Why are you walking like old aunts? Move your asses!'

Three hours later, the six men reached the Maaskar at the top of Abdulla Mountain. Sahil and the others were greeted by the sight of a large plateau, across which the camp was spread. Three men with AK-47s stood outside a nearby tent and asked to see the permits that Yusuf had given to Hussein for the five recruits.

The three guards frisked the five recruits after ordering them to throw any tobacco, cigarettes or narcotics they were carrying into a large red drum that had 'Dustbin' written on it in blue.

The six were thereafter taken to a tent where they were served a hot meal. Finally, at 1 a.m., after a frugal dinner comprising chicken curry, chapatis and dried dates, the five recruits crashed on to their beds, exhausted after what had been a long, tiring day.

'Wake up, *nikamme log*!' somebody shouted at the top of his voice, issuing commands like an army instructor. 'Get up, get going, start running!'

Sahil felt a rough hand on his shoulder. He opened his eyes, looked at his wristwatch and said, 'At 3 a.m.?' He was irritated. 'Bhai sahib, we slept just an hour ago.'

'Yes, 3 a.m., Badshah Suleiman. At 3 a.m. a poor man begins his search for food,' the instructor said, pointing his torch at Sahil, aka Zafar.

'Most importantly, at 3 a.m. the day begins for us, the soldiers of the qaum, and for the lakhs of Kashmiris who need our help,' the man, who stood erect in his black jacket, declared.

'At 3 a.m. the Indian Army troops begin their search-and-cordon operations in the Kashmir Valley and Muslim-dominated villages, keeping an eye out for our soldiers, our mujahideens. I don't know how to tell you what can happen there during such operations,' the man spat out. 'You can't be sleeping like a rock at 3 a.m. if our brothers and sisters are awake in Kashmir and suffering.'

He then introduced himself. 'I am Mustafa; call me Ustaad ji. Now start running. Your day has just begun as a soldier of the community.'

37

RPGs AND DUCKING
LIVE BULLETS

At the physical training ground of Abdulla bin Masood Maaskar, Sahil and the four others from the CTC squad were inducted into a group of 100-strong trainees.

'I am your Ustaad. I have no other name as far as you are concerned. Another Ustaad will join you later in the day for weapons training,' the instructor said by way of introduction shortly after Sahil and the rest of the trainees had dragged themselves to the ground for what promised to be a long day.

'I will teach you everything, from the best teachings of our elders, which will make you a worthy man, to karate and how to handle AK-47s. If you finish this course, the Daura-e-Aam, it means you have the strength and the heart to fight for justice and the community,' the Ustaad said.

'This is a basic course spread over twenty-one days and after this are tougher courses that turn coal into Koh-i-Noor. So let's not waste any more time and begin with a prayer. We are going to offer the night prayer, which is offered after the nightly prayer and before the first prayer of the day. It is an optional prayer, beyond the five daily obligatory prayers. Even though it is optional, its observance will give you divine inner strength and understanding,' the Ustaad said.

The recruits knelt in prayer. Thereafter, they offered the dawn prayer, which is performed just before dawn. It is the first of the five daily prayers.

'The time of the dawn prayer is a time of light and spiritual blessings,' the Ustaad explained. 'There is a saying that whoever performs the dawn prayer and the prayer before sunset will get blessed.'

Thereafter, it was time for prayers and requests. 'To stay on the path of justice and holy struggle, to undo the wrongs done to the community. Repeat after me,' the Ustaad instructed.

As the prayers ended, the Ustaad bellowed, 'Now join me for a run, boys!' and led the trainees around the perimeter of the plateau. Twelve rounds later, during which a few recruits slumped to the ground with exhaustion and had to be carried off the track to recuperate in a tent, the boys returned to the PT ground.

'Now that your bodies have warmed up, it's time to do some physical exercises,' the Ustaad said. His aide, Kamal Afridi, stepped up and faced the trainees, who stood lined up in ten rows, each of which had ten recruits.

'We begin with spot-jogging for three minutes, then we will do crunches and sit-ups,' Afridi shouted at the top of his voice.

After the arduous physical training session, the recruits were given a simple but nourishing breakfast of milk, eggs and fruit. This was followed by a class on religious education and current affairs, which was taken by a cleric.

After that was a class on the handling of weapons. The Ustaad was joined by another instructor, who told the recruits to address him as 'Chhote Ustaad ji'. Both the ustaads were almost identical in height (six feet), form (muscled) and the precise way in which they carried themselves.

'Are they from the ISI or the Pakistani army?' Sahil whispered to Atharv.

'They must be from the Pakistani army. They look like professionals. But what's the difference?' Atharv responded.

There was a range of weapons laid out on tables draped with white sheets: AK-47s, AK-56s, AK-74s, Mauser pistols, .303 rifles, self-loading rifles and M16 automatic rifles, among several other kinds.

The two expert trainers and their ten-odd aides familiarized the trainees with each of the weapons, explaining to them how they worked, how to assemble and disassemble them and their comparative weaknesses and strengths. The trainees were then taken to a small, open-air, twenty-metre firing range where they got to fire ten rounds from any weapon of their choice.

Atharv and his fellow CTC operatives performed well at the range. They silently thanked the CTC for the training they had received at the underground firing range in Delhi, where they had practised enough to feel comfortable with the weapons on offer at the camp.

The class on weapons handling was followed by the Zuhr prayer, the second of the five obligatory prayers.

At 1.30 p.m., it was time for lunch. The tired trainees tucked into their mutton biryani while keeping an eye out for what was being offered for dessert – Karachi halwa. After lunch, the trainees were told to retire to their tents, each of which accommodated ten men. The tents were pitched in an area close to the PT ground. Both sections were connected via a gravel path.

After their midday siesta, the recruits returned to the PT ground to offer the afternoon prayer, Asr, the third of the five prayers. Following the prayer, they learned about some of the finer points of the traditions and jihad from another cleric.

'Jihad is an Arabic word, and it means to strive or work hard for justice,' the cleric said. He did not introduce himself and came straight to the point.

'A man once asked a maulana which kind of jihad was better. He was told, a word of truth spoken in front of an oppressive ruler. Jihad is more than just fighting your oppressors. A man wanted to join jihad. He was told, do jihad by serving your parents.'

After the cleric finished his session, the two trainers taught the trainees defensive techniques in unarmed combat, especially those based on karate, judo and street-style boxing.

It was then time for the fourth of the five obligatory prayers, which is offered after the sun sets. This was followed by a session on current affairs at 6.30 p.m. It was led by the maulana who had spoken to them about jihad, along with the senior trainer.

'The senior Ustaad seems to be a Jack-of-all-trades,' Atharv chuckled on seeing him again.

The maulana spoke about the loss of Muslim lives and the destruction of their property during Partition, about how provinces such as Kashmir, Junagadh and Hyderabad had been 'denied' to

Pakistan due to the Hindu Congress's wily ways, about the razing of the Babri Masjid and, finally, about India's continued occupation of Kashmir. The session was thrown open to questions.

'How can young men from our community participate in the jihad to liberate Kashmir?' Atharv asked the maulana.

But it was the trainer who answered. 'Offer your lives for the cause; dedicate yourself to LeT, which is fighting for Kashmir.'

The current affairs session went on for a long time as many of the trainees asked the maulana questions. Later, the boys continued discussing the issues raised in the class during the dinner that followed.

Half an hour after dinner, the trainees offered the last prayer, the Isha, which is offered before midnight.

The trainers then took the trainees out for a quick march into the jungle, which was a trek of five kilometres, before allowing them to call it a day.

'It was a mind-bogglingly long day, brother. Let's hope tomorrow is better,' Sahil told Atharv before falling into an exhausted sleep.

But the next twenty days of the Daura-e-Aam training course went exactly like the first one. Sahil, Atharv, Nirav, Anant and Rohit did well and received special appreciation for standing out among the others in shooting, debating, unarmed combat, and assembling and disassembling weapons.

Three days after the trainees passed the Daura-e-Aam course, they were sent to another training facility in Muzaffarabad, known as the Aqsa Maaskar. The Aqsa trainers put the recruits through the advanced course, the Daura-e-Khaas, also known as the commando course, which was a four-month course. For the first two months, the daily training schedule was similar to that of the Daura-e-Aam course. The last two months, however, were dedicated to teaching the recruits a few additional special skills. These pertained to guerrilla warfare techniques against the Indian Army's assets in Jammu and Kashmir, surviving in the treacherous terrain of J&K during harsh weather conditions and using a wider range of weapons and explosives.

The instructors were a new set of six trainers. They taught the recruits how to lay an ambush for the army and security forces' convoys on highways, and how to cross the Line of Control undetected. Classes on river-crossing, reconnaissance, taking cover during exchange of fire and rock-climbing were also conducted.

Mock drills were held so the recruits could hone their skills. These often involved the firing of live bullets on those attempting to cross obstacles. Night time was preferred for such drills. As part of their survival training, Sahil and Anant were sent into the nearby jungle for three days. They had to remain unseen and attack a mock Indian Army convoy on the third day. An 'Indian Army' team, also comprising two fellow trainees, was hot on their trail with rubber bullets to 'kill' them.

Sahil and Anant managed to pull off the ambush and also 'killed' one of the members of the Indian Army team.

The second half of the Daura-e-Khaas course was conducted at an ISI facility at Marwah in Pakistani Punjab. It included an added emphasis on weapons handling and reconnaissance. The trainees were exposed to military-grade weapons such as rocket-propelled grenades (RPGs); 60 mm, 90 mm and 120 mm mortar; hand grenades; land mines; anti-tank mines and claymore mines; Russian sniper rifles such as the Draganov; and anti-aircraft guns.

The trainers gave extensive live training in firing AK-47s, anti-aircraft guns, heavy and light machine guns and RPGs.

Of the seventy trainees who had come to Aqsa Maaskar from Abdulla Maaskar, forty-five passed the tough Daura-e-Khaas course, including the CTC squad members. Atharv sustained a bullet injury in his right shoulder during one of the 'live' mock drills.

The covert CTC operatives were then told they needed to report back to the LeT's top-tier leadership in Islamabad. They had to meet Umar-Qama, Abu-Muzammil and Abu-Lakhvi.

'The time of reckoning has come. They want to evaluate us one last time before deploying us as their resources in India,' Atharv told Anant.

38

SAFFRON MILK AND
A GAME OF CHESS

Tucked behind dense thickets and adjoining the ruins of a seventeenth-century serai, or travellers' lodge, the Firdaus Masjid in Islamabad was small in size but not in fame. It was built in allegiance to the all-mighty Mughal Empire in Delhi. Tourists flocked to the mosque and the serai three days a week: Mondays, Thursdays and Saturdays. On Tuesdays, Wednesdays and Fridays, the complex attracted the faithful, who would come to offer prayers, especially on special occasions.

The mosque, which was smaller than most other mosques in Islamabad, rose thirty feet from the ground and was conspicuous by its perfectly circular dome. It was built on an elevated stone base that was square in shape and measured fifty feet on all sides. It was 8 p.m. on a Tuesday night and pitch dark. Thanks to the three electric poles erected inside, however, the mosque complex was bathed in a pale, milky-white light.

Standing in front of the seventeenth-century mosque, Atharv could see through the tall arched front entrance and the three other successive arched entrances that got progressively smaller.

Five hours ago, when Atharv and his comrades from the CTC were on their way to Islamabad from Muzaffarabad, Hamza had blurted out their destination. 'We are going to Firdaus Masjid to offer prayers for two Lashkar martyrs,' he had said.

The funeral prayer was to be offered in absentia as the men had died far from their homeland and their bodies were not present. Hamza had also told them that Abu-Lakhvi, LeT's operational commander, would be at the mosque that evening to oversee the performance of the funeral rites for the two suicide attackers. They had died during an exchange of fire with the Special Operations Cell (SOC) in Sopore, Jammu and Kashmir.

The two Pakistani youth, Aftab and Qayyum, both aged twenty-two, had been sent as reinforcements to Kashmir after six other Lashkar operatives had died in firefights with the Indian Army in Jammu and Kashmir. The Indian Army and SOC had gotten wind of the two boys' arrival and had sent a QRT to storm their hideout. Aftab and Qayyum had been killed in the ensuing fight, while two others, a Pakistani and a local operative, had escaped under the cover of darkness.

Inside the mosque, the smell of incense hung heavily in the air. Around two dozen men sat on the mattresses covering the cold stone floor of the mosque. Most were in white Pathani suits. Some spoke in hushed whispers; a few preferred silence.

But all had their eyes on Abu-Lakhvi, who was clad in a black Pathani suit.

'We have gathered here to offer our prayers. We have gathered here to remember our fallen soldiers, our brethren, Aftab and Qayyum,' Abu-Lakhvi addressed the gathering.

'Aftab and Qayyum did not lead very comfortable lives. They were both sons of parents who had to work hard to get two meals a day for their large families. And yet they heard the call of humanity. They cried when their sisters were being insulted in Bosnia, Kashmir, the West Bank and Chechnya,' Abu-Lakhvi said in a low, choked voice.

'The young men left their ordinary lives and devoted themselves to the cause of the community. They gave themselves up for our organization's mission. Because while their young Muslim sisters lived under the shadow of bayonets in Kashmir, Aftab and Qayyum could not spend their lives chasing US dollars, British pounds, girls in jeans, cars, Bollywood movies and land.

'Instead, they came to us and learned what it means to be truly valiant. They learned to run, climb and swim. They learned how to fire guns, fight with swords and sticks. By the time they left for Kashmir to fight against India's army, which occupies that piece of heaven, Aftab and Qayyum had been turned into lions.

'Yesterday, those lions were put to sleep forever by the army. They were not defeated in the battlefield. They were outsmarted and taken by surprise. Aftab and Qayyum gave up their lives, turning into shaheeds, but not before taking out four Indian soldiers in their final, deadly encounter with the enemy.

'Mehjabeen Khaala, this is the name of Qayyum's mother. I fell at her feet. I said to her, "Ammi, congratulations, you gave birth to a lion, not a man of blood and flesh. Forgive me, Ammi, as I could not bring your son back alive from Kashmir."

'But Qayyum's mother scolded me. "You congratulate me and abuse me in the same breath? My son was Pakistan's lion, and I am proud that he laid down his life fighting the battle for the weak and innocent Kashmiris. If I had another son, I would have prepared him myself for his departure to Kashmir, to renew the battle his brother could not complete," she said to me.

'The two brave-hearts are not here. They have been accepted in Paradise because of their sacrifice, while their mortal bodies are dragged from one mortuary to another in India. Let us pray for their souls.' Abu-Lakhvi paused and took a sip of water before leading the gathering in prayers.

Even as Abu-Lakhvi was offering the prayer, many in the congregation were weeping openly. Tears were trickling down Abu-Lakhvi's cheeks as well.

The veteran of many a terror campaign, Abu-Lakhvi, who had had his first taste of guerrilla warfare when he led a band of mujahideens in Afghanistan in the 1980s against the 'infidel, communist' USSR army, was still deeply affected by the death of the two youths and did not make any attempt to hide his mourning.

An hour later, in the basement of bungalow number D-13 in Khuda Baksh Enclave, Abu-Lakhvi met Atharv aka Imran and the other four CTC operatives. They had all just returned from Firdaus Masjid and Abu-Lakhvi's grief was yet to lose its sharp edge. No one spoke for a few minutes. Finally, Abu-Lakhvi offered the five boys glasses of saffron milk.

'How was your experience at the Daura-e-Aam and Daura-e-Khaas training, Imran?' he asked.

'We learned a few useful things: the need to stay fit, the magic of AK-47 automatics and what we must do for the ummat,' Atharv said, choosing to keep his response short.

At the Maaskar, the recruits had often talked about Abu-Lakhvi's sixth sense. This sixth sense, coupled with his sharp analytical skills, enabled him to spot trouble and phony jihadis. Atharv did not want to test him.

'Whatever you were so far, whatever you did or did not do, forget it all. None of that matters to me, to Lashkar, and to you. What you do now is what will make you. Dedicate your life to jihad. If your life or its sacrifice can wipe the tears of even one Kashmiri Muslim girl, then your life will have met its supreme end.'

'*Haan, janaab,*' Atharv said.

'We must restore the honour of the community by taking up arms and sacrificing the self. We have to liberate Kashmir, Hyderabad, Uttar Pradesh, Assam, Bengal and Junagadh. India will be given just two options: the sword or conversion. To set India right, Lashkar needs brave-hearts who are willing to die for the cause,' Abu-Lakhvi declared, looking Atharv straight in the eye.

'Tell us, what are we supposed to do? We are ready,' Atharv said, returning Abu-Lakhvi's gaze without blinking. 'Give us targets, show us the way. We will smash the community of stone worshippers.'

Abu-Lakhvi remained silent for a few moments. '*Merey veer*, have you ever played chess?' he eventually asked.

'Yes, of course,' Atharv replied.

'Then you will know that the game is won if you kill your rival's king. The king can be killed by any of the five types of chess pieces – the pawn, rook, knight, bishop and queen. The piece that kills gets all the attention, but actually it plays the least significant role in the rout of the enemy, in the win,' Abu-Lakhvi said.

'It is the other chess pieces that lay the trap, the plan to kill the king, and thus actually win the war. These pieces are the planners, the organizers, the masterminds. As a planner of the plot, you should have dexterity, manoeuvrability and intelligence of the highest order. You should have the ability to think through the entire operation, including how the enemy will respond and all that can go wrong.

'You must be what is required as per the situation. So, at times you could be a pawn, which strikes diagonally to kill, or a bishop, which moves only diagonally, or a rook, which moves along straight lines horizontally and vertically, or a knight, which moves two steps along a straight line and can then move left or right. Or, you could be a queen, which can move along straight as well as diagonal lines.

'Adapt, adjust, get the target. *Operation ko kamyaab karo kisi bhi keemat pe.* Understood?' Abu-Lakhvi asked.

'I think so,' said Atharv, unsure of what was being asked of him.

'See, Imran. You and your fellow recruits here have been trained well in the operational as well as the theoretical aspects of an operation; you can plan an assassination or an ambush of an army convoy, guide such an operation from afar or be the strike team that executes it on the ground.

'As you will realize, being the attacker is the easiest part. Being the planner, the one who masterminds one operation after another while being anonymous and undetected, is the important and difficult part. We need such men in India,' Abu-Lakhvi elaborated.

'The five of you will be able to stay in India comfortably as you are Indians. Assume Hindu identities to stay off the radar. Then, lay the trap and procure the necessary resources, such as weapons, to execute the operation, say from Kashmir or Nepal. When your preparations are done, we will send you the strike team, the fidayeen to execute the operation. The fidayeen will take instructions from you, and you may be required to be at ground zero to ensure all goes well.

'After the mission, you will vanish and lie low. Till you rise again to oversee another mission. You will be our sleeper cells that are at work 24x7, but whose presence is felt only when they destroy the enemy out of the blue,' Abu-Lakhvi said.

'Understood, janaab,' Atharv said.

'Umar-Qama will prepare you for this role. ISI also needs dedicated jihadis like you in India. So you will work for the LeT as well as the ISI.'

'Initially, you will settle in Mumbai and Delhi. You will have to procure government documents in the name of your assumed Hindu identities.

'We will communicate via telephone calls made from PCOs; no mobile phones. We may at times call you at designated PCO booths using satellite phones. If there is a need, we will provide you with a satellite phone for specific missions.

'We have men in Dubai. You will be given their numbers. You will call those numbers and our boys will put you in touch with us – Umar-Qama bhai or Al-Wali bhai, who are your commanders. I am there, of course, in cases of emergency.

'And finally, you will visit the ISI office in Lahore before leaving for India via Nepal.'

39

RETURN TO INDIA

'You will choose Hindu names to create a cover in India,' Umar-Qama told Atharv. On seeing Atharv's brow furrow, he added, 'It's nothing, brother. You see, Hindus are a very big, diverse community. It's like an ocean, you will just vanish. With a Hindu identity you will easily melt into the crowd.'

Abu-Lakhvi had left for Muzaffarabad after meeting Atharv and the other four CTC operatives. The five were thereafter taken to another location, a bungalow on the outskirts of Khuda Baksh Enclave, which was also an LeT safehouse.

'I will be Atharv Iyer,' said Atharv. 'The others have chosen their assumed names too,' he added. 'Sadiq will be Anant Ramakrishnan, Tahir will be Nirav Reddy, while Usman will be Rohit Kumar and Zafar, Sahil Sharma.'

'Okay. Make sure you all learn every aspect of your cover identities. Update Al-Wali about the cover profiles you create for yourselves. You will get them cleared by him,' Umar-Qama instructed them.

'But remember, you will not disobey us, come what may. You will execute what gets decided upon and cleared from here. Al-Wali will instruct you on how to communicate.' With that, Umar-Qama left.

Al-Wali created email IDs for the five and gave them his own email ID. 'The email service provider we have chosen to use is AOL. Their servers are in America and are inaccessible to the Indian counter-intelligence spies,' Al-Wali said with a smile.

Al-Wali made Atharv and the other four learn an alpha-numeric code to be used for all written or verbal communication.

The code had eleven horizontal columns; each column had four vertical rows. The alpha-numeric system was complex, but a simple way to conceal information, Al-Wali told them.

THE ALPHA-NUMERIC MATRIX:

```
-----9-----8----3-----7----2----0----6----4-----5----1
1----A----B----C----D----E----F----G----H----I----J
2----K----L----M----N----O----P----Q----R----S----T
3----U----V----W----X----Y----Z
```

'So, Bangalore will get encoded as "819172619182224221",' Al-Wali said. 'Here, B is equal to 81 as per the matrix. A is 91, N is 72, G is 61, A is 91, L is 82, O is 22, R is 42 and E is 21,' he explained.

'The numerical code is like this:

```
5----2----1----4----8
0----3----6----7----9
```

For example, 9980309883 is coded as 8895258992.'

Al-Wali told the boys that they would have to undergo a fifteen-day training period at the safehouse. 'You will be put through a series of crash courses, which will equip you with additional knowledge and skills,' he informed them.

Over the next fortnight, a battery of ustaads and clerics came to the safehouse to instruct the trainees.

The first course was Daura-e-Sufa and dealt with Salafi teachings.

'The word Salafism comes from an Arabic term which means pious predecessors,' said Abdul Sayeed, the cleric who had come to the safehouse to teach the recruits. 'Salafism is considered to be the purest form of the religion.'

After the Daura-e-Sufa, the five trainees were put through the five-day Bait-ul-Rizwan and Daura-e-Ribat courses. The first entailed training in unarmed combat. A fighting technique drawn from karate, judo, boxing and wrestling was taught to the five.

Daura-e-Ribat was an instruction on how to make safe contact, or 'raabta' in Arabic, and included conducting surveillance, tailing, taking photographs covertly and befriending 'targets' who could be sources of information.

'Making contact, whether with your commanders, fellow brothers or even your family members, must be done safely and as per the guidelines given to you,' said Iqbal, the LeT ustaad who was training them. 'Even in emergencies, the safety protocols must not be breached,' he warned them.

'For instance, you may never make a call to Pakistan from India. You also never contact a satellite phone number from India. You always contact your brothers in Dubai or Muscat or Riyadh, and they will put you in touch with whoever you need to contact,' Iqbal said.

The five men also underwent the Daura-e-Tadribul Muslimeen, which was a workshop on leadership and character building.

After the fifteen-day training ended, Al-Wali sent the five to an ISI training facility in Marwah, in Pakistani Punjab. There, a team of five non-commissioned officers trained them for another seventy-five days.

Once the ISI training was over, Al-Wali took Atharv to the Nepalese embassy in Islamabad to apply for visas for the five recruits. Atharv was introduced as the owner of Shafiz Carpets, a Karachi-based exporter of carpets. The four others were described on the visa forms as employees of Atharv's firm.

Armed with the required paperwork, the five took a PIA flight to Kathmandu. On reaching Kathmandu, Atharv went to a PCO booth and called a number that Al-Wali had given him. The number belonged to 'Krishna', who would help them enter India from Nepal.

'Be ready with Rs 1.5 lakh in Nepalese currency. Reach the bus terminal tomorrow at 1 p.m.,' Krishna instructed Atharv.

At the bus terminal the next day, Krishna, accompanied by two men, met the five CTC operatives. He collected the Rs 1.5 lakh in Nepalese rupiah from Atharv.

Krishna then asked, 'Are you guys Pakistanis?'

'No, we are Indians. I am Atharv.'

'Write what I say on a piece of paper. Let me see if you are who you claim to be. I don't deal with bloody Pakistanis,' Krishna said.

He is an LeT mule but has no clue about it, Atharv chuckled to himself.

Krishna asked Atharv to write his name in Hindi. Krishna passed Atharv in the little nationality test on seeing the paper.

The recruits were then driven away on motorcycles by Krishna and his companions. After a ride of almost six hours, much of which involved travelling on narrow dirt paths off the main roads, they arrived at the small town of Piparpati Parchrouwa close to the India–Nepal border. Ten kilometres from the town was a forested area within which lay an unmanned, unmarked stretch of the border. With Krishna's help, Atharv and the four other CTC operatives were able to cross the border undetected. They then took a bus to Varanasi, from where they took another bus to Patna in Bihar.

The next day, as directed by Al-Wali, Atharv, Anant and Nirav took a train to Mumbai while Rohit and Sahil took a train to Delhi.

Atharv and his four associates were back in India over a year after they had left for Pakistan from Kathmandu. 'Posing' as Hindus, they were back to act as part of the LeT's sleeper cells in India. Atharv tried to suppress his laughter.

It was now 5 September 2004.

40

THE FIRST ASSIGNMENT

'*Tabiyat kaisi hai? Pahunch gaye khairiyat se?*' asked a man with a raspy voice.

'Everything is fine, sir,' said Atharv to his handler from the LeT.

Atharv was standing inside Vasant Communications, a cramped PCO booth. It was right next to the Shri Krishna Kirana provision store located behind a Jain temple on Reay Road. This was a suburban area that had been developed commercially in the early twentieth century due to its proximity to the port and jetties at Ballard Estate and Ballard Pier in south Mumbai.

Prakash Pawar, forty-six, who ran the provision store and the telephone booth, was a busy man and loved sharing his opinions on everything under the sun. From 9 a.m. to 11 p.m., his shop was crowded with customers from the nearby Shri Ganesha Rahiwasi Sangh, a sprawling slum that housed families belonging to the lower and lower-middle income groups. It also had a few cooperative housing societies, such as the six-storey 'Anwarat', where Atharv was staying with Anant and Nirav in a two-bedroom flat on the third floor.

Pawar's PCO did decent business, according to him. He had a theory on who used his PCO through the day. 'The times are bad in our society, Atharv ji. People, especially boys and girls and young men and women, have low morals nowadays. The boys and girls whispering into the phone in my PCO are mostly those whose relationships are secret and undesirable, or else they would be using their own mobile sets,' Pawar had once told Atharv. Lighting a Dunhill cigarette, standing just outside the shop, Atharv had burst out laughing at Pawar's reasoning.

Atharv, Anant and Nirav had arrived in the city five days ago. Atharv was talking to Rehan, who had been tasked by Abu-Lakhvi to handle him and the four other CTC men. He had called a Dubai mobile phone number at 11 a.m. as he had been instructed to do every Tuesday. The man in Dubai who received Atharv's call had in turn arranged for him to speak to Al-Wali, via teleconferencing.

'Yes, we are settled here, on Reay Road. We will most likely enrol in a computer programming diploma course at MapTech Computer Training Institute tomorrow,' Atharv said.

'How much will it cost, this MapTech?'

'We will have to pay around Rs 1.6 lakh for the three admissions,' Atharv said.

'Do you have a currency note on you?

'I have a ten-rupee note.'

'Look at the bottom,' Al-Wali instructed him. 'What are the last two numbers of the note's unique number?'

Atharv quickly scanned the note. 'Six and seven.'

'Okay. Go to Zaveri Bazaar two days from today. A number will be sent to you today. Call it. It belongs to Vinod; he is a cousin and will help. When you meet him, tell him the two numbers you just told me.'

'Thank you, sir,' Atharv said.

'Atharv, there is one more thing. If there are other young men like you in Mumbai, then send them here, to the university.'

Al-Wali was referring to Bayt al-Mujahideen.

'I am trying; I am sure there are eager learners here. I will update you,' Atharv reassured Al-Wali before hanging up.

Two days later, Atharv collected Rs 1.6 lakh from 'Vinod' at Zaveri Bazaar. Al-Wali had emailed Vinod's phone number to Atharv, who had then called him to set up a rendezvous to collect the money. Vinod, clad in a red T-shirt, black trousers and sneakers, sporting a thick gold chain and clutching a white cell phone, was businesslike and handed over the money the moment Atharv said, 'Six, seven.'

The following Tuesday, at 11 a.m., Atharv dialled the Dubai number again and was put in touch with Al-Wali.

'Prepare to go to Nanihal. There, you will receive the project file, which you have to hand over to a trainee. It is an easy task, so do it quickly.'

As per the code used by his Lashkar commanders, 'Nanihal' referred to Jammu and Kashmir. 'Project file' referred to weapons, while 'trainee' was a fidayeen.

'Yes, sir,' Atharv said.

Later, Atharv received an email from Al-Wali: 'Go to Brilliant PCO, opposite the gate of the out-patient department of District

General Hospital in Rajouri. Ask the owner, "Where is Atif? I hope he is well.""

∽

Shekhar's cell phone buzzed. It was 1.50 p.m. Seated in his cabin at the CTC headquarters in Delhi, he was reading the interrogation report of a terror accused, looking for a chink in his narrative to breach his defence. The accused had not revealed anything of value so far to his CTC interrogators. It made Shekhar wonder whether he was genuinely cooperating or hiding as much as he could without getting hurt.

Shekhar looked at the screen of his phone. 'We are in play.' The text message was from Somaiya, CTC's designated handler for Atharv, Anant and Nirav.

Shekhar smiled and lit up a cigarette. He then called his boss on the encrypted phone line.

'Operation Trojan Horse enters the critical phase. Our response must be quick,' Shekhar told him.

Next, Shekhar called Somaiya and asked him to take a flight to Delhi from Mumbai that evening. Somaiya spent half a month in Mumbai to coordinate the operation with Atharv, and the other half in Delhi.

'Meet me at the safehouse in Chanakyapuri to discuss a possible plan of action for whatever is happening. You can then return to Mumbai via the 12.50 a.m. flight since Atharv will need you there,' Shekhar instructed Somaiya.

That evening, Somaiya was on a plane to Delhi, while Atharv was on the Rajdhani Express train to Delhi. The train reached

Delhi around 11 a.m. the next day. After eating lunch at a cheap hotel at Paharganj, near the railway station, Atharv went to Old Delhi to loiter around its streets and alleys, which he loved. He bought a bus ticket for Jammu from Janata Tours and Travels, located near the iconic Red Fort. The bus left at 6.30 p.m. and, by 5 a.m., Atharv was in Jammu. He then bought a bus ticket for Sopore, which was around ten hours by road. After a light breakfast at a nearby restaurant, he boarded the bus for Sopore at 7.30 a.m. At 4 p.m., he got off at the Sopore bus terminal. Half an hour later, Atharv was at Brilliant PCO.

41

LOOKING FOR ATIF

'Where is Atif? I hope he is well,' Atharv told the man seated inside Brilliant PCO. The owner, who seemed to be in his mid-thirties, had sad, weary eyes that tried to focus on Atharv. 'Wait,' was all he said. He then shuttered the shop and, telling Atharv to wait outside, left. Ten minutes later, he was back in a white Maruti van and asked Atharv to get in.

The man introduced himself as Zahid but did not ask Atharv to identify himself. Zahid took Atharv to his home, where he lived with his wife, parents and two daughters, aged three and five. Atharv was given a tasty but simple dinner of rotis and mutton stew. His host then took him to a room in the basement, where he was to spend the night. The room had a flask of warm water and at least three blankets to keep him warm during what was a chilly night, even by Kashmir's standards.

The next morning, Zahid took Atharv to an undisclosed destination. After travelling for around two hours, the car turned off the highway on to a road leading to the foothills of a local range. The van stopped in front of a tea shop. While Atharv was drinking his tea, Zahid crossed the road to speak to an old man sitting on a cot and smoking a hookah outside a small, shabby cottage with half a dozen bleating goats on its porch. After a brief conversation, he returned to the tea shop and told Atharv to accompany him to the old man's cottage.

'You have to stay here tonight. Atif will send somebody tomorrow,' he said. He then shook hands with Atharv, nodded to the old man and walked briskly back to his van and drove away.

The old man gestured to Atharv to sit with him on the cot. He pointed to a tiny outhouse built next to the cottage, saying, 'Make yourself comfortable there. You will get dinner in an hour. Atif will send somebody tomorrow at 8 a.m.'

After dinner, Atharv retired to bed. Half an hour later, he awoke to the howling of the wind. It was cold in the small room. He muttered his appreciation for the old man, his host for the night, for having generously kept a flask of hot soup by his bed. Shutting the outhouse's lone window, he gratefully drank the soup.

The next morning, at 8 a.m. sharp, two young men arrived at the cottage. They introduced themselves as Abu Hanzala, nineteen, and Abu Faisal, twenty-two. The three of them set off for the hill behind the old man's cottage. They walked for around seven hours, making their way through dense thickets and scaling hill after hill.

Around 7 p.m. they reached a small hut. Opposite the hut was a cave. Atharv's companions led him inside, where they found a lone occupant. He obviously knew Hanzala and Faisal and greeted them warmly. The four men spent the night in the cave, sleeping on straw beds after a frugal dinner of apples and bananas.

The next morning, Hanzala and Faisal fished out their AK-47s, the guns' black barrels gleaming in the sliver of sunlight that had made its way through the cave's entrance. The three men soon set off again, bound for a destination that Atharv had not been told about.

Three hours later, after crossing snow-clad heights and low valleys covered with tiny pink and white flowers and dotted with cottages, they reached another cave whose floors and walls seemed reinforced with concrete. This was the home of Atif, alias Abu Saqlain, the LeT's commander in Rajouri. The weary travellers were treated to mutton kebabs, rotis and glasses of goat's milk. Many cups of tea later, Atif took Atharv aside.

'Imran, from where have you come, brother?'

'From Mumbai. Al-Wali sir must have told you why I have been sent here.'

Atif merely asked instead, 'Tell me, what are you planning?'

Atharv did not know the answer. He just shrugged, nodded and broke into a half-smile, as if to say, 'I am not that important yet. Knowing such things is beyond my pay grade.'

Before Atif could ask him anything else, his phone rang. He reached for the Thuraya satellite phone and, after a brief exchange, handed it to Atharv, saying, 'It is Abu-Muzammil. He wants to talk to you.'

Abu-Muzammil instructed Atharv to return to Mumbai with the 'project files' as soon as possible.

When Atharv told Atif this, the latter said that it would be tough to ensure his safe return to Mumbai with weapons. There had been a terrorist attack on an army facility in Jammu recently and a large number of barricades had been set up on the roads and highways in the region to catch the perpetrators.

'Imran will have to wait till things cool down,' Atif told Al-Wali when the latter called for the third time that week to ask about Atharv's departure for Mumbai. Abu-Muzammil also expressed his displeasure at Atif not being able to send Atharv with the weapons to Mumbai soon enough.

'I am sure the operation can't wait a day more, considering the calls coming from Pakistan,' Atharv told Atif. He expected Atif to do something to speed things along, but nothing happened.

Finally, a week later, as directed by Abu-Muzammil, Atif took Atharv to the hideout of his superior, the divisional commander of LeT, Abu Osama. Two days later, Osama's contact, Ishtiyaq Shah, came to his hideout. Shah ran a travel agency in Srinagar and had a fleet of four wheelers.

'Osama bhai, here is the rucksack you asked me to get,' he said, handing over an olive-green bag to him. 'Once you have checked them, give me the weapons, I will set them up in the van.'

Osama took the bag and disappeared into a room at the back of the cottage.

'Here is the stuff – two AK-47s, eight hand grenades and eighty rounds of ammunition,' Osama said to Atharv, who was waiting in the room.

Shah hid the weapons and the ammunition in secret cavities built inside the van. Soon after, he and Atharv left for Ludhiana, sticking to interior roads. Atharv was carrying a MapTech identity card, which he produced at barricades and told the security men that he was from Mumbai, where he was pursuing a programming course, and had come to Kashmir to seek admission in a college in the state. The van was rigorously checked on three occasions by security men, but they did not find the concealed cavities.

Twelve hours after they had left Osama's hideout, Shah dropped Atharv off at the Ludhiana railway station. Atharv bought two sweaters at the railway station and stuffed them inside the rucksack, which had two disassembled AK-47s, grenades and ammunition. He then bought a ticket for the Ludhiana–Borivali Tejasvi Express, scheduled to depart an hour later for Mumbai. At 11 p.m., he found a seat by the window inside a coach meant for passengers with no reservation.

Almost all his co-passengers had several pieces of luggage. Among the suitcases, baskets, rolled-up mattresses and quilts, Atharv's rucksack was inconspicuous.

On reaching Borivali station in Mumbai, Atharv stuck close to a Gujarati family that was travelling with a lot of luggage. As they were leaving the platform, two railway policemen gestured to Atharv and the head of the Gujarati family to stop. One of the policemen asked the family man to show him what they had in their ten-odd bags and suitcases.

'We had gone to Kashmir for sightseeing. The bags have our belongings – clothes, dried fruit, picture frames, etc.,' the man said and offered a bag for inspection. The policeman peered inside intently. Finally, he nodded and told him and Atharv that they could go.

An hour later, as Atharv was on his way to Reay Road, his phone rang. It was a call from Dubai.

'Hello, this is Atharv,' he said and paused, listening. 'Okay, yes, please connect me to him,' he then responded. The man, who looked after the Lashkar's safehouses in Dubai, had informed him that Al-Wali wanted to speak to him.

'Atharv, take the project files to Bandra. Drop them off at room number 201, Nilgiri Hotel, near Himalaya Studio, in Bandra West,' he said curtly.

'Okay, I am on my way to Reay Road,' Atharv said.

'Go to Bandra first,' Al-Wali instructed him. 'At Nilgiri Hotel, tell the person at the reception desk that you are their guest Shrikant Joshi's brother and that Joshi left the room's key for you at the reception. Keep the file inside the small water tank on the shelf near the bathroom. The tank is empty. Call on this number at 6 p.m. today.'

'Okay, sure,' Atharv said.

He issued fresh instructions to the cab driver, asking him to take him to the well-known Himalaya Studio. From the studio, Atharv quickly walked to the hotel, where he took the key for room number 201 from the reception and deposited the rucksack inside the water tank in the room, as directed by Al-Wali. Before he left, Atharv quickly scanned the articles in the room. Two English newspapers, three empty packets of potato chips, several packets of biscuits, half a dozen bananas and a small piece of paper, roughly three inches by one inch. Atharv picked up the piece of paper. It was a bus ticket issued by Mumbai's BEST, which ran the city's iconic flaming-red buses and double-deckers. The ticket was bought for Rs 10 at Andheri East railway station with 'IIS&T, Powai' as the destination. He kept the ticket in his wallet. He then left the hotel and took a cab to Reay Road.

On reaching Anwarat, Atharv ran to Vasant Communications and called Somaiya.

'They sent me to Kashmir, which they call Nanihal. I just returned with two AK-47s, eighty rounds of ammunition and two grenades,' Atharv gave the update on his debut Lashkar mission to his CTC handler.

'Do you know what this operation is all about?' Somaiya asked him.

'No, but two AKs, eighty rounds and grenades mean they could be planning to kill several VIPs. Or they need them to deal with a counterattack from security personnel after they kill whoever they mean to kill,' Atharv said.

'The bus ticket is our best clue,' Somaiya said. 'Meet me outside Reay Road railway station in an hour.'

'Yes, sir,' Atharv said and hung up. He took another cab to Reay Road railway station.

∾

'Son, have you reached Mumbai, where are you? Check out from Nilgiri Hotel at once. Keep the project files safely,' Al-Wali said into the phone.

'*Trainees aa gaye kya?*' he asked.

42

TERROR ON A PLATE

'Tell me, Mr Siddhant Sharma, why should we give you a chance? You have not shown me even one A-list event that was handled by your catering agency, about which I have never heard in any case,' a middle-aged man, square, metal-rimmed spectacles perched on his nose, said to the young man.

'Do you think we are some government welfare department offering blankets to the needy?' he continued.

The young man, clad in black jeans and a dark brown shirt, stood opposite the black leather chair occupied by the bespectacled man.

'This is the Indian Institute of Science and Technology. IIS&T is India's premier institution for engineering education and research,' the middle-aged man said, his voice rising slightly.

The name plate outside the cabin where this conversation, which was currently a monologue, was taking place stated that the man in the black leather chair was Deputy Administrator, IIS&T,

Joseph Dias. Dias had worked with the Powai-based institution for the past thirty years.

'Do you even know who all are coming to our event on 5 January?' he was seething. 'Nobel laureate Samuel Price, an American physicist, will address a gathering of top scientists, including from the Bharat Atomic Science and Research Centre, and our students. If anything goes wrong, God forbid, I will be sacked and this renowned institution will lose face in the scientific community and among peer institutions around the world,' he thundered. 'I can't do anything for you. Stop dropping in every day to plead. You have no case.'

Siddhant was speechless and was fumbling for words. 'No ma'am – sorry, sir … sir – yes, you are right. I have great respect for you and IIS&T … But just one chance I am asking for,' he blurted out.

Then, gathering his courage, he continued, 'I won't take any profit for our deal if I get the contract. Just pay for the raw materials, food and beverages. I will do it on a no-loss-no-profit basis. Instead, give us the contract for the students' canteen, which is due for renewal.'

'What free? You will hike the rates for the food and the beverages to get your cut, you bugger, I know your type,' Dias said, not impressed.

After roasting Siddhant, he now warmed up to him, as if he had done his due diligence to test the former's catering capabilities. In any case, Siddhant was now offering a better deal. Dias decided he would take it. He was now in a mood to give him a slice of the pie. If all went well with the event on 5 January, he would even consider awarding Siddhant the lucrative students' canteen contract, he thought.

'Do one thing; leave your proposal and the rate list there. There will be a high tea and a lunch for the guests at the Convention Centre on 5 January,' Dias said, his tone now businesslike. 'I will see if you can get the high tea contract; let me talk to the boss.' Breaking into a smile, he wrapped up the meeting, rising from his chair as he said: 'Wait for my call tomorrow. But remember one thing, Siddhant, if you screw us on 5 January, I will destroy your career.'

The call came two hours later, in fact. 'Congrats, Siddhant, we have accepted your proposal for the high tea part of the event. Meet my team tomorrow to understand what all you need to do, and how.' Dias sounded happy on the phone.

'Thank you, sir, I will be there tomorrow,' Siddhant said, sounding overjoyed. 'You gave me a chance, you made my life.'

Siddhant was having cutting chai at the Marina Restaurant and Bar. It was barely 300 metres from IIS&T's main gate and abutted the Mata Amritabai Rahiwasi Sangh, a crowded slum that housed hundreds of underprivileged and lower-middle-class families.

After finishing his tea and ordering another cup, Siddhant fished out a second mobile phone from his trouser pocket.

'Good evening, janaab. *Babar bol raha hoon*,' Siddhant said in a low voice. 'I will be going to the temple and will make sure to ring its bells,' he said and disconnected the call. He was smiling as he took a sip of his tea.

Babar Irfan, an Indian recruit of the LeT, was one of Abu-Lakhvi's sharpest operatives in India and was part of a sleeper module controlled by Abu-Muzammil and Al-Wali for Abu-Lakhvi. Babar had not come under the radar of the Indian enforcement agencies or police so far. Being an unknown entity, he could travel anywhere.

Al-Wali had chosen Babar to execute the operation for which Atharv had been sent to 'Nanihal'. As per the code, 'temple' referred to IIS&T and 'ring its bells' referred to completing the mission he had been tasked with by Al-Wali and Abu-Lakhvi.

Two days ago, after receiving an alert from Al-Wali, he had collected the 'project files' – the weapons, ammunition and grenades – from Nilgiri Hotel and moved them to a flat in Mata Amritabai Rahiwasi Sangh. The cacophonous, bustling world of the slum would give him the space and anonymity required to execute the operation. He had already tied up with a catering agency in Kalbadevi in south Mumbai to handle the 5 January event at IIS&T.

A year ago, Babar had arrived in Pakistan from Lucknow in Uttar Pradesh. Originally from Kishanganj, Bihar, he was then a student at a college in Lucknow. He was doing well in academics and took a keen interest in current affairs and issues related to the Muslim community. The loss of Muslim lives in the Gujarat riots of 2002 gave him sleepless nights.

Babar's classmate, Mustaq Ansari, felt deeply for the Gujarat riot victims as well and had introduced him to a senior college student, Tariq Ansari. Tariq was a firebrand and spewed venom at the pro-Hindu right-wing groups that were being accused of orchestrating the anti-Muslim riots in Gujarat. Noticing that Babar was enraged by the slaughter, Tariq had invited him to his hostel room to meet some of his 'like-minded' friends.

At multiple such gatherings in Tariq's hostel room, several young men, including Babar, swore revenge and talked about jihad as the only option for the embattled Muslim community in India.

'Are you using jihad to make a name for yourself? Do you understand what jihad means?' Tariq had ambushed Babar and asked after one such meeting.

'Jaan de sakta hoon community ke liye,' Babar had responded without hesitating.

'You are emotional right now, brother. Think about the path of jihad carefully and then let me know how you feel when we meet again,' Tariq had said softly.

Babar had hated the patronizing tone Tariq had adopted when speaking to him about jihad.

He was at Tariq's door at 8 a.m. the following morning. Tariq was surprised to see him but ushered him in.

'Jihad is not just an emotion, it is my life's goal,' Babar had declared as soon as he sat down. 'I will avenge the death of those whose bodies are strewn in the lanes of Gujarat, just show me the way.'

Babar had no clue that Tariq had ties with LeT recruiters.

Tariq had then sent Babar to an LeT resident agent living in Kanpur, known only by his alias, 'Doctor'. The Doctor had dispatched Babar with a letter addressed to the LeT district commander of Rajouri, Atif alias Abu Saqlain. As instructed by the Doctor, Babar had left for Jammu, from where he took a bus to Poonch to meet Atif.

Atif had sent Babar and five other aspiring terrorist recruits to Muzaffarabad, where they had met Umar-Qama, Al-Wali, Abu-Muzammil and Abu-Lakhvi. For the next six months, the six were trained at the two Maaskar near Bayt al-Mujahideen, just like Atharv and the four other CTC operatives.

Like Atharv, Babar too was commended for his skills with an AK-47 automatic.

43

MURDER IN THE DARK

The two-storey structure was missing sections of its walls and floors. A faded signboard with 'Seth Govardhandas English High School' written on it lay near the entrance.

A peepal tree grew near the entrance, its branches climbing along the wall to emerge through the roof of the second floor.

The building was shrouded in darkness and not a soul was around, except Babar. Standing at the entrance, which was locked, he fished out a tiny pencil torch from a bag slung across his shoulder. Using the torch, he surveyed his surroundings and then jumped to grab a branch of the peepal tree. Slowly, he climbed the tree, reaching the first floor and finally the roof of the building. The rock-climbing lessons that were part of the Daura-e-Khaas commando course stood him in good stead here, he thought.

He took out a pair of sleek binoculars from his bag and studied the surrounding area. The view from the roof of the structure was breathtaking. All round him, a thousand lights twinkled.

Suddenly, the silence enveloping the place was pierced by a shriek.

'*Kaun hai re tu*? You fucker, are you the son of a thief that you have come here like this?'

Babar turned around in a flash to see who was shouting. He could not afford to be discovered here. A man dressed in rags was lurching towards him.

'Stop! Do you want to die?' Babar asked even as he adopted a defensive karate stance.

When the man continued to approach him, Babar took three quick steps towards him and waited. The moment the stranger came within range, Babar struck out at him, dealing a sharp blow to his neck. The stranger crashed to the floor, making indecipherable guttural sounds.

Babar hoisted the stranger on his shoulder and dropped him over the edge of the roof, near the peepal tree. The man fell to the ground with a thud. Babar pulled out a 9 mm pistol from his bag and waited for any further sounds. But there were none. He then climbed down the peepal tree, landing near the stranger's body. It stank of vomit, alcohol and marijuana. He checked it for signs of life, but the man made no sound or movement. Nor was he breathing, and Babar could feel no pulse either.

He searched the area and found a pile of garbage, broken school furniture and mattresses at the back of the school compound. He dug out a space large enough to accommodate the body, and then deposited it in the hollow, covering it up with rubbish and broken furniture.

Minutes later, he was back on the roof.

Using his binoculars, he examined the sprawling campus of IIS&T, which lay just beyond the Mata Amritabai slum, on the fringes of which was located the abandoned school building. He made a sketch of the layout of the IIS&T campus on a piece of paper, taking care to mark the point at its rear where a series of water pipes emerged out of the boundary wall through specially made cavities.

He went back to the main road and took a cab to Dadar. From there he took a bus to Pune. He would spend the following day there, perhaps watch a movie in the afternoon, before returning to Mumbai at night. He wanted to stay away from the slum in case the alcoholic's body was discovered in the school grounds.

Babar needed to arrange for the arrival of the two 'trainees' who would be assisting him in the operation and wanted no distractions till then. A day away from Mumbai would calm his nerves as well, he thought. He had not factored in having to kill somebody.

Al-Wali had told Babar time and again to avoid being noticed by the police and enforcement authorities by refraining from committing ordinary crimes that were 'fuelled by the lust for money, land, tobacco, alcohol and women'. Al-Wali had told him that as the 'soldiers of the community', they ought to be above petty crime.

'Anonymity in our work is as essential as water is for the existence of fish,' Al-Wali had said to him.

'And here I am, I just killed a drunken wastrel. My bad!' Babar chuckled.

౷

'Good morning, the admissions have been done and we are attending lectures,' Atharv told Al-Wali on the phone at the Sixty-Feet Road PCO. 'I delivered the project files,' he added.

'Good, I hope the courses are interesting,' Al-Wali said.

'They are for now; it is too early to tell. But one can get a job in the private sector afterwards.'

'Great. Now scan and email me copies of Anant's, Nirav's and your voter ID cards. I will try to get you admission in other colleges as well.'

'Okay. By when?'

'In a day.'

'Sure, anything else?'

'Have a good day, brother, and take care. Say my hello to the other two brothers,' Al-Wali said before hanging up.

∾

'Who is this Shrikant Joshi? Where is he? Vanished into thin air? And what is the operation that Al-Wali is working on? What is Atharv doing? We have no concrete leads as yet!' Shekhar was fuming and restless.

The lack of information on what Al-Wali's Lashkar sleeper module was up to was killing him, and he hurled a barrage of questions at Somaiya.

The two were having tea in a spacious south Mumbai flat.

'Atharv dropped the weapons off at Joshi's hotel. He has no idea about the operation beyond that,' Somaiya said.

'One more thing, Al-Wali has asked for scans of the voter ID cards of Atharv, Nirav and Anant. They could be for use either in this operation, or they might be kept in reserve for use in some other operation in the future. Or, they are still checking out our boys' authenticity,' Somaiya added.

'If the cards are for other Lashkar men, they will be used to forge IDs using other names and photographs,' Shekhar mused. 'We made discreet inquiries and roped in Mumbai Police to help. Joshi took the room in Nilgiri Hotel a day before Atharv's visit and did not return to it after Atharv deposited the weapons there. But the weapons are gone. Is Joshi a buyer of weapons or is he an arms carrier for Lashkar?'

'Did the police discover anything useful?' Somaiya asked.

'The hotel people told the police Joshi was heavily bearded and wore black sunglasses and had a gold chain around his neck. They said he is a politician from Pune and had come to Mumbai for business. He was not carrying any ID but paid for the room in cash for ten days. It is a third class, shady hotel, where customers give cash to book rooms and enter whatever they feel like in the register. There is no CCTV in the hotel, no lift, nothing.

'But, based on the description given by the hotel staff, a sketch has been prepared. However, Joshi was most likely in disguise and in reality looks nothing like the sketch. And Shrikant Joshi is definitely not his real name.' Shekhar sighed.

'We picked up fingerprints from the hotel room, and the forensic laboratory is trying to confirm if they match with any known criminal in the records. We have to keep this a secret exercise as Atharv may have left fingerprints there as well.'

'What about the bus ticket?' Somaiya asked.

'The destination on the ticket was IIS&T. If the ticket belonged to Joshi, it is likely he got off at that bus stop. But did he get off there to go to IIS&T? We don't know. But we cannot take a chance, in case he did go there, as he is clearly a man on a mission. The local police have been alerted and they are in touch with IIS&T to ramp up security there. We have also shared Joshi's sketch with IIS&T and the police, but we cannot put it up on roads and in public places as that will make the LeT suspicious. Atharv was probably one of the few who met him. So, he might get busted.'

'Why would Joshi be interested in IIS&T?' Somaiya wondered.

'We have asked IIS&T if there is anything happening at their campus that the LeT may want to target, but we have not heard from them yet.'

'There is also the possibility that IIS&T was not Joshi's final destination. Is there anything nearby that could be a potential LeT target?' Somaiya asked.

'Yes, there is an HPCL refinery about six kilometres from the bus stop. We have ramped up security there, especially as the facility has been on LeT's radar before. Security and surveillance have also been on high alert at the Bharat Atomic Science and Research Centre. Mumbai and the rest of Maharashtra and Goa are on high alert too. But so far we only have the sketch to go on, which, as I said, is unlikely to resemble him,' Shekhar said, sounding tired.

'Let's see, we will have to wait for a break,' said Somaiya as he finished his tea.

44

RING THE BELLS

The phone rang. Shekhar and Somaiya were still at the CTC safehouse in south Mumbai, discussing ways to intercept the Lashkar operation that was clearly under way. The call was for Shekhar.

As soon as he got off the phone, he turned to Somaiya. 'It seems IIS&T is the LeT target after all. The call was from the dean of the institution. He said that on 5 January there is a lecture by a Nobel laureate, an American physicist, and scientists from Bharat Atomic Science and Research Centre will be in attendance as the American is a respected authority on nuclear energy.'

'Is Shrikant Joshi targeting the American scientist or our BASRC scientists?' Somaiya wondered. 'I suppose it doesn't matter. Either way, it'll make a splash.'

'The event is a pot of honey, if LeT is the bear.'

'No chance can be taken with the security for this event,' Somaiya said.

'I agree,' Shekhar said as he punched a number into his phone. He was dialling the Mumbai police commissioner, A.P. Saxena.

'Sir, Shekhar here from CTC … I am fine, how are you sir? Sir, the LeT target could most likely be a high-profile event at IIS&T. We have to provide foolproof proximate and perimeter security, sir, and raid hotels and lodges across the city looking for suspects.'

'Oh, that's bad, really bad! Are you sure? We will verify too. Yes, of course, we can take no chances,' Saxena said.

'I will coordinate with the joint commissioners of police for crime and law and order, sir,' Shekhar suggested.

'Fine. And let's update each other regularly,' the commissioner said before hanging up.

In Pune, Babar alias Shrikant Joshi updated Al-Wali about the operation. Al-Wali was worried that the alcoholic's body would be discovered and lead the police to Babar. But Babar was more worried about the missing operations' strike team, the two fidayeen or 'trainees' who were supposed to arrive soon.

'The trainees have never been to India and are waiting at the place from where you picked up the trainees for your last operation. Understood?' Al-Wali reassured Babar.

'Yes, but it is late already.'

'Leave right away. After you pick them up, take them to the temple so that they can offer prayers and write the test,' Al-Wali instructed.

Al-Wali then shared two sets of email IDs with Babar. One set was to be activated to confirm the arrival of the fidayeen for the operation. The second was to be used after the completion of the operation and the fidayeen's safe return to the LeT's base in Karachi.

'The email IDs are to be deleted on the completion of each of the two stages of the operation,' Al-Wali told Babar. 'Do not send the email. Just write it and save it in the drafts folder. We both have the same passwords, so we can read what we save in the drafts. Since the email will not be sent to any other email account, our account will not come under any kind of surveillance,' Al-Wali explained.

Babar took a cab to the Pune airport and bought a ticket for Kolkata. From there, he flew to Patna. Upon reaching Patna, he took a bus to Raxaul, located on Bihar's border with Nepal. Eight hours later, on reaching Raxaul, Babar took a cab to Birat Nagar, across the border in Nepal, to finally reach the Mahendra Niwas Residency Hotel.

Two young Pakistanis in Pathani suits were waiting in the hotel lobby. One of them was carrying a rucksack and wearing a yellow baseball cap. The cap and the rucksack were the signals for him, as decided by Al-Wali.

Babar approached them. 'I am Babar. You have come to see the Red Fort?'

'Yes, we want to see the Red Fort. I am Usman Ali, and this is my friend Rehmat Shah. We are trainees and have been waiting for you.'

Babar nodded. 'Let's move, the cab is waiting.'

Babar took the two Pakistani terrorists back to Pune after returning to Raxaul in a cab from Birat Nagar. From Raxaul, the trio had boarded a private passenger bus to reach Patna, after which they travelled on fake identity particulars – made in the name of Hindus – on a passenger train to Pune. From Pune, Babar hired a cab to take Usman and Rehmat to Vikhroli railway station in

Mumbai. From the railway station, they took a bus to the Mata Amritabai slum, where Babar had rented a room.

'Both of you are to stay in this room at all times. Please don't step out. Whatever you need, I will get for you,' he instructed the two young men.

'How far is the IIS&T from here?' asked Usman.

'It is just a kilometre away.'

'And what is the plan?' Rehmat wanted to know.

Babar pulled out the sketch he had made of the IIS&T campus. 'At the back of the campus is a breach in the wall for water pipes. The breach is narrow but good enough for a man of normal build to squeeze through,' he said and pointed out the spot on the sketch.

'Around 400 metres away from the breach, across the campus wall that separates it from this slum, lies an abandoned school. No one goes there. Apparently, there was a fire there years ago and many people died. It is considered haunted or unlucky, which is why no one goes there, except alcoholics at times.

'On the night of 4 January, both of you will shift to that school building. At 6 a.m. the following morning, you are to enter the IIS&T campus via the breach. Once inside, you will make your way to a nearby building that is no longer in use,' he showed the boys the structure on the sketch. 'You will hide in a water tank on the roof of this building. Any questions?'

'No. What do we do once we are situated in the campus?' asked Usman.

'The American scientist, Samuel Price, will begin his lecture at 9.30 a.m. This will be followed by high tea at 11 a.m. and lunch at 12.30 p.m. in the convention centre. I will be supervising the high tea.

'By around 1.30 p.m., Price and the Indian scientists will come out of the convention centre, which is close to where you will be hiding. You are to take up your positions on the roof by 1.15. As soon as you see them, fire at the white man and all those surrounding him, then go back the same way you slipped into IIS&T.'

'What about the guns?' asked Rehmat.

'Leave them in the water tank. Once you exit the campus, mingle with the crowds in the slum so you are not spotted, then take a cab to Vikhroli railway station. From there, take another cab to Mumbai Central railway station.

'Here, take these two tickets for the Mumbai–Delhi Rajdhani Express. And keep these $200 as well. The train leaves arrives in New Delhi the next morning. On reaching Delhi, exit the station via the eastern side and go to Paharganj. Go to Hotel Enclave Supreme there. A room, No. 101, is booked for you for two days. The same evening, a man named Mustafa will meet you there around 6 p.m. He will ask you, "Are you ready for the marathon?" You have to reply, "Sure, we love marathons."

'Mustafa will accompany you on your train and bus journeys to Raxaul. From there, you know the drill. Take a cab to Birat Nagar. Al-Wali's man Vinod will meet you in the lobby of the Mahendra Residency. He will give you your air tickets for the flight to Karachi. When you reach Karachi, call the Dubai number you were given by Al-Wali. Use a PCO. You will be put in touch with Al-Wali; tell him your location and his man will meet you at the PCO and take both of you to wherever they require you to be.

'Is everything clear?' Babar finally asked.

'Yes, bhai, thank you. Your arrangements are excellent. May the operation attain success,' said Usman.

45

THE TOAST OF LeT

At 9.30 a.m. on 5 January, Samuel Price, a pioneer in research on using nuclear energy for civilian purposes, rose to address the distinguished gathering at IIS&T.

Price's work had encouraged many countries to study the peaceful use of nuclear energy. He had many admirers around the world, especially in the Indian scientific community, so it was little wonder that the entire top brass of the Bharat Atomic Science and Research Centre, which leads India's nuclear research, was in attendance.

'Ladies and gentleman, good morning, may God bless you,' Price said and paused.

As if on cue, the convention centre rang with applause.

'Nuclear energy is a boon, a gift from God himself, and shows the awe-inspiring power of nature and what the human mind can do. Never doubt the power of nuclear energy. It can light up a thousand homes and a hundred cities without producing too much waste, unlike, say, electricity that is produced through nonrenewable resources such as coal. It is also a low emission energy, with a relatively low cost of production. However, this powerful gift has an ugly side too,' Price said.

'The problem, apart from the desire of power-drunk countries to utilize nuclear energy to make bombs, is that though the waste produced when generating nuclear power is little, it is highly toxic, and frankly no one has a complete solution yet for handling it in a safe and environmentally friendly manner,' Price laid out the challenge.

'Today, at this august gathering, let us begin the process of coming up with a plan to handle the toxic waste being produced by your dozen-odd civilian reactors and by the scores of reactors globally. Let us constitute a panel of scientists to produce a white paper on the challenges before us in the field of nuclear energy and a plan to address the challenges,' Price exhorted his keen listeners.

Babar was seated in the last row in the convention centre.

At 9 a.m., he had checked on the arrangements for the high tea for the final time, the third check since he had arrived with the team of the Kalbadevi-based caterer to whom he had outsourced the contract from IIS&T. It crossed Babar's mind that the only things he could make were tea, omelette and Maggi. And yet here he was, at the helm of the catering arrangements for one of the most high-profile events in India.

What an ace I am, Babar thought to himself and laughed.

After Price's lecture was over, Babar made sure that the scientists and the guest of honour enjoyed the spread that had been organized.

Babar was worried about how the two fidayeen, Usman and Rehmat, were faring. He would have loved to receive an update on their status, but Al-Wali had instructed Babar to ensure that the fidayeen did not carry any phones on their person during the mission as the Indian agencies could track them via the phones in the event that their numbers were compromised.

∽

Shekhar was on his phone, speaking to A.P. Saxena, the commissioner of Mumbai Police.

'Saxena sir, over the past five days we have tracked almost 1.4 lakh calls in Powai. There were a few suspicious ones, and each of them was traced back to the callers by special teams. In fact, a few absconders in pending probes of the Mumbai Police were tracked in the bargain, and were picked up and handed over to the police authorities concerned.'

'At least some good has come of the surveillance. But what about the main target?'

'Nothing so far, sir. We have found no trace of Shrikant Joshi. But we will not stop looking,' Shekhar assured the commissioner.

∽

Usman crawled through the breach in the IIS&T compound wall without a problem. Rehmat, who was bulkier than him, got stuck in the gap, however. Minutes passed, but he could not move an inch even as he felt he would suffocate to death.

Usman called out to Rehmat in a low voice. He was pacing up and down near the boundary wall, keeping an eye out for any movement or sound while waiting for Rehmat to join him. When he didn't get a response, he quickly walked back to the breach and realized immediately what had happened. He pulled Rehmat out, dragging him by the fabric of his khakis. Once Rehmat was through the breach, he knelt down on the ground and thanked the Almighty for helping him.

It was 4.03 a.m. and still dark, except for a few lights dotting the IIS&T campus and the slum.

'Good we did not wait till 6 a.m. as Babar told us,' Usman said. 'Just imagine. At 6 a.m., that American, Dr Samuel Price himself, would have come to rescue you, thanks to the racket you were creating,' Usman laughed.

Rehmat punched Usman playfully on his shoulder. 'I got scared; it was too small a breach, brother.'

The fidayeen, clad in khakis with fake Maharashtra Police insignia, followed the road by the boundary wall for fifty metres. Then they stepped off the road and, as instructed by Babar, ran to the right towards an abandoned building, earlier a part of the mechanical engineering department. They took the stairs up to the terrace of the single-storey building and ducked into a spacious concrete overhead water tank that was lying empty.

They were to lie inside till 1.15 p.m., at which time they would emerge to take up their positions to attack Price and the other scientists, as per Babar's plan.

From their small backpacks, the fidayeen took out their AK-47s and their hand grenades, eight for each of them. The convention centre's entrance was just across the road from the building they were hiding in, around thirty metres away. The spot where Price and the others would get into their bulletproof vehicles, which were introduced into their security detail at the last moment on the orders of Commissioner Saxena, was within the range of the fidayeen's AK-47s and also the grenades.

Rehmat and Usman took turns to sleep and keep a vigil while waiting for the action to begin.

∾

At 1.30 p.m., Dr Price, along with a group of scientists, emerged from the convention centre and walked towards a fleet of reinforced white Ambassador cars. Just as the chauffeur opened the door for the tall, bespectacled American luminary, there was a deafening blast near the car, followed by shock waves and a blizzard of metal shrapnel and glass.

The blast was followed by another explosion, even as bullets began raining down on all those around Dr Price. There were two more blasts and three bursts of gunfire. Price lay on the ground, face down, while two other men lay motionless near him.

After Rehmat and Usman had thrown four grenades and emptied three magazines at Price and his companions, they shoved the remaining grenades and their AK-47s inside their backpacks, which they then threw into the water tank and took the staircase to exit the building.

The duo ran towards the spot in the boundary wall where they had entered the campus. Bullets whizzed past the fleeing fidayeen. One of the bullets hit Usman, who crashed to the ground.

Rehmat paused, but Usman shouted, 'Run, run!' With little choice, Rehmat ran, squeezing out of the breach like an expert this time. He ran towards the vegetable market located inside the Mata Amritabai slum and vanished into the milling crowd of buyers.

Minutes later, police and ambulance sirens could be heard approaching the campus. Indecipherable commands and shouts rang out. Suresh Mane, senior police inspector, Powai police, spoke on the wireless set in his official jeep.

'Alfa to Tiger One,' Mane barked into the wireless.

Tiger One was at the city police's 24x7 control room, located in its south Mumbai headquarters at Crawford Market.

'Tiger One to Alfa. Go ahead.'

'There have been several rounds of firing inside the IIS&T campus. Two intruders spotted. They shot using AK-47s and threw grenades at VIP guests outside the convention centre. Two guests are dead, American scientist Dr Samuel Price and Dr N. Srinivasan, a scientist from the Bharat Atomic Science and Research Centre.

'I am at the spot with my team. I shot dead one of the intruders, the other ran away and is being chased by two police teams, on foot and on bikes. Please set up roadblocks across the city and conduct checks at all ingress and exit points of the city with immediate effect.'

'Understood, Alpha.'

'Alpha, Roger and out.'

'Tiger One, Roger and out.'

Two hours later, Rehmat was at the Mumbai Central railway station. He sat on a bench on the platform, ostensibly reading an English newspaper as he waited for the Rajdhani Express going to Delhi. Tears trickled down his cheeks. He was grieving for Usman.

Meanwhile, Babar left a cryptic message in the drafts folder of the email account that he shared with Al-Wali: 'The temple bells rang twice.'

Six hours later, at CTC's safehouse in south Mumbai, Shekhar was visibly upset. 'Pakistani gunmen sneak into India and kill two high-value targets, including an American Nobel laureate.

A Lashkar fidayeen is dead, but nothing was recovered from his person and we all know they are fucking foot-soldiers. Morons! Are we are sitting on our haunches? Were you sleeping?

'Why did we not know more about this than we did? The Lashkar operative who was posing as Shrikant Joshi is at large and probably already planning his next hit – since he is clearly an ace and we are schmucks!' Shekhar shouted at Somaiya.

'The AK-47s and grenades recovered from the roof of the disused building will yield details such as their origin and hopefully the fingerprints of the two fidayeen. We knew their game and fought back, but they were better than us this time,' Somaiya said.

'Too little, too late?' Shekhar spat. 'What is the use of Atharv and the others in our team if we could not save Price and our own scientist? If we could not stop the attack? If Shrikant is missing and so is the second attacker?'

'Let's look at it with a cool mind. By not drawing the correct lessons from the way this counter-terror response has panned out, we will be doing a grave mistake and also injustice to the efforts of CTC and men like Atharv!

'These operations take time to ripen fully, as you only always tell us. We are all upset that two eminent scientists were murdered by the LeT in an operation we had a whiff of before it happened. But it is also true that we are on the right track, we are betting on the right horse, as they say. We knew the plot was taking shape; we had guessed them right and were prepared for them but the one who plans the attack always holds the advantage. We were tracking Shrikant Joshi, the LeT mastermind with an alias. Aren't these the first time ever in our experience? Operation Trojan Horse has hit the ground running, sir! These are early days; tomorrow we will be able to stop their terror attacks or kill all their fidayeen.'

Shekhar took a deep breath, as if to calm himself. 'True. But Atharv and the others will have to dig deep into Lashkar's heart to learn everything possible about such unfolding conspiracies. Knowing about them superficially is not enough. We can't afford to remain clueless about master Lashkar commanders like the man who set up the attack here. Within a day or two, he will exit the country and reach Pakistan to evade capture.'

'I agree. I will tell Atharv about your valid concerns. They can't swim on the surface of LeT's terror plans, and we need to have full and adequate information to intervene and kill their operations in the future.'

'Tell them to be careful.' Shekhar paused before breaking into a smile. 'Ironically, while we mourn the two deaths and get roasted by the centre, Atharv's team will be toasted for playing a key part in this deadly, successful attack. In their maiden mission.'

'Maybe they can use the celebrations in LeT to open doors that currently lie shut for them in that evil organization,' Somaiya said.

46

BACK TO THE DEN

'US Nobel laureate, BASRC scientist killed in suspected LeT terror attack'; 'Two Pak gunmen breach high-security cordon at IIS&T to rain bullets, grenades; security agencies suspect role of local sleeper cell in assisting attack' – so screamed the headlines of the daily with the largest circulation in the country.

At his flat, Atharv's head had been buried in the newspaper for the past ten minutes. The cup of tea that he had made for himself lay untouched on a small table by his armchair.

Atharv had a gut feeling that Al-Wali's demand for their voter ID cards had had something to do with the terror attack at IIS&T. The Pakistani attackers who were 'suspected LeT operatives' as per police sources quoted in the newspaper reports had probably used the covert CTC team's identity particulars to enter India. A chill ran down his spine and Atharv shuddered at the thought of having been an accomplice. The newspaper reflected the sense of shock and horror that the city and the rest of India was experiencing on learning about the audacious terror strike at IIS&T, which had killed America's most famous nuclear scientist and a top BASRC scientist. The two had been part of a team that was overseeing the construction of Sarika-2, an upcoming civilian nuclear reactor at Ratnagiri in Maharashtra.

Sarika-2 was also under the scanner of the global atomic energy regulatory authority, the International Atomic Energy Agency (IAEA), for its suspected dual end-use. While the reactor was to provide 800 megawatts of electricity to the region's horticulture-based enterprises, which exported delicacies such as the Alphonso mango, its spent fuel could also be used to produce nuclear weapons, according to IAEA secretary Thomas Burns.

Burns, an Austrian physicist, was reckoned to be a US-backed appointee to the IAEA, and was insisting upon the enforcement of the non-proliferation regime against de facto nuclear weapon states such as India and Pakistan, which had conducted underground nuclear tests in 1998. Meanwhile, China, a veto-wielding member of the United Nations Security Council, wanted to control IAEA to strangle India's nuclear ambitions as part of its strategy to contain the latter's growth as a regional power in South Asia. It was for the same reason that it was aiding Pakistan's clandestine imports to buttress that country's weaponization programme.

An hour later, Atharv rushed to a nearby PCO. He dialled Somaiya's pre-paid mobile number. Somaiya's number, Atharv smiled, had changed thrice in the last three months since he had arrived from Pakistan. 'Atharv, did you know?' Somaiya asked as soon as he answered his phone.

'No, sir, the fuckers kept it all hush-hush. We are of course assuming that it was an LeT operation at IIS&T. But, sir, you know those identity documents that Al-Wali had asked me to send to him? I think they were for this operation!' Atharv shared his apprehensions.

'I think you're right. Do you know if the attackers came by sea, Bangladesh or Nepal?' Somaiya asked.

'If they made use of the ID cards, it must mean they used land and air routes, sir,' Atharv said after a pause.

Somaiya agreed. 'Atharv, we need to identify and pick up the local support module and the attacker who fled. We must know all possible details about the next attack. You have to pump Al-Wali for information.'

'Yes, sir,' Atharv said, thinking of ways to trap Al-Wali into revealing something about the IIS&T operation.

'But please be careful. As one of the Pakistani fidayeen was shot dead by us, Al-Wali might be in a dangerous mood. He might suspect that we had an inkling of the attack and that we were prepared for them. He might even suspect you. To be safe, don't go to Pakistan if they call you there,' Somaiya advised Atharv.

'How are you, brother?' Al-Wali asked Atharv when the latter called him up via the Dubai intermediary.

'I am well, sir. There were Diwali-like celebrations in Powai yesterday,' Atharv said, hinting at the Powai attack.

'I heard and read about it. *Badhai ho, aapne bhi sajayi thi roshni*,' Al-Wali said.

Al-Wali has just owned up to the IIS&T attack, Atharv thought. But he did not say anything.

'Come here, where I am,' Al-Wali asked him to travel to Pakistan.

'Janaab, it will be risky because of what has happened,' Atharv said.

'Okay, then come to the temple in two or three days. To pray, meditate,' Al-Wali said. As per the code used by Al-Wali and his LeT compatriots, 'temple' referred to Nepal and 'pray and meditate' meant planning and analysis.

'Yes, sir.'

'Come alone via Calcutta. If there is a problem, just email me your location and wait for my man for help. Stay safe,' Al-Wali said. 'Check your emails thrice a day once you leave,' Al-Wali instructed him and hung up.

'Calcutta' referred to Dhaka as per the Lashkar code. Al-Wali did not want to risk Nepal's status as Lashkar's key spur for anti-India operations, Atharv thought to himself. And Al-Wali was testing his skills and intelligence by making him travel to Nepal via Bangladesh. Atharv decided to leave that same evening and booked a train ticket to Calcutta.

Then he arranged to meet Somaiya so he could inform him about his trip to Nepal.

'Al-Wali is offering no help in crossing into Bangladesh then Nepal, or for the trip back to Mumbai. He is acting strangely,' Atharv said, chuckling.

He was seated on a pale pink concrete bench on Carter Road, Bandra West's beach front where hundreds of young and not-so-young men and women gathered every evening for fresh air and relaxed conversations in cafés, bars and restaurants. Clad in blue jeans and a white T-shirt, Atharv spoke softly while seemingly reading the newspaper he was holding.

'Al-Wali is testing your capabilities as a resource. What route are you planning to take?' Somaiya was in a white T-shirt and brown shorts. He held a mobile phone to his right ear and appeared to be busy conversing with someone.

'I have booked a train ticket to Calcutta. From there I'll go to Guwahati, and then work out how to reach Dhaka.'

'Head to Agartala from Guwahati. Look for Abbas Ahmed at Agartala's Narsingarh cattle market. He is a cross-border trader and has contacts on both sides of the border,' said Somaiya, who was sitting next to him on the bench.

'Yes,' said Atharv in an undertone as he stood up and left.

Somaiya later updated Shekhar about Atharv's trip to Nepal via Dhaka.

Meanwhile, Atharv was on his way. From Calcutta, he took a train to Guwahati and then another to Agartala.

On reaching Agartala, he booked a room at the Delight Hotel, which was adjacent to the city's famous cattle market at Narsingarh. The first thing Atharv noticed on entering the market was the overpowering stench of dung. All types of domesticated animals, including buffaloes, goats and bulls, were being traded there amid loud conversations, shouts and other indistinguishable noises.

Abbas was easy to locate. He was the secretary of the cattle traders' association, Atharv learned after asking around for him.

'Bhaijaan, my name is Mukhtar Ahmed, and I am from Kishanganj. I am a student at Dhaka University and am returning after vacation. Unfortunately, my passport got stolen, and I can't call my teachers for help as they would skin me for my lapse,' Atharv explained his problem to Abbas.

Abbas looked at him for a few seconds, then asked Atharv to write his name and residential address in Hindi on a piece of paper. Atharv scribbled down his fake details in Hindi.

Reading it, Abbas said, 'Fine, I was just checking to see if you were a Pakistani or a Bangladeshi fraud attempting to exploit my generosity. How much can you give?'

Somaiya had prepared Atharv for this question.

'I am a student, sir. I can't give you more than a thousand rupees,' Atharv said.

'Do you plan to beg for alms in Dhaka as well?' Abbas asked. He clearly disapproved of Atharv's offer.

'That's all I have, sir,' Atharv said.

Abbas shook his head but relented. 'Be at the railway station's entrance at 4 a.m. I will come and get you from there. Carry just one bag, nothing else. Don't carry any weapons, matches or explosives,' he instructed Atharv, and taking the Rs 1,000 in advance, he disappeared.

Atharv was waiting at the appointed spot at 4 a.m., but there was no sign of Abbas. A boy, probably aged ten or twelve, who was looking at him intently from a little distance away, finally came up to him.

'Go to the back gate and wait there,' the boy said and ran out of the station.

At the back gate of the railway station, Abbas appeared five minutes after Atharv got there. He was on a black bike with a pillion rider.

'Come, hop on to the bike,' he said.

For the next hour, Abbas sped through the deserted roads, not uttering a word. Finally, he stopped near a roadside eatery on what looked like a highway.

'This is called Border Road. The international border is roughly 250 metres to the west from here,' Abbas told Atharv, gesturing at him to follow. The duo and the third man, who had not been introduced to Atharv, walked towards the back of the eatery. Behind it lay a trail that led to a nearby forested tract. About 300 metres ahead, the trail stopped at a fortified border check post.

'Murshid, you take over now,' Abbas said.

Abbas's companion nodded and took Atharv straight up to a man in khaki who was seated at the check post. A sentry with an AK-47 stood by him.

'Sir, please help this man. He is student, he lost passport, he study in college in Dhaka,' Murshid said in halting, broken English.

The man in khaki stared at the duo before snarling, 'Have you brought another fraudulent client here?' Turning to Atharv, he barked, 'Who is your father? Dial his number and make him talk to me.'

Atharv dialled the number of the Reay Road PCO, which was near his flat and which he frequented on an almost daily basis, taking a chance. There was no answer, so he called again. The PCO owner, whom he sometimes addressed as 'Anna', would never pick up the phone at 5 a.m.

'Too early, sir, my father is sleeping,' Atharv said.

'Then get lost and come later when your father is bloody up,' the man said. He seemed in a foul mood.

A second later, he said, 'Never mind. I will see what can be done.'

He said something inaudible to the sentry, who nodded and then took Atharv through the check post. He let out a shrill whistle and raised his hand. Thirty seconds later, an answering whistle was heard from the Bangladeshi check post across the border.

The sentry spoke to the Bangladeshi trooper, who came and stood at the edge of the no-man's land between the two check posts. The Indian sentry explained Atharv's predicament to his counterpart. After arguing for a while, the Bangladeshi trooper asked Atharv to cross over the fences on the Indian side and get to his side across the stretch of no-man's land.

Once he was safely across, the Bangladeshi trooper guided Atharv to the nearest bus stop, from where the latter took a bus to the small town of Shahbazpur. From there, Atharv took a bus to Dhaka. He had already booked an air ticket from Dhaka to Kathmandu, using his Indian passport.

47

'YOU COULD KILL
JUST TWO, BABAR?'

On reaching Kathmandu from Dhaka, Atharv checked into Hotel Everest in Thamel and thereafter went to an internet café located next to it. He checked his email accounts, looking for an email from Al-Wali. It was waiting for him in the drafts folder, with the subject, 'pls check'.

'Send a reply the moment you see this email, and then wait for details,' the email read.

Atharv sent an 'Okay'. The reply came five minutes later.

'Open the attachment to find a telephone number. Call it,' the email instructed. Atharv did as he was told.

The man who answered his call just said, 'Come to Atithi Deluxe, 302, Thamel,' before hanging up.

Half an hour later, Atharv was outside room number 302 at Atithi Deluxe Hotel. He knocked.

'Come in, Atharv,' a voice boomed.

As Atharv entered, he saw the speaker was Al-Wali himself. He was then stunned to see LeT operational commander Abu-Lakhvi in the room as well. Abu-Lakhvi was sitting on a black sofa, his eyes fixed on Atharv, while two men in black hoods stood in a corner of the room.

'I hope your journey was smooth, Imran?' Al-Wali asked.

'No problems, all okay, sir,' Atharv was curt.

'Your small but crucial assistance is appreciated by us. The American rat, Price, is rotting in his grave, and the Indian scientist is dead too,' Al-Wali said.

'Thank you, janaab, let me know if you have any further instructions for me,' said Atharv.

'Go to the other room and help yourself to some food,' Al-Wali said.

Obediently, Atharv went to the other room of the suite. As he was tucking into the food, loud voices suddenly startled him. A voice rose sharply in the adjacent room.

'What do you mean the mission went all right, Babar?' Al-Wali screamed.

'Samuel Price, the target, is dead. A senior BASRC scientist is dead as well. What more were you looking for?' replied the man in an even tone. The man was probably 'Babar', Atharv thought.

'What more?' Al-Wali shrieked. 'Such a big operation, for which we toiled day in and day out for months, was in play, yet you could kill only two scientists? Just two men? And we lost our commando, Usman, in the operation! What a waste of a life and the efforts that went into making him the lion that he was. What a bloody joke!' Al-Wali was furious.

'Rehmat, what do you have to say? Did Babar set you up well for the attack? The reconnaissance and target identification were done properly?' Al-Wali spoke again.

'The preparations were thorough, my heartfelt thanks to Babar bhai. The hideouts in the slum and inside the IIS&T premises were safe and impeccable,' the man called Rehmat said.

'We may have killed only two but they were two important persons, and we both survived to fight another battle for the qaum,' Rehmat offered.

'Yes, you survived, but the meagre casualties insult us,' Al-Wali snubbed Rehmat.

'Had Rehmat stood his ground for a few more minutes, there would have been more casualties, but he was probably in too much of a hurry to run away from the site, unlike what a true jihadi should do,' Babar said.

Babar's comments were met with a deafening silence. Babar was obviously someone who gave as good as he got and he would not make an exception in the case of his Lashkar bosses as well.

'Rehmat should bear part of the responsibility for the low casualties. A true soldier of jihad cannot be worried about his own skin instead of the tanzeem's goals,' Babar added for good measure.

Then Abu-Lakhvi spoke for the first time since the showdown had begun.

'Who told you a true jihadi's job is to die alone? Are you talking of a jihadi or a vain man bent on attaining martyrdom alone? A true jihadi is one who completes his missions without care for his own life. So you, as the planner, and Rehmat, as the actual attacker, executed the mission well for the tanzeem and so are both true jihadis,' Abu-Lakhvi said.

'Since Rehmat showed tremendous courage and innovativeness in entering India, carrying out the Powai mission, then returning unscathed to Pakistan, his feat is worth applauding. To execute the mission and return unscathed is a bigger jihad than dying while executing a mission. *Shabash*, Rehmat,' Abu-Lakhvi said.

'Babar, prepare for a new mission. I have a new Indian jihadi who will assist you. Go back to Birat Nagar, Imran will meet you there,' Abu-Lakhvi instructed. 'You will now handle the Nepal station for the Lashkar. You have passed the test with flying colours, all praise be upon the Almighty.

'Al-Wali has too much on his plate; he assists me in overseeing dozens of operations, apart from his own setup's operations, of which you have been a part. Now, you will have your own setup and Imran will be part of it,' Abu-Lakhvi continued. 'Al-Wali will now look after our operations in Bangladesh but not Nepal. Both of you will look after Sri Lanka and Maldives, as and when there is a need, on my orders.'

In Lashkar's parlance, a 'setup' referred to a unit personally under the command of a mid- to senior-level operative.

Abu-Lakhvi's announcements were met with murmurs, then loud words of congratulations.

As if to placate Al-Wali after what seemed like his demotion in the face of the purported failure of the IIS&T operation due to the low casualty figure, Abu-Lakhvi said, 'Babar, you will report to me, but as Al-Wali is a senior leader, you will be under his command on a day-to-day basis. Only on critical issues will I or Abu-Muzammil step in.

'Leave for Birat Nagar, go to our safehouse there, Babar. Be careful when you begin work on the operation. Once you have a plan in place, send it to us for approval,' Abu-Lakhvi said.

Given the potential of Birat Nagar as a springboard for entering India due to its proximity to the Moreng-Jogbani customs check point, LeT had set up at least five safehouses in that city, each of which had a caretaker-cum-local agent of the LeT.

'What are we looking to do this time, janaab?' Babar's voice rang out after a while.

'To break India's backbone, to break the morale and pride of its army ... Al-Wali will explain to you the details of the mission,' Abu-Lakhvi said.

'Babar, you will get the weapons from our safehouses in Nepal. Al-Wali will arrange for two of our own jihadis who will be taken to India by Imran,' Abu-Lakhvi continued. By 'own' he meant Pakistani.

'You can station yourself, as always, close to where the action will unfold,' Abu-Lakhvi told Babar.

Listening to the conversation, Atharv had long since stopped eating. He was absorbing each and every word that was being spoken in the adjoining room. The excited, at times angry, words had filled Atharv's heart with dark fears about what lay next for his motherland. As a trained counter-terror operative, the challenges that lay ahead in seeking to protect India from the designs of Abu-Lakhvi and Babar had also got his adrenaline flowing.

48

FIRST TARGET

'Bravery and wisdom, determination to win, and blood and steel – these are sublime ideals and principles that define how a life must be led for the greater good.

'These mantras of a noble, chivalrous life seem so much like slices from our own lives and ideology. They befit us as we are the soldiers of the community and Pakistan and think nothing about sacrificing our lives for religion and the community,' Al-Wali said.

He was addressing the two other men in the room, Babar and Atharv. Both had heard of each other but had yet to be introduced. The meeting was taking place in a six-bedroom flat on Arunodaya Street in central Birat Nagar. It was a day after Abu-Lakhvi had given Babar his new mission.

'But these are the slogans of the Indian Army officers – even though they are contrary to what these high ideals of bravery, victory and wisdom embody,' Al-Wali poured out hatred for India.

'But we will show them. We will make the ISI and the Pakistani rulers proud of us and our accomplishments. This will happen once we succeed in our mission. The fidayeen of Lashkar-e-Taiba will strike at the Indian officers' training headquarters, the Indian Military Academy, like a lightning bolt,' Al-Wali declared, revealing the objective of their mission.

Atharv was stunned but tried to show no reaction.

'But why the Indian Military Academy, in particular, janaab?' Babar asked.

'The IMA is an officers' training academy that churns out future military leaders; it is the cradle from where their so-called legendary military leaders, the former army chiefs Sam Manekshaw, K.S. Cariappa and K.S. Thimayya, graduated. Also, the end of the training course is marked by a grand Passing Out Parade, and India's President, Prime Minister and chiefs of the armed forces often participate in this spectacle. So it is the perfect target to hit – attacking it will be like striking at the very heart of India,' Al-Wali explained.

'Brilliant,' said Babar softly. 'But it won't be easy.'

'No, it won't,' Al-Wali agreed. 'There is water-tight security in place both inside and outside the campus in view of the latest terror threat emanating from us. And in any case, we have had our eyes on Dehradun for a long time due to the other strategic establishments there, including the Ordnance Factory and the Western India Petroleum Research Institute. Paramilitary organizations such as the Indo-Tibetan Border Police and the Central Reserve Police Force also have their barracks near IMA.

'We will be riding headlong into a fortress, into the jaws of death. But that is what the Lashkar mujahideen do, for their love of the ummah. It will be a suicide mission though, Babar, I am sure you will come up with a robust escape plan,' Al-Wali said, turning to him.

Babar smiled and nodded, his eyes gleaming with excitement.

'Babar, Imran, you will bring four mujahideen from Bayt al-Mujahideen. The weapons for them are stashed here. Imran, you have to make arrangements to accommodate the mujahideen in Dehradun and hand over the weapons,' Al-Wali said.

At the mention of Imran, Babar narrowed his eyes and stared at Atharv, then looked at Al-Wali. Al-Wali met Babar's gaze but did not flinch. Atharv looked back at Babar coolly.

'Stick to PCOs and the email mode of communication,' Al-Wali said, adding, 'For any immediate decision, Imran, you will take orders from Babar. Do not wait for me and lose critical time.

'Our objective will be to inflict as much harm as possible; preferably target men of high rank and of the Indian Army. Storm into their fortress, blast your way in and, if you manage to go deep, throw grenades and IEDs at the IMA museum. It will please our ISI contacts,' Al-Wali said.

He paused and looked at the two men, who looked a little confused at the mention of the museum. 'What is the worth of the museum? Should the mujahideen not focus instead on killing as many as possible in the IMA campus, you two must be wondering, isn't it?' Al-Wali asked.

Babar and Atharv remained silent. Both knew they were not supposed to question or argue with their commanders, nor could they speak out of turn.

'That red brick building has two prized historic artifacts that the Indians make sure to show off to important foreign dignitaries,' Al-Wali said, his voice hard.

'One is a US-built Patton tank that the Indian Army seized from a defeated Pakistani battalion in Rajasthan during the 1965 war. It is on display in front of the museum building.'

'And on the ground floor, inside a glass case, is the personal service revolver of former Lieutenant General Amir Abdullah Khan Niazi of the Pakistan army, who lost the 1971 war in East Pakistan. He had handed over his weapon to India's Lieutenant General Jagjit Singh Aurora.'

'They have preserved our shame in that museum. Destroy that structure if you get the chance,' Al-Wali exhorted the two men.

'You have a month to prepare – 11 February 2006 is when the IMA should be drowned in Indian blood,' Al-Wali said, wrapping up the meeting.

He then stood up and left the flat, accompanied by four bodyguards, who were trained LeT operatives stationed at the safehouses in Kathmandu.

The chosen date, 11 February, Babar remembered, would be the twenty-second death anniversary of Kashmiri pro-independence leader Maqbool Bhat, who was hanged in Delhi's Tihar Jail in 1984. He smiled grimly.

49

DEHRADUN

After Al-Wali left the safehouse, Babar told Atharv that the fate of the IMA mission depended on the latter and that therefore he could not let him screw up.

'Wherever you are otherwise stationed – and I will not ask you anything about that as per the LeT code of conduct – you will not go back there till the mission is over. Do not call any of your associates, acquaintances or friends. Speak to none about what we heard here today. Tell your family, if there is one, that you will be away on work for over a month.'

Atharv merely nodded.

'We will create three separate email IDs to communicate. Each of them will be created before a specific job and, once that job is performed, the email account is to be shut down.

'The first email account will be used to communicate regarding the procuring and setting up of weapons for the IMA attack. The second will be for stationing the four suicide attackers, who will be sent to Dehradun from Pakistan. And the third will be used to update each other once the operation is complete. Understood?'

'Yes,' said Atharv.

'Good. Now note down the codes we will be using for the mission. Then, memorize them, burn the paper and flush it down the toilet. The codes are as follows: "language course" is the code for reconnaissance, "project file" refers to weapons, "USB drives" is for the four fidayeen, "visa registration" signifies the attack on IMA, "Rohit" is for the one who will receive the weapons, "Abhilash" refers to the weapons carrier, and "Kushal" is the one who will provide the weapons,' Babar said.

'You will use your Indian ID documents, just in case, though no one will ask you on the Indo-Nepal border checkpoint at Jogbani. You know what you have to do to set yourself up in Dehradun,' Babar said. 'Your vehicle is ready with the material.'

'What all do we have?' Atharv asked.

'Four AK-47s, four IEDs, eight hand grenades each for the four fidayeen, four sets of Indian Army uniforms and four knives. And Rs 3 lakh in Indian currency, 20 per cent of which is fake.

'Besides, you will be given a document that identifies you as the owner of a transport firm, Jai Ambe Tours and Travels, just in case you need this cover,' Babar said.

A battered Qualis SUV was parked inside one of the garages attached to the safehouse. Babar first showed him the faux flooring inside the vehicle. Then the two moved some cartons to cover the floor. The cartons contained clothing and decorative items.

'Tell the customs people if they ask that you have a transport firm in Dehradun and intend to sell these to your regular customers. You came to Kathmandu for an excursion but could not help splurging in Thamel's irresistible shopping arcades,' Babar said.

'Gift sweaters to the border guards, if required. Once you enter India, say the same thing. If you get caught, stick to the story of being a covert supplier to criminal gangs in Dehradun,' he added.

The two were joined by another man.

'This is Sameer Gupta, he is our own man. It's a cover name,' Babar introduced the newcomer.

'He is an expert driver, knows the terrain here, and will take you to Dehradun and stay with you through the mission. He is also one of the four fidayeen. He came earlier than the other three to help you with the reconnaissance,' Babar said.

The two travellers, Sameer and Atharv, barely spoke during the two-day trip to Dehradun. What little conversation they had was limited to discussing the roads and byroads they should take to stay off the security radar. Atharv usually suggested that they take interior roads instead of main roads, while Sameer did not think much of either of the options. 'We have no control over such things, brother. If something has to happen, it will,' was his philosophical response. 'Otherwise, highways and lanes are both equally safe or unsafe.'

Neither Atharv nor Sameer mentioned the IMA attack or how they needed to prepare for it. Sameer took the East–West Highway AH2 to reach the border checkpoint at Bhimdatta, 942 kilometres from Birat Nagar. Bhimdatta lay at the western edge of Nepal along the border with Uttarakhand, the Indian side of the border checkpoint being Banbasa.

After crossing into India, roughly twenty hours after they left Birat Nagar, the Qualis travelled another eight hours, and 342 kilometres, to finally reach Dehradun late on the second night. They drove straight to the IMA campus to do a blink-and-miss drive-by, then drove on to Prem Nagar, a major residential-cum-commercial enclave in Dehradun. There, they checked into the Happy Valley Hotel, which was plain but tidy and had a sprawling parking space at the back.

'Bhai, can you please get us a guide for a city tour? For tomorrow morning? We are on a business trip from Delhi, but who does not want to explore this beautiful city on their first trip?' Atharv laughed to the bellboy who showed the two men to their room.

'Of course, sir, no problem,' the bellboy responded before bidding the duo a good night.

～

'Good morning, sir, this is Dhaval Singh. Sorry to wake you at 8 in the morning,' the man at the door said and gave a toothy smile.

'Yes? Good morning,' a bleary-eyed Atharv could barely come up with a response. They had checked into the hotel at 2 a.m., so sleep, more than anything else, was on his mind.

'I am the tour guide, sir,' Dhaval said.

'Oh yes, sure. Please give me half an hour, then we will leave. You have a cab?'

'Yes, sir. The agency provides a car, a driver and me, all at your cost,' Dhaval said.

The smile never leaves his face, Atharv thought.

'Okay, thank you,' Atharv said and closed the door.

Atharv could hear Sameer snoring.

Half an hour later, the two men were in the hotel parking lot.

'Dehradun is at an elevation of 435 metres above sea level and is the most breathtaking gift of nature in the lower Himalayan mountain ranges. It is the gateway to the famous hill station of Mussoorie and to the pilgrimage sites of Haridwar and Rishikesh. Dehradun is the capital of Uttarakhand and was the apple of the British Raj's eye,' Dhaval began as soon as the car, a blue Wagon R, drove out of the Happy Valley Hotel's parking lot.

Fifteen minutes later, on the Chakrata–Dehradun highway, the Wagon R stopped on the side of the road. They were outside the IMA campus, which was split into two sections, one on either side of the road. On both sides, the view was enchanting. To the left was the north campus, its red boundary wall stretching out on either side of an impressive entrance gate flanked by cannons. This was the famous Drona Dwar. Beyond the parade ground was a rectangular official complex with a dark sloping roof. From the middle of the roof, a white watchtower rose at least twenty feet high.

'This is the Indian Army's cradle of leadership, the IMA. Since the early 1930s, around 90,000 officers have been trained here, including many from west Asia, southeast Asia, Afghanistan, Iraq, Sri Lanka and Nepal,' Dhaval said proudly. 'That big building with the grey sloping roof is known as Chetwode Hall, while the ground in front of it is the Drill Square. The famous Passing Out Parade happens there.'

'Right. Do they allow visitors inside?' Atharv asked.

'No, you need special permission to go inside,' Dhaval said.

'Okay,' Atharv said. As they drove on past IMA, Atharv noticed the sporadic presence of military personnel and, further away, the local police.

Two hours later, after visiting the city's popular sites, including a sixteenth-century gurdwara and an eighteenth-century church, Atharv asked the guide to take them to an eatery as it was lunch time and he was hungry. They stopped at Desi Grill in the eastern part of the city. As soon as they were shown to their table, Atharv excused himself, saying he needed to find a public restroom as the small eatery did not have one of its own.

As soon as he left the restaurant, Atharv walked quickly to a nearby PCO that he had spotted from the car. He found a restroom and a shop specializing in make-up, memorabilia and dresses. Atharv bought stars and stripes of army ranks and army caps and toupees.

'Somaiya sir, alert Shekhar sir. I am in Dehradun with Al-Wali's men. Four Pakistani fidayeen will attack IMA on 11 Febraury to inflict maximum casualties. More attacks may be in the offing as, twenty-two years ago, on the same date, separatist Maqbool Bhat was hanged at Tihar,' Atharv blurted out in one breath.

'How will they attack?' Somaiya asked.

'Sir, they will be armed with AK-47s, bombs and grenades and will probably use the main entrance, the Drona Dwar. The LeT terrorist codenamed Shrikant, who masterminded the IIS&T attack, is a Pakistani, or maybe an Indian, and his name is Babar. One fidayeen came with me to Dehradun and is conducting reconnaissance of the IMA. Three more will come with Babar later. He is again masterminding the attack – setting the field, as we say in cricket,' Atharv said.

'I understood what you meant. What else do you know?' Somaiya asked.

'The terrorists will be dressed in Indian Army fatigues and will arrive at the IMA campus in a vehicle, which they may ram into the Drona Dwar to turn the vehicle into a fireball. They will be armed to the teeth. Killing the maximum number of army officers is their objective to demoralize the Indian Army and humiliate it by striking at its heart,' Atharv said.

Somaiya was silent for a few moments as he digested this valuable information. 'Well done, Atharv,' he said softly.

'Thank you, sir. I will not be in touch much as one of the fidayeen is shadowing me 24x7,' Atharv said and hung up.

An anxious Somaiya called Shekhar, who almost fell off his chair on hearing about the planned LeT strike on the IMA. A flurry of calls were made, including to the top bosses of the army, military intelligence, the Uttarakhand police, and Delhi Police's crack anti-terrorism outfit, the Special Cell.

Within two hours, a sixty-strong contingent of the National Security Guard (NSG) – also known as the Black Cats, India's vanguard against asymmetric warfare including terrorism, hijacking and sabotage – and a team of Special Cell officers was rushed to Dehradun by air.

Two days later, as directed by Babar, Atharv had the weapons ready for him. Babar came to meet him at the hotel and was briefed on the preparations. He and the three fidayeen came by the same route that Atharv and Sameer had taken.

Satisfied that things were in order, he began to explain the plan of attack that had been approved by Al-Wali. 'We will hit IMA at 11 a.m. on 11 February. The four fidayeen will split into two teams of two each and head to the north and south campuses respectively. They will be armed to the teeth and clad in Indian Army fatigues bearing the insignias of the lieutenant and captain ranks. They will inform the guards that they have come from Jammu with an important alert about an impending terror strike by Pakistani terrorists.

'The bluff may carry them in or else they will kill all the army and police personnel at the entrance gate and drive into the IMA complex to kill more. Once their mission is complete, the fidayeen will escape into the Doon valley, which lies to the west of IMA, from where they will make their way to Ludhiana by road. From Ludhiana, they will take a bus to Jammu, then Sopore, where the district commander will have them escorted back to Pakistan.'

'If the Almighty wills,' Atharv said.

'Finalize the preparations and check the weapons one last time,' Babar instructed Atharv before ending the meeting.

Babar did not tell him, but Atharv found out later from Sameer that Babar had taken three additional rooms in the same hotel.

Realizing that Atharv had not been aware that the other fidayeen were staying in the same hotel, Sameer confided, 'You know Babar, na? He is a secretive fellow by nature. He does not trust even his own shadow, to tell you the truth.

'Also, separate rooms will ensure that even if, somehow, the authorities manage to track you down, we will still have a chance to escape and carry out the operation.'

'Of course, brother, may the Almighty will it so,' Atharv said.

On 11 Febraury, at 11 a.m. sharp, the battered Qualis pulled up outside the Drona Dwar of the IMA. For a few minutes, nothing moved. Shekhar, his eyes glued to a pair of military-grade binoculars, stood on a watchtower 100 metres from Drona Dwar inside the south campus and could feel his heart pounding.

A man in army fatigues jumped out from the driver's side of the Qualis, followed by the three other occupants of the vehicle, who emerged from the back.

Whoosh ... whoosh.

Sameer was startled on hearing a faint sound and turned back to the Qualis to check the source. But it was too late. He and the three fidayeen crashed to the ground. Blood was oozing out of their heads, chests and necks.

It was all over in a few seconds. The battle-hardened snipers of the NSG, who had taken up positions around all the exit and ingress points of the campus, had hit the bull's eye in their first attempt. The bodies of the four LeT fidayeen lay still and lifeless on the road outside the IMA, even as dozens of vehicles, including ambulances, pulled up, their sirens blaring.

Apart from the AK-47s, explosives and grenades, the search of the terrorists' bodies yielded maps of the IMA complex and Dehradun, with the latter's entry and exit points marked in red. One of the terrorists was carrying maps of India and of Delhi and Srinagar as well. Each of them was carrying Rs 10,000 apart from small pouches of dried fruit. Under their military caps, the four dead men had bald heads and hairless bodies.

'They were fidayeen and had prepared, mentally and physically, to lay down their lives as per the LeT's protocol,' Shekhar later reported to his superior.

50

TIME FOR REVENGE

On the morning of 1 February 2006, ten days before the planned attack on IMA in Dehradun, LeT's newly-appointed commander of Nepal operations, Babar, was watching video footage that Abu-Lakhvi had sent him a week ago via courier.

Taken from the rooftop of a flat in Ahmedabad, the amateur mobile video clip showed a mob of middle-aged and young men at work in Nizampura, a lower-middle-class residential hub. Below the flat from where the video was shot lay an alley that had chawl-like buildings on either side. The men were raising slogans – 'Blood for blood' and 'Eye for an eye'. A few others could be seen in the grainy video displaying the weapons they carried, swords and spears, while seemingly challenging local residents to come out into the lane. Five or six of them were pummelling a man on a cycle who was passing by. Screams, wails and loud prayers coupled with pleas for mercy rang out.

The message from Abu-Lakhvi that the courier had passed on to Babar was, 'Watch the 2002 Gujarat riots video to remember those who suffered. It is time for revenge.'

The 'mob', the video's narrator claimed, was incensed as just a few hours before, a train carrying pilgrims from Uttar Pradesh had been intercepted and torched at Godhra in Gujarat. The crime was followed by several days of rioting across the state by mobs. A large number of lives were lost in the communal violence and preventive actions by the police, amidst allegations of police inaction and the collusion and complicity of state functionaries.

Babar seethed with anger after watching the video. He held on to the edge of a nearby table to steady himself. He agreed with Abu-Lakhvi. It was time for revenge.

Later that day, he was to meet Abu-Muzammil, Abu-Lakhvi's deputy, in Kathmandu's Serai Residency Hotel in Thamel. Babar himself had arrived in Kathmandu the night before and had checked into another hotel in Thamel, Lhasa Suites. Abu-Muzammil had come to Kathmandu from Karachi to inform Babar about the latest operation to avenge the Gujarat riots.

At 2 p.m. that afternoon, Abu-Muzammil and Babar were seated on the balcony of Abu-Muzammil's room on the second floor of the Serai Residency.

'In Pune's Rajmahal area lies Himalaya Bhavan, which is spread across sixty acres. It contains several one-room flats, an auditorium, a museum, lecture halls and meditation centres. There are no apparent signs of weapons being stored there or armed men on guard inside the complex. And yet, despite the peace and calm that prevails around Himalaya Bhavan, it is the headquarters of the violence perpetrated by Hindu groups. Keshavgiri is the headquarters of the BVP, the so-called vanguard of that community,' Abu-Muzammil told Babar.

'The plans for riots and the harassment of our community, and at times Christian missionaries, are given shape at Himalaya Bhavan. We suspect that the BVP was involved in the Gujarat riots along with other such right-wing outfits,' he continued.

'They must pay for what they have done. We will storm into Himalaya Bhavan and flatten it, kill all there. Our ISI handler has given his go-ahead to this project of ours as well,' Abu-Muzammil declared.

There was a twinkle in Babar's eyes on hearing Abu-Muzammil's diatribe. 'Tell me what the plan is, janaab.'

'You will reach Pune in two days. A room will be booked for you at the Chancellor Hotel in Baner,' Abu-Muzammil instructed him. 'Three days from today, two mujahideen will meet you at the hotel. Rohit, who is a computer expert, and Sahil, a practitioner of unani medicine. Both did well in the Daura-e-Khaas and Baitul Rizwan courses and are promising boys. They have conducted a recce on Keshavgiri and will update you.'

Babar nodded.

Abu-Muzammil then stood up and walked back into the room. He was a tall man and walked with a slight limp due to an old bullet injury sustained in his right leg during his five-year stint in Kashmir for LeT.

Babar could hear him on the phone, asking for 'Akbar'.

Two minutes later, there was a knock on the door. Abu-Muzammil opened it and ushered in three young men in pathani suits.

'Babar, meet Akbar, Sohail and Irfan. They came with me on the PIA flight from Karachi, posing as my employees. I came here as the head of a carpet manufacturing firm, seeking clients in Kathmandu,' Abu-Muzammil introduced the men.

'These three were the best trainees at Bayt al-Mujahideen. They will go with you to Pune. The operation will happen on 11 February, Babar. Let India suffer on the day they hanged Maqbool Bhat,' Abu-Muzammil said, his voice rising.

After his meeting with Abu-Muzammil, Babar went to the Everest Presidency Hotel in Thamel, where he booked two rooms for the three fidayeen. By booking them into a separate hotel, he ensured that if any one of the three hotels where the Lashkar operatives were staying was searched by the Nepalese police or counter-terror authorities, at least two of the three sets would have time to escape.

That evening, Babar checked out of his hotel and took a cab to the bus stop in Thamel on Lekhnath Marg. On the way, he picked up the three fidayeen from the Everest Presidency. Abu-Muzammil had earlier given him the Indian identity documents that had been made for the three Pakistani fidayeen by forging the voter ID cards taken from Atharv and his two associates. The documents would help the three enter India.

The twenty-one-seater deluxe bus left at 8.30 p.m. from Leknath Marg for Birgunj on the Nepal–India border. Each of the four tickets cost around 960 Nepalese rupees.

'Sleep easy, brother. In two hours, we will stop to drink tea and eat tandoori chicken,' Sohail said soon after they boarded. Akbar and Irfan broke into hearty laughter. Sohail and Babar joined them. Sohail's comment had broken the ice between the fidayeen and Babar.

As the bus zipped past forests with the silhouettes of mountains rising darkly behind them, Babar, who was drifting off to sleep, suddenly saw the fair, cheery face of Rifaat in front of him. He jerked awake and sat up in his seat as he remembered Rifaat – Rifaat, whose smile spread like the aroma of earth after rains, the one who smelt of jasmine, whose voice sounded like a distant waterfall in the forest, who said unexpected things, whose beauty was like that of a valley of flowers. Rifaat – who had asked him to choose between her and jihad, whom he had left in the cold, whom he had abandoned for jihad…

'What happened, brother? All well?' Sohail asked with concern.

'I am fine, just got jolted out of sleep suddenly, and some memories rushed back,' Babar offered, attempting to shrug off his companion's concern.

'I hope you did not remember someone? Your face has turned pale. You look like a ghost! Memories are bad, memories inflict pain. Especially if they are of those who live in you,' Sohail said, his voice trailing away.

'Okay, Devdas, good night,' Babar said lightly.

'Good night,' Sohail responded and smiled.

Babar was trying to sleep when Sohail began humming:

Aa bhi jaa, aa bhi jaa, ae sub-aah aa bhi jaa
Raat ko kar vida,
Dilruba aa bhi jaa
Aa bhi jaa, aa bhi jaa, ae sub-aah aa bhi jaa
Raat ko kar vida,
Dilruba aa bhi jaa …

The haunting lyrics were from a song that was a 2002 chartbuster from the Bollywood movie *Sur* and spoke of unrequited love.

When Babar finally fell asleep, it was Rifaat's tear-stained face, her large brown eyes peering into his, which refused to fade away from his mind's eye.

The bus stopped four times but the four men did not get off even once. At 6.30 a.m. the bus reached Birgunj, bordering Raxaul in Bihar. The four men took an autorickshaw across the border. From Raxaul, they took a bus to Patna and went straight to the railway station. Babar bought four tickets.

'For Pune, sir. We are four of us. Any type of tickets will do. Our uncle is hospitalized there and reaching there in time is the only concern right now,' Babar pleaded with the booking clerk.

'Everyone has the same story. You should book the tickets in time so that you get the reservation and can travel well,' the booking clerk said, clearly unimpressed.

'Rs 3,200, ordinary tickets, for the general compartment,' the clerk said.

'*Badi meherbaani, duaon mein yaad rakhna, sir,*' Sohail said, jumping into the testy exchange that Babar was having with the clerk.

The Danapur–Pune Express left at 8.50 p.m. and would take thirty-one hours to reach Pune.

51

TERROR AT BVP HEADQUARTERS

'We were probably trained by the same set of ustaads at Bayt al-Mujahideen. Sahil, who taught you firing and marksmanship during the Daura-e-Khaas?' Babar asked.

'Ustaad Zakir. He knew so much. What a shooter, as if guns were an extension of his hands. He was probably on deputation from the ISI; he had the bearing of a typical fauji,' Sahil said.

'Ustaad Zakir. What a teacher! But very stern! I did so many extra rounds of the training-cum-football ground during a particular combat course in LeT conducted by him that I was more familiar with its features than even the designated maali,' Babar laughed.

'True,' Sahil agreed.

Babar was sitting with Sahil and Rohit in their room in the Aamantran Lodge in Pune's Budhwar Peth. 'What did you find during your survey of Himalaya Bhavan? What are the gaps we can exploit?' he asked, getting down to business.

'None on the surface. The complex is really big and has good perimeter security. There is a three-tier security system. If we can barge into the campus, break through the layers of guards and commandos, it would be a gold mine for us as the top leadership of BVP can be found there,' Rohit replied.

'How soon can we rent a big car? We will also need to rent two flats and arrange for police uniforms,' Babar said.

'I can get the uniforms,' Rohit volunteered.

'And I will get the car,' Sahil said. 'A friend of mine runs a garage here at Budhwar Peth. I will get a car from one of his mechanics who deals in stolen vehicles. But I may need Rs 1 lakh for that.'

'Fine. Please get a red beacon as well,' Babar said.

'There is a shop that sells props for film and theatre productions. I will get a dummy red beacon from there, but of course it won't work,' Rohit said.

'That is all right, brother. The siren is not required actually. It will only attract more attention. A red beacon is just to intimidate the policemen who are on duty at the barricades,' Babar said.

'Our three brothers who have come from Pakistan will lead the assault on the BVP headquarters. Let's check the place out again tomorrow, Rohit,' Babar said. 'I will also get the weapons tomorrow.'

Rohit nodded.

'Now note down the codes for this operation. The attack will be known as "match", targets are "wickets", fidayeen are "bowlers", weapons are "bat", the one who gets the weapons is the "batsman", the one who gets the fidayeen from Pakistan to Pune is the "captain", reconnaissance is "net practice", danger is "baarish",

Maharashtra ATCS and police are "umpire", Bangladesh is "mama ghar", bus is "aaram se", train is "maje se", bag is "kit", Delhi is "chachi ka ghar", Pakistan is "dadihaal", Raxaul is "cousin", Patna is "teacher", Kathmandu is "dost", Mumbai is "Stylebhai", Abu Dhabi is "Prakash", Nepal is "Ravi's house", flight is "bike", and Abu-Muzammil is "ghar ki baat",' Babar rattled off.

Rohit smiled. 'So much of cricket. These words remind me of the times spent on the cricket grounds during school and college.'

'*Match pe nazar rakho.*' Babar smiled back.

'Sahil, aren't you a computer professional?' Babar asked.

'Yes, sir,' Sahil said.

'Please see if you can get copies online of police IDs, even if inferior copies. Here are the copies of the passports of the three Pakistani brothers who came with me. See if you can make police IDs for them,' Babar said.

'I will try, janaab.'

After meeting with Rohit and Sahil, Babar went to a PCO in Baner to make a call to Abu Dhabi. The call was made to a 5,000-square-foot villa in Al Bateen Park on King Abdullah bin Abdulaziz Al Saud Street. The villa had been an LeT safehouse for the past decade and was under the control of operatives of Abu-Muzammil's setup.

'Irshad bhai, as-salaam-alaikum, Babar this side,' Babar said.

'Wa-alaikum-salaam, Babar bhai, please wait for a minute,' Irshad said and connected the call to Abu-Muzammil's number in Rawalpindi.

'Babar here, salaam. *Batsman kab aayenge?*' he asked, enquiring about the delivery of AK-47s, grenades and other weapons for the fidayeen.

'Go to the Namaste India Lodge at Swargate. Go to room number 107, you will meet Shafiq there. The bats for the match are kept there. *Bowlers thik hain?*'

'Yes, janaab. They are enjoying themselves but preparing hard. The match is a few days away and their only focus currently is the match,' Babar said.

'Umpires were seen?'

'They are sleeping and will come after the match,' Babar laughed.

Abu-Muzammil joined him.

'How did you get the bats? Are they in good shape?' Babar asked.

'They were used in two matches earlier, but they are new. They were in Hyderabad. Shafiq took a bus to Mumbai, then Pune. After the match, you have to return them to Hyderabad,' Abu-Muzammil said. 'The bowlers will go to Ravi's house?' he confirmed.

'Yes, I have made all the arrangements. *Pune se aaram se Stylebhai ke ghar.* Then on the same day *chachi ke ghar.* The next day, they will go to the teacher's house and from there to Ravi's house,' Babar said.

'Okay, good,' Abu-Muzammil said and ended the call.

Babar next went to the Namaste India Lodge to meet Shafiq, as instructed by Abu-Muzammil.

Shafiq was terse. 'From where?' he asked.

'*Ghar ki baat.* Prakash. I need the bats,' Babar said. He handed over the 'kit' to Shafiq.

After taking delivery of the 'bats', Babar, who was clad in cricket whites and had a baseball cap on, took a state transport bus from the bus stand opposite his hotel. He knew that public transport vehicles were only lightly checked by security personnel manning check posts on the streets and highways.

～

Rohit called up Shekhar directly and not Sawant, despite CTC's instructions not to do so. He used a PCO located in Kothrud, Pune. Such calls were allowed only in cases of an emergency and Rohit thought now was such a time.

'Hello?' Shekhar took the call after two rings.

'Trojan.'

'Speak,' Shekhar said.

'There isn't much time. The Lashkar conspiracy to hit Himalaya is in an advanced stage. Three specialists have arrived from Pakistan, others are here too in Pune. Sahil is here and so am I. The date is 11 February, time not decided,' Rohit said in one breath.

'Will they reach the targeted site in a vehicle? What kind of car? Will the gunmen spray bullets indiscriminately or do they plan to go for targeted killings? Will they throw bombs?' Shekhar asked.

'They will be driving a big sedan. The terrorists will be in fake police uniforms; the car will have a red beacon to evade checks and get easy access. They will be armed with AK-47s and plenty of grenades,' Rohit said.

'Will they hit and run or will they stand and fight till death?'

'Hit and run.'

'Why BVP?'

'Abu-Muzammil thinks BVP was part of the groups suspected of involvement in the 2002 Gujarat riots and that therefore its top leaders must pay. He calls it eye for an eye, revenge,' Rohit said.

'Revenge. Of course! As if they kill hundreds in India for the welfare of anybody! Their job, which the ISI decides for them, is to kill Indians in the name of any propaganda! Look out for any alarming signal or development,' Shekhar said and hung up.

Shekhar took the next flight to Pune. Within an hour of landing, he was in the cabin of the commissioner of Pune police, Rakesh Goswami.

'Good evening, sir. I am Shekhar Singh, from CTC Delhi, operations,' Shekhar introduced himself.

'Hello, Shekhar. We met in Delhi last year at an event at the President's house,' Goswami said.

'Yes, sir, that's correct. I was among the awardees that day,' Shekhar said.

'If I remember correctly, you bagged a medal for bravery? You had taken down three Pakistani terrorists during a raid at their hideout in Ramnagar in Uttarakhand two days before they were to launch a suicide attack on the state's secretariat where the chief minister sits,' Goswami said.

'Correct, sir, I must appreciate your memory.'

'What is the emergency in Pune?' Goswami came to the point.

'Sir, we have reliable information that the LeT is in the final stages of executing a major terrorist attack on BVP's headquarters here, in Keshavgiri, on 11 February. They could be looking at wiping out the entire top leadership which resides there, as we know.

'Three LeT Pakistani operatives, who are suspected of being armed with AK-47s and grenades, will attempt to break into the headquarters to kill as many as they can. If they are able to kill any big personalities, it will grab media attention globally and LeT will love that,' Shekhar said.

'Why BVP leaders?'

'As you know, sir, LeT's goal is to destroy India and kill as many Indians as they can. They want to make Muslim-dominated territories secede from India. To this end, they conduct operations all the time. For each operation, they cite a different reason. The BVP, which was under the scanner along with a clutch of other right-wing outfits for their alleged roles in the Gujarat riots, has been a target for the LeT. A hit on them could give it international publicity as well.'

'I see,' said Goswami, deep in thought. 'What do you have in mind to prevent this attack?'

'There is three-tier security around the BVP headquarters, sir. Please issue an order that from 9 to 12 February, no red beacons will be allowed on police cars. As the LeT fidayeen will be wearing police uniforms and will arrive in a sedan with a red beacon, it will be easy to spot them,' Shekhar said.

'Done. What else?'

'From Sadashiv Patel Marg in central Pune, a narrow 250-metre road, Deeksha Marg, splits off to the left. At the end of Deeksha Marg lies Himalaya Bhavan. The complex's entrance must be protected by commandos from the Swift Reaction Team of Maharashtra ATCS, to strengthen the deployed police personnel in outer layers. The security team must not allow any cars inside the Himalaya Bhavan campus, and all visitors must be frisked and put through metal detectors,' Shekhar said.

'Also, set up barricades along the road leading to Keshavgiri,' Shekhar continued. A senior police officer must be deployed at these barricades to check IDs, and commandos need to be there with their fingers on the triggers. The police officers at the barricades should be empowered to give orders to fire at suspicious persons if they do not obey orders and proceed towards Himalaya Bhavan. They should fire to injure them for preventive arrests or neutralize them if that is required. And finally, please have snipers positioned around the building to pluck out the terrorists if they can,' Shekhar said.

'I see you have covered the basics well. I will see what can be done and with immediate effect,' Goswami said.

At 10.30 a.m. on 11 February, the three fidayeen, dressed in police uniform and carrying a white kit bag, were waiting at a roadside eatery near the Sarasbaug Ganesh temple on Bajirao Street, which attracted hundreds of devotees daily.

Two days earlier, on 9 February, Babar had instructed the fidayeen to check out from their hotel on the evening of 10 February. Since 6 p.m. on 10 February, the three men had been staying in the waiting room of the Pune railway station. Babar had given them train tickets for Mumbai, scheduled for departure on 10 February. The tickets would give them access to the waiting room and create an alibi for the three fidayeen, as per Babar's calculations.

Also on 9 February, Babar had taken an 11 a.m. flight to Delhi, then hopped on to another flight to reach Dehradun to run a check on the preparations to mount the attack on IMA. He had used a forged voter ID card, which had his photograph but a fake name and address, to buy the air tickets.

Around 10.40 a.m. on 11 February, a white ambassador with a red beacon atop its roof pulled up outside the eatery. Rohit was in the driver's seat, accompanied by Sahil, who exited the car and gestured at the three fidayeen to get in. Rohit and Sahil walked away from the car, taking quick steps, and melted into the crowd. The fidayeen got into the car, with Sohail at the steering wheel praying for success in their mission.

As the fidayeen had learned during their triple reconnaissance of the target and the route to be taken to it, Bajirao Street met up with Patel Road. At the junction, one had to turn left on to Patel Road and keep going straight for another 1.5 kilometres to reach the point where the road turned left on to Deeksha Marg. At the end of Deeksha Marg was the entrance to Himalaya Bhavan.

The fidayeen had been told to bluff their way past the guards stationed at the entrance, telling them that they were policemen on an official visit for an emergency situation. Once inside the premises, they were to head to the first floor of the residential building, to flat number 107, which was the home of the BVP chief, eighty-one-year-old Dattatrey Shirke.

'Throw two grenades at the door of 107, storm in and kill the old bastard,' Babar had earlier told them when going over the plan of action for the attack. 'Kill anyone you see on the way in and on your way out. Each of you has four additional magazines. Drop the weapons into bushes or in a water body while escaping, but remember the disposal spots.'

'Now is the time for action. The time to pay your debt to the ummah. We offer our lives here, to avenge the atrocities committed against our mothers and sisters and elders and children,' Babar had told them.

The white ambassador, fitted with the dummy red beacon, zipped to the Patel Road junction in no time and turned left on to the road. Once the car hit Patel Road, however, it had to slow down to a crawl, thanks to the traffic. Twenty minutes later, they reached the point where the road turned towards Keshavgiri. Sohail and his associates were shocked to see barricades at the Deeksha Marg turn.

'From where have these appeared?' Sohail shouted to Akbar.

'How does it matter? It is a high-profile building, so this could be a routine deployment,' Akbar said. 'Stay calm.'

The car, with its red beacon, had caught the attention of the security men at the barricades. The men, some of whom were in the deep blue dungarees of the Swift Reaction Team commandos, were armed with automatics, AK-47s or MP-5s, their hawk-like gazes trained on the car.

'Sohail, some of the security men at the barricade seem to be commandos. Prepare to fire at them at will when they stop us,' Akbar said.

'Stop!' one of the security men at the barricade shouted as the ambassador neared it, gesturing wildly at it to stop. The others at the barricade trained their guns at the occupants of the car. The car came to a halt.

'Who are you?' a security man, who seemed like an officer, asked sternly.

'We are from the police headquarters. DCP Suraj Pawar sent us here on emergency work,' Sohail said, fishing out an ID card.

'I am DCP Suraj Pawar, and I did not send you here,' the officer took out his Glock pistol and pointed it at Sohail.

At this, Akbar and Irfan grabbed their AK-47s from the floor of the car and pressed the triggers. As soon as the security personnel saw Irfan and Akbar with their AK-47s, they opened fire at the car's occupants.

Rat-tat-tat … Rat-tat-tat … Rat-tat-tat … Rat-tat-tat

The AK-47s boomed. The fidayeen's bodies were punctured with holes and were oozing blood. Akbar's burst of fire had hit the DCP, who took five bullets in his right shoulder.

Ambulances and forensic experts began arriving at the site of the encounter. The fidayeen's bodies were frisked and then taken to a local government hospital, where they were declared brought dead on arrival by a senior doctor. The bodies were taken to the morgue to await autopsy. The car was searched thoroughly for incriminating objects and later seized. The DCP survived and was discharged from hospital a week later.

52

KARACHI IN MOURNING

'Good evening. This is Mark Dwight from the BBC. Four years after religious riots erupted in India's western state of Gujarat, the central government has for the first time published detailed data on the number of people killed. The junior home minister, S. Shankar, told Parliament that in all over a thousand lost their lives, 223 persons were reported missing and around 2,500 were injured. The riots were sparked by a fire on a train in Godhra in Gujarat that burnt to death fifty-nine passengers. The probe by Gujarat's state government said that a mob attacked the Godhra train, causing the fire and the subsequent riots.

'The state government under Chief Minister Ramkrushna Solanki paid out Rs 2.04 billion towards rehabilitation and relief measures, the minister told Parliament.

'In other news from South Asia, Bangladesh's prime minister ... '

The screen of the TV set, which was hung on a grey wall, flickered in the dim light. Barring the voice of the BBC news anchor, there was pin-drop silence in the room. LeT's operations chief Abu-Lakhvi, his second-in-command for Indian operations Abu-Muzammil, Abu-Muzammil's top aide Al-Wali, and Babar were present in the room, sitting opposite the TV screen, their unblinking eyes on Dwight.

Abu-Lakhvi sat erect on a large sofa made of sheesham wood with brown faux leather upholstery. Abu-Muzammil sat on a carpet on Abu-Lakhvi's right, his back against a wall. Al-Wali sat on the carpet too, with Babar seated next to him.

A month after the LeT's audacious, synchronized double attacks on India on 11 February at Dehradun's IMA and Pune's BVP headquarters had proved to be spectacular failures, the terror outfit's top leadership was yet to emerge out of the resultant sense of mourning.

Both the attacks, concluded this group in its deliberations over the past two days, were cases of 'near misses'. Whose fault was it then that the two attacks had not achieved their respective objectives: eliminating a large number of Indian Army officers and BVP office-bearers, including its chief, Shirke?

Both the attacks had been snuffed out at the entrances of the two targeted sites, causing embarrassment to the LeT's ability to orchestrate high-value strikes in what it called India's 'hinterland', referring to the rest of the country barring Jammu and Kashmir, whose 'liberation' was LeT's raison d'etre.

Abu-Lakhvi, during the threadbare analysis of the two operations, which had looked at how the preparations had been conducted at every stage by the LeT, had dubbed Abu-Muzammil, Al-Wali and Babar 'nikammay', good-for-nothing burdens on the organization.

'The Powai operation was done well even though we failed to kill more than two people. We killed a well-known US scientist, which must have shamed India before America and the "first world", as the white-skinned call themselves. The killing of the senior BASRC scientist too was a feat, as it would have adversely affected India's nuclear armament plans, and that is why our friends in the ISI personally reached out to me to offer their appreciation,' Abu-Lakhvi had said. 'And that is why I had said that all of you who are part of Abu-Muzammil's setup did well. I even promoted Babar as a token of my appreciation.

'But why did the IMA and Pune operations fail? The planning was good, the execution was good, but six fidayeen were killed as if they were sitting ducks. What do we have to show in return? Nothing. We could not kill even one of our targets,' Abu-Lakhvi had then raged.

'Is Pakistani blood so cheap? I suspect they got wind of our plans. So from now on, use satellite phones and landlines more than mobile phones to reduce the risk of somebody intercepting our conversations. As I keep saying, PCOs are the safest.'

Abu-Lakhvi had paused and stared intently at each man in turn before continuing. 'More importantly, is there any breach in LeT, whether in our structure in Pakistan or in India, including Kashmir? Do we have any spies of India amid us? Agents from R&IW or CTC?

'Let us hope these are just my suspicions. It is better to question ourselves and keep looking to rectify our weaknesses than be ignoramuses and strut around like foolish peacocks.'

It hadn't been said in so many words to Babar, but he felt that since he was an Indian, his commitment and integrity were being doubted by Abu-Lakhvi, which pained him.

The discussion in the room had gone on for three hours and had concluded only when Abu-Lakhvi had asked an aide to switch on the 7 p.m. BBC news broadcast. He did not like to miss the BBC news broadcasts, especially those at 7 p.m. and 11 p.m. He was of the view that the BBC represented the best of the UK's neoliberal school of thought, which backed Pakistan's stance on the 'disputed' status of Jammu and Kashmir.

The twelfth-pass Abu-Lakhvi also admired Dwight for his 'perfect pronunciation' and learned from it, another reason why he did not miss the 7 p.m. bulletin.

The room they were all sitting in was quite spacious, and was in bungalow number 30 D, named Clifton, in Karachi's Defence Colony. It was one of the eight LeT safehouses in Pakistan's commercial capital, which prided itself on its cosmopolitan culture. The city, which was dotted with skyscrapers, flyovers and serene seafronts, however, stayed in a virtual state of siege, with violence erupting on its streets and alleys among the 'mohajir' – the migrants – and sectarian militias and the local underworld.

Clifton was also one of the fifteen-odd addresses of Mumbai's fugitive underworld don Dawood Ibrahim, alias Muchchad, who had orchestrated the 1993 serial blasts in India's commercial capital with the help of the ISI. Dawood and a few other top accused in the blasts, namely, co-mastermind Tiger Memon, his brother Anees Kaskar and Javed Chikna had been on the run since then.

The mention of the 2002 Gujarat riots in Dwight's bulletin brought back the focus of those assembled in the room to their jihad. Abu-Lakhvi's terror outfit, along with its mentors in the ISI and the Pakistani establishment, had repeatedly exploited the incident to instigate and cajole Muslim Indian youth into rebellion and subversion. None uttered a word in the room, as Abu-Lakhvi and the others remain glued to the TV screen. After the news bulletin, there was a panel discussion, where a background on the riots was being given.

'Abu-Muzammil, we have to return to hitting India hard, to knock it out of its senses. It seems there is again a buzz in that country over the controversial Gujarat riots issue thanks to the disclosure of official figures by the government, four years after the incident,' Abu-Lakhvi finally said while sipping from a teacup. 'You can't let this opportunity go as well. Prepare, I want a plan. We meet here again at 6 p.m. tomorrow.'

∾

'BVP has a two hundred-acre campus in Naigaon, on the outskirts of Mumbai, named Kundan Sarvoday Sansthan, which is run in the name of an allied charitable entity. The campus is truly remarkable. Sixty per cent of the land is used to grow organic vegetables, fruits and medicinal herbs. There are renewable energy-tapping resources at the campus, including solar panels, windmills and hydroelectricity plants,' Abu-Muzammil addressed the men gathered in the Clifton safehouse the following evening.

Abu-Lakhvi, Al-Wali and Babar listened with rapt attention.

'NGOs for women, underprivileged children, Dalit workers and farmers run programmes at the campus on behalf of the charity's management. One of the NGOs working for women's empowerment has organized a grand felicitation ceremony on 25 March to honour a group of a hundred beneficiaries who are running small-scale industrial manufacturing units.

'The group will be felicitated by the chief minister of Gujarat, Ramkrushna Solanki, who has long been our target number one.

BVP chief Dattatrey Shirke will be on the dais too and so will ministers from Maharashtra and Gujarat. This is an opportunity that we cannot afford to miss,' Abu-Muzammil said.

Abu-Lakhvi felt a rush of excitement. 'It is the perfect opportunity to get some of our top targets. Imagine the sensation it will create among members of our community in India, Bangladesh and Pakistan if we manage to hit Solanki and Shirke. It will mean more recruits, support and funds for our war to liberate Kashmir from India's stranglehold,' he said gleefully.

'So, what is the plan?' he asked, turning to Abu-Muzammil.

The meeting continued for several hours, during which Abu-Muzammil laid out the entire plan in minute detail.

Al-Wali and Babar, it was decided, would assist Abu-Muzammil. They would rope in two sleeper modules in India, the one in Mumbai led by Atharv and the one in Delhi led by Rohit, as per the plan presented in the meeting.

After the meeting, Abu-Lakhvi called up his ISI handler and updated him about the meeting's deliberations. The ISI handler, a lieutenant general in the Pakistani army, Farooq Shah, told Abu-Lakhvi, 'Make sure you do not screw up this action like the IMA and Pune projects.'

'Not at all, janaab. It will all go well.'

'Get verifications done on your own; find out if you have moles inside your tanzeem. Use men who report only to you. And update me on this regularly.'

53

GUNNING FOR THE CM

'Good morning, janaab. Anant here.'

As directed by his LeT handlers, Anant was making the mandatory weekly call to his immediate commander, Al-Wali. Lashkar had devised such a protocol to monitor its agents in foreign lands and 'behind enemy lines', as it referred to India, to assign them tasks as part of ongoing operations and keep them motivated for jihad. Anant was at the Reay Road PCO that was used by Atharv to contact Al-Wali. It was around 10.30 a.m. on 14 March 2006.

'Good morning, brother,' said Al-Wali. 'Where is Atharv?'

'He is unwell, so he sent me to speak to you. He has typhoid.'

'Oh, sorry to hear. May the Almighty keep him safe and grant him a speedy recovery. How are the classes going in Mumbai?'

'Quite well, we are learning new things. I will convey your greetings to Atharv.'

'I have some work for you. How big is your flat? Some more brothers will be coming to Mumbai for sightseeing; can they stay with you?'

'Our flat is quite small, it can only accommodate three people. We are three already,' said Anant.

'Okay, then please arrange for a flat on rent for a fortnight. Make sure there is no CCTV on the premises. And it should have a garage big enough to accommodate a goods transport vehicle, like a minivan.'

'Consider it done. When should I take the room on rent?'

'From 15 March. The five brothers will arrive on the seventeenth. Pay the landlord half now and half later. But if he insists, pay him in full, that's okay. You'll need money. I will send Rs 5 lakh via Western Union. Send Nirav tomorrow to the Western Union kiosk at Zaveri Bazaar with his ID papers.'

'Done, I will update you tomorrow morning.'

'Leave for Kundan Sansthan, Naigaon. You were taught to conduct reconnaissance here, so use those skills there. Find out how secure the campus entrances are and the best ways to gain entry. Don't get caught.'

'Call me tomorrow, brother, with the details,' Al-Wali said and hung up.

Al-Wali is planning something big and ghastly at Kundan Sansthan, CTC must be told about it at once, Anant thought to himself as he dialled Somaiya's landline minutes after talking to Al-Wali.

Anant repeated the conversation he had had with Al-Wali to Somaiya, word for word.

'What are you saying, Anant? Those LeT bastards are planning to unleash another operation in Mumbai?'

'Yes, that is what it sounds like. Atharv is unwell, so Nirav and I will have to carry out Al-Wali's orders.'

'Fine. Also, I must alert you – Al-Wali is also known as Junaid to some of the recruits.'

'Okay. As Al-Wali – or Junaid – wants me to rent the room for the five brothers from 15 March for a fortnight, whatever grand attack they are planning will happen between 15 and 30 March.'

'Yes, that makes sense. Keep your eyes and ears open to find out whatever else you can. Did Al-Wali drop any hint whatsoever regarding what or who the target is this time?'

'Yes, some Kundan Sansthan in Naigaon is the target, where the fidayeen will storm in with heavy weaponry, it seems. I am yet to find out who will get targeted at Kundan Sansthan. I am going there now to conduct a reconnaissance as I have to report about the security arrangements to Al-Wali tomorrow.'

'Oh! What did you say, Anant? Kundan Sansthan, Naigaon? Isn't that the name of the BVP facility where the Gujarat CM and the BVP chief are scheduled to attend a function on 25 March? I read the news this morning!'

He added, 'Don't worry, keep up the good work. You may again save the precious lives of our countrymen, like the three times in the past. And, of course, give an inaccurate report to Al-Wali; do not identify the gaps in the security at the Naigaon campus. From Mumbai's northern city limits – that is the Dahisar toll plaza – Naigaon is some 20 kilometres away.'

'Yes, sir. Let's smash the LeT project again,' said Anant.

'Let's do that,' replied Somaiya.

At Himalayan Paradise, there was everything but mutton or chicken for Babar. The daily provisions were yet to arrive for the modest two-star hotel located on Jain Bazaar Road near Peer Mitha Bazaar in Jammu.

According to All India Radio's 8 a.m. news bulletin, a fierce encounter had broken out between the Indian Army's Rashtriya Rifles and LeT terrorists following a search and cordon operation around Nagrota. The search operation had been launched on the basis of intelligence that five recently arrived Pakistani terrorists were being given shelter in a village, Shakarpur.

But Babar was not waiting for the provisions truck to arrive, like the other hotel guests. Instead, he was waiting for Abu Saqlain. It was 14 March. There were just eleven days to go for LeT's attack on the Naigaon complex of the BVP.

Losing no time, Abu-Muzammil had on 13 March itself, the day the attack was conceived, sent Babar with Rehmat Shah, one of the attackers who had led the attack on IIS&T and had survived to tell the tale, to Jammu by flight.

Meanwhile, at Himalayan Paradise, Babar had booked two more rooms, telling the hotel's manager that he was part of a 'baraat' party for a 15 March wedding in the city. Al-Wali had used a satellite phone to call up LeT's Kashmir-based divisional commander, Abu Saqlain, who looked after Poonch and Rajouri, to deliver three fidayeen. One fidayeen, Rehmat, was there already with Babar for the Naigoan operation.

Al-Wali had directed Saqlain to give a cache of arms, ammunition and explosives – fifteen AK-47s, 35 kilos of the deadly military-grade explosive RDX and thirty grenades – concealed inside a medium-sized goods transport vehicle to Babar in Jammu.

'No problem, I will provide fidayeen and the materials by tomorrow in Jammu. I will draw from a stockpile that we created two years ago, inside a mountain cave deep inside a Poonch forest,' Saqlain had told Abu-Muzammil.

Since 1990, when LeT cadres began infiltrating into Jammu and Kashmir, the Lashkar had been creating several clandestine stores of weapons like AK-47s, explosives like RDX and grenades for use in their operations. Such stores optimized efficiency and provided weapons and explosives instantly for an operation. Otherwise, men and weapons were sent to India from Pakistan and Bangladesh via Kashmir, Nepal or Sri Lanka, which took time and involved a lot of risk.

At 3.45 p.m., Saqlain finally called Babar to inform him that he had arrived along with four fidayeen and asked for the keys to the rooms that Babar had booked for them.

As Babar began mumbling his thanks to Saqlain, the latter laughed and said, 'I am happy to be of any help to you, brother. You must be up to something truly big!'

Babar was unsure if Saqlain was taunting him about his last two failures, but then realized that in the secrecy-obsessed LeT, the left hand did not know what the right hand was up to.

'Thank you, commander sahib,' he said warmly.

Saqlain and the four fidayeen – Sakib, Saquib, Rehmat and Faroukh, from Gujranwala in western Punjab – had arrived in Jammu in a dark green Eicher van.

'The cache is concealed inside a fake ceiling above the driver's seat. The ceiling is rarely checked during searches,' Saqlain informed Babar. 'Good luck, brother.'

∽

At the Mumbai Police headquarters near Crawford Market in south Mumbai, Shekhar was sitting with the police commissioner, A.P. Saxena. He had just apprised the commissioner of what Somaiya had told him about the LeT's latest terror conspiracy.

The police chief, his forehead furrowed, was judging the time available to foil the terror plot and the best way to achieve that objective. He had already called the additional commissioner, Pulkit Narula, of the ATCS of Maharashtra Police. He, along with two assistant commissioners of police, would be supervising the investigations. One of the two ACPs was Sunil Deshmukh. Deshmukh had been with the counter-terror agency since its inception and possessed a wide repertoire of informants.

Shekhar and Saxena were now waiting for the counter-terror agency's officials to arrive.

Twenty minutes later, Narula and Deshmukh walked into Saxena's office.

Shekhar told the counter-terror agency's officers all that he knew about the Lashkar plot to kill Gujarat CM Solanki and BVP chief Shirke, who had both survived terrorist bids on their lives in the past. The two were scheduled to attend a function at Naigaon's Kundan Sansthan on 25 March, he told them.

Shekhar, of course, did not disclose anything about CTC's source of information or about Operation Trojan Horse. When prodded about the source of the information, he said, 'A friendly foreign ally told us.'

Saxena asked the two ACPs for their assessment of the situation as well as whether they would lead the operation to locate the five Lashkar terrorists.

'If the five terrorists are expected in Mumbai on or after 15 March, we should set up a watch for them at least two or three days prior to pick up any early signals or breakthroughs,' Deshmukh suggested. 'If they are coming in a vehicle, the vehicle could be carrying something crucial to their upcoming operation, like weapons, ammunition or explosives.

'I have a hunch that the fidayeen will come from Kashmir as the LeT has a cadre of trained fidayeen there. LeT usually uses Pakistani fidayeen, under the assumption that Indian operatives are not that motivated to make the "supreme sacrifice". Such a team can come from Kashmir on short notice,' Deshmukh said.

'What if the fidayeen are already in Mumbai or Pune?' Saxena asked.

'I will ask for details on vehicles that leave for Mumbai from several states, including Jammu and Kashmir, Punjab, Andhra Pradesh, Rajasthan, Uttar Pradesh, Bihar and Madhya Pradesh from 15 March onwards. There are several CCTV-fitted toll booths at interstate check posts en route to Mumbai, and if we have the suspects' profiles, it will help,' Deshmukh said.

'Gentlemen, we have a hunch that one of the five terrorists who will come to Mumbai is a man known just as Babar. This is because he has had the experience of operating here in the past too. CTC has a sketch of him, based on witness accounts. Babar is LeT's Nepal-based commander whose job it is to execute, coordinate and support terror attacks in India,' said Shekhar.

'Babar is the one who orchestrated the IIS&T attack in Mumbai, then the attacks on IMA and the BVP headquarters in Pune. For the IIS&T attack, he used the cover name of Shrikant Joshi. We don't know if Babar is an Indian or a Pakistani, but in any case he must have a Pakistani passport. I will ensure that Babar's sketch is sent immediately to all the check posts that fall on the routes taken for Mumbai,' he added.

'Terrific, please provide us with copies of Babar's sketch and any other leads you may have as we proceed,' said Narula.

∽

A pair of military-grade binoculars with night-vision capability by his side, Deshmukh was waiting with three others inside a black Tavera SUV, with tinted glasses, on National Highway 48, which connects western Gujarat with Mumbai and the rest of Maharashtra. It was around 3 a.m. on 16 March.

The officers had been there since 15 March, taking turns in twelve-hour shifts to keep a watch on the vehicles coming from the Bhilad checkpoint in Valsad district in Gujarat. Deshmukh's team had taken position near Talasari, which was barely eight kilometres from Bhilad.

Deshmukh's phone started buzzing. It was Shekhar. It must be about something urgent, thought Deshmukh.

'The registration number has been confirmed. They are using a Punjab licence plate, number PB-03-MN-6867. It's an Eicher van, colour deep green,' Shekhar informed him.

'The Bhilad check post has CCTV cameras and Babar has been identified. He is sitting next to the driver of the van. There are three other youths in the back seat. Be careful, and don't hesitate to shoot them first, Mr Deshmukh – though catching them alive will give us tremendous leads.'

'Understood, sir. We will do our best,' Deshmukh said.

After crossing the Bhilad checkpost, Babar told Saquib to pull over to the side of the highway. He got out of the van, saying, 'I will carry on in a cab, around 500 metres ahead of you, to alert you if there is any danger. If you see the emergency lights of my cab go on, you should stop and take a diversion or a U-turn, whatever may be possible at that point,' he said.

The men in the van waited as Babar hired a white Wagon R cab from a nearby taxi stand and drove away, taking care, however, to stay about 500 metres ahead of the Eicher van.

But Babar missed spotting the black Tavera that was parked on the service road off the highway and passed by it. When the dark green Eicher van came within 200 metres of the Tavera, Deshmukh, who was watching the highway through his binoculars, shouted, 'Our target has arrived, that green van far away is what we are looking for!'

Deshmukh and his colleagues took up positions along vehicles parked on both sides of the highway and waited for the Eicher van to come within the firing range of their AK-47s and Glock pistols.

When the van was only 100 metres away, Deshmukh and two other officers stepped on to the road and gestured at the van to stop. Saquib, who had seen them the moment the officers came on to the road, accelerated instead. Outsmarted, Deshmukh and his colleagues jumped back into their Tavera and began chasing the Eicher van. Five kilometres on, Deshmukh got a clear view of the Eicher van and he let loose a volley of AK-47 bullets at one of its tyres.

The van's rear tyres took the shots, causing the wobbling van to veer off the road and turn turtle.

Deshmukh's team reached the van and pointed their guns at the vehicle, then began extricating the occupants one by one. The fidayeen had all sustained minor concussions and were groggy.

Thanks to the impact of the accident, the cover concealing the cavity in which the weapons cache was stashed came loose. A shower of AK-47 ammunition came cascading out, even as Deshmukh was dialling Narula to update him about the interception. He requested the bomb disposal and detection squad and a forensics team to be sent as soon as possible to handle the cache and gather evidence.

After the bomb disposal squad arrived, the cavity was opened up entirely. The search yielded fifteen AK-47s, thirty-five kilos of RDX and thirty grenades. The ATCS officers were stunned to see the deadly stockpile that was being brought into Mumbai to unleash bloodshed and destruction. In the 1993 serial blasts, only twenty-seven kilos of RDX had been used, killing 257 people and destroying dozens of buildings.

The four fidayeen, who were barely conscious, were taken into ATCS custody and rushed to Parel's KEM Hospital. The four would be questioned about the details related to their targets and the conspiracy, the masterminds and the source of the cache. Most importantly, they would be asked about the whereabouts of Babar, who had slipped out of the grasp of ATCS and CTC. He had managed to do so for the fourth time over the last three months.

Deshmukh then called up the Mumbai Police commissioner and Shekhar to update them. The fact that Babar had evaded the police net yet again irked both of them as by now they knew that Babar had the capability to rejig the LeT operation to deal a heavy blow despite the setback dealt to it.

54

A SUMMONS TO KARACHI

Babar realized he had lost the Eicher van, which was supposed to stay only a few hundred metres behind his Wagon R cab, and decided to take a U-turn to find out what was wrong.

As the cab took the next U-turn, Babar's eyes wandered down the highway and he saw the Eicher van standing on its head a little distance ahead. Policemen carrying AK-47s and pistols were swarming around it. An ambulance stood near the van. He could see the four fidayeen in the back of the ambulance. They seemed dazed and hurt.

The precious cache of weapons, ammunition and explosives they had brought to Mumbai for the operation was strewn all over the highway. The arms were being collected, piece by piece, and taken to a blue police wagon parked nearby. The sight filled Babar with a sense of doom and acute disappointment. All the planning and effort behind the operation had come to naught, he thought.

The operation was blown. He needed to retreat and retrieve whatever was not lost yet, he thought. He was worried about how Abu-Lakhvi would react to this debacle.

'Drop me at the Bhilad check post on the Gujarat border. My friends are stuck, one of them has fallen ill there,' Babar told the cab driver coolly.

After crossing the Bhilad check post, Babar hired another cab for Surat airport, Gujarat's second busiest after Ahmedabad. The cab took around two hours to reach the Surat airport, which was around 95 kilometres away. Once there, Babar bought a ticket for a noon flight to Delhi. He used fake identity documents in the name of Dipankar Bose as his earlier assumed identity, Shrikant Joshi, had been exposed in the IIS&T attack.

On reaching Delhi, he would catch a Nepal Airlines flight for Kathmandu, his operational base. From there, he would take an Emirates flight to Abu Dhabi, and then switch to another flight to reach Karachi. By taking such a circuitous route, Babar would be doing what he had been trained to do by the LeT – avoiding any links with Pakistan to the extent possible.

Hungry and shaken, Babar bought a coffee and a chicken wrap from an eatery at Surat airport after purchasing the ticket. The disastrous end to the ambitious operation had left him dazed. He knew there would be consequences in Karachi.

More than the loss of the cache, which must be worth at least Rs 2–3 crore, Abu-Lakhvi would feel the loss of the four trained fidayeen. Babar knew the enormous resources and manpower Abu-Lakhvi spent to prepare just one fidayeen.

But for now, he focused on sipping his coffee and tucking into the chicken wrap. It gave him a moment of respite from the crisis.

A few minutes later, his thoughts wandered back to his last three operations, all of which had ended in failure. Six fidayeen had been gunned down. Four, including the IIS&T attacker Rehmat, were in the custody of the Maharashtra ATCS, along with a weapons stockpile that could have enabled at least ten more attacks in India against its security forces and VIPs. He would have to face the wrath of Abu-Lakhvi. Babar panicked at the thought.

∽

'How did the Maharashtra ATCS come to know of our consignment's entry into Maharashtra via the Bhilad check post?' Abu-Lakhvi asked sharply. His forehead was creased and his eyes were bloodshot.

'The checkpoint is located at a major gateway between Maharashtra and Gujarat and is a sensitive spot as far as the entry and exit of suspicious persons and consignments are concerned,' Babar said without flinching.

'But why was the ATCS, an anti-terror force, monitoring the check post? I can understand if it was just a police team,' Abu-Lakhvi said.

'I have heard that ATCS is also tasked with intercepting narcotics and counterfeit currency,' Babar said. 'Also, the consignment was handed over by Saqlain's unit in Kashmir, and we don't know if they are under surveillance, which could have led to the bust at Bhilad. Perhaps men and material leaving Kashmir are under routine surveillance.'

'You could have a point there,' Abu-Lakhvi conceded. 'I have alerted Saqlain to see if there is a black sheep in our tanzeem in Kashmir, or if we are being tracked at some level unknowingly.'

Abu-Lakhvi was meeting with Babar at Lashkar's Clifton safehouse in Defence Colony in Karachi.

'Abu-Muzammil, see if we can move men and material into India's hinterland from other transit points instead of Jammu and Kashmir, which is crawling with Indian spies and security personnel,' Abu-Lakhvi instructed. 'Could it be that there is a breach elsewhere? Abu-Muzammil? Babar? Al-Wali?' he mused.

Abu-Lakhvi was worried and livid at the latest failures. Four Pakistani LeT operatives were in the custody of the ATCS in Mumbai after being caught with a massive cache of arms, ammunition and explosives. The only other such instance, Abu-Lakhvi had been reminded by his ISI handler, Lieutenant General Shah, was after the 1993 Bombay serial blasts, when 1,500 kilos of RDX had been seized. The 1993 consignment was part of the stock that had been shipped to Bombay from Karachi by the ISI and a smugglers' cartel in the wake of the demolition of Babri Masjid.

'How have the Indian recruits been in the field? Is there any reason to doubt their commitment to LeT and Pakistan?' Abu-Lakhvi asked.

'They have been committed and steadfast. I can't think of a reason to suspect them,' Abu-Muzammil said emphatically. He considered the five Indian recruits – Atharv, Nirav, Anant, Rohit and Sahil – to be valuable assets in his setup. Unlike typical Pakistani LeT operatives, the Indian recruits were all educated and understood their responsibilities well, a fact that Abu-Muzammil had often mentioned in his discussions with Abu-Lakhvi and Al-Wali.

'Yes. But the fact is that from the time they have been made operational in India – and I am not accusing them of anything, at least for now – Lashkar-e-Taiba has suffered costly failures, including the loss of precious trained fidayeen and war stores. Is there any connection between their entry and our downward slide? We should raise the question and do the due diligence in this regard,' Abu-Lakhvi said.

'*Shikast pe shikast pe shikast*,' he murmured, almost to himself. Then, as if coming to a decision, he said, 'Abu-Muzammil, call the five Indians back to Pakistan. They need to explain to us what went wrong in the last three operations.'

'Ji janaab.'

Abu-Lakhvi then turned to Babar. 'I want you to be part of the scrutiny.'

He did not make it clear, however, if Babar was also under the scanner. Would he be there to appraise the five Indians' performance along with Abu-Lakhvi and the others, or would he be appraised himself?

'Babar, stay at Bayt al-Mujahideen for a few months. Help us plan a few operations from here. Also, Abu-Muzammil will show you our two electronic explosives laboratories there. You should learn how to make bomb timers and switches,' Abu-Lakhvi said.

∾

'Anant, how are you? *Kaam kharab hua*. You need to lie low. Seniors are asking questions. They are also worried about your safety as we have been facing failures, one after another,' Al-Wali spoke softly.

'*Ji, janaab*,' Anant said. He was making the mandatory call to LeT, although Atharv, the designated contact person to interface with Al-Wali, was better. In fact, he had emptied a few bottles of beer with Anant and Nirav the previous night to celebrate the seizure of LeT's cache at Bhilad by the Maharashtra ATCS. Operation Trojan Horse, as Sawant had said, was truly in 'play'.

'Bhai, come to Karachi. Go to Patna and then Raxaul. Cross into Nepal and fly to Karachi via UAE. We need to discuss why we have been failing continuously over the last few months. The flaws, if any, need to be spotted and dealt with. Only then will you and I be able to wage jihad in India,' Al-Wali said. 'I will also assign you a very sensitive work once you meet me,' he lied to ensure Anant did not get alarmed.

'*Ji, janaab*. I will convey your instructions to Atharv. As you know, those in custody here are singing like parrots. There is still a state of high alert. There is enhanced surveillance on the country's key entry and exit routes. We need to be careful when coming to you,' Anant explained, trying to be reasonable and not defiant.

'Hundred per cent. I am glad you are using the training we gave you to think on your feet. But don't delay too much; come here after a week,' Al-Wali said and hung up abruptly.

Anant quickly dialled Somaiya.

'Al-Wali wants to meet us in Karachi to find out why their operations have ended in disaster one after another of late,' Anant informed him. 'He is going to give an important assignment too.'

'What is the assignment?'

'Al-Wali did not say anything about it.'

'Okay, but sit tight for now. I must first consult with Shekhar sir,' Somaiya said.

Shekhar was not happy about the news Somaiya gave him.

'No, the boys must not go to Pakistan. The LeT is probably suspicious of their five Indian recruits. Multiple LeT operations have of late met with spectacular failure. We knew what they were up to and the CTC could destroy their missions. Our agents shot them in their heart and Abu-Lakhvi's fury is understandable. They will be watching every move of all the new recruits to try and spot a leak,' Shekhar was adamant.

'What's the harm in going there, sir? The LeT is insisting that the boys appear in Karachi, and not going there will further raise their suspicions,' Somaiya said.

'Tell the team to keep delaying their departure on one pretext or another, but not to say directly that they won't go there,' said Shekhar. 'Abu-Lakhvi wants to kill these five recruits, our agents. That is why they must not go. I hope I have answered your question, Somaiya ji.'

'Yes, sir,' said Somaiya, his voice heavy with worry.

'Somaiya ji, let me also tell you that I already knew our five agents were in mortal danger before you called me,' Shekhar said.

'How?'

'Two days ago, thanks to technical surveillance, CTC nabbed a Pakistani Lashkar terrorist in Ghaziabad,' Shekhar said.

'Then?'

'The rascal, Ali Reza, from Sialkot, was a hard nut to crack, but eventually he broke. He had been assigned to conduct surveillance on Rohit and Sahil by none other than Abu-Lakhvi himself. Abu-Lakhvi kept Abu-Muzammil, Al-Wali and Babar out of the loop on this operation to conduct surveillance on their Indian recruits, our boys. The fact that Abu-Lakhvi sidestepped Abu-Muzammil and his entire setup shows that he is very serious about verifying if Rohit and Sahil are genuine jihadis, and he doesn't trust Al-Wali and Abu-Muzammil to do the job.

'Reza was seen loitering around the cyber café that Rohit and Sahil run as their front business in Ghaziabad. He was spotted by one of our surveillance teams and subsequently nabbed.'

'What exactly was Reza up to there?'

'Abu-Lakhvi had asked him to verify details about Rohit and Sahil – if they actually run a cyber café, if they live at the address that they had provided to the LeT. The recruits are under the scanner, and it does not look good. Reza said the LeT has been suffering losses and failures, and they are checking for breaches.'

'Understood, sir. I will tell Anant and Rohit to be careful and to do whatever they can to avoid walking into the lion's den,' Somaiya reassured his boss.

55

A SERIES OF BOMBINGS

The stone courtyards and steps encircling the old Hanuman temple at Dashashwamedh Ghat by the river Ganga in Uttar Pradesh's Varanasi were packed to the brim with devotees. It was around 4 p.m. on a February evening in 2005.

Dashashwamedh is among the eighty-four such ghats along a seven-kilometre stretch on the banks of the Ganga. It comes alive before sundown, with the Ganga aarti being performed by young pundits dressed in saffron every evening. The aarti is marked by the chanting of hymns in Sanskrit, the sight of flaming lamps and the smell of sandalwood and ghee, making for a mesmerizing experience for visitors and devotees.

On this particular evening, as the Vedic chants rang out over the water, two booming explosions rattled the surroundings, followed by shrieks, wailing and panicked voices.

The police initially attributed the explosions to the accidental bursting of a liquefied petroleum gas cylinder in an adjacent tea kiosk. Subsequent forensic findings, however, indicated that the blast was caused by IEDs. It was suspected that the IEDs were made of ammonium nitrate and iron nails. Two bombs, packed in aluminium containers, had been clandestinely planted by the perpetrators. The police later changed their stand and called it a 'terror strike'. They suspected the involvement of the LeT, though they had no hard evidence to confirm this.

A few weeks later, there was another terror incident in Uttar Pradesh. Twelve people were killed and dozens injured when a blast ripped apart a coach of the Shramjeevi Express near Jaunpur railway station. Forensic tests indicated the use of military-grade RDX in the bomb, which was hidden in the compartment's toilet.

According to eyewitness accounts reported in the media, two young men had boarded the train at Jaunpur with a white suitcase and leapt off shortly thereafter without it. The explosion had followed soon. The media reported that the police had no definite leads, though they were investigating the involvement of the LeT and Bangladesh's Harkat-ul-Jihad-al-Islami (HuJI), which had a following in certain pockets of Bangladesh.

Two days before Diwali in October 2005, blasts tore through the shopping precincts of Paharganj and Sarojini Nagar in Delhi and in a bus at Govindpuri in south Delhi. The blasts killed sixty-two people and injured at least 210. Investigators suspected that pressure-cooker bombs had been used in Paharganj and Sarojini Nagar, and a tiffin-bomb in Govindpuri.

In March 2006, a series of blasts ripped through Varanasi's Sankat Mochan Hanuman Temple and the cantonment railway station, killing twenty-one people and injuring over a hundred. It was suspected that pressure-cooker bombs were used. One of the bombs was kept in the waiting room of the railway station.

All these blasts took place in northern India – the national capital Delhi and the country's most populous state, Uttar Pradesh, in particular – killing and maiming innocent civilians. The bombs were planted in crowded public places and sites of worship. The investigating agencies did not have any clear leads on the identities of the culprits or their motives.

No one claimed responsibility for the series of blasts, which were probably orchestrated by two sets of terror outfits, and CTC was worried about the need to unmask the new masterminds. Initially, LeT also did not know the exact identities of those who were responsible and later told its members, including Atharv and Rohit, to not talk about them. Al-Wali, though, indicated to Atharv once that some ISI-controlled cells most probably could be behind the blasts. But he did not have any actual information on this. Abu-Lakhvi would periodically probe Atharv, fishing for any scrap of information that the latter may have acquired on the subject.

In one of the weekly telephone calls with Atharv, Al-Wali handed over the phone to Abu-Lakhvi after a few cursory queries.

'How are you Atharv? How are your studies?' Abu-Lakhvi said.

'We are well here, thanks to your best wishes.'

'Brother, when did you go to Varanasi? To Dashashwamedha Ghat?' Abu-Lakhvi asked him.

'I have not gone to Varanasi in my life, janaab.'

'It's okay; you can tell me if you went.'

'I have never been there, janaab.'

'So, what about the Shramjeevi Express?'

Abu-Lakhvi was being indirect, but Atharv was not on the same page, it appeared.

'If you mean that … ? No, janaab, those two blasts were not our work.'

'Oh? I thought they were by your team. I asked Abu-Muzammil about them, and he said he will get back with all the facts. I will find out then who is behind them if it's not us,' Abu-Lakhvi declared before hanging up.

∾

'Hello, Atharv.' It was Shekhar who answered the call on his office landline. Atharv had called him on Somaiya's instructions.

'Sir, you wanted to speak to me?' Atharv said.

'I asked Somaiya if the LeT was behind the blasts in UP and Delhi. The Dashashwamedh blast, the blast in a coach of the Shramjeevi Express, the Sankat Mochan temple and the Delhi Diwali blasts.'

'Sir, my team was not involved in those blasts.'

'Have you heard anything at all about the orchestration of these blasts?'

'No, sir. Not even a whisper.'

'This is disturbing. It means that we are dealing with another powerful terrorist outfit, which is probably sponsored by Pakistan's ISI. The way the blasts were carried out at carefully selected, crowded spots indicates that these terrorists are well-trained, stocked with weapons and know how to kill with deathly efficiency.'

'Yes, sir, it seems that way.'

'Atharv, we are dealing with a new, unknown entity. But what is troubling me also is the fact that you know nothing about it. You are trained to be one of them, and you must be one up on them. You are supposed to be my eyes and ears in the Pakistan-sponsored terror factories, and yet we are drawing a blank on these blasts. What is the point of running an elaborate, time-consuming and expensive covert mission like Operation Trojan Horse then?'

Shekhar was venting his frustration at not having any solid leads on the blasts' perpetrators even as the weight of expectations from the public and the government increased. The media was skinning the counter-terror and intelligence organizations for their 'failure' to prevent terror. Shekhar hung up abruptly.

Minutes later, Shekhar received a call from Rohit.

'Rohit, do you have any idea who was behind the blasts in Delhi and UP? Are you and LeT behind them? Did you help them?' Shekhar shot the questions at him.

'No, sir, my unit did not provide any assistance whatsoever. I have no idea about these blasts actually.'

'Well, get on with your work then. You are supposed to know about and tell me such things. Information-gathering to protect India is what we do for our bread and butter. We are not nine-to-five file pushers.' Shekhar banged the phone down.

'Rohit, were you there for the Sankat Mochan and Sarojini Nagar works?' Abu-Lakhvi asked.

'No, sir. Sahil and I had no role to play in those blasts,' Rohit said.

'Were you there at the Varanasi ghat or at the Shramjeevi Express events?'

'No, janaab.'

'So, the Lashkar-e-Taiba, which prides itself on being the premier anti-India terrorist organization based in Pakistan, a status that guarantees it enormous funds from the ISI for conducting operations, has no clue who is behind the spate of bombings that have killed dozens in India's heartland.' Abu-Lakhvi was baffled and embarrassed at not knowing who the perpetrators were.

'Fine, Rohit. What about the work given to you in Dehradun?' Abu-Lakhvi changed tack seamlessly. He was referring to the reconnaissance work Abu-Muzammil had tasked Rohit with. He was to scope out Dehradun's Indian Institute of Petroleum Research.

'I did that, sir. The place is full of security personnel,' Rohit said.

Rohit had told Abu-Muzammil that the institute had enhanced, five-tier security, which would make it difficult to enter the premises for an attack. Abu-Muzammil had dropped the plan, which Abu-Lakhvi did not know.

'Send your list of the next targets,' Abu-Lakhvi said and hung up.

All Lashkar handlers asked for lists from ground operatives. The 'list' was a reference to an operative's own choice of targets.

'Yes, sir,' Rohit said.

∾

'Babar, what is this new terror outfit behind the blasts in Dashashwamedh Ghat, Shramjeevi Express, Sankat Mochan temple and Delhi's Govindpuri and Sarojini Nagar?' Abu-Lakhvi asked.

That Abu-Lakhvi had called him directly, instead of communicating through Al-Wali or Abu-Muzammil, alarmed Babar. Usually, Abu-Lakhvi's instructions were relayed to him via Al-Wali, Abu-Muzammil or the latter's aide, Ibrahim.

Abu-Lakhvi had used his satellite phone to call on Babar's newly acquired satellite phone – which by then had become the preferred mode of communication globally for organized crime/narcotics/terror syndicates to avoid interception by government agencies. A month earlier, Abu-Muzammil had sent a Thuraya brand satellite phone set to Babar.

'No idea, janaab. I thought it's us or the Jaish-e-Mohammed,' Babar said, surprised by the question.

Abu-Lakhvi then decided he would check with ISI's Shah if it was the Pakistani spy agency that was running a newly spawned terror outfit on its own – if it had only Indian members to provide Pakistan the space to deny any link with the terror it was sponsoring in India. Shah confirmed to Abu-Lakhvi in a meeting they subsequently had that the latter's suspicions were correct about the blasts in India having been orchestrated by a new ISI-run terror entity. But Shah did not part with any more details and instead warned Abu-Lakhvi against meddling in the spy agency's affairs.

56

BREACHING THE BASTION

'Three of your key operations bombed spectacularly two years ago, in 2006, costing the lives of our precious fidayeen and crores of rupees that went into the planning. They brought us infamy and ridicule, Babar, and that rankles the most. As our Nepal commander, you did perform with diligence and competence, I must say, though. You have helped us handle several sensitive operations that brought us success.

'But, as far as individual operations are concerned, I hope you get back to your successful ways. The IIS&T attack must not be your last act of glory as a planner and organizer for Lashkar,' the rasping voice with a thick Punjabi accent boomed. It was Abu-Lakhvi calling Babar directly again, and he was in full flow.

'Listen carefully, Babar, here is your chance to redeem yourself. I am giving you an operation and the men and material required to pull it off. I am entrusting to you the charge of two Indian jihadis, Sohrab and Janbaaz Ansari, who are from the Pilibhit district of Uttar Pradesh and have been with us for the past few years. These two are cousins and have done combat training with us in Pakistan – the Daura-e-Aam, the Daura-e-Khaas and even the advanced Daura-e-Ribat at Bayt al-Mujahideen,' Abu-Lakhvi said.

'Ji janaab, I am ready to do whatever is required,' said Babar, relieved that he was not to be punished for his failures.

'You are to organize a devastating attack on a convoy of Indian Army vehicles carrying soldiers near Bareilly in Uttar Pradesh, which is a big strategic hub. It has a few regimental headquarters, an air force station and a British-era cantonment,' Abu-Lakhvi explained the mission.

'Kill as many as possible. The attack should put the fear of death in each Indian soldier's heart. The ones passing through Bareilly are those returning to their bases from Kashmir. Just imagine the buzz it will create internationally if we are able to kill fifty soldiers returning from Kashmir duty.'

'Yes, it will certainly make everyone sit up and take notice and show the world we mean business,' said Babar. 'What about the two Indian jihadis? Where are they now?'

'We have settled Sohrab and Janbaaz at Bhairava, the gateway to Nepal at the Indo-Nepal border. Over the last two years, we helped Sohrab establish himself and earn a livelihood there so he could melt into local society. We first bought him two trucks to run a transport business. Later, we helped him set up a manufacturing unit for shoe soles.

'Twice we tasked him to kill Kanwariyas, who are Shiva devotees and travel great distances on foot to offer holy water to the Shiva linga, but they could not kill a single pilgrim. The plan was leaked, the man ferrying AK-47s from Kashmir was killed in a police encounter in Badaun in Uttar Pradesh, and the security forces increased their presence on the route.

'Their trucks are currently more valuable to us than the two cousins,' Abu-Lakhvi laughed. He was someone who hardly ever laughed, yet today he did. What was so special about today, Babar thought.

'They will meet you today in Kathmandu, at 4 p.m., at our safehouse in Battisputali. Be there on time. I didn't want to compromise your residential address, so I did not send them there.'

Babar had successfully set himself up in Kathmandu by this time. As part of his cover, he had enrolled himself in an engineering course at Paramount Computer Academy. A small sum of 1,000 rupees had ensured that he was not required to furnish documents for the admission. Using his student ID card, which bore the name of Sanjay Sharma, he had procured a voter's card with the help of the academy's guard, who knew somebody in Nepal's Office of Voters' Registration. Using the voter's card, he had rented a two-bedroom flat in Bhimsengola, which was a short distance from the academy.

'Yes, janaab, fine,' Babar said.

'You can get the weapons you will need from Saqlain in Kashmir now. Saqlain checked and found no breach in his setup during the verifications ordered by me after the Mumbai operation to kill the chief minister of Gujarat bombed,' Abu-Lakhvi said.

'Abu-Muzammil will send you two Pakistani fidayeen from Baithul for the Bareilly operation.'

'Ji, janaab. And I will send Sohrab to Commander Saqlain.'

57

THE LAST HURRAH

'What is your problem, why are you such a shame upon Lashkar-e-Taiba's Indian operatives? There are so many Indian mujahideens in the LeT and they have always carried out audacious, complicated attacks. You guys can't do even a simple recce properly? Speak up!' LeT's Nepal commander came to the point brutally.

'We tried our best, sir, but could not achieve our goal,' Sohrab said.

'That is what I am asking. Why? It's not like the stars of the universe are conspiring against you,' Babar snarled, then turned to Sohrab's cousin Janbaaz.

'Janbaaz miyan, are you just brave in name or do you have it in you as well?' Babar mocked him.

'Sir, please test us just once,' Janbaaz offered, blood rushing to his ears in response to Babar's biting sarcasm.

'I will give you a final opportunity to earn some respect for the first time in LeT,' Babar said.

'Sohrab, have you been to Rajouri and Poonch in Kashmir in your truck?' Babar asked.

'Yes, twice, for operational reasons. To transport something there and get something back from there,' Sohrab said.

'How did you manage the trips?'

'I drove my truck, which has an all-India permit for transporting goods, to Kashmir to meet Commander Abu Saqlain. I carried wooden trinkets and carpets, which were financed by Al-Wali sir, to Kashmir, and brought AK-47s and RDX that Commander Saqlain gave me back from there and dropped them off at locations in Uttar Pradesh.'

'Now you are talking like a trained professional,' said Babar.

He whipped out his blue satellite phone – which startled the two 'failed' jihadis as they had never seen such a communication device before – and made a call.

'Babar here. As-salaam-alaikum, Saqlain sahab. Do you remember Sohrab bhai?' He listened for a moment, then continued, 'Yes, that one only. He will be coming to you in four days, on the direction of commander Abu-Lakhvi. Please provide him with two AK-47s and the two Pakistani fidayeen that the commander will send you in the next two days.' Babar paused, then said, 'Shukriya, commander sahib,' before hanging up.

He turned to Sohrab. 'As you heard, you need to leave for Kashmir in two days. I am giving you Rs 50,000 to fill your truck with whatever can be easily traded there. Come back with the two fidayeen and the two AK-47s that he will provide you with. Hide the two fidayeen and the weapons near Bareilly or in your hometown of Pilibhit. Take a house on rent for three months there. In fact, you let it be, Janbaaz will take the house on rent.'

'Yes, janaab,' Sohrab said.

'Janbaaz, go to Pilibhit, take a flat there for the operation. Find out the best day and location to conduct a massive suicide attack on the Indian Army convoy passing through Bareilly, which has a huge presence of armed forces personnel through the year. There is an Indian Air Force station there and also a unit of the Indian Army,' Babar said.

'I will set out today,' Janbaaz said.

Janbaaz and Sohrab left the flat immediately after collecting the cash from Babar.

∽

'Atharv, what's happening? What is brewing in Abu-Lakhvi's terror kitchen?' Somaiya asked.

'There are no fresh instructions about any operation,' Atharv said.

'There must be something?'

'I have been asked to study the perimeter security of the Bharat Atomic Science Research Centre in Mumbai. I have done a recce of the site twice since last week.'

'Okay, good, that's something. Who will handle the operation?'

'Al-Wali may ask me to handle it in case they like my report on the chinks in the security.'

'What are they focusing on?' Somaiya asked.

'I have been asked to concentrate on the security layers around the residential accommodations of the scientists and staff inside the BASRC campus.'

'Bastards!' Somaiya exclaimed. 'Tell them the security is tight.'

'It is indeed watertight, and I have told them already.'

'Good. Remain alert. Where is Babar?'

'No idea.'

'Based on the arrested fidayeen Rehmat Shah's interrogations, we put the Clifton bungalow in Karachi under technical surveillance. The residents have been using mobile phones, landlines and also two satellite phones. One of them uses the satellite phone, specially to place calls to Kathmandu.

'I believe that it is Abu-Lakhvi himself at the Karachi end and Babar at the Kathmandu end, and they are planning a big operation against the army in Bareilly. The weapons and fidayeen are coming from Abu Saqlain in Kashmir.'

'This is valuable information, sir.'

'Yes, but we need more details. Let me know if you hear anything.'

'Yes, sir.'

Somaiya hung up.

58

ATTACKING THE CRPF CITADEL

Fifteen days after Babar had tasked Sohrab and Janbaaz, he met them again on 25 December at the Lashkar safehouse in Kathmandu. The duo arrived on time. Babar served them tea and helped himself to a can of coke.

'So, where are the weapons and our Pakistani fidayeen brothers, Sohrab?' Babar asked, his head bent over his laptop.

'The Pakistanis, Imran Ahmed and Mohammed Shabbir, are armed with two AK-47s and ten hand grenades. They are lodged at a flat we rented at Raju Paraspur in Bareilly. I brought the two fidayeen and the weapons smoothly from Kashmir three days ago. Saqlain sent his best wishes to you,' Sohrab said.

The Bareilly army cantonment is one of the oldest in the country and was set up by the British Indian army in 1811. The Jat regiment centre is located in Bareilly, a city that grew in prominence during the Mughal period and lies around 250 kilometres west of Delhi and roughly 115 kilometres south of the Indo-Nepal border check post of Bhimdatta.

'Two major highways, the Bareilly highway and the Nainital highway, intersect in Bareilly at a place called Bilawa. I kept a watch on this intersection for a week, but I spotted only three small army convoys, which were under tight security,' Janbaaz said.

'I see. It is not a good or viable idea to target them then as we don't know of a pattern of movement,' Babar mused.

'Yes, sir,' Janbaaz agreed.

'Do you have any other target in mind?' Babar asked.

'There is a group centre headquarters of the Central Reserve Police Force in Pilibhit that can be attacked instead. It would yield a good number of casualties,' Janbaaz replied.

'Where is it exactly?' asked Babar.

'Pilibhit lies around fifty kilometres north of Bareilly. It is also the same distance from the Bhimdatta check post. The headquarters is spread over sixty acres and lies on Yashwantri Mandir Marg adjoining the Yashwantri Lake.'

'Okay. Have you carried out proper reconnaissance of the site?' Babar asked.

'Yes, sir,' said Janbaaz.

'And what did you learn? What is the best way to attack and when?'

'At night. The guards have eight-hour shifts beginning at 3 a.m. At 2 a.m., the guards on duty will be tired after their seven-hour vigil. Those who have to replace them at 3 a.m. will still be drowsy at 2 a.m. and getting ready. Besides, the darkness will provide the two fidayeen cover to escape,' said Janbaaz.

'What would be the focus of the attack?'

'They have to look at killing the maximum number of guards at the headquarters' heavily guarded entrance. They must fire bursts from their AK-47s and they can lob as many hand grenades as possible,' Janbaaz outlined the plan of attack.

'After the attack, they should cross the road and take cover in the forested tract that runs parallel to Yashwantri Marg. They should drop their weapons, run eastward and take a bus or a cab to the Indo-Nepal border. They can cross the border at Banbasa– Bhimadatta and return to Kathmandu,' added Sohrab.

Babar nodded. 'So far, so good. Seems like a viable plan. The fidayeen are ready?'

'Yes,' confirmed Jaanbaaz.

'How will they reach the CRPF headquarters?'

'They will carry rucksacks that will have their guns and grenades, and will take a cab on Yashwantri Marg so as not to leave an obvious trail.'

'Fine. Be ready. I will get the approval and the date of the attack from the bosses in Pakistan.'

The same evening, at 6 p.m., Babar tried but could not contact Abu-Lakhvi via satellite or mobile phone. Finally, he called up Abu-Lakhvi's aide Ibrahim from a PCO near the safehouse. Babar told him about the proposed attack on the CRPF base. He asked Ibrahim to seek Abu-Lakhvi's approval and get a date for the attack. He also explained why he had chosen the CRPF base as the target and not an army convoy passing through Bareilly, as originally planned.

Ibrahim called Babar back around midnight. Abu-Lakhvi had approved the attack on the CRPF base and wanted it to happen early on 1 January 2008, at 2 a.m., he informed Babar.

Babar's use of a PCO to talk to Ibrahim, rather than a satellite or mobile phone, meant that the crucial conversation on the date and time of the attack was not intercepted by the CTC, which had been keenly listening in on identified mobile and satellite communications. So, while the CTC was aware that the LeT would be unleashing a fidayeen attack on the CRPF base thanks to the intercepted satellite and mobile communications between Babar and Abu-Lakhvi, Abu-Muzammil, Al-Wali, Sohrab and Janbaaz, they did not know the details. The talks included references to renting a house in Pilibhit, a trip to Bareilly and Pilibhit, and stray references to 'group HQ' and 'Yashwantri Marg'. But the exact time and date of the attack was not known and that was a gaping hole in the information they had about the impending attack.

Nonetheless, they had enough to go on for Shekhar to send an alert to the top brass of the Uttar Pradesh police. He asked that the security forces undertake all adequate precautions to foil the attack. In response, a police control room van with armed personnel was deployed outside the CRPF base.

At 2 a.m. on 1 January 2008, the two fidayeen emerged out of the bushes across the road from the CRPF base on the opposite side of Yashwantri Mandir Marg. They crossed the road, their rucksacks on their shoulders, and walked towards the entrance of the base. One of them, Shabbir, walked ahead and, when around twenty feet away from the entrance, engaged a guard in conversation.

'From where can we get a bus to Pilibhit?' he asked. A lone UP police PCR van was stationed outside the CRPF base's entrance gates but it was not clear, from where he stood, whether it was occupied at that point.

While the guard, who held an AK-47, was thinking of a response, Shabbir's buddy fidayeen, Imran, opened fire from behind. The guard took a hail of bullets and slumped to the ground. The second guard, who stood across him, trained his INSAS 5.56 mm automatic rifle at the two attackers and pressed the trigger. In the same instant, however, the attackers dropped to the ground and fired back at the second guard. The second guard fell too.

The attackers stood up and began firing indiscriminately at the other guards who were gathered at the gate. They started lobbing grenades at the guards too and threw four in all. It all happened in a blur. The attackers then crossed the road again, put their AK-47s in their rucksacks and leapt into the bushes.

By the time reinforcements rushed to the gate, the attackers had fled. Seven CRPF men lay dead, along with a civilian who had got caught in the crossfire.

The Uttar Pradesh police had to face the heat for not acting on the 'specific intelligence alert' they had received from the CTC to thwart the attack on the CRPF base. A committee comprising three senior officers dealing with internal security was set up to look into the alleged lapses.

It was the second big success after the 2005 attack on IIS&T for Babar and he was ecstatic.

Abu-Lakhvi, meanwhile, was planning for more ambitious attacks.

59

A PROMOTION

At noon on 1 January 2008, Babar's phone trilled sharply. It was a text message from Abu-Lakhvi.

'Well done, Tiger! Eight killed. Seven of the dead were CRPF commandos. Fateh, the Almighty is the greatest, all praise be upon him,' the text read.

Babar reread the message after offering the afternoon namaz. Apart from the successful culmination of the operation, he was also secretly elated that he had been able to draw the best out of two known failures in the LeT, Sohrab and Janbaaz. As the Nepal commander, such a feat would reflect well on his leadership prowess, Babar thought to himself.

By midnight, as planned, his partners-in-crime, Sohrab, Janbaaz and the two fidayeen, Imran and Shabbir, were back in Kathmandu at the LeT safehouse located in Thamel.

Just after Babar had finished debriefing the four-member Pilibhit attack team, his handler Abu-Muzammil called.

'Well-planned operation and executed beautifully, brother! Congratulations. May the Almighty shower His blessings on you!'

'Whatever I did is thanks to the training you gave me.'

'Two things, Babar. Abu-Lakhvi and I have decided to let you put together your own operational unit, a setup. It will give you some space to plan on your own as per the situation at your end, and the ability to take decisions on your own if needed since you are in Kathmandu and can't wait for our nod for every minor issue.'

Babar was overwhelmed. 'Shukriya. I can't believe this. I don't know if I have the ability to run a setup.'

'We are confident that with your hard work and immaculate planning, you will be able to manage it. Also, there is the mother of all big operations on the drawing board. I need you to recommend some good fidayeen, men who won't bat an eyelid before the worst adversity and the biggest guns of the Indian commandos and the Indian Army. These fidayeen are to be our Pakistani operatives. It is for an operation on a scale that would befit the Ghazwa-e-Hind in India.'

'You can count on me to do whatever is needed,' said Babar.

'Good. You will help us in instructing the fidayeen. For the commando and military training, we have experts. You will be required to teach these men the local Indian languages, like Hindi and Marathi, so that they can pass off as Indians. Also, tell them a little about the current situation in India, the backwardness of the Muslim community there and how they are being oppressed, the security situation there, among other topics.'

'Ji janaab,' said Babar.

'It will be something similar to what you did last year, when you trained ten Pakistani fidayeen who went to help us in our jihad in Kashmir.

'Another thing, Babar,' Abu-Muzammil added. 'You have to help a Mumbai-based operative who will come to meet you. His name is Shaukat Mirza. He needs four fidayeen and weapons for them. His task is to organize a fidayeen attack on a high-profile software professionals' conference at the seaside five-star Hotel Samudra in south Mumbai. Imran and Shabbir can be used for the operation while Abu Saqlain can send two more men and weapons from Kashmir.'

'Imran and Shabbir had dropped their AK-47s in a bush near the CRPF base attack site. I will send the duo to retrieve them and take them to Mumbai,' said Babar.

'Okay, may the Almighty grant you continued success,' said Abu-Muzammil before hanging up.

Abu-Lakhvi's and LeT's ecstasy turned out to be short-lived, though. By the evening of 3 January, in a coordinated operation with the Nepalese authorities, the CTC nabbed the men who had carried out the deadly attack on the CRPF headquarters in Pilibhit.

Unknown to Babar and Abu-Lakhvi, the Indian counter-terror and intelligence agencies were tracking their conversations and activities, and those of their men who had arrived in Nepal in a staggered manner to be sheltered by Babar at Lashkar accommodations. The satellite phone conversations between Babar, his Lashkar handlers and the latter's ISI contacts were monitored by the CTC and its external counterpart, the R&IC. A discreet watch had been kept on the movements of Babar and his associates in Nepal. The CTC had been on the trail of Sohrab and his truck from the time he had returned with the two fidayeen, Imran and Shabbir, from Kashmir. This was because Imran and Shabbir were under the watch of the counter-terror units of Kashmir police and the CTC Srinagar station. When Sohrab contacted the two fidayeen, it brought him under the scanner too. For the CTC, it was time to mop up Lashkar's entire Nepal team with the help of R&IC's impressive assortment of local agents who had been keeping a watch on the Lashkar hideouts.

The CTC first picked up Sohrab, then Janbaaz, Imran, Shabbir and finally Babar. Babar was baffled to see the CTC team led by Shekhar. He knew his time was up but his ego was bruised. He had a question for Shekhar.

'Sir, welcome to Nepal!' he said. 'Be good enough to tell me where I slipped, which in turn gave you the break that you never got before. I have always been a step ahead of you amateurs otherwise! Today, I have your hands on my collars.'

'Nice question, terrorist! But ponder over it behind bars; you won't come out any time soon!'

'Hope you liked my *fankari* in carrying out complex operations,' he chuckled.

'Shut up and pack up. Prepare for the journey back home.'

'The number of casualties, however, could have been better at IIS&T. What do you think, janaab?' It was rankling Babar that he did not prove good enough to stay away from the long arm of the Indian security authorities.

'Let's hope you are as chatty when I interrogate you in India.'

∾

With the capture of Babar, who had been behind at least five major LeT attacks since 2005, the CTC could breathe easy for some time. He had been an expert in selecting the target, planning the attack to the last detail and ensuring the escape of the attackers and himself.

But Shekhar knew that in the business of counter-intelligence and counter-terrorism, one could never bet on the next moment.

For instance, it was not clear yet who was behind the recurring blasts, targeting places of Hindu religious significance in India, since the 2005 Dashashwamedh Ghat blast in Varanasi. It was also not very clear who had been bombing places of religious significance to Muslims since the September 2006 blasts in Malegaon, a textile hub in Maharashtra.

In September 2006 in Malegaon, three IEDs had exploded just after Friday prayers outside a Muslim cemetery close to a mosque, Hamidiya Masjid, on the occasion of Shab-e-Barat, causing deaths and a deadly stampede. Thirty-seven had died and 125 sustained injuries.

In May 2007, an RDX-based IED device had exploded at Hyderabad's historic Mecca Masjid, a seventeenth-century mosque in the old city, during the Friday afternoon prayers. The IED was placed near the Wazoo Khana, where the faithful perform ablutions. Nine had died in the blast, another five had died in police firing after riots broke out on the streets following the blast, which had occurred at a time when 10,000 people were gathered in the mosque.

Then in November 2007, synchronized serial blasts had ripped through the premises of the Varanasi civil court, the Faizabad district court and a Lucknow court, targeting lawyers. Six bombs had gone off in all, while an unexploded one was discovered. The blasts killed eighteen people while eighty-one sustained injuries.

After these blasts, for the first time since the Dashashwamedh Ghat one, a claim emerged to own up even as it offered a defence for the attacks, using a complex narrative of religious and social issues to justify them as valid retaliation in response to the perceived wrongs done to the Muslim community.

An email, ostensibly in the name of the unknown 'Al-Hind Mujahideen' was sent to a few news channels from the account of 'guru_alhindi@yahoo.fr'. It talked of the alleged 'wounds inflicted by the idol worshippers', the December 1992 destruction of the Babri Masjid and the 2002 riots in Gujarat. It was suspected that the outfit was old wine in a new bottle, which drew elements from the LeT and HuJI and hoped to provide adequate deniability to the ISI and its puppets in the LeT, JeM and a radical Muslim students' body that was proscribed in the early 2000s.

But who were the members of the Al-Hind Mujahideen and who were part of its leadership? Who trained its men, financed them, and provided weapons and explosives to them? Were they answerable to the ISI or the LeT/HuJI? There were many queries but no clear answers.

The Al-Hind Mujahideen would reinvent itself as 'Indian Mujahideen' (IM), vowing to shed more blood of the 'infidels', taunting and ridiculing India's intelligence, counter-intelligence and police agencies after orchestrating a series of synchronized blasts in India in 2008. These included nine serial blasts in Jaipur in May (sixty-three killed), twenty-two blasts within ninety minutes in seventeen locations in Ahmedabad in July (fifty-six dead), nine in Bangalore also in July (one dead) and nine in Delhi in September (twenty killed). The arrest of an accused in the Ahmedabad blasts, Anwar Shaukat Basheerpuri, threw some light on who constituted the Indian Mujahideen.

Quoting co-accused Usman Sheikh Qureshi, who led the banned Hindustani Majlis outfit after the arrest of thirteen of its top leaders, including then chief Malik, Basheerpuri claimed that 'Indian Mujahideen will conduct serial blasts in Ahmedabad as revenge for Gujarat riots' during his interrogations by the Gujarat police. 'He asked Qayyum bhai as to what this Indian Mujahideen is. He said that some of them are old hard-core elements from the banned outfit and some new young people have also joined.'

Even as they picked up pieces from the ruins left by the deadly blasts, Shekhar and his bosses in the CTC sorely missed having any information on how the terror masterminds functioned. They missed having a project in place like Operation Trojan Horse, which had succeeded in embedding counter-terror Indian operatives deep into the LeT's South Asian framework to thwart, pre-empt and defang its ceaseless terror plots.

60

THE NIGHT OF 26/11

When the explosions rocked India from 2005 to 2008, for which there were no clear leads on the identities of the perpetrators, Shekhar grilled Atharv about the blasts in the Mecca mosque and Malegaon, but he claimed ignorance about who could have executed them.

'Atharv, have you heard anything at all that can provide us with a lead on who was behind the Malegaon and Mecca mosque blasts?'

'No, sir, I have no idea who was responsible for them, and it seems the LeT may also be clueless.'

'Well, that's a pity,' said Shekhar.

'But there is something else that I have come across, thanks to a stray query by Abu-Muzammil. He asked me if I could get Indian prepaid SIM cards for a group of thirty to thirty-five fidayeen. I told him I would try. But he never broached the topic again. Once, when I raised it, he snubbed me and did not give me a straight answer. He never raised the subject again.'

Shekhar was immediately on alert. 'Indian prepaid SIM cards for Pakistani fidayeen? It seems they are planning a big terror attack in India outside Kashmir. Any idea where?'

'No idea, sir.'

'Thanks, Atharv. Be alert and on the move. Keep your eyes and ears open.'

'Yes, sir.'

After hanging up, Shekhar was immersed in deep thought. Convinced that the LeT was planning something very big, he went to meet the CTC chief to apprise him of LeT's search for Indian SIM cards for a large number of Pakistani fidayeen.

Months later, members of Abhinav Bharat came under the scanner of investigating agencies for their alleged involvement in bomb blasts at Hyderabad in May 2007 (Mecca mosque, nine people dead), Ajmer in October 2007 (the shrine of Sufi saint Khwaja Moinuddin Chishti, three people dead) and Malegaon in September 2008 (opposite a goods transport firm office, four people dead).

A few weeks later, the opportunity to act on the intelligence provided by Atharv presented itself before the CTC.

Rakesh Sharma, a senior Kashmir police officer who had run several counter-terror operations against Pakistani terror outfits active in the Valley, most of them in collaboration with the CTC, got in touch with Shekhar.

It was around 11.30 p.m. on 30 August 2008 when Shekhar got a call from Rakesh.

'How are you, sir?'

'Hello, Sharma, I'm fine, thanks. It's good to hear from you. Tell me, what is new?'

'A covert intelligence operative of ours, "Mongoose", who is embedded in the LeT, got a valuable scrap of information. A local LeT commander asked him to procure thirty-five Indian prepaid SIM cards, but not from Kashmir. They will be sent to Pakistan via special human couriers.'

'This is valuable intelligence,' Shekhar said. 'Mongoose is a great find, a real talent. I want to make the most of this opportunity. I want to send some of my own SIMs in the lot that will go to LeT in Pakistan.' Shekhar couldn't believe his luck.

'Yes, sir. That is exactly why I called you.'

'I will send you three SIMs from Delhi. LeT might use them if and when an attack is launched in India.'

'Yes, sir. Please send the SIMs, and I will ensure they get to LeT.'

Shekhar's aide bought the three SIM cards, using fake identity particulars, from a SIM retailer in Delhi. The SIM cards were sent to Mongoose in Kashmir through covert channels.

It was one of the three SIM cards, number 91-99107194XY, which became active around 9.50 p.m., three months later, on 26 November 2008, when LeT's ten-man fidayeen squad, including Ajmal Amir Kasab, took the 550-nautical-mile-long sea route from Karachi's Keti Bunder creek to land at Mumbai's Budhwar Park seashore at Cuffe Parade.

The SIM was being used by one of the ten fidayeen. Till then, the three numbers had been dormant.

Over the next fifty-nine hours, the Pakistani Lashkar terrorists, who were armed with AK-47s, RDX-based eight-kilo bombs, and grenades, attacked five iconic spots in Mumbai: the Taj Mahal Hotel, the Oberoi–Trident Hotel, Leopold Bar and Café, Chhatrapati Shivaji Terminus and the Jewish Chabad.

The intercepted number gave the first breakthrough in listening in to the real-time commands being relayed to the Mumbai attackers by their Karachi-based command centre, manned by senior commanders including Abu-Lakhvi, Abu-Muzammil, Umar-Qama, Sajid Mir alias Wassi and Hamza.

At 1.26 a.m. the same night, the conversations that were tapped into yielded a lead that proved crucial in analysing the nature and source of the attacks.

Controller (C): Are you setting the fire or not?

Mumbai attacker (MA): Not yet. I am getting a mattress ready for burning.

C: What did you do with the body?

MA: Left it behind in the boat.

C: Did you not open the locks for the water below?

MA: No, we did not open the locks. We left in a hurry. We made a big mistake.

C: What big mistake?

MA: When we were getting into the boat, the waves were quite high. Another boat came. Everyone raised the alarm that the navy had come. In the confusion, [team captain Abu] Ismail's satellite phone got left behind.

❧

Kasab was arrested at Girgaum Chowpatty on the night of 26 November, while his buddy, Ismail, who was also the leader of the ten-man Lashkar team in Mumbai, subsequently succumbed to bullet injuries received in a desperate encounter with policemen and officers of the D.B. Marg police station. Assistant Sub-Inspector Tukaram Ombale attained martyrdom while overpowering Kasab. Kasab and Ismail were travelling in a stolen Skoda car after killing three senior police officers in an ambush in the lane adjoining St Xavier's College near Azad Maidan in south Mumbai.

Ismail was the man who had earlier handled the sole satellite phone given by the Pakistani Lashkar commanders to the ten-man fidayeen team for communication purposes. He was among the three fidayeen added to the Mumbai attack team at the last minute and was suspected of being a Pakistani naval commando. The ten-man team was selected from a specially selected group of thirty-two trained Lashkar suicide attackers, for which, the CTC later realized, Abu-Muzammil had approached Atharv as well for prepaid SIM cards.

The LeT attack team had its sea route to Mumbai from Karachi marked on the GPS sets its members were carrying. When the gunmen began their journey on 22 November, they activated their GPS sets in the sea at a point named Man on Board (MOB), which was around twenty kilometres southwest of Kajhar Creek in Keti Bunder, Pakistan. MOB is roughly 130 kilometres southeast of Karachi. The original route ran close to the Indian coastline, and Ismail, as the team leader, took a call to intervene. He discarded the route and charted a new route that was around eighty kilometres off the Indian coastline to evade detection. The terrorists' GPS sets showed the culmination of their journey to be at Budhwar Park in Cuffe Parade in south Mumbai, from where they could hire cabs to reach their destinations.

Lashkar recruit Abu Ammar, a native of Beed in Maharashtra, had been used by Abu-Lakhvi to train the team members in picking up the nuances of colloquial Hindi and Marathi and on how to talk on Indian electronic channels during the siege they were going to lay at the targeted spots.

Kasab's interrogations by CTC would reveal that the ten-man team had left Karachi in a small boat around 8 a.m. on 22 November 2008. Forty minutes later, they had transferred to a bigger boat, the Abu-Lakhvi-owned 'Al Husseini', which was carrying seven senior Lashkar commanders.

The next day at 3 p.m., they seized an Indian fishing trawler, the MV Kuber. Its four crew members were moved to Al Husseini while its captain, Amar Singh Solanki, was kept on board to navigate the trawler to Mumbai. The four crewmen were later killed and dumped in the sea by the Lashkar team.

Ismail asked Solanki to steer the MV Kuber till it reached a point just four nautical miles off Mumbai. It was then 4 p.m. on 26 November. Beyond the turquoise sea waters, the drone of the fishing boat's engine and the smell of dead fish in the air, the outline of a skyscraper began taking shape amid the haze. As the trawler cruised towards the shore, the cherry-coloured dome by the skyscraper could be seen too by Kasab, the stocky young man leaning on the deck's metal railings.

The sun escaped from the clouds, sprinkling gold dust over the skyscraper and the bud-shaped dome. The wind howled, the waves splashed against the boat, but the sight hushed the otherwise boisterous Kasab into silence. A group of seagulls flying by the boat squawked.

Kasab let out a shout. 'Bombay! We have reached Bombay! I can see the Taj Mahal Hotel and the adjoining tower too!'

Ismail picked up his AK-47, pointed it towards Mumbai's shoreline and let out a burst of fire.

The seven Lashkar attack controllers, who sat in a specially equipped command centre in Karachi, asked the team to wait till dark before going ashore. The fidayeen transferred to an inflatable dinghy with an outboard motor and set off for the Mumbai shore at 7.15 p.m. They reached Mumbai's Budhwar Park beach at 8.30 p.m.

∾

'Ask the navy and the coast guard to be on the lookout for a boat or a motor launch having a satellite phone,' Shekhar instructed a senior Mumbai police officer involved in the 26/11 fightback.

'The interception of the terror instructions being given by top Lashkar bosses and one "Major General" from Karachi to their ten fidayeen in Mumbai helped the CTC and Indian security forces eventually neutralize the LeT's terror attack on Mumbai.

'The tapping was a watershed event. It laid bare before the entire world the Pakistani state's deep, direct participation in sponsoring terror in India through its tools like the LeT like never before,' Shekhar told a senior bureaucrat in the Prime Minister's Office a day after NSG commandos had killed eight of the ten Lashkar terrorists who had set sail from Karachi on 22 November. As part of India's fightback during the 26/11 attack, a team of NSG commandos was flown in on a chopper from a naval base and dropped atop Nariman House in south Mumbai, which housed a Jewish institution, amid heavy gunfire. It was the first airborne operation the NSG conducted in an urban, densely populated theatre. Two LeT terrorists, Babar Imran alias Abu Aakasha and Nasir alias Abu Umar, were killed in the operation at Nariman House.

In 2012, Kasab was hanged after a court that conducted his trial found him guilty of crimes, including multiple murders during the 26/11 attacks that killed 167 and injured over 1,200.

Thanks to the interception of the terror commands from Pakistan to the gunmen, one of the first crucial pieces of information that the CTC passed on to the Mumbai police and then the NSG was this: 'There are ten Lashkar fidayeen; get the ten bodies and the terrorists' personal weapons, ten AK-47s.' The 26/11 attacks continued for fifty-nine hours and were reckoned to be over when the ten gunmen and an equal number of AK-47s were accounted for.

After 26/11, Abu-Lakhvi renewed his calls to the CTC's five operatives to meet him in Pakistan for 'stock-taking' and 'consultations'. Despite his persistent summons, the five agents had cited an array of excuses over the years for not being able to meet him and his top aides in Pakistan for a debriefing on why LeT top operations had failed one after another. As per the protocol laid down by the LeT itself, the operatives were to stay in touch on their own initiative with their Pakistani handlers, indirectly, via phone numbers located in Dubai. The Pakistani handlers could not get in touch with the five if the latter chose to snap the link.

And so the five did not return to meet Abu-Lakhvi or any of their other Lashkar handlers. Atharv and Rohit both told Abu-Lakhvi that they had pending work and would come there on its completion. The CTC learned from its interceptions of conversations of Lashkar operatives located in Pakistan, Nepal and India that Abu-Lakhvi and his associates were frantically looking for the CTC operatives for several years for having given them 'deadly blows'. Abu-Lakhvi beefed up the LeT's internal mechanisms to safeguard against the recruitment of 'enemies'.

Atharv and the other four CTC operatives broke their contacts with the LeT subsequently and decided to disappear for a while – until a new assignment, a new project with the CTC, beckoned.

India's war on terror continues, within its borders and beyond. The CTC is spearheading the war. Indians like Shekhar, Somaiya, Sawant, Imran Hussein, Atharv, Rohit, Anant, Sahil and Nirav are the spear's tip.

ABOUT THE AUTHORS

Divya Prakash Sinha is a 1979-batch IPS officer who joined the Intelligence Bureau in 1987 and spent around twenty-eight years of his career there looking after counter-terrorist and security operations. He is credited with neutralizing a large number of terror modules in the country. After rising to the level of Special Director in the IB, he also served as Secretary (Security) in the Cabinet Secretariat, from where he superannuated in 2015. He is a recipient of the Indian Police Medal for Meritorious Services and the President's Police Medal for Distinguished Services.

After superannuation, he was selected for the post of Central Information Commissioner by a high-level panel headed by India's Prime Minister.

Sinha is an honours graduate in physics from Patna University. As an IPS officer, he began his career in Tripura, holding various positions, including of a district SP and SP, CID.

Abhishek Sharan is a senior crime journalist, who has spent the past twenty years roaming the gullies and mohallas of Mumbai and Delhi tracking gruesome murders, startling suicides, bomb blasts, gang wars and financial scams. He has reported from the sites of terror attacks in the national capital, Hyderabad, Jaipur, Mumbai, Bangalore and Malegaon. He has written extensively on the investigations as well as the human toll of these atrocities.

Abhishek has pursued multiple e-courses to better understand the global terror landscape, including Threat of Nuclear Terrorism (Stanford University), Terrorism and Counter-terrorism (Georgetown University) and Understanding 9/11 (Duke University).

A history graduate from Patna, Abhishek moved to Mumbai to pursue post-graduation in Advanced Media Studies from St Xavier's College. He started his career at *The Indian Express* and later went on to work for *Hindustan Times*, *The Asian Age* and, most recently, *Mumbai Mirror*, where he was Senior Assistant Editor.